BOOKS BY PETER CLOTHIER

Dirty-Down	1987
Chiaroscuro	1985

DIRTY-DOWN

____DIRTY-DOWN

_____PETER CLOTHIER

1987   *New York*   ATHENEUM

Library of Congress Cataloging-in-Publication Data

Clothier, Peter,——
Dirty-down.

I. Title.
PR6053.L57D5   1987   823'.914   86-47946
ISBN 0-689-11876-7

Copyright © 1987 by Peter Clothier
All rights reserved
Published simultaneously in Canada by Collier Macmillan Canada, Inc.
Composition by Westchester Book Composition
Manufactured by Fairfield Graphics, Fairfield, Pennsylvania
Designed by Laura Rohrer
First Editon

*For Harry and Peggy
with love and
gratitude*

It's in the blood...

ACKNOWLEDGMENTS

I acknowledge a great debt of thanks to the Los Angeles art community —a constant source of affection, inspiration, wonder and fun. And special thanks to those who gave time to help me in writing this book, chief among them Roland Reiss, the artist whose work begins and ends the story; Larry Albright; Stephanie Barron of the Los Angeles County Museum; Brian Cooke of Cooke's Crating & Fine Arts Transportation, Inc.; Denise Domergue, President, Conservation of Paintings; Michael Hayden; Howard Kaplan; and Jim Morphesis. And special thanks, also, to my wife, Ellie Blankfort Clothier, for love, expert advice, understanding—and for reading the manuscript more times than a person should have to.

DIRTY-DOWN

|

THERE IT was again. Freeze frame, then action. A kind of visual itch that eclipsed the noise and activity of the opening-night crowd, an image that spoke to him like a clear voice out of nowhere. It lasted for a single instant, then it was gone.

He heard the voice say: You shouldn't be here.

That was absurd. Wil Garretson cocked his head and squinted out across the atrium, taking advantage of what seemed like the evening's first quiet moment to scan the crowd again for a clue. He found none, and the party went on anyway.

"Hey, Wil!"

He heard the sound of a real, familiar voice but made as if he hadn't, playing for a little extra time. It would take Charlie a few more moments to shoulder through the crush.

So what was it?

Damn.

The angle of vision was an odd one. He was standing on the second stair up from the atrium floor, and it left him a head or more above the crowd. From this vantage, he gazed out over a hundred other heads toward the white-clothed table bowed with its familiar load of darkly glazed pâtés and pale yellow cheeses—Brie and Jarlsberg—deftly draped with bunches of green and pink grapes. The people, too, were gashes of restless color, flashes of jewelry, heads in motion, noisy with news and laughter. He knew them all. Knew most of them. It was a scene replayed for the hundredth time.

"Wil?"

This time, though, it was played out in his honor. A kind of landmark, in his fiftieth year.

Or, he reminded himself, it was partly his. On this occasion, the museum had managed to slip selections from the Benson collection—a tribute to a local couple who'd caught the constructivist bug, and a chance to save on the costs of another opening. So be it.

Then Charlie caught up with him. "Congratulations, Wil," he said. "I'm thrilled. The work looks great." Charles Strauss, his dealer.

Wil must have heard the same thing twenty times that evening. "You think so?" he asked.

In his bones, he knew the show had turned out well. He raised a craggy chin and scratched at the half-inch beard he should have trimmed again before setting out for the evening. When it came, the offer of a solo shot was flattering, but he'd had real doubts about a museum show at this juncture. He had doubts about summer shows generally. Usually they were fill-in stuff, grab-bag groups that smacked of debts that needed paying. Still, he'd never had a show at the County before, and Charlie had convinced him that the timing was okay. And the show looked good.

"It looks terrific. You needed this."

"Like a hole in the head." Wil laughed. Jostled from behind, he juggled his glass and steadied himself on Strauss's shoulder. "Sorry."

"No, really," said Strauss. He shook a drop of wine from his sleeve. "I know it's been a pain in the rear end to get ready, but it marks a certain point in your career—and it sure can't hurt the old stock values." He paused to study Wil approvingly. "Besides," he said, "it looks like you've found time to spend at the beach. That's wonderful. You deserve it. Lay back for a few weeks, Wil. Relax. You're looking great."

It was true, he'd never felt better. Lean and strong. After years of pounding the sidewalk, he'd given up running a couple of months before and he'd found that, along with the weights he toyed with in the studio most days, an aerobic walk and a half hour's swim did as much for him as running ever had. He was daily amazed to feel no different than he had when he was twenty-five.

"You should get out more often yourself," he told Strauss.

"Oh, Jesus, you Californians!" Strauss gave a small, rueful laugh and parted the front of his neatly tailored jacket to pat the beginnings of a paunch that swelled under a gray-and-white-striped shirt. "Some of us have to be content with being fat and pasty-faced," he added. With a fingertip, he pushed the glasses back from where they'd slipped halfway down his nose and, in the same gesture, a lank mass of brown hair from his eyes. "It goes with the turf. Too many lunches. Too many hours spent on the telephone, slaving so that you guys can get out on the beach."

"Busy, huh? I'm happy to hear that."

Strauss countered Wil's grin with a good-natured scowl. "Summer," he grumbled. "I hate it. All I get is problems. We should all pack up and leave, like they do back east." Charlie was one of the good guys, in Wil's book. He did well for his artists. He'd hit the art scene only about ten years ago, young, ambitious, and had climbed fast. Already he'd reached the point where he handled the best of the West Coast artists and those who spoke badly of him—there were always those—did it only behind his back and with more than a hint of envy.

"If I'd been smart," Wil mused, "I'd have taken the summer off myself."

"Why?" Strauss was surprised. "For God's sake, you're not teaching, are you?"

Wil dug a finger into the hollow of his temple and twisted it slowly. "I'm crazy," he laughed. For years, more out of habit and pleasure than necessity, he'd been teaching studio at Otis. Sometimes they managed to prevail on him for a summer course. He'd committed to one this year before the prospect of the show came along, and hadn't the heart to renege.

"They'd be dead without you," Strauss told him. "You're the best they've got." Wil laughed again. "I mean it," insisted Strauss. "You give too much of the creative juices to it, Wil. Are you headed for the bar?"

"Why the hell not?" said Wil.

It was a Thursday—one of those unreal, hot southern California nights, at the end of the first day of what the weather people predicted was to be a heat wave. The famous and the not-so-famous mingled in

5

the atrium in loose-fitting designer clothes. Canapés circulated on plated silver platters, proffered by the hands of sardonic black servers who observed the antics of the pretentious and the affluent with the bored amusement of visitors at the zoo.

"Well, Charlie." Wil raised his Sebastiani. "Here's to an early fall."

They waved in unison at the spare frame of Fred Aaron, the new curator of post-war art who'd proposed the Garretson show and piloted it through a dozen meetings and committees. Tall, bony, blessed with an inordinate length of nose down which he liked to gaze unblinkingly at those who bored him, Aaron was practicing this art on a docent lady, nodding his tight combed head toward her, frowning a little as though he found it hard to follow her. Wil sympathized. There's something about these events that strips the mind of the gears it usually relies on.

"Later, Wil," said Charlie. "There's business to be done here somewhere, I suppose."

Wil wrapped a long arm around his shoulder. "You take care," he said. "I need you." For himself, he found a space on the table to unload his glass and started for the elevators to the third floor, where the shows were hung. He managed half a dozen paces.

"Wil! Wil Garretson!" He peered about him, searching for a familiar face. He found a smiling one that seemed to mean him, and hoisted his look of delighted recognition.

"Well, hi!" he said. He left off the name because he couldn't remember it. She wore her shirt unbuttoned to the navel. "Peek-a-boo."

"What?" Her eyes began to cloud, doubtfully.

"Nothing," he said.

"It's been ages," she told him, confident again. She kissed him directly on the lips and stroked his beard.

"Sure has," he agreed. He stood back to survey his find, appalled by the sudden thought that they might have been lovers in a younger year, that all she'd done was change the cut of her hair. "Where was it last?" he tried.

"Acapulco?" she suggested.

"Who knows?" said Wil. He'd never been there.

They were about to explore further possibilities when a man swept up behind her, seized her hand, and stopped long enough to greet Wil with a cheerful "Hey, Wil, how's it going?" before disappearing with her back into the crowd.

Wil sighed, resuming his trek toward the elevator.

6

"Hey, Wil." The new speaker stood, arms folded, back against the wall, dressed in a dark blazer and a dark striped tie. He tilted a sympathetic head and winked. They had worked together once, in the rental gallery, in Wil's post-student days.

"Hey, Barnett, how's it going?" Barnett Newman, onetime security guard, now head of security at the museum. No kin, he used to say, to the guy that put the stripes down the middle of his paintings, but Wil enjoyed the thought of it anyway.

"It's the overtime that kills you," Newman said.

"Yeah," said Wil. "Tell me about it, Barn. How's the family?"

"Doing good, Wil. Remember Susie?"

"About so high?" asked Wil. He held a palm out, three feet from the floor.

"She's in college now."

"Jesus, Barn . . . Would you believe that?"

He decided to pay his respects and take a look at the Benson collection first, and the voice came back when he reached the Mondrian. This time it was stronger than before. It said: You don't belong here.

Wil shoved it back down where it came from and stared at the painting. He'd seen a good part of the collection at the Benson house but he'd never seen this one there. The collection included some of the greats from the early days of constructivism, along with a few of the new guys working with hard edge and relief—everything from Mangold to Frank Stella. Some good stuff. And some not so good. Wil liked the Bensons but he wasn't convinced they knew too much about painting. He stooped closer to the Mondrian and wondered why it missed. It was maybe just one of those things the artist shouldn't have let out of the studio. No special reason. Wil guessed even Mondrian was entitled to one off day.

He'd been having enough of them himself.

"You like that one?" Small, gray, and serious to the point of gravity, Herb Benson laid a tentative hand on Wil's shoulder. His glasses made heavy sad circles around his eyes.

"It's terrific, Herb," Wil lied.

"It was a big gap," Benson said. "We've been waiting a long time for a Mondrian."

Then when the chance came, Wil thought, they jumped at it. Couldn't wait for a good one. "Well, that's great," he said. "Congratulations."

7

"And you," said Benson. "A wonderful show."

He went on in, and the work looked good. "Wil Garretson: Wall to Floor." Fred Aaron had dreamed up the title and, while he worried that it was a little cute, Wil had to admit it was accurate enough.

Twenty years of work. On the walls there were maybe two dozen of the paintings he'd first gotten a name for. Very smooth, very flat, from the front they looked deeper, inviting the viewer to plunge into the spaces they suggested in the wall. Like open cities even from above, anaxometric, creating a third dimension with the manipulation of surface color and light. He'd done them until that was what the world expected of him and he couldn't do them anymore.

And then the change, ten years ago. A risky change, for an artist, at a time when many still clung to the distinction between "painter" and "sculptor." Those were the pieces on the floor, a row of them ranged in plexi boxes, thigh-high, so that you had to look down into the microcosms they created. It was a slow, sometimes painful affair, the process of bringing some of those spatial concerns out into the third dimension, scaling down to radical smallness and introducing, tentatively at first, that teasing play of images in "mysteries" that he never fully allowed to tell the whole story.

Until that was what the world expected of him.

He looked along the row and was brought face-to-face with the source of his discomfort. The work was good. He had no quarrel with it. But there was not one ounce of mystery or surprise for him anymore. It was finished. What the show had done was simply prove it to him. What counted now was the work he still had to do—a terrifying emptiness.

The voice was right. It was easier to be here than at the studio, where he belonged. He'd been avoiding it. A small, dark pain began to eat at his gut, somewhere close in behind the bottom rib.

Wil would have made it out through the atrium if it hadn't been for Sally.

He had missed her until now. He had wondered if she'd be there. And now the crowd had thinned considerably, toward nine o'clock. She stood slightly in profile to him, light shimmering on the deep lavender of her silk blouse, her brown hair bobbed to shoulder length, pushed back to reveal the slender O of a silver earring. She held her hand up in front of her mouth, fingers turned out, her lips saying "No!"

That image in itself was surprising, enough to stop Wil in his tracks.

And focusing on her so intensely, he took a moment to register the second figure as a part of the tableau, looming suddenly close, too close, and staggering slightly. A kid. Drunk, Wil thought. And somehow shocking in the intimacy of his gesture. An Otis graduate of maybe five or six years back. Wil found the name: Jim Sewell.

The kid was rigged out in gray Guess jeans and a white shirt, collar turned up, with that chic crumpled look. A light, high-shouldered jacket with narrow lapels à la thirty years ago. He'd pushed the sleeves up to his elbows.

He leaned into Sally as though, Wil imagined, to whisper something in her ear, and Sally was trying simply to say no.

Where was Rick, for Christ's sake? Working?

Goddamn the man.

"Sally?" Wil crossed the floor and used his body like a quiet wedge, shifting the kid back with his shoulder, returning the belligerence in his eyes with a quiet, cold stare.

"Oh, Wil!"

He brought an arm around her shoulder, turning their backs deliberately to the kid and walking her away from him. Then he stopped and held her.

"How's Rick?" he asked.

She shrugged, avoiding his eyes. "He couldn't make it," she said.

"Too bad," said Wil. "You need any help?"

Green eyes. They met his briefly and moved on. Wil wondered that he'd ever believed he could read them.

"Help?" she said. "You mean Jimmy?"

Wil shrugged. "From across the room..." he started.

"He's harmless," she said.

Still, there was a tension between them Wil hadn't felt in years. He dropped his arm and folded her hands between his two. "You liked the show?" he asked.

That did the trick. Sally arrived back from wherever it was she'd been. "Oh, God," she said. "I'm sorry. I loved it, Wil." She leaned forward to kiss him. "You're a genius."

2

T HE CLIMBER started at first light.
    He loved the morning better than any other time of day, loved
the mountain in the morning. He stretched and grinned. Better than
making love. Grabbing the heap of clothes and boots he had left by the
camper door, he slipped out naked into the near darkness.

The chill of the air braced his skin as he stretched out the sleep from
his arms and legs. Yawning, he walked a short way down toward the
woods and pissed a long arc into a patch of ferns.

He pulled the heavy sweater over his head, stepped into the shorts
and corduroy pants and stooped to lace up his boots. He knew the trail
well and didn't think he'd need a rope, but he slung one across his
shoulder anyway.

There was a ledge he liked to reach before the sun rose. It was an easy
climb, a path that wandered out of the forest on the valley floor and up
through sparse pines to where the steeper slope began. Here the trail
narrowed. Dirt and pine needles gave way to a footing of solid rock and
the slope dropped sharply away to his left. Beyond, the desert stretched
out into a darkness whose distances were soon suffused with a vague
pink glow.

Dawn. He reached the ledge and crouched there, pulling a thermos of

10

coffee from his backpack. The plastic cup steamed in his hand as he squinted to watch the shifts of light and color.

The horizon slowly defined itself and stabilized. The fluffy pinks intensified, reflecting their colors on the vast, flat reaches of Mojave sand and brush. Within minutes they turned to rich golds and yellows as the sun's rays cracked the horizon and the tip of its brilliant disc appeared and disappeared, and rose again.

Then the incredible flood of light that raced backward, toward the sun, across the desert floor.

When the sun had risen, all he wanted to do was get to the top and back to the camper. Make love. Start the day.

From here on up, the face was sheer, a rock climber's dream, with satisfying hand- and footholds that made the going smooth, but enough of a challenge to make it worth the effort. He worked fast, economical in his movements, and paused only briefly on a higher ledge to look back down toward where the camper stood among the trees.

She was still sleeping there.

A distant hum turned into the insistent putter of a motor.

He was thirty feet from the top of the cliff when he heard it, and he cursed it aloud for breaking his concentration and destroying the peace. He turned his head away from the rock and found it approaching out of the low sunlight, hard to see, but growing louder.

What the fuck, he thought, would the goddamn thing be doing here?

He moved to secure his grip and his foothold, to compensate for the turn of his head and its movement out and away from the cliff.

After a brief pause over the camp site, the chopper lurched up out of the sun's line not a quarter mile away. It hung there for a moment, glinting, then lunged crazily forward with a deafening din, directly toward him, as though to plunge into the cliff.

"What the fuck?" he said aloud.

It was fifty feet from him when it swung about, broadside, and paused again. He squinted out at it. Cops? Rangers? He had never heard of a climber being bothered by the law. Yet the thing was definitely there for him. The door slid back. Against the light he could barely make out the figure of a man pointing something at him.

Then suddenly he knew.

They had come to kill him, simple as that. He couldn't believe it, they were going to kill him. Exposed and clinging to the rock face, there was nothing he could do to stop them.

He gathered all the breath he had left in his lungs.

"Wait!" he yelled. "No!"

The words were swallowed into the roar of the helicopter's engine and he sobbed and tried to yell again.

"Wait! Wait!" It was pointless, Jesus. What could he do to them? "Wait!"

Sally Horan was awakened by the helicopter, coming in fast over the camp site and thundering down from the sky like the wrath of God. Gripped by the sound, the camper was a rattling toy and her first wild thought was that Rick had found out about them.

But that was ridiculous.

She heard the helicopter keel away in the direction of the cliff and searched around in panic, unable to remember where he had stowed her clothes. Impatient, she did without them and grabbed, instead, for the sleeping bag and wrapped it around her shoulders.

The grass in the clearing was white with early dew and her feet froze, gathering dirt and pine needles as she ran toward where the yellow machine hovered, half visible through the trees against the cliff face.

Instinctively she sensed the attack before it came, and she yelled as she thought she would never yell in her life. She yelled from a full throat up the echoing rock face and her voice came back tiny, powerless. She yelled at the helicopter, two hundred feet above her, impervious, hanging like a furious, steel yellowjacket.

High up, she saw a black speck huddled against the rock, and there was nothing she could do. She stood there in a daze of nausea and incomprehension as she heard repeated snaps of gunfire, barely audible above the aircraft's motor. The bullets slammed into the rock above the man's head, splintering chips out of the mountainside. He lost his grip, and Sally screamed again as she watched the distant body peel away from the rock and tumble through two hundred feet of space.

He spun off again on first contact with the steep slope, and landed somewhere beyond her range of vision with a thud that she not only heard but felt, like a tiny earthquake, in her feet.

This time, the scream stuck somewhere in her throat.

3

SHE STARTED forward but the chopper was moving again, dropping toward her in another infernal storm of noise—bigger, somehow, than she'd imagined, a mass of deafening steel. She bundled her head in the sleeping bag and ran for the shelter of the pines, watching from there as the machine swooped close to the ground and hovered for several seconds before it keeled off with a final surge of power and headed back toward the desert floor.

The silence that followed was almost more chilling than the sound. For several moments Sally was paralyzed with fear and shock and pain. Then she was half-crying, half-talking to herself as she scrambled toward where he had to be. She climbed and stumbled, clawing her way across the boulders. Her feet started to bleed. Along the way, the sleeping bag caught on the sharp, jutting edge of a rock and ripped, spilling its guts out over the path.

"Oh, shit!" She swore and panted, paused for breath, and stumbled on.

The crows had found him before she did. Two of them were perched on boulders, eyeing him with nervous caws. Others were circling in the air.

The thermos had fallen separately, cracking open on the rocks like an egg and smashing into a thousand glinting pieces. The brown liquid still steamed where it had spilled.

Jimmy looked strangely comfortable—until she got close and saw that one leg was folded completely back under his body, broken at the joint. Otherwise, he was still as perfect as before: no blood or wounds, not a scratch on him anywhere that she could see.

Inside, he was bleeding to death. As she crouched beside him, he opened his eyes and she watched the pupils wander, searching for her somewhere in the distant expanses of the sky.

"Oh, God, Jimmy!"

Such a boy! So beautiful! She cradled his head in her lap, rocking, keening. "For Christ's sake, Jimmy. Don't go. Not now, not now."

There was a sound, barely human, as his lips moved, and she leaned down over him, watching, her own lips working along with his as she tried to understand. It could have been "Love!" he said. Or "Leave!" Then more of that strange, inhuman sound that came from his throat as he closed his eyes and slipped gently away from behind them.

Oh, Jesus, Jesus.

Sally closed her own eyes and was dazzled by the sudden, blinding light. She prayed like she'd never known she could. Oh, God help us. God help me, she prayed. Oh, God, take Jimmy. Take him, wherever you are. And the light turned into darkness, which she entered, thankfully.

It was the sun that brought her back, the first heat of the day, where it struck her neck. The tears had left her bruised inside but the panic was gone. She needed to get help.

No hysteria.

Stupidly, before she'd even begun to act, she found herself rehearsing words. They kept coming, she heard herself saying them: A man's been killed. I have to report an accident. A death. A killing. I have to report a murder....

Jim's head still lay in her lap, turned out from her, his face chalk-white, his lips parted. Sally pulled her cramped knees out from under him and laid the head gently on the ground.

Rick!

Thoughts came in the form of sudden shooting pains that she felt in the right side of her head, and Sally shoved them out impatiently.

Okay. One thing at a time.

Jim was dead. Sally touched his face to make herself believe it and pulled her hand away at once. It wasn't his face.

She stood up, tottering, kicking the soreness from her joints, and looked around.

The helicopter was long gone, now, improbable as a dream. Had it been there? The narrow valley was as silent and deserted as yesterday, when they had arrived. She took the sleeping bag from her shoulders and laid it over Jim's body, double folded. Then she ran back—a small naked figure among rocks and pines.

Fast. Careful.

The clearing was deserted, too.

She'd never been there. As she opened the camper door and looked inside at the bed the two of them had mussed with love and sleep, the thought arrived full-formed, uninvited, without her having worked it through: There was no need for anyone to know about her. There was no need for Rick to know. Ashamed, she tried to push the notion back behind her, but it kept surfacing. *She'd never been there.*

More hurried, now, she dressed and went through the camper quickly, stuffing the rest of her clothes back into the duffel bag she'd brought. Some stupid, sexy underwear from Fredericks. Tight jeans and sweaters. She stuffed them all in and crammed them down to close the zipper. She made a final check to be sure she had left nothing behind.

The valley was in full and brilliant sunlight, but its silence seemed unnatural and hostile now. She waited, holding her breath and listening with irrational expectation, yet she was startled by the cough of a motor starting, way up by the highway.

Shading her eyes, she scanned the ridge where she knew the highway ran. A person would have a perfect vantage point from there.

Her heart was pounding. The tears were coming back and she gulped them down. She had to move. *I want to report a murder.*

Jim had left the cab door unlocked, but the ignition key was not where he'd put it, under the mat. She fumbled with the fixture on the glove compartment and ripped it open. Nothing. Sally felt the panic coming back. Jim surely wouldn't have taken them, not to climb a mountain. She tried the inside of the camper. She turned every storage locker inside out, her hands trembling, uncontrollably. Nothing.

Sally forced herself to stop. She stood and held on to herself, shivering. She folded her hands across her chest and tucked them under her armpits. Hugging. Tight.

Logic. Okay, so there were two choices left: Climb back up to where Jim lay to search his pockets for the keys. Sally shuddered. Or hike up the trail to where they'd left her car. It was off the road, perhaps three miles away.

Shouldering the duffel bag, she headed for the steep track to the highway.

Then she remembered. *She'd never been there.* Had she?

Hollow with the growing awareness of her pain, she turned back to the camper, using her scarf to wipe the door handles and the steering wheel. With tears in her eyes, she rubbed down every last place she thought she might have left a fingerprint until, by the time she was through, her whole body seemed to shudder uncontrollably with the numbing ravages of shock, and disbelief, and fear.

Even when she reached the car, the nightmare wouldn't end. She fought the steering wheel down the rough track to the highway and knew that something else was wrong.

The moment she turned onto the highway, she knew: The car had a flat. She couldn't believe it. The rim of the wheel was rattling on the asphalt and the steering wheel shuddered in her hands.

"Oh, Jesus! Please, no!"

She saw a turnout a hundred yards ahead and edged the car onto the gravel. It was a crescent, wide enough, allowing a panoramic view of the valley. Shivering, she looked down over the parapet into the huge stillness where Jim lay alone.

She looked back down the road and up ahead. There was nothing. How often did people pass this way?

She had to move.

Her hands refused to do what they were told. First it was the hatchback that wouldn't open, then she fumbled with the floor covering and ripped the nail half off her thumb as she grabbed at the jack. The spare wheel wasn't a wheel at all, but a wafer-thin gismo with what looked to be a solid-rubber tire. The operating instructions, when she got to them, read like a foreign language. Ten times she started over.

Once she got the jack fixed in where it was supposed to go, she managed to get the wheel off the ground. She was still struggling with the lugs when the gray limousine pulled in beside her.

At first it was the crunch of gravel that she heard and hardly wanted to believe it. Then, when she looked up, the vehicle seemed to be a part of the nightmare, arriving like a silver apparition. For a moment, its tinted windows simply stared at her like blind, dead eyes.

The driver's door opened. If the man was somebody's chauffeur, he didn't come with the conventional image. He was tall, well built, with blue jeans and a blue workshirt that was lined with Western piping. Brown cowboy boots, polished to a high shine, and blond hair, all in place. A lariat, set with a milky turquoise. His watch band was a chunky silver-and-turquoise cuff and he wore a Navaho ring. A Walkman tape deck was attached to his waist, and the orange ear pads fitted snugly over his ears.

"You need help?" he asked. He didn't touch the headset, and looked down at her without a smile. The cheekbones, unusually high and prominent, were offset with startlingly blond brows and pale blue eyes. Too pale. And the man seemed purposefully to convey an arrogance in his bearing that froze Sally's sudden hope into suspicion.

"You have a telephone? A radio?" she asked.

This time he adjusted the sound on his Walkman as he shook his head slowly. "Boss doesn't believe in them," he said. "Says it's the one place he gets privacy."

Sally glanced at the aerial on the limousine. It was identical to the one they had installed for Rick's car phone. The man was smiling at her now. He stood quietly, legs akimbo, and returned her gaze. "I can give you a ride," he said.

She controlled the physical pain that tightened her gut like a cramp and simply shook her head. "You could help me with this tire," she said.

He hesitated, shrugged, unbuttoned his shirt and threw it on the seat of her car. "It's hot," he said. "No point in messing it." The wires of the Walkman draped down over his torso. It was muscular, tan, and Sally couldn't help but read the message in the way he showed it to her. She was mortified to see how easily the lugs came off. He slid the wheel from the bolts and rolled it around.

"Who did it?" he asked.

"Who did what?"

"You thought you had a flat?" he asked, shaking his head. "Jesus!"

Sally nodded. "It wasn't a flat?" she asked. She couldn't think.

He rolled the tire again and squeezed it down, pointing to a dark slit in the wall. "Somebody put a knife in there," he said, smirking as

17

though it happened every day. "Somebody slit it. Kids, maybe." He looked around with a grin, as though they might materialize from the trees. "Where's the spare?"

She watched him, her head bursting with the pressure, thinking about Rick. Trying not to think. And Jim. She saw Jim's face again and she was empty. She was sick with emptiness. Rick. She couldn't tell him and she knew she had to.

The man's nude torso was repulsive. When he had finished, he helped himself to a rag he found in the trunk and wiped himself down with it, grinning at her. He rubbed at the oil stains on his hands and forearms, then dried the light sweat from his underarms.

If Rick knew, it would destroy him. Destroy them.

Absurdly, Sally found herself wondering what music the man was listening to. He handed her the rag to hold for him like a servant, and reached past her into the car for his shirt.

"You got to be careful, lady," he said, buttoning it. "The places you go. Glad to have been of service, now."

The limousine's motor burst into action and the car moved quietly away. Sally watched it go, with the realization that she had never known if someone else was in it, looking out at her through the tinted glass.

There was Jim. Beyond help.

She already had the motor started when she saw the keys on the passenger seat. Jim's keys. The miniature death's head he had once carved from a tiny block of rosewood still dangled from the chain. She hadn't seen them there before. They couldn't have been there; surely she couldn't have missed them.

She thought of the blue-eyed driver. Light-headed, clammy with cold sweat, she looked at her watch. Ten-thirty. She shut out the thoughts and put the car in gear and drove.

It took another twenty minutes to get down from the mountain to the desert floor, watching the S-bends up ahead and the long straight cuts in the hillside for a glimpse of the gray limousine. If it wasn't ahead of her, it had to be behind her.

She pulled off the road at a country general store with a pay phone on the covered porch outside. Bald tires were heaped up by an ancient gas pump, and the yellow-green mass of a thirsty vine sprawled over rusty farm equipment and decaying furniture. A string of bells clattered as she pushed the door.

"Can you give me some change? For the telephone?"

The woman at the counter looked her over without special interest, despite the dried sweat and dirt she had dabbed at with a handkerchief in the car mirror. Somewhere she had picked up a scratch that left a smudge of dried blood on her forehead.

"Quarters?" said the woman comfortably. "You bet." She took Sally's dollar bill and snapped it out on the till, opened the register with a clang and sorted out a dollar in change.

"Have a good one, now," she said, but Sally was already out the door.

She dialed the emergency number given on the pay phone.

"Rescue," the voice said.

Sally took a breath, forgetting all the words she had rehearsed. "I just saw a man shot off a mountain," she said. "From a helicopter. He must be hurt. I mean, I think he's dead."

"What's your location, ma'am?" The question was toneless, automatic, read off from a checklist.

"Location?" said Sally. Somehow, the name Jim had mentioned surfaced in her head. "Nine Pines," she said. "He's at the foot of the cliff. But I'm not there," she hurried on, falling over the words, "he's there. I had to leave. To get to a phone."

"Is the party unattended?" the voice continued. The party. Jim.

"Yes," she said. "Well, he's alone now. I was with him. Please get someone there fast."

"Your name, please?"

"Name?" she said.

"Your name," repeated the voice.

Sally hesitated, agonized. "Just get to him," she said. "Get to him fast."

She hung up, looked back down the highway, and listened to the blood pulse in her ears. She slipped another quarter in the machine, dug in her bag, and pulled her Pac Bell credit card from its plastic folder.

4 _____

THE WHISTLE in the kitchen shrilled. Wil Garretson let the weights
drop to the floor beside the bench, grabbed a knee to help him roll
up from his back, and draped the sweat towel around his neck.

From the kitchen, he yelled: "You want coffee?"

"Decaf, okay?"

He poured water over the fine grind in the drip machine and reached
into the closet for a jar.

"Will you settle for instant?"

"Instant what?"

MaryJo came out of the bathroom and shook the water from her
hair. She studied his bare chest and grinned.

"Sweaty, huh?" she said.

"I thought you went for that kind of stuff," said Wil. MaryJo had
opened up her aerobic dance studio on Main Street the year before and
taught most of the classes herself. She was too tall to dance professionally, she said. Bullshit, said Wil. But this was the next best thing.

She came over to the kitchen counter now and leaned over the coffeepot. "Smells good," she said.

He turned her toward him and put both arms around her. "You,
too." He unhooked the towel she'd wrapped herself in, let it fall to the
floor, and stood back to admire. "Incredible," he said.

20

It was. Breathtaking. A source of never-ending wonder to him, an incredible machine she kept tuned to the finest point of fitness every day. He'd been surprised, when he first knew her, to discover that under the leotard lay a body that had none of the meager skinniness of dancers. Without any extras, it managed to be generous and full, with breasts and hips that were real breasts and hips—but tight, economical, supple, lithe. He followed the circle of a wide brown nipple with his finger and watched it respond.

"I have a class," she warned him. "It starts at eleven-thirty."

"It's Sunday." The towel had fallen from his shoulders, too, and the light swimming trunks did little to hide his rapidly expanding plans for the morning.

"My best day," she said, escaping him.

"Mine, too."

"At the studio, I mean. Sunday's my bread and butter. What about last night? You didn't get enough?"

"That was last night," he said. "This is today."

She laughed and would have kissed him but the telephone rang, and she grabbed the chance to recover her towel.

"Goddamn," said Wil. He picked the wall phone off the hook and grumbled, "Garretson." MaryJo disappeared into the bedroom.

"Wil, is that you?"

"Sally?" It was an odd time for her to call. It was odd for her to call at all.

"Wil. Thank God you're there."

He sensed the edge of careful control that covered some other expression in her voice, and pulled a kitchen stool from underneath the counter. "I'm here," he said. "What's the problem?"

There was a silence at the other end. Then she spoke quickly. "I need to see you, Wil. I need your help."

Wil looked over the kitchen counter and squinted into the intense white light of the studio. He had his time cut out to get it cleared of the clutter, half-finished pieces that he knew he'd never finish now. It all had to go. He needed space. New space.

"You want me," he said, "you got me, sweetie. You know that." The Thursday opening was the first he'd seen of Sally in months, but she'd been on his mind long before that chance encounter.

"Who called?" MaryJo poked her head around the bedroom door and Wil covered the receiver.

"Old friend," he said. She disappeared again.

"Today, Wil?" said Sally.

"You mean now?"

"As soon as I can make it."

"So when should I expect you?"

"Maybe three hours," she said. She was hell and gone, she told him. In the mountains. She sounded near hysteria.

"The mountains? Christ, Sally..."

"Don't ask," she said. "I'll tell you when I see you."

"I'll be here," said Wil.

"And, Wil..." she said.

"Yeah?"

"Don't mention this to anyone, okay?"

"Not a word," he said.

"I mean it, Wil." Had he sounded flippant? "I'm scared out of my mind."

Scared? Sally? Wil hooked the receiver back up on the wall and propped his head in his hand. He knew—rather, he sensed—that things weren't going well with her. He'd always assumed she had simply married too well, for an artist. Money does strange things to the need to produce, and Rick had plenty of it. The motive for her work—what little Wil had seen of it in recent years—was coming from the head, not from the heart. Guilt, not gut.

Reaching for the coffee maker, he threw the filter in the trash and filled a mug. MaryJo was finished in the bedroom now and he poured water on her instant, adding Sweet 'n Low.

"Well, fess up. Who was she, this old friend?" She was in work clothes: a black leotard and a wide turquoise belt, and her hair was pulled back in a pony tail. Sometimes, he thought, her eyes were proud and distant. Sometimes they danced.

"Smart ass," said Wil. She came close and he kissed her, slipping an arm around her waist. "You're looking great."

"You changed the subject."

He let her go. "A very old friend," he said. "Sally Horan." MaryJo shook her head. "You never met her," he added.

"Lover?"

"That was the funny part," said Wil. "We were in love. We weren't lovers." He laughed and let his fingers run through the pony tail. "I was much younger then," he added. No collusion, she'd said. That was the catch phrase that year. Translated, it meant: Don't sleep with anyone until you've got your earlier business sorted out.

"It doesn't sound much fun to me."

Back then was another life. "It wasn't," he said. "I was married. She didn't want to feel she was breaking us up. She wasn't—we were doing a great job by ourselves. But by the time I was free, she wasn't."

She took a seat across the counter and put her coffee down in front of her. "And you were so noble, love? I didn't know you had it in you. She didn't wait around for long, then?"

"Not her fault. It took me a long time to make up my mind, those days. Maybe I was just screwed up," he added, laughing.

"And she got married?"

"You're too young," Wil said. "The way you say it, it sounds like some quaint Victorian custom. Yes, she got married. She was right. Rick Horan. A solid guy. Ivy League, fresh out to California. He came straw-haired and charming, with a pedigree up to here. Not only that, he's a money whiz who handles business for half the artists in Los Angeles—the successful ones. When you need a good tax shelter, Rick's the man who knows what's on the right side of the law. Roughly, that is. He's done well."

"Happy ever after?"

"Well, you know." He made equivocal gestures with his hands and shrugged.

"So why did she call?"

"She needs to see me."

"Why?"

"She asked me not to say."

"Come on, Wil, this is me. MaryJo. It's not going any farther."

Wil shook his head slowly. "The truth is, I don't know," he said. "She says she's scared."

"Scared? What's she scared of?"

"That's it. I haven't the first idea."

"Well . . ." MaryJo checked her watch and bent to kiss him, rumpling his hair with her fingers. "Got to go," she said. "You'll tell me?"

"Do I see you tonight?" asked Wil.

"Not tonight," she said. "But I'll call you."

Wil kept his promise to himself and spent two hours in the studio, dismantling everything he'd put together in the last few weeks. At ten grand a shot, with half a dozen works in progress, he knew how delighted Charlie Strauss would be to know they were headed for the scrap heap. But now that Wil had made the decision, it came as an immense relief. The things had been sitting there for weeks, expecting something from him. It was the only way he knew to shake himself free. In his experience, new things only came from freedom. Not slavery to the past.

When he'd finished, he surveyed the clearance with something like exhilaration. The two storerooms in back were more cluttered than before, but here, in his working space, there was nothing. Emptiness. Pure space. It was a good first step. He picked up a pair of sunglasses from the kitchen counter and left the studio, locking the door behind him.

Outside, the boardwalk was alive with the sounds of hairy people hawking leather bags and beads, as though the sixties had never died. Hot dogs, hot radios, mimes and acrobats, street drugs, the sticky smell of grass. The perpetual carnival of reedy, costumed skate freaks, the air filled with the continual quiet thunder of their wheels and the blare of ghetto blasters.

Venice. Last refuge of the California crazies.

You had to be as crazy as the rest of them to love it. Today, a wicked Santa Ana blew down from the desert and pushed the smog back from the foothills over the basin. It brought a million city folks with it to the beach. There were those who hated the annual invasion. But for Wil, after years of Venice life, it had become a part of the natural rhythm of things. He liked the circus.

"Hey, Wil!"

He was barely a block from the studio when he was overtaken by Bernard Trost, un-hip in white shorts and an open-necked white shirt. Dark-haired, brown-eyed, he had one of those complexions that seem in permanent blush and turn to a beetroot-red in the heat. Even the V in his alligator shirt was scarlet.

"Walk with you awhile?" he asked. They fell into step and together dodged the skaters on the boardwalk, heading out past the palms to the pier where the bicycle path does a wiggle on its way south to the marina.

"How's things?" asked Wil.

Bernie paused in mid-stride and turned to look at him. "They've been after me to move," he said.

"Oh, Jesus. You too? Rent, is that it?"

Bernie nodded. "They tried that first. The guy wanted another two hundred a month," he said. "It didn't work." It wouldn't, Wil knew.

24

Not with Bernie. A writer, his work never brought him more than beer money, but Bernie had never needed to worry about that. He had a private income of some kind, a trust. "I told them I'd pay," he said.

Most of Wil's friends weren't so lucky, and many had already been forced to move. "Another two hundred a month can do a person in," he said. "So you met their increase. What's the problem?"

"They tried to worm out of their own terms. They wanted to buy me out next. They offered me fifteen grand to relocate. I told them to get screwed."

It's a familiar story. Artists ferret after space and improve it. Before you know, there's a couple of galleries moved in and the neighborhood shapes up. Then the developers bring capital and chase the artists out. They'd held out longer than many had expected in Venice—the last undeveloped beach property along the coast. And now, in the past ten years, no more, it seemed, even Venice had gotten fashionable. A half mile up on Main, boutiques and restaurants had elbowed out what had been a row of artists' studios in renovated nineteenth-century storefronts. Farther south, good spaces on streets like Market and Windward were going to sound stages for commercials and rock videos, design and architectural studios.

"Is it the landlord that you're dealing with?" Wil asked.

Down at the edge of the beach, fine sand had blown across the bicycle path, leaving little dunes at the edges. They paused a moment to watch the surfers finding the curl of the wave, ducking under, wiping out. The wind had brought out the sailboats, too, a thousand of them, flashing their white sails against the blue of the Pacific.

Bernie shrugged. "My guess is, the landlord's just the patsy. I plan to find out."

"Could Lee Lawrence be behind it?" Wil asked.

"The designer?"

Wil nodded. Lawrence had started out taking studio space on Windward, and the empire had continued to expand from there. He put out a line that combined old-fashioned macho with a bold, incongruous diversity of styles in everything from clothes to living room furniture. The first studio had been a Venice landmark for some time. Then came the restaurant on Market. Now, rumor had it, a boutique.

"That's pushing it. I doubt he has the power," Bernie said.

"You're going to follow it up?" asked Wil.

Bernie looked at him briefly and nodded. "They started eviction proceedings," he said. "Damned if I'll go without a fight. Besides, it's one for the files."

Wil grinned. Trost's collection of clippings on art-world anomalies was legendary. Crooked deals and dealers, fakes and frauds. Auctions and record prices. He kept files full of the stuff. One day, he threatened, he would write a book.

They paused, backs to the wind, and watched the skaters for a while. A blond girl, pony-tailed like MaryJo, drifted by, traveling backward, right leg raised. Her light-mauve shorts were shorter than the trim cheeks they were supposed to cover. Wil realized suddenly that Bernie had been talking at him, and he hadn't been listening. They had reached the pier.

"Turning back?" he asked.

"Can't sit around and mope," said Bernie. "Maybe I'll make it over to your place later this afternoon."

And Wil struck his forehead, remembering it was Sunday.

5

SUNDAY AFTERNOON was always open house for a small group of artist friends at Wil's place. He couldn't remember how the ritual had started, but for years there had been a bunch who drifted in uninvited for a beer or a glass of wine. It was a way to finish the weekend, a way to get started on the following week.

"Hey, Wil. Bring you a beer?"

Wil nodded absently and looked at his watch, wondering what he was going to do with his friends when Sally arrived.

Maybe he could take her back into the workspace.

He'd converted the front part of the building for his living space, walling it off from the work and storage areas and leaving access to them only through the kitchen. You reached the open loft and the bathroom by stairways either from the living room or the studio, and from there you could look down each way into the space below.

He'd built just about everything himself. The living room was centered around a fireplace that he'd added, the high white walls leading up to a long row of clerestory windows that filtered the Venice sunlight into an even glow. Aside from the occasional tall green cactus and the three long couches arranged in a wide square around the fireplace, he'd gotten almost everything in trade from friends: the centerpiece, a Navaho rug that hung about the fireplace from Tony Berlant, the airy, painted screen from Billy Al, a coffee table in glass designed by Larry Bell.

Someone set down a can of beer in front of him and he reached forward to pop the tab.

"Are you with us, Wil?"

Whatever was eating people, it was in the air. Maybe the Santa Ana. A craziness. Barbara Corton had just arrived in a neon-blue jumpsuit, her long black hair electric as her artwork, blown out with wind and static. Wil watched her cross to the icebox, pouring herself a glass of Mondavi. Leon Drake took a long, deep swallow from his own new can and waved it in Wil's direction.

"Lost them!" he snorted, rubbing a stray drop into the fabric of his brilliant Hawaiian shirt. "That's what they've done, they lost the motherfuckers! Can you believe it?" Wil shook his head and made appropriate noises. They had started out together in the late fifties, fresh out of Chouinard. Leon, Wil, and Stu Ray, a threesome. Wil found it hard to believe in a forty-nine-year-old Leon Drake. His friend looked young, smooth-faced, a little pink in the cheeks. The gray hairs mixed in among the light brown and the finely etched wear lines only accentuated the youth of his face. Flamboyantly handsome, Leon's fine features were familiar to anyone who knew their way around the LA art world.

"Lost what?" asked Barbara.

"Two paintings." Wil brought her up-to-date. "The County was supposed to deliver them back and they never showed." He kicked his heels up over the arm of the couch.

"Insured, I hope?" Barbara was practical, as well as mystically inclined. In her spare time, she read Tarot cards and palms. Leon shrugged. Money wasn't the problem. If sales counted for success, he had done better than most. His trademark paintings were filled with biomorphic images floating like magic in paradoxical spaces, ambiguously defined by hard-edge grounds. Since the early sixties they had been a feature on the international market. Expensive, always in demand, never unreservedly praised by critics but loved by the hip collector, they were the essence of what people think of as California light and color.

"Maybe you're not much used to them, Leon," said Barbara. "But the rest of us don't take the imperfections of the real world as a personal insult." Leon was one of those people to whom most things come easy —art, fame, women, money. His studio a few miles up the coast was fabled, written up in architecture journals. Out of town, in the Coachella Valley, he'd also bought a ranch. It all flowed in, and Leon accepted it with good grace and an eighteen-carat Malibu smile.

"Was that from 'Contemporary West Coast Painters'?" Dave Lyman had been silent until now. "That's a laugh." Dave was Chairman of Painting at Otis. He was one of the many artists who'd never quite made it in the public eye. An ardent hater of fads and fashions, he scoffed at Leon's habitual white cotton pants and flowered shirts, and still wore paint-spattered jeans and plaids. Even so, he had followed the drift back to representational painting and recently had been doing gloomy landscapes, hills and fields with heavily overlaid paint. Good painting, everyone agreed, but still nobody bought it.

"Come on, Dave," snorted Leon. "Your nose was out of joint from the start about this show."

Dave bristled. "Listen," he said, "for ten years they forget there's any such thing as a West Coast artist, and then the best thing they can do is mount this goddamn blockbuster with you and a couple other Hollywood stars and call it 'West Coast Painters.'"

Even Dave had caught the bug. He was angrier than he needed to be. Wil Garretson swung his leg back over the arm and yawned to release the tension. He studied the design on the red can of Tecate. It was a good three hours since Sally called.

"What does Charlie say?" asked Barbara. Charlie Strauss was Leon's dealer, too.

"He was at the opening Thursday," Wil said, trying to get back into the drift of things. "He didn't mention it."

"He hasn't said boo," said Leon. "He's a dealer." They were silent for a minute. Dealers was a subject on which most of them could agree.

"Well, anyway, who's counting?" Dave Lyman asked. "Which are they, Leon? Untitled three thousand five hundred fifty-four and Untitled three thousand five hundred and fifty-five?"

The others laughed and Leon glanced around with a sheepish grin. He produced great quantities of work and had long since run out of titles. Art by the square foot, Lyman called it.

"I don't understand," said Barbara. "Did Stu Ray ship them for you?" Stu Ray had given up on art soon after Chouinard, and gone into the transportation business.

"Sure did," said Leon.

"And?"

Leon laughed. "You know Stu," he said. "You question his people's performance, he goes purple around the collar and starts to froth at the mouth."

Wil joined in the laughter. He could see it. Stu had a tendency toward apoplexy. Still and all, they had stayed good friends, the three of them, even though they saw each other rarely.

"What about the County? What's the story there?" Bernie Trost had been nursing his own problems, off in the corner of the sofa, and spoke for the first time, quietly.

"Story?" said Leon. "They claim that Stu picked them up. They think. I spoke to Fred Aaron down at the museum. He was amazed. Embarrassed. Thunderstruck...well, you know Fred. He swore they would check into it for me. They better; I'll sue the bastards' ass."

Bernie chuckled. "God knows what they think they're doing down there," he said. "It's a total fuck-up. They found those fakes last year—the Pollock and the de Kooning, remember?" Someone laughed. "They weren't half bad, at that," said Bernie. "I saw them before they managed to get them off the walls."

There was a silence. Barbara was the first to break it: "Well, there's MOCA," she said.

"The great hope of the future," Leon joked.

And while the usual parade of more-or-less good-natured gripes about the new museum was trotted out, Wil yawned again and stretched, and went to the icebox for another beer. Then the doorbell rang. "I'll get it," he yelled.

The moment he opened the door the déjà vu kicked in like the next line in the enigmatic narrative of a dream. A blue car parked across the alley, the texture of brick in the opposing wall, a patch of pale green where ice plant sprouted unexpectedly from dirty sand, a beer can, rusting and half buried. It was all familiar but it seemed to be wanting to say something particular, if only he could hear.

And Sally. The strange thing was that he wasn't surprised. There was a scratch on her forehead, smudged brown with dried blood, and the whites of her eyes were tired and yellow, lined with red, their sockets dark and painful as new bruises. She'd been crying, and the tears began to well again when she saw him. She stumbled forward into his arms.

30

"Easy," Wil said. "Take it easy." He stood at the door for a moment, supporting her weight. The sweat had dried on her body and her clothes, caking accumulated dust and oil into uneven black ridges.

"I'm sorry," she said. With visible effort, she pulled things back into near control. She searched the length of the alley and, as though they were the first words coming into her head, she said, "I think I need something to eat." Then she frowned, puzzled.

"Of course." Wil glanced back over his shoulder. She started into the studio and stopped abruptly on the threshold.

"Oh, Jesus, Wil. You're having a party?"

"Party?" said Wil. "Hell, no. Just some of the guys over for a Sunday beer. I'll send them home. Come on in."

"No, wait," she said. She grabbed his arm and held him by the door. "Listen, it's Jim," she whispered. "Jim Sewell. He's been killed."

Wil stared at her.

"He fell," she went on. Her eyes refused to settle and she ended up gazing down the alley again. "He was climbing. You know he liked to climb?"

Wil nodded. "Some damn-fool thing," he said. "I did know that." He eased her in past the doorjamb. "Were you there?" he asked.

She didn't answer. "I shouldn't have come," she said.

Wil shook his head. "Were you with him?" he asked again. Sally Horan with Jim Sewell? Out in the mountains?

Her eyes lost focus, somewhere beyond his shoulder, then sharpened to meet his directly. "Jim was my lover," she said. "I think you're the only person I can trust."

There was laughter from behind and someone yelled, "Wil!" He ignored the sound and took her cheeks between his hands. "Okay," he said. "Then trust me. You want to clean up?" She nodded. "The shower is through there." He pointed. "And there's a robe on the back of the door. It's going to take ten minutes to get rid of this gang. Pretend they're not there."

The room was suddenly dead silent as he led her in and brought her to the bottom of the stairs. "Turn right at the top," he told her.

Watching her upstairs, he waited until he heard the door close.

"Is she okay?" Dave asked.

"Can I do something?" Barbara Corton was ready to follow her up to the bathroom.

"No, listen," said Wil. "Thanks, folks, but it's all taken care of. The best thing you can do is leave me to help her. Okay? Next week?"

He stood there, waiting for the silence to go away. For a moment everyone seemed too stunned to move.

"Am I crazy?" Leon wasn't known for his sense of timing. "Wasn't that Sally Horan? Rick's wife?" Rick handled Leon's business and taxes.

"None of your goddamn business, Leon," said Barbara cheerfully. She was the first to get up to leave. "Bye, Wil," she said. She shook out her black hair, kissed him lightly on the lips and grabbed the floppy bag she lugged with her everywhere. "But listen, you guys, I'm expecting you all this Wednesday. Okay?"

"Wednesday?" said Dave. "What's with Wednesday?"

"Oh, for Christ's sake, Lyman! Where have you been?" Leon pointed a finger to his forehead and rolled his eyes. "Wednesday? The ranch?" It was the first night of a new piece Barbara had been working on.

"I've got a whole mountain lit up for you guys."

"Neon?" asked Dave.

"And klieg," she said. "I'd use laser if I could afford it."

"I'll be there, Barbara." Bernie Trost was a faithful. One time, Wil remembered, there had been a closer relationship between the two of them. It was Barbara, not Bernie, who had opted for independence. "You got enough help?"

"Plenty, thanks, Bernie. A lot of the work's been done. I'll have some of Stu Ray's shipping people coming out on the day, and then there's a gang of students driving up with me tomorrow." Barbara taught a graduate class at UCLA.

"Fair enough, then."

"Ciao, Wil," she said. "Take care, all." She paused at the door to wave.

Leon swallowed down the rest of his beer as he watched the others leave. "Hey, Wil," he said, "I guess you know what you're doing. Good luck, I say."

"Shut up, Leon," said Wil.

"Hey man, the taxman's wife. Take what you can, I say." Leon had taken his share. "Lovely woman, huh?"

"Shut up," said Wil with a sigh. "And leave."

6

WATER HAD never felt so good, streaming in a hot cascade from the shower head through her hair and down over her body. She soaped and resoaped and then soaped again. Sally wanted to be cleaner than she'd ever been in her life. She wanted new skin. She wanted a new head.

An image kept returning despite herself—and by now she'd found it was easier to focus on the images that came than to try and block them out—Jim's nude body when she had showered with him, running her fingers the full length of it. The shock was to discover she could remember its tiniest details but couldn't recall his face. Worse, when she tried, the face that kept recurring clearly and unwanted in the place of Jim's was the driver's, up in the mountain, tan and healthy, with the light blue eyes.

Sally dried herself fast and put on the terry-cloth robe, wrapping it tight to the collar and knotting the belt firmly at the waist. She rubbed steam from the mirror with the towel and watched herself fade out again in the rapidly re-misting circle. Nothing. She felt like nothing. Numb.

When she came downstairs, there was a glass of straight amber liquid waiting on the glass-top coffee table and the single sip she took from it exploded dizzyingly inside her head. The room began to turn and she momentarily closed her eyes.

"Better?" Wil asked. He brought a white plate from the kitchen and set it down beside the glass. "Pizza," he said. "Frozen. It was all I could find."

She missed what it was he'd said and gazed around absently. "You've changed this place," she answered.

Wil laughed. "It's been a real long time since you were here." She had come as a student, with a class, and had stayed on afterward. They'd sat in two director's chairs in what was then the studio and talked into the night. It was little more than raw space in those days.

"It's been years." She stared through the glass tabletop to the rug beneath, floating. "I feel like I just stepped off a jumbo jet from Europe," she said. "The ground won't hold." Day seemed as if it should already be night.

The timer on the kitchen stove began a relentless ding and Wil left silently to retrieve the packaged pizza from the oven and brought it back on a tray. "Eat," he said. He moved a stringy slice over to her plate. "It'll help."

She leaned forward and tried a bite. "I can't believe I'm sitting here eating this," she said.

He watched her hand and the memory came back whole-cloth, brilliant: the light in the drawing studio at Otis, the one above the gallery where he taught his figure class, the torque of the model's body, contrapposto, the soft, squeaky sound of twenty charcoals on twenty sheets of paper. "Loosen up," he'd told her. "Forget the wrist. It's the action in the shoulder that counts." Standing behind her, his arm lined up with hers where it held the charcoal, sweeping the line across the paper, giving her the feel of gesture.

"Do you want me to call Rick?" he asked.

Sally started on a second piece and shook her head. "No," she said. "I took care of it. I left a message on the tape." She licked the hot paste from her fingers. "Wil...I don't want you to think..."

"You don't owe me any explanations," he said.

But she waited, insisting, searching for what it was she wanted to say. "It wasn't easy. It took years."

"Rick seems like a terrific guy."

She gave a small gesture of annoyance. "That was a part of the problem. He's great. He's wonderful. He'd do anything for anyone. Everybody loves him."

"Except you?"

She took a deep breath, and it came out as a sigh. "It's not even that," she said. "I guess I needed more of what he gave to everyone else. More time. You know...more care."

She looked at her hands. Instead, saw Jim's letting go their grip on the sheer rock face.

"You told me once he was a workaholic," said Wil.

The image went away and she frowned. Concentrate.

It was true, there'd been enough times she thought she was going crazy, she was so goddamn lonely. "I guess," she said slowly. "He's always out. I mean, he'll leave the house at six in the morning and not be back for food until ten at night. Then he lays off the guilt on me. I'm always the selfish one. I'm the one who's never satisfied. I'm the one who can't get focused. It got so that I believed him. I mean, there had to be something wrong with me, right? This great guy...I got smaller and smaller." She paused. "He was so goddamn right, it got to where I couldn't bear to have him touch me anymore. He couldn't understand that, either."

Again, the silence. Beyond the walls and windows, the distant sound of traffic leaving the beach and heading back for the city.

"The strange thing was," she went on after a moment, "the tougher he came off to everyone around us, the weaker he seemed to me. And passive. There were times he didn't care if we made love for weeks." She tailed off for a moment and came back, changing her tone abruptly: "But that doesn't help much, does it? It's foolish to blame Rick for my own mistakes."

"And Jim? He was one of them?"

Sally smiled a bleak smile. "Jim stopped by the house one day to deliver a painting. I'd met him in a class at Otis. Your class." He wasn't likely to forget: She'd been one of those students they call "mature"—coming back to college in her late twenties. Jim Sewell must have been all of nineteen himself. "So this was, what?—seven, eight years later, it must be. He walked in that day and the guy was sweet and strong and free and so darn young—he's twenty-eight, right?" She shook her head. "I seduced him—I guess that's the word. I mean, I literally jumped on him."

She disappeared for a moment, chasing after the memory, and Wil reached forward for the glass of cognac that she'd neglected.

"Will you help me hang it?" she'd asked. She'd come around to the front door barefoot, braless, in loose shirt and shorts, from the studio.

"Okay," he said. "Where should it go?"

It was an Ed Moses. It went in the bedroom. They'd worked on it together, close, Jim sweating slightly with the heat of the day. She eyeballed it for height while he held it against the wall and went back to hold it up for him while he marked the top level. Then he dropped the hook and they both went down for it together . . . Sally ended up on top.

"I never felt better," she said. She was choking back tears again now, laughing and crying together. "Honest to God, I never felt better in my life. I didn't even feel guilty."

Wil waited quietly, swirling the cognac in the glass, and waited for her to find the thread again: "After that it was an addiction. The more I had, the more I seemed to need. It went on for, well . . . more than a year." She turned to him. "I started making art again."

"I never knew you'd stopped."

"Yes. Oh, for months . . ." The little studio Rick had built for her in back of their house was a gem—tall walls with even light and not much else, but marvelously proportioned. Wil had been there, not often, but sometimes when she called to have him see the work. She made intricate, rich tapestries in acrylic paint on canvas, huge illuminations, mazes of pattern and color and anthropomorphic form.

The telephone broke into the long silence. Wil waited for it to stop, but it went on ringing until he got up to answer it. It was MaryJo. "Hi, babe," he said. He gazed into the elegant black depths of the Bengston screen. "How was the day?"

"In this heat? Grueling," she said.

He laughed.

"And you?" she asked.

"Oh, terrific."

"How's your girl friend?"

"Just fine."

"That's it? Just fine?"

"Listen, babe, this isn't the best time, okay? I'm going to have to call you back."

"Wil . . ."

"Later, MaryJo, okay? I love you."

He hung up and came to sit back on the sofa.

"Girl friend?" asked Sally.

Wil nodded. "We're lucky," he said. "It's a good fit."

"Does she..." Sally's eyes wandered to the loft.

"Live in? No." Wil laughed. "I guess we're both too wise for that. Two artists in one space."

"She's an artist?"

"Dancer," he said. She nodded absently as though she hadn't heard. "Don't you think it's time you got around to telling me?" he added.

"Telling you?"

"What happened. On the phone you told me you were scared."

She'd been stalling, enjoying the luxury of letting it all out. That wasn't why she'd come. "Jim didn't just fall off the mountain, Wil," she told him. She held his eyes steadily. "He was murdered...."

The word dropped into the quiet comfort of his living room like a boulder from the ceiling, bringing Wil to his feet. "Jesus, Sally..."

"Wait...It happened right in front of my eyes...."

"You called in the cops?"

"I think it was the mountain-rescue number I called. I was scared out of my wits. I told them what I'd seen and where to find him. Then I hung up."

"They don't know who you are?"

Sally shook her head. "That's the thing, Wil. It's Rick I've been worried about...."

Wil started to pace. "You think it was Rick?" he asked. "That's crazy."

She shook her head again, positive. "Rick never knew about Jim and me."

"You're sure?"

"It would have broken him," she said simply. "You don't know him like I do. He looks as tough as nails, but underneath, he's strung together with high-tension wire."

"If you're sure about that, then..."

"Listen," she said, interrupting him. "Wait. There's another thing I haven't told you...and this is what really scared me stupid. It was like some kind of warning...."

"Warning?"

"There was this limo...."

Wil held up a hand and shook his head. "Whoa, whoa! Let's back up to the beginning, Sally. Tell me the whole thing from the top."

She told him the gritty details, not the magic. She left out the days of planning, the story she had concocted to spend the weekend with her friend Paula. She left out her walk with Jim in the twilight and the incredible night sky, the return, almost, to that great illusion of perfect union with the universe. That all looked silly now, and childish. Instead, she told him what had happened in the morning when the helicopter awakened her. She told him about the gunshots and the broken body, the thermos flask in pieces and the coil of rope. He was shaken. She told him about the slashed tire, the limo driver and his cowboy boots, how she found the keys and the tiny rosewood death's head, and he sat there chilled to the base of his spine.

"It's incredible," he said. The story was unbelievable, but what chilled him were the images coming home to roost. Ten years later. His head was spinning.

"I can't believe it myself," she said.

His own thoughts would keep, though; he'd check into them later. The first question was this: Was Sally safe? "You drove straight down here after calling?"

"I stopped for gas."

"And the limo couldn't have followed you here? You didn't see it again?"

"No." Sally weighed the notion. "I didn't see it again. But I gave up watching after I hit the freeway. I guess it's possible. Wil," she said, "you don't think I'm in danger?"

The melodrama should have seemed absurdly out of place. And yet...

"Listen," he said. "It's small comfort, but, whoever it was, if they wanted to kill you, they could have done it, easy. They wanted to scare you off."

"They did a good job," she said.

But Wil was already thinking ahead. "They have to know Jim pretty well, if they knew his plans and they knew his weekend haunts. If you've been with Jim awhile, it's a good bet they know you, too. They can find you whenever they want."

She shuddered. "Thanks, Wil."

The variables dazzled the mind, but Wil's was in high gear now, and racing. "What the hell was Jim up to, Sally? Choppers and limos sound like serious business. I mean, that's not a crime of passion, for Christ's sake. That's planning, organization. Drugs? Did Jim do drugs?"

Sally shook her head slowly. "A guy with that love for his body? A guy who spent so much time and energy keeping in shape? I don't see it. Beside, I'd have known."

Wil wasn't so sure. A teacher who got to know his students better than most, he was past being surprised by drugs and what they do to people—and coke persisted in hanging around the higher regions of the art world like a silver-lined Hollywood cloud. It wasn't enough to love your body. People he'd known had worshiped their bodies and still done coke.

"Was he making money?" he asked. The kid had looked like some fashion model at the County opening on Thursday, and he sure wasn't living off his art. "He didn't even have a gallery yet, did he?" She shook her head. "So how was he getting by?"

"That's how I met him again. You know Stu Ray?"

Wil nodded. "Old friend," he said.

"Rick handles his accounts," she added. "Anyway, Jim worked for him, out at the Raiders."

"Oh God, one of those," said Wil. The art shipping business. He had seen enough students go that route. With all the kids coming out of art school, they had to eat. Usually they didn't stay for long in jobs like Ray's. The rare few would find a gallery and start to make enough to live. Others would drift away from art forever. Some found teaching jobs. And a few did what Stu Ray had done: start their own business and get rich. The world is full of artists doing what they don't want to do to get by.

"And there's nothing else? No dark secrets? Nothing dramatic or unusual in his life? Death in the family?"

"His family's somewhere in the Midwest, I think. He barely ever mentioned them."

There was silence. Wil closed his eyes and returned ten years in time. He saw the square surface of the table. There was a landscape there, with figures. There was a rifle, a climbing rope, a thermos flask, a bunch of keys. Nothing that quite fit together, yet everything related.

"You know what the irony is," she said, "of this whole thing? This was to be the weekend... Honest to God, I'd finally decided I just couldn't live with it anymore. I was going to tell Jim good-bye and try to make things right with Rick."

It never worked. When things had gone this far, in Wil's experience, they were impossible to patch. "He's going to find out now, Sally. You can't fuck around with murder."

Her eyes began to well with tears again. "I can't do it, Wil," she said. "All other things being equal, I'd go running to the cops. But look, I just don't see that I know anything that's useful. Dammit, Wil, I had an affair. What happened to Jim...it didn't happen because of me; I just happened to be there. Do I really have to ruin Rick's life now to pay for it? If only I could tell you how it's ripping me apart."

Another irony, Wil thought. But something, he had to admit, that strangely turned him on. He needed to move. Move on. The world outside the studio smelled good, it was time to head out and reap another crop of information. "That's it then? That's why you came? You want me to help keep you out of it?"

She was silent.

"I don't know if it can be done."

"Could it hurt to try? A day? Two days? Just see what the police come up with?"

"Isn't that what they call withholding evidence? You think you can show up two days later: 'Gee, I'm sorry, Captain...I didn't realize...'"

"I panicked. Lost my head."

Wil considered. "Are you sure there's nothing that could lead the cops to you directly? No fingerprints? No clothes? No one who saw the two of you together?"

"Not a hundred percent," she said. "There must have been people at the gas station where we stopped, out beyond San Bernardino. Then there was the woman I got change from, out in the sticks. She'd recognize me, I guess. But how? Unless they had a picture."

"Pictures," said Wil. Another image he'd used: a tiny photograph left abandoned on the ground. "Did he carry one in his wallet?"

"No," she said slowly. "He didn't do that. But...Oh, Jesus!" She brought her head forward between the palms of her hands and pressed in at the temples. "Pictures. I didn't think of that. The studio must be full of them."

"The studio?"

"Jim's place. And there's other things of mine there." She turned to him. "I couldn't bear it, Wil. Can you get them for me?"

40

"That's breaking and entering, Sally. Another crime."

"It's not a crime to walk in with a key, is it?" She took the ring with the rosewood death's head from her purse and held it out to him.

Of course. The skull. That was there, too.

7

WIL SLAMMED the door of the old silver Le Sabre and bounced down out of the sandy parking lot onto Brooks. The walls reflected his headlights in the gathering dusk.

It didn't make sense. Jim Sewell, barely five years out of school and working at Ray's Raiders. What could be more normal? But then there was Thursday night. Guess jeans. An affair with Sally, who had ten years and a lot of class and money on him. And a helicopter with a gun on Sunday morning. In some way he didn't yet fully understand, it called on him. Because of Sally. Because of a piece he'd done ten years ago that changed the direction of his work. Because he needed to get back to that source.

"Goddamn," said Wil, aloud, and banged the steering wheel with the flat of his hand. He squirted through the yellow light and made a right on Pacific, heading for the freeway.

It was twenty minutes to Jim's studio, a couple of miles west of downtown on Washington Boulevard, in one of the new low-rent areas —not much of a neighborhood for safety. The original population had been ousted over the years, first by Armenians and Greeks, then by blacks, and more recently by southeast Asian immigrants, Koreans and Vietnamese. The artists had come last. Some of each kind had stayed and they all lived in uneasy proximity, selling their particular wares in shops and restaurants and fighting, like elsewhere, mainly over parking spots.

Wil found one close to the street address and pulled in to the curb. It was eight o'clock. The best part of the light had gone and the air was heavy with remnant heat and chemical particles. It was the kind of weather that made Wil glad he had held out against the tide of artists moving east for the lower downtown rentals.

The studio was dark, and Wil found the street door boarded up with long-rusted nails. A note scrawled years ago in felt pen on the chipping paint read: "Studio entrance in back."

Picking his way past the trash cans, he turned behind the building to find an alley leading past a row of entrances. No windows here, just a sheer brick wall with loading doors the length of the block. Opposite, on the other side of the alley, was a row of doorless garages. The one behind Jim Sewell's door was dark and empty.

An open dumpster stood beside the loading door, casting an even deeper shadow where the lock was. Wil was still fumbling for the key when he heard the sound.

A shuffle. A rustle of debris.

He froze with the key in his hand, and realized suddenly that he'd taken no precautions to protect himself.

Silence. Still, he couldn't shake the feeling there was someone there. Holding his breath, he edged around the side of the dumpster and peered out into the alley.

Tensed as he was, he was still caught off guard by the charge from the darkness opposite. He hardly had time to bring his hands up to his body when he felt the impact.

He went straight down. Hit the concrete with a crunch that jarred his bones and, with the wind knocked out of him, Wil found himself pinned to the ground by a mass of solid weight. It was a moment before he could think to react, squirming and shifting, flailing with whatever limbs he could free.

It was useless. He lay still, panting, listening to the panting weight on top of him.

"Who the fuck are you, man?" The voice came close to his ear and with huge relief Wil sensed a panic equal to his own.

"A friend," he said. "I'm a friend of Jim Sewell's. Let me up and I can tell you, okay?"

"Show me," the voice said. "Prove it."

"Listen," said Wil, "I was his teacher. At Otis. Wil Garretson. If you know Jim Sewell, you'll have heard of me." He felt the weight shift slowly from his back.

"Wil Garretson, huh? What the fuck brought you here, this time of night?"

He still couldn't move for a moment when the weight was lifted from him, and lay there, cheek to the stinking concrete. Then he was helped into a roughly sitting posture and propped against the wall.

His attacker was a young black guy, burly and bearded. He had one knee on the concrete and examined his victim anxiously.

"Christ," said Wil. "That's some way to greet a visitor." He nursed the knee that had hit the concrete hardest.

"Listen, man, we stick together around here. I have the space next door. Jim and I were friends."

Wil looked at him.

"You heard about Jim?" he asked.

"Yeah, I heard. I saw it on TV. Dead when they found him. I couldn't believe it, man. The guy was a friend. . . ."

Wil put out a hand.

"Wil Garretson," he said again.

"Yeah, I heard about you. Madison. Madison Grant." He produced a sheepish grin and pulled Wil to his feet. "The stuff of Presidents," he added, with a shrug. "Too bad about Jim."

"What did they say?"

"Who say?"

"On the news."

"They said who he was and they said he fell off the cliff, is all."

"They had tape?"

"Well, yeah, sure. Just a quick shot of the guys with the stretcher and a pan up the mountain, where he fell."

Had Sally made it clear? If there'd been mention of murder on the news, that would have been at the top of Madison's mind. "I thought he knew what he was doing," Wil said.

Madison shook his head. "The guy was an ace. Ace climber," he said. "It's crazy."

Wil stopped to fit the key in the lock. "Do you mind?" he asked.

"Sure, be my guest. Where'd you get the key?"

Wil ignored the question and opened the door, reaching around the

44

sill for the light switch, then stepped in and glanced around the studio he had come to see.

"Good God," he said.

Come to think of it, Jim Sewell's place wasn't too much different from his Venice studio when he'd first moved in there many years ago. The place had only the basics to convert it from a storefront into habitable space. Here at the back, a kitchen was separated from the bathroom with a simple dry wall, the studs still exposed and water-stained on the bathroom side. Above them, a rough platform had been erected on a scaffolding of two-by-fours to create a loft, with a ladder leading up to it. That was it. Most everywhere, the wiring and the plumbing were exposed.

"So much for code," said Wil.

"Don't complain," said Madison. "It works."

Wil smiled. Much of an age with Jim, his friend was built broad and strong yet his eyes were gentle, his face almost academic with its gold-rimmed glasses and its serious, straight lines across the forehead. His hairline was already well receded, leaving only an island of fuzz toward the center of the skull. He wore a gray T-shirt with navy sweat pants and, around his neck, a thin gold chain with a crescent moon. For all his bulk, he moved lightly on his feet.

You wouldn't have a hard time liking Madison Grant, Wil thought. Or trusting him. "Lead on," he said.

In contrast with the living area, Jim's studio space was palatial—large, high-ceilinged and immaculately painted. Even in artificial light, it glowed.

"Where did the key come from?" asked Madison again. "I didn't know you knew Jim that well."

"Friend of a friend," said Wil.

Madison nodded. It took him a couple of seconds to work it through. "The chick?" he said.

The chick, thought Wil. Good God! Sally Horan, Jim Sewell's chick?

"Was she here often?" he asked.

"Two—three times a week," said Madison. "She fucked Jim over good."

"She did?" said Wil.

"Guy was never the same, once he started up with her," said Madison. "It happens. He was beginning to make it, see. He was just beginning to get there. Then this broad comes in and, zap, he's lost it. Jim got to the point where he thought of nothing but money anymore."

Wil shrugged. Maybe the kid was just growing up.

The track lights flooded the walls with an even wash of brightness and several paintings in different stages of completion were propped or hung against them. In one corner, a rack housed dozens of large canvases. Too much, thought Wil, too fast. He gazed at the paintings that lined the walls. Using a single, flat horizon line, Jim had been working to open the painting up at this point to a source of light that seemed to come from behind and within. He could see what Madison meant. The new work seemed to have reached a plateau. It wasn't going anywhere much, and the painting was still thin. The potential was there, but Jim was struggling with the same issues he had been working with in art school.

"Was there anything else you noticed?" asked Wil. "I mean, any other changes. Aside from his art?"

"Just that he used to be a friend. We used to rap a lot, you know. We worked together, too, down at the Raiders. I helped him get the job there. Past couple of months, he's been weird. That's the only word for it, man. Weird. Into himself. He hasn't had time for anyone or anything. Almost like he was getting ready to go, you know what I mean?"

Wil turned away from the paintings to look at Madison, impressed by the accuracy of the perception.

"Listen," he said, "I'm going to look around. For Sally, okay? She's married, you understand. She just didn't want any of her things found here, and she thought the cops might come. They haven't been here yet?"

"For an accident? In the middle of the night?"

"Yeah," said Wil. "I see what you mean. Well, for some reason she thought they might."

Madison shrugged. "They haven't been here since I've been home. I guess I would have known; I've been working in the studio since early afternoon. Which reminds me," he added, looking at his watch. "There's something I promised to have done tonight."

"Listen," said Wil. "I was thinking. I might just see you tomorrow. Don't be surprised, okay?"

"Tomorrow?"

"Maybe," said Wil. "Meantime, can you forget you saw me here tonight—for Jim?"

"Saw who?" said Madison. "You lock up, now, when you leave."

Wil closed the door behind him. In the large silence of the studio, he was strangely conscious of Jim's presence—Jim's and Sally's. He climbed the vertical ladder into the sleeping loft and hauled himself over the edge.

It was almost funny, the thought of Sally shinning up here, ready to tumble into bed. There were signs of her touch: the double mattress on the floor was made up with fresh, patterned sheets and pillowcases and a covered quilt that looked more like Bullocks Wilshire than J. C. Penney's. A vase of flowers stood on the orange crate used for a bedside table. Dead now, the blossoms had dropped pollen on the doily that was spread out under them, and dusted the cover of a book. Jim's bedtime reading: Nietzsche. That figured.

No pictures anywhere. That was all, except for a row of concrete-block shelves with Jim's clothes and a silk robe hanging on a wall hook, all soft and redolent of Sally. Wil checked the shelves, then took the robe and slung it over his shoulder.

He climbed back down and started in the bathroom. There were a sink and a rusty shower with a couple of cockroaches scurrying for cover. It had been painted recently and a new shower curtain hung, to hide the worst of the corrosion. On the bottom shelf of the mirror cabinet, he found a little row of feminine items: Jean Naté After Shower, some talcum powder, same brand, and a handful of cotton balls. They could have been anyone's but they weren't, they were Sally's and Wil pulled them out, making a stack of things to take home on the kitchen table.

In the refrigerator he found half a six-pack and a couple cans of Tab, some plastic-wrapped cheeses, salami, a loaf of bread and an opened carton of milk. There were a few anonymous packages in the freezer, whose door was jammed with several months of ice. Sally had not had much to say in the food department. She probably had enough of that at home.

Wil grabbed a can of beer and went back to the studio. There was a big old kitchen table Jim must have used for drawing, covered with stacks of paper. Wil popped open the beer can, set it down, and started to sort through them.

There must have been two hundred drawings and watercolor sketches—nice enough, some of them, but mostly not the slightest interest to anyone anymore, studies for work that would never be com-

47

pleted. He found a number of his-and-her drawings in nude poses and went through them carefully, pulling the ones that were recognizable as Sally. The pictures of Jim he left, pausing only long enough to recognize the results of his teaching. There wasn't the raw talent for the figure you could find in Jim's, but they were well enough done—with loving attention to detail in the private parts. Wil grinned. He could see the two of them, sitting around making pictures of each other.

He made a pile of drawings and left them with Sally's robe and the stack of toiletries.

Working some more on the beer, he turned to the drawers in the desk. The file drawer was stuffed with journals—black books, crammed with drawings and notes. He flipped through a couple, checking the dates on the flyleaves, and picked out the most recent: The first date was in March, and it ended with a handful of blank pages at the back.

No doubt the kid had been goofy for his lady. Wil found pages of erotica, little sketches where he had reinvented every position known to man. There were poems, too, that made Wil wince. He hoped they would have made Sally wince if she'd seen them. It was straight ejaculatory stuff, pyrotechnical sex reduced to absurdity by art-school spelling.

In other notes, there was a kind of anguish. It ranged from the maudlin self-pity of a teenager to rank social cynicism and anger. The old, tired art-and-money bind. Fuck art. Fuck the rich. Wil would have expected better if he hadn't been teaching twenty years.

Between the pages, around about March, Wil found a folded note on an old piece of Otis stationery—ripped off, no doubt, from someone's office years before. It was undated. "Sally," it started, "Youre husband is such an asshole, I can't beleive it. A man devotes his entire life to sucking the blood of artist's and you say you love him. . . . How can you live with yourself and this man? How can you tell me . . ." Mercifully, moral outrage had peaked into impotence at that point. Clearly the thing had never been mailed—a blessing for all concerned. Wil stuck the paper in his pocket.

Around mid-April, he found a single page with a telephone number, written large, in black, circled three times in red. He ripped a page from a notepad and copied down the number.

The other desk drawers were mostly filled with materials: pencils and colors, various inks, a box of watercolor tubes. Two of them were stuffed with papers. In one, there was a sack of unsorted letters, business

48

and personal, which yielded little of any interest at first glance—and nothing on the distinctive stationery Wil would have recognized as Sally's. The other drawer contained a shoe box with bank statements, mostly in unopened envelopes, along with stacks of used checks and blanks and a savings book.

Wil hesitated. The job he'd come to do was done, wasn't it? Still, now that he was here, there could be no harm in satisfying his remaining curiosity. He went carefully through the box. Within an hour, he knew from the employee's wage stubs that Jim earned between two and three hundred a week and, from the heap of canceled checks, that he bought his clothes at funky shops on Melrose and his groceries at Lucky's. He had been through the gas and electric bills and Pac Bell: no long distance calls, but a list of toll calls in the 213 dialing area and a few 818's, the area code for the Valley. He checked the April billing against the number he had found in the notebook: There were several calls. Wil jotted down dates, along with a couple of other recurring numbers.

He opened the little bankbook. It dated from two years ago, but until April this year there had been at most two, three hundred dollars in the account. Then two deposits of five thousand dollars each in April and May, along with a few cash withdrawals, brought the current total to $6,229.57. Wil raised an eyebrow. Jim Sewell seemed to have found a way to relieve his money problems.

He pushed the drawers closed and stuck his feet up on the tabletop.

Sifting through his thoughts, Wil might have missed the sound of the truck in the alley if it hadn't stopped right at the studio. The cab door slammed. Boots made an easy pattern of footsteps on the concrete, chains and bolts clattered against metal.

Caught off guard for the second time, Wil hadn't time to switch off the studio lights. He barely had his feet off the table when the man unlocked the door, cracked it open, and froze on the threshold, unprepared for the light.

He hesitated, framed for a second in the door, then turned and ran.

Wil reached the door in time to see the cab door crash closed. The engine caught and roared, and the panel truck lumbered off down the alley with its rear doors swinging wide. It lurched into a hard right at the intersection and hauled off into the darkness.

"Fuck it!" Madison Grant appeared from behind the dumpster. "I tried to jump him, man. Too late."

"You did a better job on me," said Wil.

"Did you see him?"

"Not worth anything. He was half in the shadow, just a blur."

They stood side by side in the alley and stared at the corner where the truck had turned.

"A truck?" said Madison. "The guy dies, and they come out here to rip off his paintings at midnight?"

Wil's head started to throb. Jim's paintings weren't worth a damn on the market, God knows. But aside from that, there was nothing in the studio that would have needed a truck.

Madison followed him back in. "You thinking what I'm thinking?" he asked.

Together, they sorted through the canvases stacked in Jim's racks. It was a couple of minutes before they found what the truck had come for. Stashed between Jim's own paintings, surface to surface, protected with polyethylene wrapping, were two Leon Drakes. Market value maybe seventy grand between them.

"Holy shit!" said Madison. He pointed to the length of two-inch tape holding down the plastic wrapping at the edge. It was marked in black felt pen with a series of identifying numbers. "They're Raiders marks," he said. "These things disappeared a few days back. Goddamn Jim ripped them off? Jesus! The guy was crazier than I thought."

They pulled them out and leaned them against the wall, then stood there for a moment and looked at them in silence.

"Listen," said Wil, on impulse. "Maybe we'd better not mention this to anyone. Maybe not till we've thought it through, okay?"

"Hey, man, my job's on the line. Stu Ray would kill me."

"Stu Ray's about my oldest friend. I'll square it with him, if he ever finds out. A couple of days, okay? Help me get Sally off the hook?"

Madison hesitated. "What makes you think they won't be back? It looks like they think they own the stuff. Just where do you plan to put this, man?"

Wil thought for a while and smiled. "Your studio?" he said.

50

8

BACK AT his own place, Wil stopped in the kitchen long enough to pull the tab off another can of beer and went on through to his worktable to get some thoughts on paper. His habit was to work from a plastic tray of three-by-five note sheets, pinning them to the celotex board in rows as he developed his ideas. Tonight, he cleared the board of everything that remained there, clipping stacks of old notes together and setting them aside.

There was an uncomfortable twinge that dogged his conscience, somewhere—something that was left undone, or something done that should have been left undone. He couldn't bring it into focus and abandoned it. It would come when it was ready.

Clean sheet.

Then he opened the third drawer of the steel cabinet and flipped back through the tabulated files, stopping at one of them and sliding it out. Inside, there was a plastic sheet of color slides and a small stack of black-and-white glossies. Wil held the slides up to the light and squinted through. Then he slipped the sheet back in the file and pulled out the whole sheaf of glossies, lining them up on the celotex board with push-pins.

Up close, through his half-moons, he inspected the detail shots of the construction one by one, his heart beating. He'd been right. Now what?

Out front, the street door opened quietly and Wil looked at his watch, surprised.

"MaryJo?" he called.

It was a moment before she put her head around the kitchen door. "What the hell's been happening?" she asked.

She didn't wait for the answer, though, and Wil listened with half an ear to kitchen noises, studying the pictures on the board in front of him until she appeared with a spoon in her mouth, a steaming mug of chocolate in one hand and a brim-filled dessert bowl in the other. "I'm hungry," she explained.

He wheeled over the second office chair next to his own and helped her down with a kiss. "You taste of ice cream," he said. "I thought you were staying home?"

"I was." She set the cup down on the floor and attacked the bowl as though she'd fasted for a week. "I got worried," she managed, between mouthfuls.

"Worried?"

"Good God," she said. "I leave you for an hour and this broad's all over you." She waved the spoon at him. "I called five times this evening. You weren't home."

"You want to hear?"

She nodded.

"Then eat your chemicals and listen, okay?"

"Okay."

"First the preamble..." He started three weeks ago, the first of the signals he remembered clearly. It had no meaning that he could identify. It was simply there. He'd been headed back from Palm Springs, from an installation he'd been doing at the museum, and there it was—the particular angle of vision from the Le Sabre, westbound on the freeway; the peculiar quality of light at sunset, and the line of the mountains; the lazy turn of the blades of the tall wind towers, where they stood in rows on the crest of a nearby hill, creating electric current.

There it was, with the chill and the unquestionable visual certainty of a déjà vu. And for no reason that he understood, the whole was powerfully tied in his mind with this other image, the memory of the woman he'd once known, still knew, but differently, occasionally only, as a dear, close friend.

"You know when you're dry?" he went on. "When you're coming to an absolute dead end in your work? When you know that you've just

52

been going through the motions?" MaryJo nodded, spooning the last of the ice cream slowly. "After times like that, when it starts to come back, I get to feel like some kind of an open channel," he said. "It's electric. Everything around me seems to conspire, and I don't know what it's trying to tell me. The harder I try, the less sense I can make of it all." He paused. "I've learned to leave it alone and follow it."

He paused again and watched her nodding that it made some sense. "It's been like that," he said. He told her about the opening, Thursday night. The telephone call that morning. He told her about Sally's visit and her story, plus his own foray into Jim Sewell's studio.

When he was through, she'd finished her ice cream and had come to stand behind him, breaking the knots of muscles in his neck with the balls of her thumbs.

"Okay," she said, working. "So what's this?" She nodded toward the pictures on the celotex board.

"It's more of the same," he said. "Except that I did this piece ten years ago. Long before we met. Around the time I first knew Sally, as a mater of fact. It was a leap—the transition between the paintings and the floor pieces. It pulled me out of the last long drought. The piece was called—get this—*Murder at Flat Rock Springs*." He laughed uncomfortably. The title had been intended to raise a smile, evoking the element of pastiche he'd been playing with at the time.

She looked at the pictures. "A déjà vu in reverse?"

"That kind of thing. But this is really enough to spook you. Come over here, take a look at it." He brought her close to the board and pointed. "This one's the whole piece, okay?"

Substantially, it looked much the same as the long row of boxes in the County show—a little bigger in scale, a little clumsier in concept and execution. A kind of diorama that you looked down into from above, two levels, split horizontally by the wandering curves of plexi sheet, echoing and responding to each other.

"A mystery, huh?"

"Right. It was kind of a tease—a take-off on the whole notion of the 'mystery.' A narrative with no particular start or ending, a whodunit with only the clues, no characters. Now take a look at the images."

They moved on. The objects were arranged like "clues," all tiny in scale and proportionate to each other: a footprint in the sand; a barrel cactus. "Oh, shoot," said MaryJo. "I see what you mean." A rifle, leaned against the trunk of a tiny tree. A coil of rope. A pair of empty cowboy boots, one half-buried in the sand. A key ring with three keys. A tiny thermos with scattered shards of glass. A torn sleeping bag. A death's head. "You think...?"

"Listen," said Wil. "I don't make too much of it, okay? I'm no psychic, and there's nothing here that's that unusual for a kind of rustic campground scene. This isn't the answer to Sally's problem, that's for sure."

"So what is it, then?"

"It's a puzzle. Maybe a sense of destiny, if that's not too big a word. Something that seems to make me a part of what's happening. A direction..."

"Wil...?"

He was absorbed again, sifting through the images.

"Yeah, babe?"

She sucked the spoon. "You won't get confused between life and some dumb artwork, will you? This business of Sally's is police stuff."

"Well, they know the facts. Let them get on with it. I want to help her if I can, you understand?"

MaryJo laughed at that. "You think this is helping Sally? Or Jim? You're dreaming, Wil."

"I just want to do something...."

"For them? Or for you?"

He thought it through. "Okay," he said. "So maybe I need this as much as she needs me. It's a goddamn boring life, if you're never ready to take a risk."

"What kind of a risk, for Christ's sake, Wil? And 'destiny'? Come on. That sounds so fucking pompous. You're not talking about some theoretical problem in the studio."

The flash of anger should have been a warning to him, but he plowed ahead. "So I need to get out of the studio. I've been sitting here making tight-ass little boxes for ten fucking years."

"Be honest," she said. "You're still in love with her."

"Are you kidding? Are we having a fight?" He wanted to pull back now, too late, laughing and reaching out to put his arm around her waist, but she ducked away.

"No, seriously," she said. "Are you?"

"In love with her? No. But as a friend... You never lose those kind of feelings for a person, do you?"

MaryJo picked up her mug and the ice cream bowl. "You sleep on it, Wil," she said. "I'm off."

"You won't stay?"

She was already halfway out to the kitchen. "Listen," she said. "You've got things on your mind. I'll see you later, okay?"

Wil listened to the front door close behind her, then stared at the board and worried after the tag ends of her thoughts. Even assuming she was right, she'd blown the whole thing way out of proportion.

He reached for the note tray, starting slowly at first, making notes of random thoughts and images in neat calligraphic print and pinning them to the board. In a few minutes, though, he was working fast, without leaving time for reflection, easily, allowing his instinct to work for the other processes, waiting for things to take shape as they did when he started out with a new art piece. After forty minutes, for reasons he hadn't paused to analyze or question, he ended up with one note near the middle of the board that called out for attention. It was printed large: RAY'S RAIDERS. The others seemed to be grouped around it, in various stages of proximity.

"Goddammit," he said to himself. "Why not?" He stared at it for some minutes, then went to the telephone and dialed Dave Lyman's number. Go for broke. It felt right, too. Aside from anything else, his teaching was getting stale. Charlie Strauss was right. He should have taken the time anyway.

"Dave," he said, "Garretson. I need to take the rest of the summer off."

There was a silence. Wil studied the pattern of notes against the celotex. It was there.

"Jesus, Wil, what time is it? What did you say?"

"You heard. I'm sorry, I need the time. It's only another three-four weeks, for Christ's sake."

"Wil, are you drunk or something? What happened since I left?"

"Stone sober, Dave. Listen, I'm asking this as a favor. I wish I didn't have to."

"Starting when?"

"Starting tomorrow."

"What do you expect me to tell all the folks who signed up just because you were teaching, Wil? You don't owe them something?"

"Dave," he said wearily. "Don't lay the guilt on me. I'm reliable, huh? Usually? Just this once. Tell them I'm sick. Whatever."

"And how do you think I'm going to replace you, at this notice? My God, Wil, this is ridiculous."

"Come on, Dave. I know you've got a list as long as your arm, people just lining up for teaching jobs—the poor sods are breaking down the doors. They don't even know what they're in for. You tell me you can't find someone to fill in for me before Tuesday?"

"Tuesday?"

"Tuesday noon. It's my first class from now. Do me a favor?"

There was a silence at the other end of the line. Then Dave said: "Okay, I'll do it for you, Wil. You're going to owe me one on this."

"Right. So I owe you. I won't forget. And, Dave, thanks, I appreciate it."

He only realized after hanging up that it was well past midnight. Spreading Jim's drawings on the studio floor, he went over them carefully. There were perhaps a dozen of them. Whatever else, the kid had been able to catch some small part of the spirit of this woman he'd stumbled on. Beyond their technical facility, the drawings were infused with a passion Wil could never have taught him. A shame, he thought.

Then he searched around in the studio for one of his own sketch pads. He hadn't used them in years.

9

DAY BROKE with incredible slowness, defining the frills of the bedroom draperies, the edge of the armoire, the long arc of the standing lamp. Sally struggled to adjust her eyes, forcing them to dwell on the familiar detail.

And Rick.

He snored lightly, easily as he slept. Whatever he may have noticed when she got home at eight, the only comment he made was that she looked tired. Even so, she'd encouraged him to get to bed in good time, feigning interest in a movie that she didn't watch. Later, all night, she had huddled on the far side of the bed, sprung tight as a dam to hold back the flood of grief she felt inside, for fear of waking him. She'd tried to switch off the feelings.

Toward dawn she must have dozed off into a restless sleep, for she woke from a nightmare thinking about the sleeping bag. With that special clarity of dream, she saw it catch and tear on the rock and watched the stuffing billow out like clouds against an impossibly blue sky, engulfing her. She couldn't breathe.

Once she was sure she was awake, she lay motionless awhile and stared up at the ceiling fan that made slow circles overhead.

The image resisted her attempts to shake it. It didn't take much to figure out that a man who had fallen two hundred feet on solid rock wasn't about to get up, walk a half mile to his camper, come back and cover himself with a sleeping bag before dying. It was something she badly needed to tell Wil.

Sally turned her head quietly to watch Rick sleep. At forty-three—five years ahead of her—he still had the youthful, no-frills good looks of a well-bred Easterner, along with that perennial small-boy quality of the Eagle Scout. A frank, open face—but you could measure the distance between eyes and mind in oceans. The friendliness, people found as they got to know him, was always on the surface, and many had given up on the frustrating business of trying to get him to open up—a notion he found to be absurdly Californian anyway. For all that, he wore a perpetual air of innocence that left Sally with a curious blend of tenderness and irritation.

His habit was to sleep like a baby until he woke, and then he was wide awake, in gear, and driving.

The alarm read just past six. She had to get up. She slipped from the bed and wrapped a robe around her as she went downstairs. Sourdough was already yowling on the sun porch and she opened a can of tuna for him, setting down his bowl and scratching his head before going out for the newspaper.

The day was painfully brilliant for her aching eyes, its edges blurred only slightly by the haze which the summer day would soon turn into smog. The street had a glazed, ephemeral quality, the orange-tiled roofs set at multiple angles to each other, the soft pastels of Spanish houses blending with the green palette of palms and yucca, dark cypress and pale grass.

My street, she had to tell herself. I live here. Then, as she stooped by the wrought-iron gate for the newspaper, her robe fell open and Sally was startled by the intense and physical feeling of exposure. She straightened quickly, bringing her body back into the folds and tightening the belt as she smoothed her robe and glanced up and down the street. Then she hurried back to the house.

She pulled the string off the *Times* on the porch and an envelope slipped out—a simple white envelope without stamp or street address. Her name was written in big, childish writing that could have been the mailman's: Mrs. Sally Horan. She opened it absent-mindedly and pulled out a single sheet of paper with what felt like a small, square card inside.

Not a bill. Then what?

Oh, Jesus. She closed her eyes for a moment, propping herself against the washing machine and fighting back a sudden dizziness as she unfolded the paper.

Please no. The Polaroid print showed her naked, laughing, lascivious on a pile of pillows. Legs parted, she pointed a finger down into the bunch of hair. It was a terrible print, but there was no mistaking her. Her skin was blanched from the flash and her eyes glowed strangely, yellow as a cat's.

"Oh, Jesus," she said aloud. She had to run to the downstairs bathroom gasping, and leaned down over the bowl, an instant dull, sick headache throbbing in her temples. She wanted to throw up and her stomach heaved and retched but nothing came. Ripping the picture into tiny pieces, she flushed the toilet and watched them disappear down the drain.

Another thing forgotten. Jimmy had taken a dozen of them one day, it must have been months ago. She couldn't remember why she had the camera with her, but he found Rick's SX70 in her bag and pounced on it like a toy. There had to be at least ten others that he'd taken and kept— for blackmail purposes, he told her. So she could never leave him.

There were pictures of Jimmy, too—pictures of whatever nude parts of both of them they could bring together in one picture, giggling, with the camera at arm's length.

Where were they?

Sally's head reeled. She sat on the toilet, waiting for the nausea to pass, then ran upstairs to where the guest-bedroom window overlooked the street and parted the slats of the Levelor an inch to look up and down the street.

Nothing. There were all the familiar cars, and the quiet of early morning.

"Sally!"

She jumped, her heart racing again. Rick stood at the door in brown-striped pajamas. He rubbed his eyes.

"Oh, Jesus," she said. "You scared me."

Rick's smile was tentative, puzzled. "I'm sorry," he said. "What's going on?" He stepped into the room and she froze there, waiting.

"It's okay," she said. "I'm sorry. Just checking the street."

"Checking the street?" He reached for the pull and raised the Levelor abruptly, letting in more sunlight than her eyes could stand. "What's to check?" He turned to look at her again and frowned. "You don't look okay. I'm sorry, sweetie, but you look plain terrible."

When he put her arm around her she couldn't help it, she shuddered at the touch. "I guess I'm not feeling great," she said.

"Maybe you should have stayed in bed?"

"No, really, I'll be fine."

"Really? You mean that, now?"

"Really."

He looked at her. "Well, fine." Whether he believed it or not, she knew he was relieved to be off the hook. He didn't trust himself with the overt signs of human failings. "Maybe a bite of breakfast wouldn't hurt?" he added, his voice more cheerful, losing its morning burr. He looked at his watch.

"Sounds good." She forced herself to match his tone.

That had been the trouble from the start. If he could only unbend. If he could only have forgotten the damn clock from time to time, along with his goddamn sense of obligation to everyone else. Sally hurried downstairs to make coffee and steeled herself against the next shock when she found Jim's picture featured on the first page of the Metro section of the *Times*. Her eyes ran to the caption: "Climber Found Dead."

The picture was an old one. His face looked narrower with the beard she remembered only from art-school days, his smile thinner, his eyes tighter and somehow more intense.

Heart pounding, she followed the lines of the short article with her finger until she came to the final paragraph: "Local police," it read, "are asking the public's help in tracing an unidentified female companion." You read these things about other people, not yourself. "An LAPD spokesman working with the sheriff's office would say only that officials believe this individual can help them in their inquiries."

Deliberately, she folded the section and tucked it back in the folds of the front page. Then she cracked a single egg over the poacher and slipped two whole-wheat slices in the toaster oven before Rick made it down to the kitchen in his terry-cloth robe and slippers. Sitting down, he folded one leg across the other, revealing a V of golden hairs the length of his thighs. She turned away.

"Coffee?" she asked.

"Thanks, hon," he said. In a gesture she felt to be awkward, stilted, dishonest in some way, she straightened the haystack on his head and poured coffee into the mug with RICK printed on the side. Rick reached a hand around her waist and smiled. "How was the trip?"

"Terrific," she lied.

"And Paula?"

"She's just great." It was a mistake to have used Paula for her alibi. It had seemed like a perfect idea at the time, since Paula had needed one too. But then Paula often did. "Driving poor Kenneth crazy, as usual."

Rick laughed and stirred his coffee, shaking out the front page of the *Times* for the usual quick glance with which he seemed to be able to take in all the news.

Sally came to the table and sat down to watch him eat. "Are things going well?" she asked. "At work, I mean?"

Folding the front section back, he picked up the Metro and paused to look at her curiously. "Terrific," he said. Would he notice? "Everything's just fine. What's special about today?" The edge of irony was barely perceptible, yet familiar as dirty socks on the floor beside the bed.

He'd met Jim only a couple of times, casually. If he noticed the picture, though, he made no comment, opening out the big sheets to the op-ed page. Jim's picture dangled from his hand. "You seem, well, out of it, these past few weeks," she said hurriedly. "I was worried."

"I've got a lot on me, hon, is all. You know how it is." He lowered the wall of paper that he'd propped between them. Beyond the smile, she saw the sheer concentration of accumulated pain and tension in his eyes and reached out for his hand across the table.

"Anything I can do?" she asked.

She wanted to cry. There was a brief moment when it could all have come unstuck—but the moment passed.

"You can be a love and bring me some more coffee."

By the time she did, he was past the op-ed and ready to move on to the Monday Business section.

Sally drank coffee. She hated the stuff because it hyped her up, but she drank it anyway, watching and waiting for Rick to be through with breakfast. By the time he was ready for his shower, she noticed that her hands were trembling. She dialed Wil's number.

"Garretson."

She heard the water start and the shower door close. "Wil," she said. "Thank God! Jesus, Wil, I can't believe this is happening." The break-fast tension spilled out in a mess of words, the Polaroid, the envelope with the newspaper, waiting at the gate.

"Whoa," he said. "Hold up."

"What do I do, Wil?" she asked. "For Christ's sake, tell me, what do I do now?"

He took a minute to think it through. "Don't let them scare you. They're trying to make you believe they'll somehow move in on you if you talk."

"I figured that out."

"Or at least they want to show you they can fuck your life up for you."

"No more than I already have." Sally set her jaw and held back the emotions. She wasn't going to lose it now.

"That's the point. I know you won't like this, Sally, but I think you have to go to the cops. If you like, I'll go with you. Tell Rick. Then go tell the whole damn story to the cops. What can I say?"

She shook her head. "No way," she said. "Not now. Listen, Wil, I'm scared. If I could help Jim, it would be different. As it is, all I want is to run away and hide."

"Right. I would, too. But you need more help than I can give you, love."

"Did you get to the studio?" she asked.

"Sure, I got there. I found some pretty interesting pictures myself. Life drawings. His and hers."

A brief stab of pain, then there was a flash of color at the window, where a blue jay landed for its morning crumbs. "What did you do with them?" she asked.

"I brought them back with me," he said. "They're here, along with a few other things I picked up. Got any idea where Jim might have laid his hands on an extra ten grand?"

"Ten thousand dollars?" The jay's eyes stared at her accusingly from its perch in the back yard.

"Ten thousand in the past three months. I found his financial records. There were two deposits on a savings account at the Wilshire National. One on May 4 and one on June 12, five grand apiece. Any ideas?"

"None."

"Another thing," said Wil. "You may as well know it all: I found a couple of stolen paintings in his studio. Did Jim make a habit of stealing art?"

"Jimmy? Steal? You're crazy, Wil. He had no reason to."

"Ten thousand bucks ain't bad. I could bet he'd never even dreamed of that much money before."

"But what would he need it for?"

"For you."

Sally was silent, thinking. There had been times Jim wanted her to get divorced and live with him. When he swore he was going to make it big. She'd thought he was joking.

"So what were the paintings?"

"A couple of Leon Drakes. Strangely enough, I knew about them before. They got lost in transit, somewhere between the County and Leon's studio. He's been screaming about them for days."

He focused with sudden clarity on the thought that had nagged at him last night. He shouldn't have moved them. He should have left them where they were, for the police to find. He'd gotten caught up in the momentum of the thing.

"And they were in Jimmy's studio? I just can't see him stealing." The jay preened, turning his attention from the missing crumbs to Sourdough, and the cat put on his best show of disinterest, stalking away through the yard.

"So what other ideas do you have?"

"He might have sold something," she said doubtfully. "There was some talk of a gallery taking him on. I think it was Charles Strauss, he said..."

"Charlie? He wouldn't touch the work."

She heard the shower door close upstairs and pulled the extension out to the back porch. "I seem to remember him saying he had some kind of an in. Well, maybe it was someplace else. I don't remember."

"You know damn well that Jim's work wasn't near ready for any gallery show, let alone Strauss. What else is there, Sally? A MacArthur grant? Let's be serious. A great new benefactor who cottons to his budding genius? You say it couldn't be dope. What are we left with? Two stolen paintings, ten grand in the bank, and a kid who transports art works for a job. Jesus, Sally, you tell me how to put that together. You knew the guy."

Did she? She'd always thought that Jim had told her everything.

"On the other hand, there's blackmail and extortion," Wil went on. "It it weren't for the Leon Drakes, to someone standing outside this thing, there'd be one nice, juicy answer: Horny wife of wealthy accountant falls for young gigolo and coughs up when he says he'll send the pictures to the old man."

She concentrated on the sounds from upstairs. Five minutes, maybe. "That's rubbish," she said.

"You know that, Sally, and you tell me that it's so. I'm with you, love. but if the police start putting things together, we're going to have to hope like hell that they'll go along with you as trustingly as I do."

"I thought of that. It's one more reason to steer clear of them."

"It'll look a whole lot worse if they figure it out for themselves."

Rick's closet door closed. "Wil," said Sally. "I've got to go."

"You want to go on with this thing?"

"I have to."

"I'm not convinced. But let's say one more day. I guess for that long you can fake it, if the cops want explanations. Will you do something for me?"

"Of course."

"I picked a few numbers from Jim's telephone bill around the time those payments were made. Why don't you take the time today to dial the numbers and see what you can get. If worse comes to worst, you can always claim a wrong number. But see if you can find who's at the other end. Okay?"

She wrote down the numbers he gave her. One of them was the studio number that she kept unlisted.

"Anything else?" she asked.

"Yes. Take care of yourself. Look over your shoulder a lot. Watch out for a gray limousine."

"You'll stay in touch?"

"I have these things of yours. I'll stop by with them, late afternoon, okay? Around five-thirty, six. Your place. Oh, I forgot to tell you, don't try calling me at Otis; I won't be there. I quit."

"You quit?"

"Yeah. I'll tell you more later."

Rick was finished. She heard his footsteps on the stairs and in the hall. She came back into the kitchen. "Okay, then," she said loudly. "Good-bye."

"Bye, Sally. You take care."

But she'd already hung up and Rick breezed in with his briefcase. "On the phone already?" he asked. "Who do you find to talk to at this time of day?"

64

She used the same lie she'd used once in the past. "Oh, just Blanca." Remembering how guilty she'd felt. A little lie. "She was supposed to be here today. Rick?"

"Yes, Sally?"

She laid an arm on his sleeve.

"Stay home. You're working too hard. Stay home with me, just today."

He laughed. "Are you kidding, lady? I've got work stacked on my desk this deep, and I'm leaving for Chicago in the morning."

"You're leaving?" Sally felt a cold void in her stomach.

"Don't tell me you forgot? Jesus!" Rick was incredulous. It was true, she'd forgotten. Chicago. Some national meeting.

"You really have to go?" she asked. She meant it.

"Sure I have to go. Are you crazy?" Then Rick was out the door with nothing more than a peck, and Sourdough came rubbing his neck against her ankle. She picked him up and scratched him under the chin.

"That's it," she told him, listening to Rick's car leave the driveway. "We're alone. You and me, cat." The difference was, he didn't seem to mind.

10

A MOTHER SOW sprawled on her belly in the mud and offered a row of teats to a dozen squealing piglets. Beyond, a grinning farm hand sloshed a pail of pig swill into the feeder. Pig heaven, thought Wil. The skies were blue and all the hillsides green.

That was the story of the block-long mural at the Farmer John meat-packing plant. But the idyl stopped at the walls. Out here in Vernon in the gathering heat and smog of an August day, the stench of animal blood and slaughter pervaded square miles of colorless city. So much for art and life.

He was going too fast. He eased his foot back from the gas pedal on the Le Sabre and pumped gently at the brakes. So whence, he asked himself, amid such torpor, his growing inner sense of things beginning to rocket out of his control?

Slow down, he told himself.

Stu Ray's warehouse was south and east of downtown Los Angeles, a long haul out through the industrial east side. Up in the maze of telegraph and power lines above the endless rows of gray industrial cinder blocks, the air was already heavy with the poisonous brown haze. Wil sneezed and winced as he turned the big car into the Raiders parking lot.

The operation had expanded since he was last out this way. A couple of brand-new trucks with Stuart's logo were parked at the loading bay,

66

and the entrance to the office area had been treated to a face-lift: The glass door opened of its own accord as Will approached, and he found himself in an air-conditioned lobby where one of Stu's own early pieces, a massive, shaped canvas with large, geometric areas of flat monochrome—brown, orange, purple—hung above chrome furniture and plants. he must have been happy to find a place to put it.

"I'm looking for Stu Ray," Wil told the receptionist. A blonde who might have walked off the set of a 1940s movie, she had full, scarlet lips, big breasts, and a waist compressed to a wasp's width by a wide black patent leather belt studded with rhinestones. The liberation movement had left no appreciable mark on Stu.

"You have an appointment?" She sounded as if she'd rehearsed the line.

"No appointment," said Wil.

"Mr. Ray's not available this morning," she decided. A tiny voice was all that piped out from that generous pair of lungs. "Can his assistant help?"

Wil blinked at her for a moment, and looked at the open office doors behind her.

"Stu," he bellowed. "Come out here, goddammit, you bastard. What's the matter, you haven't got time for your friends? Get your ass out here, Mr. Ray!"

Stu Ray put his head around a door and grinned.

"Hey, Wil!" he said. "How's it going? Come on in, for Christ's sake! What are you waiting for?"

Wil raised a wicked eyebrow at the receptionist. "What can I say?" he said. "The master calls."

He edged around the desk and grabbed the hand that Stuart Ray held out for him. Stu had come west from Philadelphia in the fifties, when Chouinard was still the hottest art school in Los Angeles. He'd always been a wiry character, short, slight of build, but tough. And ambitious. It showed in his face—a knotty structure of muscles at the jaw, steely blue eyes that looked at you head-on. He needed things that Wil had never needed and never set much store by—like money and security. Sure Wil would have liked them, but with him they'd never come easy and they'd never come first. With Stu, they did.

Looking around him, Wil's first impression was confirmed: Stu had got plenty of what he wanted. He'd started out working for Cart & Crate, at that time the biggest and best in the business. Stu built their packing crates and drove their trucks. Fifteen years ago, he'd surprised the art community by branching out on his own in a field where no one other than himself saw the need for competition. He started small, in a single corner of his studio, but it wasn't long before the business had taken over the whole space—and pushed the painting out.

In the past three years, he'd lost some hair but gained in other respects. He had his own building, with a suite of offices and stacks of four-drawer filing cabinets, computer terminals. The works.

Converted from a corner of the warehouse, Stu's office made it clear that he set great store by image. He'd designed the space himself, and there were penthouse executives downtown who would have paid an arm and an leg for the look. Cool and white, it was fitted out sparsely with clean, custom furniture and lamps. What made the difference was the art. It was everywhere—on walls and floors and tables. You tripped on it as you walked.

"You're doing well, Stu," said Wil.

His friend shrugged and grinned, waving a hand grandly to describe the extent of his empire, then running his fingers back through thin, wavy salt-and-pepper hair.

"As you see, Wil."

"Yeah, well, you need to make a buck. Did you give up finally on art, or do you still do some in the closet, now and then?"

Stu pulled a pack of unfiltered cigarettes from the pocket of his shirt and lit one. He blew out the smoke and chased it with his hand, hoisting a boot up on the desk in front of him.

"Listen, Wil," he said, "you get to be a little cynical, you know? Especially handling the stuff like I do, every day. You see some idiot's paintings sell for fifty thousand bucks in New York, you get to handle a few of them up close and you find out what they're made of. You know what they're made of, Wil? Piss and shit. You're lucky if the damn thing doesn't fall apart. I mean aside from questions of meaning or value, a lot of it's no more than a piece of schlock. Just as an object. Shit, I wouldn't give a dime for half that stuff. No, I don't do any of it now. It isn't worth my time. That's it, Wil. It isn't worth the time you spend on it."

"I know how you feel, Stu, I really do. I guess there's those of us who are dumb enough to do it anyway."

Stu laughed and fought down a cough. "I'm happy to know it, Wil, my friend. There's got to be someone out there making the stuff for me to keep shifting around. And how's the teaching business? You doing okay?"

"Doing great. I took the summer off."

Stu's brow wrinkled. "I could have sworn I heard you were doing a summer session down at Otis."

"Right," said Wil. "I was, until yesterday. I took an early retirement."

"So?" The eyebrows went up. "Good for you, man. I'm delighted." As always, Stu's mental computer was humming along somewhere behind the clear blue eyes. "What brings you out to my part of the world? Don't tell me you've been missing old Stu?"

Wil smiled. "A favor," he said.

"I should have known." Stu Ray's boot crashed down from the desktop and he leaned forward, stroking his mustache with fine fingertips. "What can I do?"

"Ask rather," said Wil, "what I can do for you."

"Now you're talking." Behind the laugh, Wil sensed an uneasiness in the eyes. "So tell me, Wil. What can you do for me?"

He'd tried to rehearse this before coming. He needed to call on a very old friendship. He needed Stu's cooperation, not the defensive anger that was always close to the surface. "I think you've got trouble here, Stu," he said. Hold the eyes. There it was, a dark flash, a tightening round the lids.

"We've all got troubles, Wil." Stu was wary.

"Not like yours." Keep holding. "Don't shine it on with me. You're too smart not to know what's happening under your nose, and dammit, Stu, you're too honest to let it happen."

He crushed the half-smoked cigarette in the ashtray, keeping his cool. "You're out of line, Wil."

"I'm a friend."

"My friends are known for keeping their noses out of my affairs."

"This one's not. This one likes his old friends too much to believe in shit like that."

Stu's face was set hard and angry. "So tell me."

No way he could put them back now. "Let's try two Leon Drakes for openers. You hear about them?"

That blew it. "Hear about them!" he yelled. "Jesus Christ, can you believe those mothers, trying to lay it off on me! They screw up on their fucking consignment sheets and they have the goddamn balls to call me up when they can't find the paintings anymore. Where's the Leon Drakes, they ask? The Leon Drakes? What Leon Drakes, I say? The ones you were supposed to ship back to the studio, they say, from the West Coast Painters show. Just show me the consignment sheets, I tell them. I guess they're still looking."

Stu trailed off and swung gloomily back in his chair. The worst moment—the explosive one—was past. Be direct, Wil thought. "I think I can help you find them," he said quietly. "What's it worth to you?"

"You know where they are?"

"I didn't say that. I said I could help you find them."

"You heard me say I lost them?"

"Come on, Stu. It's me, Wil Garretson. Trust me."

"I should trust you? You beat me too often at the poker table, friend." It was years since they'd played. He leaned across the desk again. "Okay," he said. "Suppose I were interested. Suppose I believed you. What is it you want?"

"A job."

"You're shitting me?" Stuart snorted, suspicious, and sat there shaking his head. Wil wasn't sure if it was disbelief or outright refusal. "You don't want what I've got, Wil. I hire kid artists here. It's minimum-wage stuff, you know that...."

"That's not the point."

"So what is?"

"Your other problem. Jim Sewell."

"Jim Sewell?" asked Stu. The shadow of a scowl appeared around his eyes. Wil nodded.

"Too bad about Jim," Stu said slowly. "He was a good kid."

"You'll need someone to stand in for him," Wil pointed out. "Just let me hang out with the team for a couple of days. You know damn well I can do anything your kids can do, and better. I know all that stuff backward. I could do it in my sleep. A favor, huh? Look, I put my work clothes on." He patted the knees of his worn jeans. "I came ready to do a job."

Stu Ray was shaking his head. "Wil Garretson working for the Raiders? No one's going to believe that for a minute."

"What the fuck does it matter whether they do or not? You're the boss. We're talking a couple of days here, Stu."

He hesitated. "Why?"

70

"Jim Sewell was screwing you over, you must have known that, Stu."

He took another cigarette from the pack and held it unlit between two fingers, shaking them, no. "I didn't. I still don't believe it, on your say-so. Besides, that doesn't answer the question. What's your stake?"

"Personal. I need to hang out with the crew. Ask some questions. I'm doing a favor for a friend."

"I'm not convinced I need it."

"Aside from you. For another friend."

Stu Ray heaved in a breath and blew it out again in a soundless whistle. "And you're not going to tell me who."

"I can't. You're going to have to trust me. I'm trading on twenty years of friendship, pal. Besides, the truth never hurts unless you have something to hide."

"Goddammit, Wil, you don't know what you're asking." Somewhere outside the window a truck's horn blared. Staring out in the direction of the sound, Stu stubbed out the length of his unlit cigarette, swore disgustedly and sighed. "Have it your own way, then. You want the job, you've got the fucker. Two days, max. And only on condition that you level with me, with anything that affects me."

"It's a deal."

"Okay, let's go."

11

THE WAREHOUSE was a huge space—twelve, maybe fifteen thousand square feet, at Wil's guess. Stu strode ahead between rack after rack of paintings, his footsteps echoing back down off the metal roof. Madison had been right about the serials: The lengths of two-inch masking tape attached to the plastic cover at the edge of each painting were marked with black lettering and numerals identical to those on the Leon Drakes in Jim Sewell's studio.

Aside from that, Wil was astonished by the sheer number and diversity of the works in storage. "My God, Stu," he said. "You have half the art in LA in this place." At a glance, he picked out some large-scale Poons and Olitskys from the Bradley collection, a broad selection of pieces by some half dozen pop art heavyweights from the Conners in Beverly Hills, and a bevy of the new international superstars—the Baselitzes and Clementes, the Fischls, Salles and Schnabels from Bob Rooney's collection up in Malibu.

"Too big to hang over the fireplace?" he suggested.

"Some of them," said Stu briskly. "Either that, or they're not good enough to unload on some museum before tax time."

Wil laughed. They passed a clear space in the middle of the warehouse where the massive hulks of sculptures under plastic wraps stood

72

mute and shapeless as ghosts. "You need climate controls for this lot, I take it?"

"Temperature," said Stu. "And humidity." Relenting slightly, he slowed his pace for Wil to catch up. "This here's a growth industry these days, pal. I need those amenities to bring in the heavies. Those guys don't fool around. They aren't about to leave their stuff to rot in an uncontrolled space. You can't keep ahead of the competition, my friend, you're dead in your tracks."

Whatever the competition, there was probably no one in Los Angeles who knew as much about the movement of artworks as Stu Ray—including the museums he often worked for. Wil couldn't begin to guess at the value of what passed through Stu's hands in a year.

"What's this lot worth?" he asked. "Just what you have in storage? Twenty million? Thirty?"

"Maybe more. That's conservative, I'd guess. Tell you the truth, Wil, I never have the time to stop and count it. The insurance folks get their jollies doing that."

"I'd hate to think what their bill has to be."

"The only ones who enjoy that thought," Stu said, "are the folks down at California Farm Assurance. It's one of those extras that get passed on to the client."

He blasted ahead between the racks, arms waving, red at the nape of the neck, until they came to a small enclosed office area down by the loading dock. "Here, Wil," he said. "I want you to meet Fred Clusky. He's my super. Fred, this is Wil Garretson. He's an artist. God knows he should know better than to want to work with us at his age, but he does. He'll take Jim's place for a while. Just have him do what you had Jim down for. Trust him. He can do anything, okay?"

He turned to Wil and put out his hand.

"Okay, Wil," he said. "It's all yours. I'm too busy to spend time talking to the help. Take care." He shook Wil's hand and stalked back between the racks, the heels of his boots slapping down on the concrete floor.

"Pissed, huh?" Fred Clusky was a burly character with short blond hair and small blue eyes. He gave Wil a quick once-over and led him into the office without comment. Pulling a clipboard from the nail beside the door, he thumbed through a neat stack of worksheets for the day.

"Sewell," he mumbled. "He was to work with the crating crew this morning until lunch. At one, he was down for a pickup with Madison. Madison Grant. He drives. Can you handle that?"

Madison? Okay. "Whatever you say."

"You'll find the crew on coffee break. Down the corridor, third door to your right."

He found them in a dingy, neon-lit lounge, fitted out with a couple of ripped sofas and a coffee table piled with the tatters of old art magazines. A dying cactus stood in the corner, beside steel-framed and barred security windows. They hadn't been cleaned for more years than he cared to guess, and only one torn yellow drapery survived. Beside a Sparkletts hot-and-cold dispenser stood a jar of instant coffee with powdered cream, stained sugar lumps and a single bent spoon. Above it, some joker had pinned an Ed Ruscha poster upside-down on the wall. *I Don't Want No Retrospective*.

"Hi, folks," he said. "I'm Wil Garretson." His effort to be casual with a name familiar to everyone in the room met with a bolt of high-tension response: mostly plain disbelief. Madison turned away without a word and shook his head slowly, making a clear patch on the dirty window with his finger. "I'm helping Stu out by standing in for Jim Sewell for a while."

There was a nervous laugh somewhere and someone said, "And Nancy Reagan's stopping by for lunch."

More laughter, followed by an embarrassed silence. Wil made as if he hadn't heard the comment and closed the door behind him. On the bulletin board, someone had fixed a snapshot framed in black tape and Wil wandered over to look at it, his movement causing a ripple reaction the room.

"This is Jim?" he asked.

"That's Jim," said one of the crew. "You knew him?"

"A little," said Wil. "He was a student of mine once." He peered at the picture. Jim stood there, a washed-out figure making narrow eyes against brilliant sunlight. There was leafy shrubbery in the background, and Wil was startled by the gun that was slung across the young guy's shoulder.

"Jim had a gun?" he asked.

"Looks like it," someone said. "What the fuck are you doing here?"

Somehow he had to defuse the outright hostility and disbelief. Wil

74

went head on. "There's two things we can do," he said. "You can resent the hell out of me, or pretend I'm not here and hope I'll go away. I won't, but you can try. Or we can get along. Why don't we try?"

The silence this time was broken by a more friendly laugh from a short, stout character, a little older than the rest, with a mess of black hair. "This is bullshit," he said, coming over, taking the hand Wil offered. "I'm Raul. Raul Ortega. This here's Madison Grant..."

"Hi, Madison. We've met somewhere..."

"Yeah, hi." Madison turned back to the window.

"Don Henschler..."

"Don..." Wil had heard the name and knew something about Henschler's work from downtown gallery shows. He was down from the north, Seattle, Wil thought, and was obviously talented—one of those perplexed young artists who look around and see that everything's been done and that the market has exploited it all, so they turn it around by appropriating styles and images from the past. The ultimate irony—or the ultimate despair. In Don Henschler's work, it was hard to tell.

"Don," he said. "I've seen your work around."

Henschler stared balefully from behind thick lenses and nodded brief thanks. Long strings of hair fell forward into his eyes and he pushed them back self-consciously. The guy looked sick. Mid-thirties, medium height, and skinny to the point of emaciation, he was pleasant enough, but soft and absorbent as a sponge. His smile was nervous, humorless, and his eyes had a distant look of tolerant surprise.

Raul, by contrast, was a butterball, filled with an excess energy that spilled over into constant banter, witty and rude. He ran his coffee mug under the tap at the sink and took Wil by the arm. "Okay, friend," he said. "Break's over. You asked for it. Grab a hammer, help yourself. Jim was down to work with me until lunch."

The crew dispersed and Wil followed Raul out to the packing area, catching the dust mask he tossed to him and fitting it over his head. An Arthur Dove landscape lay flat on the workbench, ready to be wrapped, and Wil noticed a long-tongued, creamy Georgia O'Keeffe lily propped on its side against the racks, along with a couple of Charles Sheelers.

"Thirties, huh?" he said. "Whose show?"

"Chicago. The Art Institute." Raul adjusted his own mask over his mouth and nose.

The drivers had already brought in a dozen pieces from different collections. From here, they'd be traveling in three large packing crates with labyrinthine corridors and interior chambers, each area specially tailored for a single work.

They worked for a concentrated hour, communicating not in words but signs. Aside from the masks, talk was difficult above the whine of the rip saw, the crescendoing stutter of a nearby compressor and the occasional roar and clang of the forklift. It was a while since Wil had done this kind of work himself, and he was happy to watch and follow Raul's directions.

Raul worked smoothly, fast, piecing parts together. It was artist's work, and Wil knew that Stu Ray was smart to hire a man like Raul, who knew how a painting worked, where to look for potential weaknesses and how to treat delicate surfaces.

Then, too, young artists come in plentiful supply, and cheap. They're hungry.

Satisfied with the interior, Raul picked up the power drill and countersunk the screw holes in the exterior panel. Wil watched the shavings spin away from the bit until the crate was ready and Raul rested back on his haunches, pulling the mask from his mouth and wiping the sweat from his forehead.

Wil pulled his own mask down below his chin and squatted across from Raul. "How well did you know Jim Sewell?" he asked.

"Jim?" For a moment, something fell into shadow in the distances of Raul's eyes. Then they refocused, suddenly, and the man uncoiled with a yell, launching his stubby bulk toward Wil and carrying him, skidding, the pair of them in a bundle, across the concrete floor.

Still rolling, Wil caught a glimpse of the steel blade of the forklift slicing past him and heard the passing whine and roar of the engine, the swish of rubber, turning tight and fast on concrete. Then the world spun around again, and he came to rest against a crate.

As he raised his head and wriggled to separate himself from Raul's entangled body, the machine stopped short a bare six inches from a stack of lumber they'd been working from. The engine stalled out, and for a moment the silence seemed total.

"Shit, man. Get down from there!" Clusky emerged from the office, yelling. "Where's your brains, fuckhead?"

It was Don Henschler who climbed down from the forklift, sweating and pale. Wil noticed that his hands were trembling as he pushed the glasses back up the bridge of his nose.

76

"Out! Get out of here!" yelled Clusky. "What the fuck's the matter with you these days?" Henschler cast a quick appeal toward Raul, then shrugged and walked back to the office, stumbling over the blade of his own machine.

"Close call," said Wil, getting up and watching Henschler leave. Whatever was driving him was more than the compulsion to do art. "What's with Henschler?"

Raul dusted himself off. "Listen," he said, "it happens. I'll bet it's three, four times a year some joker pokes a forklift through a painting. Hazards of transit." He looked at his watch. "Let's grab a drink from the machine, then we could maybe get that second crate measured up before lunch."

He led the way to the Coke machine by the office and rattled some coins into the slot. Coming back, he grabbed a Stanley measure, and together they took the dimensions of the paintings.

"You were going to tell me about Jim," said Wil.

Raul looked up from the heap of wood he'd been working on. "You said you barely knew him," he said. It was a question more than a statement, and Wil realized he wasn't going to get by without some kind of explanation. The tug at his gut told him he hadn't the time to pussy-foot around.

"I need to find out why he died," he said.

That sank in slowly, the dark eyes searching his. "For the cops?" Raul asked. He didn't seem surprised.

Wil shook his head. "For me." Then added, "For a friend he was going with."

Raul turned back to his work. "I don't know that I want to get involved in this," he said.

"So what was Jim doing here, for Christ's sake?"

"He was getting by, pal, like the rest of us." Raul worked angrily on the rough drawing he was making, sketching in the dimensions. He looked up at Wil again, briefly. "What the fuck else would anyone do in this dump?"

"Bitter?"

A length of one-by-four clattered to the floor as Raul stretched out the Stanley measure and marked off another. "Not bitter," he said. "A realist."

"You're an artist, too?" Wil asked.

Raul let the extended length of the measure zip back into its case and took a long drink from his Pepsi can. "You bet," he said. "Homeboy. Born with a spray can in my hand."

"Just that? Graffiti?"

He paused. "Just that. Until some white-ass painter like yourself came in with federal bucks to keep the walls nice in the barrio." He laughed, measuring off another length of one-by-four and ripping through it with the hand saw. "We washed off the graffiti and did murals to educate the masses. Then the guy helped me get into art school and I learned to make cool art. I made it for a couple of years— real nice minimal stuff, easy on the eye, easy on the mind. You know the route."

Wil fitted the new section into place and held it at right angles for Raul to tie down.

"Who was the artist?" he asked.

"You know him," said Raul. "It was Dave . . . Dave Lyman."

It sounded like Dave.

Raul offered him the can, but Wil shook his head. "You still painting, then?" he asked.

"You know, the usual, man. I do the stuff but there's not a gallery anywhere will show them. I got back to some of the images of the barrio and Latino life's not cool, in the art scene, unless your name's Almaraz or Gronk."

"So what else is new?" asked Wil. "You guys make enough money, here, to get by?"

Raul sat back on his heels and laughed again. "You kidding?" he said.

"So what does a person do, to support himself? What's the perks? What was Jim up to, Raul?"

"The perks?" Raul lost his grin.

"The scam," Wil persisted. "Come on, don't tell me there's no way you can make an extra couple of bucks? All this art around the place?"

Raul sat back on his haunches, glaring. "Listen, man. I don't know what you're after, but you got the wrong guy here, okay? I don't fuck with that shit." His voice as angry, intense. He drained the Pepsi can and crushed it between his hands. "Stay cool, Wil Garretson," he said. "It's lunchtime. I got things to do."

Wil watched as Raul sauntered out to the door.

"Raul," he called. Raul stopped and turned. "Where can I find Don Henschler during lunch?"

There was a moment's hesitation, then a shrug. "You could try his studio," he said.

"His studio?"

"In back." Raul nodded in the direction he meant. "Can't miss it. It's a small building to itself." He paused on the threshold, smiling again. "Hey, I'm thinking of getting back into graffiti," he said. "It's in again now. Or cars. There's a market for them, too. You hear the museum's maybe doing an auto show? You reckon they'll need a lowrider? I could use a recommendation."

He cackled and walked out into the sunshine. Another Jim Sewell, thought Wil. If Dave Lyman had picked him out, he would surely have the talent to make something of his art, given time. Trouble was, there was no one likely to give him the time he needed. Jim Sewell had stolen for it, and Wil could have bet that Raul knew more than he was letting on. He could have bet, too, that Raul wanted to talk.

12

"LISTEN," SAID Sally, on the studio telephone, "I've got to go now. There's someone at the door." In fact, she was relieved to have the excuse: She could listen to Paula but she couldn't talk to her. Besides, today was the wrong day to put up with her aches and gripes, her lawyer husband, and her whole damn soap-opera life. Paula was everything Sally had sworn she would never become, when she started out with Jim. Her phone calls never ran less than an hour.

The flow from the other end of the line barely rippled, and the studio extension to the front-door bell rang again. This time, Sally threw Sourdough down from her lap and got up.

"Got to go," she broke in again, mid-sentence. "Bye now. I'll call back, okay?"

Outside the air-conditioned studio, she ran into the solid heat of the day. "Who's there?" she called.

The studio had been added in back of the house, and she hurried down the side path toward the front door, gathering the robe around her waist. It was well past noon, she realized suddenly, and she hadn't yet dressed. She stubbed a toe on one of the flagstones at the corner.

"Damn!"

"Police Department, Mrs. Horan."

There was no way she could stop. She was already turning the corner of the building as she tripped and fell headlong into them. The best she could do was convert the near collision into a pretext for her shock.

"Oh, God," she said, "you scared me!"

There was a sudden stabbing pain in her chest which in seconds gave way to a heartbeat that pulsed heavily through her torso. There were two of them, a man and a woman, in street clothes. About to display their badges, they thought better of it and reached out to help her recover her balance. The woman had an arm around her waist.

"Let's find you somewhere to sit," she said.

Heat or nerves, Sally felt a drop of sweat run down the small of her back. "No," she said. "It's all right, really. I'll be fine."

"We need to talk to you, Mrs. Horan. We could come back later, if we've caught you at the wrong moment." At least there was no sense of urgency. She'd imagined immediate arrest.

"No," said Sally. "No, of course not. But you'll have to come around the back—the front door's locked. Just give me five minutes while I put on some clothes."

"There's no need..." said the woman.

"No, really."

She sat them in the breakfast room while she ran upstairs and grabbed a track suit from the shelf. Stripping off her robe, she left it where it fell, pulled on the baggy pants and the top, and stopped in the bathroom to check herself out. Her face was clammy with sweat. Her eyes were terrible. She pulled out a Kleenex from the box to dry her face, ran a lipstick around her mouth and rounded out the line with her lips.

Jesus, what could she tell them? She looked terrible.

Her heartbeat had settled to a steady five points on the Richter scale by the time she got back to the breakfast room, and her mind was made up to tell them as little as she could but make it as close as possible to the truth.

She made herself busy putting coffee on the table and brought out three mugs from the china cabinet. HAVE A NICE DAY above a sunshine face. A present from Paula and Kenneth. Stupid, normal things, they seemed to take on strange significance, like beacons beckoning from a world she'd left behind. The pictures of the two of them, Rick and Sally, pinned on the corkboard behind the kitchen phone, seemed to smile from the same lost world.

"Now," she said, "how can I help you?"

They showed their badges again, and she barely read the names.

"There's probably nothing that should concern you, Mrs. Horan," said the man. He wore a big check jacket and a woolen tie, knotted clumsily below an open collar button. "The department is helping the sheriff's office up in San Bernardino to make some routine inquiries into the death of a James Sewell. We understand you knew him?"

Even given the time she'd gained to prepare herself, the needle on the seismograph shot up to eight point three again.

"Yes," she said. "I read about it in the paper this morning. What a terrible thing!" Gushing. Too much. "But I've no idea how I could be of help."

"Mrs. Horan," said the woman, "we're looking for a woman who evidently saw Mr. Sewell fall and put in a distress call. Have you any idea who that could be?"

White blouse, gray skirt. Dark stockings and black patent leather shoes on a hot day. Eyes that were penetrating, but gave nothing away. It was time for the lie. "My God, none," Sally said. She hated herself, wondering if the truth would have hurt as much, and forced more words out. "I didn't know Jim that well. I've no idea who his friends were. But—excuse me—what I can't understand is why you came to me."

They didn't answer directly, but worked in their notebooks, both of them, with ballpoint pens. Sally turned the salt shaker in small circles inside a red square inch of the tablecloth. Outside the window, one of her blue jays hopped watchfully up on the patio table and Sourdough stretched and hauled himself up on the windowsill to keep an eye on the bird.

"Mr. Sewell had your name and telephone number in his wallet," said the man. "Have you any idea why?"

The thunder started up again in her temples. "We were students together, oh, perhaps ten years ago," she said. "Then I met him again quite a while back, when he came here to deliver a painting." They made no comment, so she began to improvise, filling the silence. "I guess I saw some of his pictures, too, and liked them, so he called to make a date and brought some things around and I ended up buying one. It's on the wall in my studio, if you'd like to take a look at it. I had it framed." It was a gift from Jim.

"Thank you, Mrs. Horan. Can you give us a date on that?"

A date? Because they'd changed the area code, his telephone bill would itemize dozens of calls to her studio number. Wil had picked the number out.

"Let's see, sometime around April, May. We had a few conversations.... I'm sure I could check."

"Did you visit him in his studio?"

Sally felt herself starting to drift. Hold on. Rubbing her fingers in taut circles at her temples, she found herself wishing she had Rick here. Wishing he knew. "Oh, yes, I was there a couple of times—I got to know him a little."

"How recently had you seen him, Mrs. Horan?"

"Let's see. Well, now you mention it, I happened to run into him just the other day. Thursday, it must have been. There was an opening at the County."

"The County?"

"The museum. I'm on the council there. It's on Wilshire."

The woman added a note at the bottom of her page and flipped it over to the next. So slow. "He seemed in good spirits? Everything seemed normal?"

Sally thought back. Jim had swung wildly from elation to dejection. "He seemed just fine," she said.

"No mention of a trip to the mountains?"

Sally shook her head. "Not that I remember." Foolishly, Jim had insisted on talking about it. He was already bombed. Sally shook her head harder, made a show of arranging her shoulders to disguise a shudder.

The detective paused to consult his list of questions and looked up at her again, his broad face unsmiling. "Mrs. Horan, we understand that you didn't know the victim very well, but did you by any chance know that Mr. Sewell had recently purchased a high-powered rifle?"

She did. Good God, and she had forgotten! She shook her head again slowly, but the memory came back in vivid detail: It was a weekend, maybe six, eight weeks ago. It had to have been a weekend, because they'd had the luxury of an afternoon in bed. Where had Rick been?

Sunday. It was a Sunday. Phoenix. He'd had some business there. She had called him from Jim's studio, charging the call to her home. Jesus, she thought, would that have shown up on the telephone bill? Her head started to whirl, and she caught the glance exchanged between the two detectives, as though they had followed her thoughts. She feigned a sudden interest to cover her confusion. "How could I possibly have known?" she asked. "That's fascinating! Jim Sewell with a gun. I just can't see it."

But she saw him clearly in the studio, playing, aiming the thing out over the loft. She heard the metal snap of the bolt as he locked it into place.

"It was in back of the driver's seat in the vehicle that was discovered at the scene," said the detective.

In the camper? Things kept on showing up where they hadn't been before. Like Jim's keys on the seat of the Celica. Sally's mind flashed to the smiling face of the limo driver, out on the prospect point. "We traced the date of purchase through the license. We're running tests on it."

Tests. Of course. She remembered having handled the thing, he had forced it on her. They were playing. "Jesus Christ, Jimmy," she asked him, "what are you doing with that thing?" "It's beautiful," he said, "here, feel it." He reached for her hand and guided it down the barrel. She remembered the fascination of its feel—smooth as silk, though hard and cold. "It's disgusting," she told him. "I hate it. Isn't one prick enough?"

"Tests," she said. "Yes." What she didn't know was if her fingerprints would stay there for that long. Would Jim have cleaned the gun? She had been curious enough to take it, when he insisted, and sight down its length toward the skylight at the far end of the studio with her finger on the trigger. He showed her the bullets, lean and clean and heavy in her hand. "So what do you need it for?" she had asked. "Protection," he said.

"Listen," she told the officers, "I know I haven't been much help, but I do have to work this afternoon. If there's anything else..."

The man ran the tip of his pen down the metal spiral of his notebook, lips moving slowly as he checked the items off.

"I guess not, ma'am." He exchanged another look with his partner, who also shrugged a negative. "But I'll leave a card with you, in case you have any other thoughts that could help us. No one you would suggest we should see?"

"No, really. You'll need to find someone who knew Jim far better than I did."

She brought them to the door and showed them out, watching

through the living room window as they backed their cruiser across the driveway. They had forgotten to look at Jim's picture, and she wondered vaguely if that would have been important.

When she went back in, the telephone rang again and this time Sally didn't answer. She couldn't face Paula.

13

WIL SWEATED in the tiny enclosure of the pay phone across the street from Ray's Raiders and tapped a coin against the plexi bubble that enclosed it. He listened to the telephone at Sally's ring eight times and hung up. He tried MaryJo with no more success. Then he leafed through his pocket diary, stopped at the Ds and punched in an unlisted studio number for Leon Drake.

The phone rang twice.

"Leon Drake's studio." It was Sandy who answered, Leon's current live-in helpmate.

"Sandy, Wil Garretson. Is Leon there?"

"Hi, Wil. Sure. I think I can get him. Hang on for a moment and I'll see."

Leon kept a wall of people around him to save time for his work. For years, Wil had scoffed at the motion of an artist with a full-time staff, but recently he'd let Leon convince him to hire at least a Kelly girl a couple of afternoons a week. Now he wondered how he could have done without help for so long. It was wonderful. She took care of the mail and kept the files in order.

"Yeah, Wil? Hi." There weren't a lot of people who could get right through to Leon. Wil was one of them. "I hear you quit your job. What's up?"

News travels fast along the art community's grapevine.

"Is there somewhere I can catch up with you this evening?" Wil asked. "Will you be in town?"

For Wil, going up the coast to the Malibu studio was going out of town. "Sure, I'll be in. Can I do something?"

"Not much; I just need to talk, okay?" There was time enough yet to tell him about the paintings. He couldn't trust Leon not to go off half-cocked.

"Sure, Wil. I'll be at the West Beach by eight."

"Okay. See you there."

"Look forward to it."

"Me, too, Leon."

He hung up again and stared across the street for a moment at Stu's big cinder-block warehouse, checking his watch to see how much of the lunch hour he had left. The compound was surrounded by a high chain-link fence that enclosed two other structures with the warehouse. One seemed to be used exclusively to house and service the small fleet of trucks and pickups Stu had put together. Wil was surprised that the second, smaller building was a studio, and still more surprised that Stu let it out to one of the crew.

What was the feeling that he got from Henschler? Something close to panic. The forklift incident fit right in with the impression he'd had earlier, in the lounge: The guy was ready to whirl off in a tailspin. Wil hurried past the loading dock and turned the handle of the door to the studio in back. It was open.

Honey.

The smell permeated the space. It stopped Wil short at the entrance, sniffing. It had been some time since he'd caught the sweet smell of encaustic—a mixture of wax and pigment that produces an unmistakable aroma when you warm it ready for use. Few artists bothered with the cumbersome stuff these days.

But Henschler was using it.

Startled by the sound of the door, Don turned quickly from the bench where he'd been working, chipping lumps of wax from a brick with hammer and screwdriver and throwing them in the pot to melt. He squinted at Wil for a moment, puzzled by the disturbance.

"This is my space," he said, getting up. Wil noted the barely controlled edge of territorial hostility in the artist's voice.

"Oh, yeah?" said Wil easily, stopping by the door. "Nice space." He ignored the tone—though he knew he might have felt much the same way about his own studio, if someone had walked in on it.

"That's okay," said Henschler hurriedly. "You can come in." He put down the screwdriver he'd been working with. "I guess I should have latched the door. But it is my space. Most of the guys who work here just know about it."

"How come you got so lucky?" Wil asked, looking around.

Henschler hesitated. "Stu rents it out to me as a part of the deal," he said. "He built it for himself but he never used it."

"That's nice," said Wil.

For his own taste, it was bleak. Nothing was done to cover the cinder blocks of the interior wall, and the aluminum ducts and ceiling struts were all exposed. The concrete floor was bare, spotted with wax chips around the paint-splattered bench. There was a drafting table in the corner by the window, a few sparse racks and a big, old-fashioned wooden easel. A pair of wheeled worktables covered with supplies defined different work areas: one for acrylics—gessos and rhoplex, fat jars of medium and color. The other was set up for oil, with gallon containers of turpentine and thinner, tubes of color, carefully squeezed from the bottom, and coffee cans stuffed with palette knives and brushes. In the center of the studio, an oil drum served as a bin for dirty rags.

"You build your own stretchers?" Wil asked the obvious to put Don at his ease: A stack of stretcher bars was propped against the wall by the door, and a roll of canvas lay partially unwound. Wil stooped to run his fingers over it. At the edge, a thin blue line of thread ran through the weave.

"My God," he said. "Where did you get this stuff? They haven't made this in years."

It was blue-line duck. Almost every painter loved it, back in the fifties and sixties. There were some Wil knew wouldn't work on anything else—until they stopped making it. He looked up and could have sworn Don was blushing.

"From a friend," he said. "He brought a stash at some warehouse sale. He sold it to me."

"Yeah?" said Wil. "If ever you want to sell, I know some guys would pay you an arm and an leg. What's with the encaustic?"

"Oh, nothing, really." Did it come out a shade too fast? Was it Wil's imagination? "I was just starting to play around with some ideas."

There was a false note there somewhere. Don's work was intricate,

88

precise—encaustic seemed an unlikely medium for him, but Wil backed off. "You do all your work here?" he asked.

Don nodded. "There's only a tiny apartment where I live," he said. "And I've always preferred to keep my work space separate. Coffee?"

Wil took the mug he offered. "What is it you're working on?" he asked.

The guy was as fretful as a deer. He showed Wil some recent drawings with trembling haste, pulling them back almost before he had looked at them. Still lifes. Incredible draftsmanship, such as Wil hadn't seen in years. At Otis, he had watched the steady decline in skills like this among young artists: Some would never learn to draw.

"Did you know Jim Sewell pretty well?" It was Don's question, coming suddenly, nervous and out of context. Wil looked at him thoughtfully.

"I knew him quite well," he said. "He was one of those students, you know, who latch on to you. I guess I had something that he needed. Anyway, we were reasonably close for a while there. Even after his time at Otis, he kept up. I would hear from him now and then."

"I can't believe it." Don's hands were busy with the pencils on his worktable, arranging and rearranging them. "I can't believe he's dead."

"That's how it hits you, yeah. You never learn to expect it. I've had friends die on me, like that...." Wil watched the pale face that wouldn't look back at him and trailed off into silence, allowing Don room to say whatever it was that was wanting to come out.

"...seeing him every day, working with him," he said.

"So what was his beef?" Wil asked gently. "Was Jim in some kind of trouble?"

There was clear desperation in the eyes now, when they met Wil's finally, briefly, darting on. Come on, Wil nodded quietly, let it out. But whatever doubts he was nursing, Don turned them out with a quick shake of his head. His fingers went to a loose end of hair behind his ear and began to curl it furiously.

"It was just such a shock," he said, ducking Wil's question. "I guess it'll take a while to adjust."

"Yeah," said Wil. Wasn't that just the way? You spend your time trying to avoid the confessions of the young, until you want one. This guy needed help. Wil had wanted to open a door, but it seemed as if he had just closed it. "I guess you're right."

Then a buzzer sounded out in the warehouse, calling them back from lunch.

"Listen, Don," said Wil. "If you need to talk to someone, give me a call. Here you go." He tore off a corner from a sheet of paper discarded in the trash and wrote down the number. "No hassle," he said. "Remember."

"Look what they stuck us with."

Wil found Madison at the loading dock, kicking the front offside tire of a battered van, the oldest vehicle of the Raiders fleet. The gold rims of his glasses glinted in the sun, and he didn't look happy. "This mother's near bald," he said.

It had to be ninety-five degrees in the shade. "Does it have air conditioning at least?" asked Wil. He wiped at his neck with a handkerchief.

"Are you kidding?" Madison grinned fleetingly at him. "The boss said I was to look out for you," he added.

"What's the matter," Wil grumbled, "my old friend doesn't trust me anymore?"

"Stu Ray never trusted anyone in his life," said Madison with a laugh. "The man's pure business." He slid his clipboard with the consignment sheets onto the seat, swung into the cab, and watched as Wil stripped down to a tank top on the passenger side. "You're in good shape," he said.

"I work at it," said Wil. "What do you do? File a written report with Ray on my condition?"

Madison started the motor and put his foot on the gas, and the van's engine produced the stuttering roar of a grounded helicopter. "Maybe," he said. He swung out through the gates and lumbered north to catch the westbound freeway where he made the left turn to the on-ramp through dense surface traffic.

"What kind of an artist are you, Madison?" Wil asked. "I don't think I ever saw your work." He watched the traffic ahead, red brake lights flashing on in rapid sequence as the freeway hit the main junction south of downtown.

"You kidding?" said Madison. "Where do you think they'd show it? I do video, mostly. Some performance, when I get the chance."

"Oh, yeah?"

Madison was evidently used to the response. "Not interested, huh?"

"Why fake it? I guess it's not my speed. Maybe the truth is that I'm lazy—I like to get it all in one shot."

"Old-fashioned, huh? You'll learn."

"Someday, maybe."

Madison turned his attention back to the road, and Wil picked up the clipboard to read through the two consignment sheets. This afternoon's run was a short one out to Santa Monica and Brentwood for pickups. Wil knew both the collections, the Singers' and the Steins', and grinned to himself in anticipation of Brenda Stein's reaction—Wil Garretson showing up with Ray's Raiders. He gazed out across the square miles of the Los Angeles flatlands, amazed how far the grid of surface roads reached north to the hills, and south toward Long Beach and the ocean.

"You mind if I ask you something?" They'd reached La Brea before Wil realized it, and Madison took his eyes from the lane in front for long enough to glance across at him.

"Ask away."

"What the fuck are you doing, man?" The question had been roiling inside him since Wil had shown up at the Raiders. "I mean, what the fuck kind of game are you playing?"

Wil stared through the windshield. He was in much deeper than he'd planned or realized. Too deep. "Listen, Madison..."

"I'm listening."

"This thing is dangerous....Deadly."

"Fuck that, man." Madison laughed. "Just plain living's deadly, where I come from. I don't like being used, okay? Does that make sense to you? You're using me, Wil."

He couldn't argue with that. He'd dealt Madison in without a syllable of explanation: The guy had the Leon Drakes sitting there in his studio to prove it. He had the right to know. "Jim was killed," Wil said bluntly. "Murdered."

"Jesus Christ." Madison's head swung so fast, the van veered dangerously toward the inside lane. The blast of a horn set him straight again. "You're shitting me?"

Wil shook his head. "It wasn't an accident—Jim didn't just fall. Someone shot him off the cliff. Sally Horan was there, watching it."

"Oh, Jesus. That's unreal."

"Sally thought so."

"They shot him? That's not what the news reported."

"Well, they didn't exactly, not as far as I can tell...." Wil gave him the short version of the story as they headed west. Free of downtown, the traffic was five miles over the speed limit in the slow lane now, and Madison wiped the sweat from his eyes, scowling with the effort of concentration.

"The cops were there this morning," he said finally, when Wil had finished. "At Jim's place."

If he'd left the Drakes where he'd found them, for the cops to find, it would have been out of his hands, Wil saw that now. "You talked to them?" he asked.

Madison shrugged. "I was just leaving. What did I have to tell them?"

They slowed again toward the Robertson exit. A half block south of the freeway, the head of a palm tree was in flames, sending out a haze of orange smoke into the laden air, and the eastbound lanes were slowed to a near standstill by the rubberneckers.

"It's beautiful," said Madison. "A flaming tree. That's LA, isn't it?" he paused. "That's Jim." It flared like a firework and the plume rose fast against the sun, reducing its light to an eerie, dark transparency.

14

THEY DROVE on in silence past a couple more exits, the van accelerating into the second lane to avoid the San Diego freeway ramps.

"Did you look at this morning's paper?" Wil asked.

"I don't follow that shit, man." They shot the elegant, long curves of the connecting overpasses, and Madison watched in his mirrors as he finally merged with the traffic from the San Diego south.

"They're looking for Sally," said Wil.

"The cops?"

"They think she can help with their inquiries."

Madison glanced at him over his shoulder and drove on without comment. The van hurtled past the Bundy off-ramp and under the big green Lincoln exit sign. "We'll take Lincoln north," he said. "There's a street map in the glove compartment."

"I don't need it. I know the way."

Once off the freeway, Madison relaxed. "So what the fuck's happening?" he asked. "Whoever did it, they wouldn't have wasted Jim for the Leon Drakes," he said. "For two lousy paintings? There had to be more to it than that."

"Listen," Wil said. "How much did Jim earn? Two, three hundred a week? Okay. So this is August. In May and June, each month, he paid five thousand bucks into a savings account. Ten grand, Madison. And that was a month before the Leon Drakes even left the museum. Does that say something?"

Madison stared ahead and frowned. "What it says is that somebody got to Jim four months ago with a juicy offer."

"Like what?" Wil asked. "Tell me. You know this business better than I do."

"Take your pick, Wil," sighed Madison. "The possibilities are endless. The business is full of them."

"Name one."

Madison scratched at his small island of hair. "Okay," he said. "Remember, about a year ago—it was in the papers—this driver just happens to make a lunch stop at a coffee shop between here and the museum in Santa Barbara. Someone just happens to know there are a couple of Monets on the truck, along with some other Impressionist shit. No courier, no escort, no alarm. Like this crate, only bigger, right —and with time locks on the two freight doors in back. Safe enough? They stole the whole damn truck and were gone before the driver finished lunch. The cops picked the truck up in Modesto three days later."

Wil remembered the story now. "Ray's Raiders?"

"It wasn't us that time. It could have been."

"What about the driver?"

"He swore he left the rig locked, and they didn't have anything to disprove it. But I'll bet he hasn't been working since. Maybe he hasn't needed to." He laughed, coming up on Wilshire, the van shuddering to a stop as the light went from yellow to red. "It could happen anywhere, if someone knew what was on the truck," he said. "It could happen right here, at the traffic light. I've had a million bucks or more in the back of this bonebreaker. A De Kooning, a couple of Motherwells...it soon adds up. Someone shows me a gun, I climb right out. Don't you?"

Wil chuckled. "I sure do," he said. "Did anyone ever make you an offer?"

"One person came to me, once," said Madison slowly.

"Who was that?"

"Jim Sewell." He spoke deliberately, with a kind of sadness.

"And?"

"He asked for help. I turned him down."

The blast of a horn from behind reminded him that his speed had dropped, and he picked it up with a jab at the gas pedal. "Screw you too!" he yelled as the car pulled out to overtake and the man leaned across to give him an angry finger. "Shithead!"

"Was this recent?" asked Wil.

"Two, maybe three weeks back. It could have been the Leon Drakes."

"Did you ask him why?"

"No. But he told me anyway," he said. "The guy said he wanted to get back at someone. I told him he was a crazy jerk."

"Did you ask him who he wanted to get back at?"

"No. Well, I asked him, but he didn't tell me. Maybe the guys that paid him the ten grand... He told me like it was some kind of joke. He was going to give the paintings back. No harm done, he said. The guy thought it was a fucking joke."

"Why didn't you tell me this last night?"

"I didn't know you last night," said Madison.

"You don't know me today."

They drove in silence, Wil giving directions to the Singer house. When they reached it, the van pulled to the side of the road before turning into the driveway, and Wil realized suddenly that Madison had tears in his eyes. He rubbed them away with the heel of his thumb, and sat there and swore.

"Let's get those fuckers, Wil," he said.

Wil shook his head slowly. It wasn't the emotional stake, he thought, that had driven him this far. What hooked him, pushed him farther than he'd planned to go was the simple urge to get the problem solved—an instinct that governed every artist's work. Once the gears are meshed, their action takes a life of its own. "The idea was to help Sally out of a jam," he said. "Leave the real work to the cops."

"Yeah." Madison managed to convey his skepticism in a single syllable. "So what are you doing at Ray's Raiders, Wil? Leaving it to the cops?" He laughed shortly, shoved the gear stick forward, and drove on.

The house was up in the canyon area, shaded with tall eucalyptus trees and twenty degrees more bearable than downtown. The van scrunched over the gravel and came to a stop in the driveway where a big old Dick Corman structure, dating from before the time he went conceptual, juxtaposed its colored steel branches with the delicate lattice of a copper birch. The rear end of an XJ Jaguar jutted from the carport.

It was the maid who opened the door.

"Mrs. Singer home?" asked Madison. The woman stood her ground at the threshold, treating him to an appraising stare. "We came for the art." He waved the consignment sheet without appreciable results.

"I'll take care of it, Alicia." Sylvia Singer pushed her way impatiently past the maid and grabbed the clipboard from Madison's hand. "You were supposed to be here half an hour ago."

A tall, cool woman of carefully cultivated beauty, she was dressed for the tearoom at the Regency Club. Her eyes flickered only briefly when they met Wil's, uncertain where she might have seen him and whether he was to be recognized now. Wil offered no help and a moment later her eyes had moved to Madison and on, into the trees behind.

"You'd better come in," she said. She led the way briskly down the corridor to the right. "It's in the dining room."

The piece was a Franz Kline, maybe three feet by two, Wil guessed, still on the wall. The single, strong black gesture on its rugged white ground managed to dominate even the elaborate crystal chandelier that hung over the polished walnut table. A dozen plate settings with white napkins and glittering glassware sat, either anticipating a dinner party for that evening, or simply gathering dust for decorative purposes.

"Well," she said. "You'd better get ahead. I did tell your people no later than one-thirty. I'm late."

"Gee, Mrs. Singer," said Madison smoothly. "I'm sure Mr. Ray would want us to apologize for the inconvenience."

She looked at him narrowly, eyes alert for the sarcasm she suspected, but found him only serious, polite. "Well," she said, "be careful with the piece, it's valuable. I have to leave. I'll ask Alicia to check and lock up after you've left." She wafted from the room and they listened to her heels click down the hallway.

"Bitch," said Madison.

"She wanted to be sure we left the silverware behind," Wil said. "That's it? That's all she has to say?"

Madison shrugged and sighed. "It's typical," he said, "of some. Wouldn't you know it, the thing's supposed to have been wrapped."

Wil checked the instructions the front desk had copied down on the consignment sheet: OWNER WILL WRAP. "Well?" he asked.

"Listen," said Madison, "it happens all the time. The damn collectors bitch about the way we handle their precious goddamn stuff, but they don't know enough to take care of it themselves. I put a couple sheets of plastic in back of the van, in case. They'll have to do."

96

Wil brought the picture down from its hook on the wall while Madison went back out to the van. It was a light stretcher, standard, store-bought, more delicate than it should have been, and close up, the surface of the paint was badly cracked. Madison returned with enough of the plastic sheeting to wrap around the face and taped it to the stretcher bars behind—good enough to keep the work protected until they got it to the warehouse.

The Jaguar was churning up gravel in the driveway when they got back out. Madison waited until the storm had passed before he opened up the doors and climbed in. Wil passed him the Kline and together they laid it flat, face up, on an outspread quilted blanket and checked to be sure it wasn't going to slip and slide.

"She didn't even ask for a receipt?" asked Wil as they left the driveway.

"I left one on the table anyway," Madison told him. "Some of these people work on the assumption that the rest of the world is there to take care of them. Or maybe they just don't care."

"Is this just private collectors, or museums, too?"

"It's different with the museums—most of them, anyway. They inspect their own stuff and send out a condition report with it. If it's valuable enough, they use a courier to escort it. But private collectors ... There's plenty of good ones, I don't say that. But there's some of them don't even have the good sense to check—until the stuff gets back with a nick in the frame or a broken glass." He laughed. "Then they come back at you and claim all kinds of damage. Maybe they like the insurance money better than they like the art."

"Does much of this stuff get lost?" asked Wil.

Madison glanced at him over his shoulder. "Just plain lost?"

"Like the Leon Drakes," said Wil. "Ripped off."

They made it to Sunset and followed the wide boulevard as it curved east past the canyons toward the Brentwood area.

"I don't know how much." Madison dropped the window to its lowest and laid his forearm out on the sill. "When it does, they try to keep it quiet, but once in a while you catch wind of something like that. It wouldn't be hard to find out the pickups and destinations without any help. At the Raiders, they're posted on a board and updated every day, a week, maybe ten days ahead."

"Where anyone can see?"

"Front office," he said. "In front of your nose."

The van swung down the concrete driveway at the Steins' in Brentwood. The consignment sheet said to pick up two framed Serra drawings, headed back for a commercial gallery in New York. Will had seen the two pictures in the house. In heavy frames, well protected under glass, they could safely wait for wrapping at the warehouse.

He rang the bell and listened to its Avon ding-dong way back in the kitchen.

"Hey, Wil, for God's sake." It was Brenda Stein herself who came to the door and reached up to lay a hand on his beard and plant a sloppy kiss on his cheek. "You working with Stu Ray? You have to be out of your mind."

Wil grinned. "A short stint," he said, his arm around her shoulder. "I'll tell you sometime. This here's my friend Madison. Madison Grant. Watch out for his videos, okay?"

"If you say so, Wil. Hi, Madison. You've been here before, haven't you? Can I get you guys some coffee?"

They turned down the offer and followed her through the house to a large conservatory where they kept the Serras. They were propped against the wall, ready to go—dark, clumsy, oppressive shapes in charcoal, drawn against large areas of smudged white.

"You're selling, Brenda? I'm surprised. These are terrific drawings."

"Trading. I'm going to miss these guys—but there's something right now that we want more."

"What's that? More Serra?"

"You'll see next time you come."

"Can't wait."

Between them, Wil and Madison hauled the big drawings one by one to the van. Heavy mothers, Wil thought, they needed the two-person crew Stu had sent. Then they set the pieces face-to-face and roped them to the exposed fretwork of the walls.

Back at Stu Ray's a few minutes past five, they found the rest of the crew had left. Besides Wil's big Buick, there were two cars left in the parking area—a second old clunker and a neat red Alfa Romeo that Wil hadn't seen before.

"Whose are those?" he asked Madison, jerking a thumb.

"The Olds belongs to Clusky," Madison said. "I think the foreign job is Brad's."

"Brad?"

"Some friend of the boss," said Madison, shrugging. "Thinks he owns the place. He hangs around."

"Some car."

"This guy has fantasies about himself."

The two of them off-loaded and racked the Serras and the Kline, and Madison backed the van into its parking stall.

"That's it, I guess," he said. He climbed out, stretching and shading his eyes against the sun to look at Wil. "You need any help?"

Wil laid a hand on his shoulder "Thanks," he said. "But why don't you get on home? I think I'll hang around awhile longer. Snoop around a bit. Maybe grab the chance to get Clusky talking, if I can. Who locks up? Is it Clusky?"

"If Stu's not around, it's Clusky. The front gate's on an electric eye," said Madison. "It'll open up for you from the inside and close automatically. But unless there's some special reason to have guys working late, they clear us all out before they leave. If Clusky sees your car out there, he'll come looking for you."

Wil watched Madison vault down from the dock and heard his car door slam out on the street. The loading area was deserted, the big steel door rolled down, the only light source now the small, high skylights in the roof, which let in light enough to see one's way. Wil's footsteps echoed quietly in the cavernous gloom as he headed back through the racks past Clusky's office. Here the window cast light in a grid of four squares on the concrete, and the sound of voices traveled indistinctly through the door. Wil paused, listening, then seized the moment to move on quickly to the front office.

Even without the overhead neon strips, the office was much brighter than the warehouse. A telephone blinked as he opened the communicating door and stepped into the carpeted reception area. Computer screens stared blankly into the open space, and the high-speed printer sat silent under its dust cover. Wil tested a few drawers in the banks of files and found them locked. Even the lap drawers in the desks, where he thought to hunt for keys, had been left secure. No notes, no papers—the desktops were swept clean of information. Even the trash was emptied, in compliance, surely, with Stu's own obsession with neatness.

The single source of information was the weekly assignment board that Madison had mentioned, posted behind the secretary's desk. Wil glanced through the list of activities for inspiration. Barbara Corton was down for Tuesday and Wednesday, out in the Coachella Valley. Then there were other names, some of them familiar—institutions, galleries. Most of the jobs were noted down in blue, but Tuesday, tomorrow, had a notation written bold in red and boxed in with strong lines: CUSTOMS —LAX. No clue as to what the difference was between blue and red, but Raul Ortega, Wil saw, was also down in red for a delivery in the Valley in the afternoon. Bird in the Bush. A gallery? Wil had never heard the name. On the other hand, he wasn't surprised. There were numerous galleries he'd never been to, and this one's name alone made it sound like a schlock operation.

He sat down at the secretary's desk and scanned the office area from this vantage point for a while, then flipped the power switch on the computer keyboard. A square of green light appeared in the top right corner of the monitor and blinked at him, followed by the two words "Enter Code." Wil swore to himself and turned the thing off again. He got up, tested Stu's door, and found it locked.

It was five-thirty. With nothing to be gleaned in the front office, he went back to the warehouse and paced down between the racks, pausing here and there to check an item on the shelves. Before he reached Clusky's office, the door burst open, spilling light across the darkened concrete floor, along with the sound of voices, louder now.

"...you don't agree with something, it's Stu Ray you talk to, not to me." Clusky was angry. "I don't give a fuck what you have to say..."

"You'll listen to me, Clusky." The anger in the second voice was controlled, almost amused. "See you in the morning."

The man came around the corner from the office so fast he couldn't avoid a direct collision with Wil, knocking the wind out of his own body with a grunt. Wil reached for his arm to bring him back to balance and held on for a moment, letting go when it was snatched away from his grasp. He had an impression of pale, angry eyes as the stranger glared at him in the darkness before turning on his heel and making for the door.

"Who's the charmer?" asked Wil, as the man vaulted down from the loading dock.

Clusky gave him the once-over, suspicious. He looked at his watch. "For Christ's sake, Garretson," he said irritably, "what are you doing here, this time of night? Where's Grant?" He was still consumed with his own anger, distracted.

"He left," said Wil. "Ten minutes ago. I just came in to see what you had me down for."

100

Clusky herded him to the door. "I don't have you down for nothing yet. Check with me in the morning."

"So who was it?"

"None of your goddamn business, Garretson."

"Clusky . . . ?" Wil tried to slow the man down without success.

"Yeah?" He was bolting the loading door from the inside, crashing the steel bars into place, anxious to be moving.

"Forget it," said Wil. "It'll wait until tomorrow."

15

D ON HENSCHLER stood back a ways from the window in his studio and watched, rolling a stray lock of hair around one finger. Despite the heat, his skin was cold and clammy, and the itch behind his eyes was impervious to the stinging rub of his fingers. Garretson bothered him. He knew something, or he wouldn't be here. Worse, there was something about the man that seemed to draw out the very things you wanted to keep hidden. His eyes. He made Don feel like a kid compelled to spill his secrets.

He shivered, watching the man climb into his big old silver car and roll out of the parking lot.

Don watched Clusky watching, too—the whole scene plotted like some photo-realist painting in the window frame, Don thought. The super threw his jacket in the car and made a last inspection of the doors and windows of the warehouse. It was a ritual Don must have witnessed a hundred times, and today he could barely wait till it was over. His eyes ached with the emptiness, staring out from semidarkness into sunlight, and the hunger ate at his belly like a pain.

Clusky locked the small door by the loading bay and checked the three trucks in their stalls, with Don swallowing down another two minutes of agony. You've got it, he told himself. If only you can wait. The call had to come this evening and he knew his nerves would be

102

scrambled until it came. What was Garretson up to, for Christ's sake? Was he for real? Kind eyes. Don cursed himself.

"Be real." He mouthed the words behind the window, realizing he was unsure what they meant anymore.

One thing was certain: Jim had fucked up in some way. What Don read in his death was a lesson for himself, and he felt vulnerable, raw, confused. Trapped. If Garretson seemed to offer a way out, there was always Jim there, to remind him . . .

Clusky slapped the roof of his car and climbed in, backing it around from his parking spot and making a wide turn into the street. Now.

But Don still waited. He waited until the electric eye brought the gate to a close, though his heart had already begun to pound in anticipation. It began to race when metal clashed against metal, and he hurried back to the studio. Ten minutes, fifteen. Then he could get to work. He was behind schedule already.

He had designed and built his cache with the obsessive attention to detail he lavished on his paintings and, like them, it fooled the eye. A locking device was built in under the window frame. The crack where the wooden sill joined the casement was invisible to the casual eye. When released, the mechanism allowed him to slide the whole sill forward from its place and reach down into a cavity between the cinder blocks below.

The space was surprisingly large: He had been able to fit two fair-sized paintings there, and still had room for the shelf where he kept his candy box. He pulled it out and stripped off the thick elastic band that held it closed. On the lid, a spry kitten leaped to trap a wind-up mouse.

Don opened the box carefully. Inside, packed neatly down, were a syringe and spoon, along with a length of rubber tubing and his last two small, transparent envelopes.

Taking the box to the burner where the encaustic was keeping warm, he removed the pot and squatted down over the stove, laying out the paraphernalia piece by piece on a white tile he kept for that purpose. He sweated cold as he watched the liquid heat. Then he loaded the syringe, wrapped the hose around his left arm at the bicep, flicked his finger at the vein to snap it up, and punctured the skin with the needle.

For a full five minutes, allowing the bliss to reach down inside of him, he sat in silence with his eyes closed. Then, with a sigh, he rewrapped the candy box and returned it to its shelf.

He had more work left to do than he cared to think about and the telephone call was about as much as he could deal with in one evening. But they would be anxious to hear about the new one and he had to get a look at it first. He had a point of his own to make, too, and felt a constriction in the belly when he thought about it. He dreaded the calls.

The back door from the studio crossed a narrow alley to the warehouse. With daily access to the system, it hadn't been hard for Don to make the key and install a circuit that simply circumvented the electronic alarms on command. Inside the warehouse, the corridor was still dimly lit by reflected daylight and Don ignored the light switch, picking his way between the racks until he came to the holding section where Garretson had stacked the Franz Kline.

It had been left for the night, covered loosely with its temporary plastic sheet. Unframed, the picture's edges were protected with thin strips of wood, and at first touch Don realized it was unusually light and fragile. He pulled the cotton gloves over his fingers and gripped the picture by the edges, sliding it carefully from the rack.

Back in the studio, he set it up on the easel.

First off, he made an inch-by-inch study of the surface. He had handled Klines before. There was nothing remarkable about this one, except perhaps that the stress marks, crisscrossing the black calligraphic gesture that was the picture's central image, were more severe than some he had seen. A mixture of cheap material—Kline had been known to use car paint or even plain house enamel—and fast work. Given time, he could handle that with a hair dryer, maybe, or the space heater.

Don's hand-held ultraviolet light was fitted with a magnifying glass, and he went back over the surface checking for underpainting or restoration work. The white ground of the painting jumped out at him as he switched it on, and the light brought out an earlier gesture, painted out and re-covered until the artist was satisfied that he had found what he was after. The weave of the canvas seemed to be intact, and the one restoration looked to have been made by the artist—a corner that had been scratched and painted back over.

Finally, he raked the front of the painting with another hand-held light, a neon he had designed himself for the purpose, highlighting areas of impasto and passages where underpainting had built up the surface.

Turning the picture around, he ran a finger along the edge of the canvas and pulled a piece back from the wood to look at the stretcher. Nothing unusual there, except that the wood was dry, almost brittle. Don scratched at one of the pegs with his fingernail. Given the small scale of the work, it was a lightweight structure, unreinforced and easy to reproduce, though the wood would have to be stressed and aged. The back of the raw canvas was stained with black smudges, and the signature and date were written large across the middle. Nineteen fifty-five.

Two weeks, maybe three, he decided. It was more time out from his own work, but he didn't have a choice.

He needed photographs to work from, and he had begun to set up lights in front of the easel when the telephone rang.

"Yes?"

There was only one person it could be. Don knew the sound well, a voice that came across, distant, muffled, impersonal: "You have the Kline?"

"It's here in the studio," he said. "I'm just setting up for the UVs. They have it scheduled for crating and shipping out tomorrow."

"Well?"

"I can make you one," said Don. "But don't plan on a substitution, not in this case. I've checked the underpainting, and there's no way I can make a duplicate. It's going to be more like a companion piece, something from the same period, say. Maybe an early trial for the same gesture. Even then, it's not going to pass a museum test. It will get past the kind of collector who doesn't know too much or look too close, but not past a smart one."

"Okay, that fits. How long?"

"Two weeks, maybe. I'd rather have three."

There was a pause. "Then forget it. I don't have that long. What about the Warhol? What's left to be done?"

"The dirty-down."

"The what?"

"It's the aging process. To make the thing look right." The piece was a straight soup can, no problems. But a white ground is bound to lose a lot of its freshness after twenty years and a brand-new copy needed a dirty-down to take the edge off it. There were various ways to go about it, and Don knew them all.

"I need it tomorrow."

He hesitated. "When do I get paid for the last job?" It was a Josef Albers, yellow, gray and white concentric squares that palpitated on the canvas. Four weeks' work, and you could barely tell it from an original. Like the Mondrian they'd hung in the museum last week. Don allowed himself a small smile at the memory.

"When I see money, fuckhead. We had it presold in Tokyo but we're waiting for cash. You'll get it when we do. Minus advances."

"Advances?"

"Come on, Henschler. We've been feeding you shit these past three weeks. You still owe us, man."

Don didn't believe what the man told him, but he hadn't kept accounts. The whole thing was confusing when you never knew how much they were going to pay, or how much they were charging for the supply. He'd simply lost count.

The pain returned to his belly, a sudden cramp that made him wince with fear. "I have something new I've been working on," he said. He glanced across at the Jasper Johns flag he'd pulled from the rack—maybe the best and the hardest thing he'd ever done. He'd started it with the idea of trying to find a buyer himself, and making ten times more than he would otherwise. Now he knew he couldn't take the risk. "Something you didn't ask for. It's good."

"Like what? How do we know we can sell it? Listen, we manufacture to order in this business. We deal, then we steal." The man laughed. "You find us a buyer, man, and we'll take what you make."

"Three more days I need. I'll arrange for a drop Thursday night, okay? I need money."

Another silence on the line and a short laugh. Then: "Yeah. Like the rest of us."

Don's heart pounded. He knew he shouldn't do it. He wouldn't have done it if he hadn't been desperate. "Like Jim Sewell," he said. He felt sick. He needed a piss.

This time the silence was longer.

"Like who?"

"Come on, I'm not stupid. I'm not blind. I could see what was happening. There had to be others. Jim was one of them."

"Jim's dead." The voice had changed tone.

He shouldn't have done it. Jesus, he knew he shouldn't have done it. It wasn't a denial. It was a confirmation. He had been right. Don's fingers went straight to his hair, curling furiously.

"And not only Ray's Raiders, huh, isn't that true? I've been reading the papers, I hear what's happening. You guys have been busy...."

"Don't push it, Henschler."

"You need me," said Don. "You need what I can do."

"Don't count on it, fuckhead. You're too late anyway. I'm closing up shop. This is it, kid. You've got two days."

Don opened his mouth but the words wouldn't come. He shouldn't have started what he knew he couldn't finish. "What do you mean?" he asked. "Closing up shop?"

"What I say. That's it. End of story."

"But..." He'd been working for them for the past two years. They couldn't close up. "Okay," he said. "Okay, sorry, let's forget it. Let me show you what I've got. I can work cheaper. Faster. You can't close up."

"Watch us."

The silence seemed to Don to last an hour. The urge to piss was suddenly unbearable and he grabbed hold of his bladder, closing his eyes. "Please," he said. "Please."

"I'll take delivery on the Warhol tomorrow. Same place."

"What about the new one?"

"The Kline? Forget it, I said. Too late."

"No, not the Kline. The other. It's a Jasper Johns flag. They're selling for more than a million dollars now."

"Wait. Hold the line."

The hold button left him in suspension. More silence. Was there a conversation at the other end that he couldn't hear? Then the voice returned. "A flag, huh? Okay, Don. You can drop it off with the Warhol tomorrow...."

"Not tomorrow. Three days, I said."

"Is it ready?"

"It still needs to dry."

"No three days. Tomorrow, and I'll take a look at it. But let's be sure of one thing...."

"Yes?"

"You don't threaten me, Don. There's no mileage in that, you understand?"

"That's not what I meant. That wasn't it at all."

But the phone went dead before he finished. Don hooked the receiver back and ran to the toilet. He ripped at his belt and pants as he ran. When he sat down on the toilet seat, the piss came slow and painful. His clothes were wet.

Closing up shop? He shouldn't have done it. When he got back to the studio and tried to screw the camera down into the tripod, his hands were trembling so much he couldn't match the threads. Then he stopped, and realized what he was doing. Christ! They didn't even want the Kline.

He should have known better.

Pushing aside the tripod, he scrabbled around in the trash barrel for the scrap of paper he'd thrown away. Frustrated, he went back to the telephone and dialed 411.

"Information," said the voice. "What city, please?"

"Venice, California. The name is Garretson. Wil Garretson."

He noted down the number on the wall beside the telephone and dialed. The ring went unanswered.

16

I T WASN'T often Wil drove past his portrait. The Kent Twitchell
mural was full-face, twenty feet high, yet a likeness so detailed that
even the follicles of his eyebrows stood out in photographic highlight.
Shoulder to shoulder with him, Barbara Corton gazed out over the traffic in similarly heroic scale. Both were unsmiling.

Wil pumped the brake on the Le Sabre as he drove past, then hit the
gas as the driver behind gave him the horn. Not that there was much
more than a car's length difference in it, in rush-hour traffic.

Twitchell liked to think of the painting as a modern altarpiece, to be
seen at fifty miles an hour. Hence the scale. But Joseph and Mary was
taking things a little far. Wil grinned and eased himself farther right to
get in lane for Hollywood.

The traffic on the four-level interchange was bumper to bumper,
crawling. Wil drummed his fingers on the steeling wheel as he thought
back over the day. So far he'd achieved what? he asked himself. There
was the itchy feeling that he'd been carried away, overstepping by far the
original limits he'd planned to set for himself. And the aching void was
there in the belly to remind him of a distinct foreboding that things were
headed out of control much faster than he could catch up with them.

But the facts were hazy. A kid who stole paintings and got himself killed in an elaborate, almost cynically cruel setup. An old friend with an art-transportation business. Young folks who needed money to support themselves in an expensive world while they pursued their art habits—and who looked around and saw an art scene where the survivors were the ones who were hyped up by a market that was literally banking on them, where everything came back to the dollar. When an Ed Ruscha goes at auction for close to a quarter million bucks, what makes much sense anymore? Not to pick on Ed, Wil thought.

So who could be surprised if Jim decided to turn the tables for a change? Even if Wil hadn't known Jim Sewell in art school, the budding artist's notebooks identified him as a hot-air radical. Rip off the art establishment, he would have argued, instead of getting taken. Play the game. Trouble was, whoever had put him up to it in the first place turned out to be playing tougher games than he ever reckoned on.

Digging down below the surface, Wil was surprised to find an anger he hadn't fully recognized before. Something like having the neighbor's dog shit in your yard. For all its quirks and faults, the art world was a good one—tight, supportive, generous to its own. People cared. Small ripples made a difference you would notice in a pond as small as this—and someone had just chucked in a boulder.

Twenty minutes from downtown, the traffic finally began to creep up the Cahuenga Pass. Near the top, Wil accelerated out along the Barham exit ramp and swung back over the Mulholland bridge toward Woodrow Wilson Drive.

Surrounded by a white-walled citrus and avocado orchard on the hillside street, the Horans' old Spanish house looked out on the other side over scrub brush and wilderness. Coyotes ruled the wildlife up here, and only the distant, subdued roar of traffic, absorbed by hills and twisting streets, betrayed the proximity of the city. Today, the house was simmering in a haze of heat, and Wil noted with relief that Rick still wasn't home when he nosed his big car in behind the Supra.

"Wil!"

Sally came out to meet him. She must have been watching at the door before he reached it.

"Thank God," she said. "I thought you'd never get here." It was the kind of day she'd normally be barefoot, wearing white cotton shorts and a light open shirt for the studio, but today she wore jeans and sneakers, her shirt buttoned to the neck. She peered out from behind the oversized round lenses of a pair of tinted glasses that he'd never seen her wear.

110

Wil put both hands on her shoulders, steadying her. "I tried to call around lunchtime," he said. "Just to check in."

"I couldn't face the phone. Listen, Wil. Rick will be home any moment. The police were here." He studied her face. For the first time since he'd known her, her eyes seemed dull and heavy behind the lenses, the muscles around them tired.

"We'll sort it out," he said.

Leaving the pile of her things in the trunk for the time being, he put an arm round her waist as they walked back to the studio. The architect who'd designed it had been sensitive to the need for balanced light: It filled the space with a soft, even glow that set it apart as a haven from the outside world. There was a single painting in progress on the opposite wall, along with half a dozen watercolor sketches pinned to the celotex beside it, absorbing light from the clerestory. Wil gravitated toward them out of habit, following the intricacies of her structure with a thoughtful eye. No doubt that the work was getting stronger, more sure of itself, unafraid of the decorative element it had always flirted with and now seemed for the first time to embrace.

"You've done a great job here," he said. Sally glanced at the painting, shook her head, and turned away. The board she used as a palette was scraped clean, and the brushes were dry.

There was a little sitting area at the far end of the studio, and Wil took a seat on the couch there, watching as Sally perched a little apart, on the stool at her drafting table.

"Wil..." she began. She hooked her heel in the crossbar, folding one leg across the other.

Wil shook the wandering thoughts from his head. "Okay, love," he said. "Let's go back over it. Tell me about the cops."

She started, and he listened, gazing at Jim's small picture on the wall beside him. A simple pastel, it split along a strong, unbroken horizon, the top-half light, the bottom-half surface and reflection. The glow that radiated from its central seam was dazzling—an effect he'd still not been able to translate into paint. Wil closed his eyes as he listened. Madison was right: It was unreal.

Images. That was the whole thing. He could see them, building into teasing patterns like a Borges story, the images he'd used in the piece he'd made so many years ago.

He left a long silence when she finished, feeling the distance between them like a concrete substance, letting her feel it, too.

"Sally," he told her. "We're doing this wrong. Your Jim was deep into the mire and I've barely been able to get a sense of what it's all about." He gave her a brief sketch of the day at the Raiders. "Besides," he said, "there's too damn much you've forgotten. It's not just the obvious things like the note with your address they found in Jim's wallet, or the gun, or the Polaroids. There's too much static in the air that's going to point to you." He paused. "Speaking of the obvious," he added, "I have your things from Jim's studio in the trunk. I'll give them back before I leave."

She put her head in her hand. "I don't need that stuff," she said.

But that was no answer.

"Okay, sure. But, Sally, if you're planning on lying to the cops, you better be damn sure they can't catch you at it. What about witnesses? Fingerprints? Pubic hairs in the sleeping bag, for Christ's sake? I mean, who knows what the experts can dig up? We're goddamn amateurs, Sally, is the point. And what are we going to tell them when and if we have to? We've already gone too far. You see what I mean?"

She said nothing. Instead, she set her jaw and stared ahead of her, as if she hadn't heard.

"You're still not ready?"

She shook her head, silent.

"Tomorrow, then? If nothing else has broken?"

Sally moved her head from side to side, equivocating.

"Well, listen," he heard himself say. Face it, Wil, the voice said, you're pleased. You're delighted. "You were going to check on a couple of things for me. The telephone numbers? From Jim's bill?"

"Of course. I took care of it." She was alive again, slipping down from the stool and crossing to the desk, where she pulled a small sheet of message paper from a spike. "These are the numbers," she told him. "One of the 818s was the studio here."

Wil looked down the list. A couple of names were familiar, artists he knew, and friends. Then there was Bird in the Bush, the name he'd seen printed in red letters on the Raiders' bulletin board. "This gallery," he asked Sally, pointing. "You know it?"

She looked over his shoulder. "Never heard of it."

"Me neither," said Wil. "Not until today."

"Today?"

"It's a hokey name," he said. "It's down for a delivery from Stu's place tomorrow."

They studied the name together for a moment. "I can find out," she said.

"What do you mean?"

And Sally was back in gear. Her eyes began to work again, behind the glasses. "I'm stifling, sitting around here waiting for someone else to do something. What's wrong with getting out and doing something useful myself, for God's sake? I'll take a drive down to the valley tomorrow and check the place out."

He realized suddenly that he was less ready for her to take the risks than to take them himself. "What's wrong," he said, "is that it gets you in deeper than you already are. And you're exposed enough as it is."

"I feel safer when I'm moving."

"Out of the house?"

She nodded. "They know where to find me here. And Wil...I'd prefer to be out, if I can."

"Why's that?"

"I hate the thought of being left here alone. Rick's leaving town tomorrow. He'll be gone for a couple of days."

"Rick's leaving? Where's he going?" Wil fought down another rush of feelings that he didn't want to recognize.

Coming just at that moment, the knock at the glass panel in the studio door startled them both. They looked around to find Rick squinting in, between cupped hands. He waved and opened it.

"Wil Garretson," he said. "This is a surprise! How's it going?" He came in and kissed Sally on the forehead, mussing her hair a little with one hand, and offering the other one to Wil. "Everything okay?" he asked. The gesture was easy, and accepted easily, on the surface. The tension was somewhere down below. "What do you think of Sally's new work?"

"I think it's great," said Wil.

Rick was wearing office clothes—a beige linen suit, blue oxford shirt loosened at the collar, and a striped navy tie. A couple of inches taller than Wil, he was well built and bronzed. He kept himself fit with tennis and racketball at the athletic club. At forty-three, he had already lost some of the wavy brown hair which he combed straight back from center, and he wore gold-framed bifocals. Otherwise, he had survived the trials of business well. Cool eyes, a little tight, Wil thought, or tired.

They still conveyed that confidence in his ability to get things taken care of—the quality that had earned his reputation as a business manager.

"What's this I hear?" he asked Wil. "You working at Ray's Raiders? How have the mighty fallen!"

Wil laughed. "Just helping out an old friend in a crisis," he said. "Nothing permanent. You talked to Stu?"

Rick took off his jacket and slung it over his shoulder. "Yeah," he said, "by coincidence. He checked in with me today. He has a lot of respect for you, Wil." He looked at his watch and back at Sally. "You going to be ready for dinner?" he asked.

"Dinner!" Sally slapped her head and winced. "I can't keep the first thing in my head. Listen, Wil, we have a date in an hour and I'm still a mess. I'll try your suggestion and give you a call, okay? Thanks for the good words."

"Anytime, Sally. Take care, okay?"

She kissed him briefly on the cheek. "You too, Wil. Stay. Have a drink. Rick, get the man a drink before he leaves."

"Sure, love."

"And don't forget you still have to pack...."

There are things between a married couple, Wil thought, so second nature that they work on autopilot even when the other things in life go crazy. He watched as Rick Horan hurried over to open the door for Sally and followed her down the steps to the back entrance of the house.

The den was sheltered from the sunlight, dark, a little muggy at the end of the day. It had always been Rick's room. The couch and easy chair were leather-covered, polished, squeaky to the touch. Even though he'd long given up smoking, his rack of favorite pipes still stood on the mahogany desktop, along with a shiny chrome perpetual-motion toy and a row of framed family pictures. The room was paneled in dark wood, the shelves on two walls packed with hardbound volumes, mostly on business and the law, some general-interest books on psychology, and a few best-sellers from recent years, mostly unread, to judge by the immaculate dust jackets. The stack of sound and video equipment in one corner looked equally unused.

Rick opened a section of the wall to reveal a wet bar. "Well," he asked, "what will it be, Wil? Scotch? Bourbon? Vodka? I hate to say it, but you look like you could use one. Tough day at the Raiders, huh?"

"A hot one. It's hideous downtown. I'll have a bourbon, if I may."

"Take the weight off."

The air sighed in the leather cushion as Wil sank back in a corner of the couch, and Rick threw ice into a clear crystal tumbler and tipped the bottle of Jack Daniels over it. The liquor spilled out over the cubes and Wil watched a splash explode into droplets as it hit the polished wood counter. "Water?" Rick asked. "Or soda?"

"On the rocks, thanks." Rick passed him the glass and reached into the small icebox for a bottle of Perrier, pouring himself a half glass over ice. "Well, cheers," he said, raising it.

"Cheers. How's business, Rick?"

"Too busy, as always." Rick hitched his jacket over the back of a chair and raised his glasses to rub at his eyes. "But who's complaining?" He sat back in the easy chair, and Sourdough sauntered in off the patio, jumping up and landing in his lap. "Damn cat," said Rick. "Leaves its hairs everywhere." He picked a few off his lap and dropped them down by the chaise.

The hell with the delicacies, Wil decided. There might never be a better moment. "Listen," he said. "A little free consultation, okay? Between friends? Interesting question—you must have clients who bring it to you once in a while. A friend has these paintings stolen, two of them. The insurance company pays up, right?"

Rick held his drink up to the sunlight through the window and squinted through it into the back yard. "Assuming the work's properly insured, of course," he said. "And once the theft's been investigated. It could take time."

Wil nodded. "No matter where it is? In transit, say. Or on loan at an institution like the County?"

"Well, I guess. For a museum show, the institution's policy would more than likely cover it door to door. You had something stolen?"

"Not me," said Wil. "Leon Drake. Me, I'm just curious."

Rick nodded slowly. "I heard about the Drakes," he said. "They must be covered some way."

"The insurance would pay full value?"

The sun was playing its light on the avocado leaves outside. There was the faintest trace of a breeze, a tremble in the leaves which brought a breath of air in from the ocean and caused the light to shimmer. Sourdough had gone to sleep.

"That depends on how you define value." Rick smiled. "In the art world, there's all kinds of ways, you know that. For insurance purposes, it would be the amount for which a specific work is insured."

"Current market?"

"Market value according to an independent estimator. Not your dealer, I can promise you! Who knows what current market value is: What some joker last paid for a Rauschenberg at Christie's, or what you could actually get for yours if you tried to sell it? There's a difference."

"But probably more than you paid for it? Forget the Leon Drakes for a moment. Say, from a private collection."

"That depends on when you bought it, doesn't it?" Rick laughed comfortably. "It's a joke. Everything's relative in the art world, right? Put it this way: Nobody buys a painting for what it's supposed to be worth. When I buy, as a collector, I get ten to twenty percent off—depending on how much I buy from that particular dealer. A whole lot more, believe me, if I can get it direct from the artist's studio."

"More than twenty?"

"Come on, Wil. You're an artist. You have a painting your dealer says is worth ten grand. I come to you with six, seven thousand, cash. How about it?"

It happened all the time, Wil knew. On a work that was priced at ten thousand dollars, you'd get maybe five from your dealer. Sell it out of your studio, you can give a whopping discount—and still make a better profit on the deal.

"You don't need me to tell you this, Wil. Besides, there's a growing number of artists who refuse to work with a dealer at all. Value's a conspiracy, not some absolute reality. This is a crazy world we work in, you and I. So, starting day one, most art is 'worth' more than you paid for it, assuming you know what you're buying and have discounts available—that's a part of the game. You never sold a piece to a friend or a special client?"

Wil set his glass down on the end table. "Sure I did," he said. "There's no reason, then, you can't make a tidy profit on having your collection ripped off?"

Rick's hand played with a corner of the cat's ear, pulling at it gently. "Conceivably, sure. There's lots of people wouldn't squawk too loud if they lost a painting—and many more who would be privately kind of pleased if it got damaged. It's a lawsuit-happy world we live in, isn't it? But in practice you'll find most people are as underinsured as me and Sally. We can't keep up with insurance rates on artificial values. Hell, most of the major museums have works they can't afford the premiums on."

116

"Is that right?"

Rick shrugged his shoulders. "Right. You read about the fire at the Huntington, a few months back? The Reynolds? No insurance. The thing was beyond any value anyway. But in case you have plans, I wouldn't advise you to try losing art too often. Insurance companies don't like that kind of thing, and they tend to sniff it out pretty fast. What are you trying to get at, Wil?"

Wil wasn't sure himself. "I think," he said with a grin, "that I'm casting about for a profit motive. By the way, do you know if there's much in the way of stolen art these days?"

Rick put his glass down on the glass tabletop, got up, and stretched. "It happens," he said. He gazed out over the lawn to where it met the scrub brush, frowning. "The biggest problem would be unloading the stuff. It's easily identified, and most of it's not easy to sell. Ask any dealer. Contemporary work, anyway. Of course, there's always the unscrupulous collector. You've met them. They're part of the art game, too. But sure, to answer your question, I get clients reporting losses on their taxes."

"Taxes?"

"Sure. You think those two won't show up on Leon's returns, if they're not found? You can write off documented thefts—or any other losses that haven't been fully covered by insurance."

"Another profit motive?"

Rick took his glasses off and held them at arm's length, examining the lenses for dust motes. "I doubt it," he said. "It's not what I would advise my clients. But I've seen people turning art into money in the weirdest ways." He laughed. "Sounds like you're cooking up a scam, my friend."

"Maybe it's not such a bad idea," said Wil. "I sure need something to help pay the rent."

"Watch out," said Rick with another laugh. "There's people who cook up scams and just get burned with the sauce. Hey, cat, get out of here." He tipped Sourdough out of his lap and brushed the hair off his pants. "Listen," he said, holding out his hand. "I've got to pack, or I'll be in trouble with the boss. Good talking to you, Wil."

17

BACK AT the studio in Venice, Wil showered and draped a robe around his body. Resting his head against the backboard of the bed in the loft, he picked up the phone and punched in Bernie Trost's number.

"Bernie? Hi, it's Wil."

"Yeah, Wil. How's it going? What's this I hear, you quitting Otis?"

Wil grinned. "It's nothing," he said. "Not much. I'll explain. But listen, I need a favor. Right up your alley."

"Shoot."

"In confidence, right?"

"Sure, Wil. Whatever you say."

"We've got something strange going on down here. I don't have time for the whole thing now, but it might have to do with a pattern of scams around the moving business. Art transportation. It could involve thefts or frauds, tax losses, insurance, or any combination of the above. Your files are full of this kind of stuff, right?"

"I've been saving them for years...."

"Right. So, listen, I'm looking at Stu Ray's...."

"Stu? Jesus, Wil, I thought the guy was a friend."

"Yeah, well, it could be he knows nothing about it. I can't see Stu mixed up in it. And this could be just a part of it, Bernie. Just a ragged end. What I'm smelling here is an organization, something that could have been going on for years, that's just beginning to surface—a game so big that someone needs to kill to protect it...."

"Holy Christ, Wil! Are you serious? Who? I mean, someone got killed?"

Wil hesitated. "Jim Sewell," he said.

"The kid that fell off the mountain?"

"Listen," said Wil. "What I'm thinking is this. If we could find some kind of pattern in your files, we'd be on to something, right?"

"Not much hope, Wil. There's acres of the stuff. If I'd managed to get it onto the word processor, we'd have something. It's a monumental task, though, getting it all onto diskettes. I've barely started."

"Will you give it a whirl? On the off-chance?"

Bernie grunted.

"Another thing," said Wil. "Have you checked on who owns your property yet?"

"I didn't get far. Some operation calls itself Tristate. I still haven't been able to find out who owns it, but they claim to have offices in the mid-Wilshire area. What does that have to do with it?"

"No idea. Just a feeling. Will you let me know when you've checked out the offices?"

"If it will help. I was planning on getting down there tomorrow. Wil? Have you thought of Leon's paintings?"

Wil paused again. He had known Bernie for enough years now. Why not? "I not only thought of them," he said. "I found the mothers."

"Found them?" Bernie was incredulous. "Where?"

"Listen," said Wil, "I have to be at the West Beach in an hour or so. Will you meet me tomorrow? Lunch? I'll tell you more then."

"How about the County?"

With luck, he could make it on his lunch break. "I'll be outside, by the temporary stairs, twelve-twenty. And listen, I'll be pushed for time. Bernie, I'm not even telling Leon yet, okay?"

There was a silence at the other end. Then Bernie started, "Wil, I just don't understand..."

"For Christ's sake, Bernie. You understand about as much as I do. Do me a favor?"

Wil stopped by the kitchen to open a can of beer on the way to his studio. He stood at the worktable for a while, looking over the drawings he'd made the night before, and was again surprised by the raw new voice he found speaking through him.

There were only two elements in the drawings: Man and rock. Life and matter. The animate and the inanimate. The two were one, perhaps, struggling to be two; or perhaps in some way he didn't yet understand they were trying to become each other.

They were looking at pain and fear and death in a way he'd never thought possible for his work to look at them. In everything he'd done to date he'd wanted to talk about those things, but he had sublimated them, playing with them like toys. These drawings were wrenched from a place inside he hadn't known about. It was Jim Sewell, clinging up there on the cliff face. Jim Sewell, twisting away.

Wil looked at his watch. There was time enough. Would it work? The telephone rang and he ignored it.

He opened the back door that led from the studio into what had once been a small back yard. For years now, it had served him as a junk yard—the single place where he could throw things to forget about them. There was twisted steel and weathered chunks of lumber, coils of rusting wire and mesh, the bric-a-brac of a working studio. He wrestled with an ungainly length of four-by-four, maybe eight feet of it, heaving its base from where the grass had laid years of roots around it, and dragging it through to the center of the studio.

Returning to the yard, he poked about for other sections, wood and metal, looking for rough solidity and bulk.

A half hour later, there was a heap of the stuff in the middle of the floor and Wil was perspiring freely with the effort of bringing it all in. He needed a real sense of what it was he was after. It had to be vertical, that was a part of it.

There was a pulley chain and a block and tackle he hadn't used in years and he pressed them into service now, swinging the chain down the rail from the end of the studio and lowering it to where he could hitch it around the lumber. Then he rattled the chain through the pulley, hoisting a single end slowly until the whole piece half-hung, half-stood at an eighty-degree angle from the floor.

Then he walked away and turned to tilt his head and look at it. He thought it could maybe work. He checked back on the drawings he'd made and flipped to a new page, pleased with the feel of the charcoal, the movement coming back to his arm.

120

"You're kidding?"

He hadn't heard MaryJo come in. He put the pad down on the worktable and reknotted the cord of his robe. There were splinters of dark wood and charcoal smudges everywhere, all over him, stuck to the white terry cloth and the hairs on his chest and legs.

"I just took a shower," he explained.

She giggled. "What in God's name are you doing?" She stood there and gaped. "I mean, this looks like...I don't know what it looks like. This is crazy."

"It's an idea. Just rattling the bars of my cage," he said. It did look funny when he thought about it. Funny and crazy. And dangerous. He felt a little light-headed. The phone rang again, and they both stood listening to it without moving.

"Some idea," she said, when the ringing stopped.

"Yeah, right. Some cage."

She padded into the studio in rubber flip-flops, looking around. "It's a mess," she said. She wore a pair of pearl-pink shorts over a turquoise unitard. Its top came down in a long curve from her shoulders. "What have you got on?"

"Got on?" asked Wil.

"Under that."

"Oh, that," he said. He showed her.

"Hmm-mm." She stood akimbo, hands resting on her hips, and inspected the revelation with an appraising eye.

"And you?" he asked.

"Me?"

"Yes," he said. "You."

She pulled the straps down from her shoulders. "Got these," she said.

"Hmm-mm."

She kept working, wriggling her hips free. "I got this."

Wil brought her close and wrapped her with him in the folds of the robe. "You sure have, babe," he said. Hugging her, he was lost for a moment in her hair.

"We could go to bed."

"Are you kidding? Who can wait that long?" He reached behind and hooked her up on his hips and carried her to the long green couch that lined the wall. And the thought came to him as he laid her down that perhaps she wanted to play longer, but for Wil the play was suddenly gone, the urgency swamped him like some dark invasion of night and he sobbed painfully, shuddering as he writhed and plunged, and shuddered massively as he felt the roots contracting, shattering, and released.

And then there was nothing. Nothing. A huge emptiness that threatened to overwhelm him. A dizzy fall. An emptiness and a pain he couldn't identify.

"Look at me, baby." MaryJo was over him, anxious, slapping his face. "You're not looking at me."

He opened his eyes and found himself looking into hers.

"Wil?"

"Yeah, babe." He waited, catching his breath. "I'm looking at you. What is it?"

"Jesus, I was worried. You passed clean out."

Wil sat up on the couch and stared at her. "I was out? How long?"

"A minute. A good minute. Are you okay?"

Lying back on the couch, he searched the studio ceiling slowly with his eyes, then looked at his watch. "I'm okay," he said. "But I'm late."

"Late for what? You're not going anywhere, Wil."

"A dinner date with Leon down at the West Beach. That never happened to me before. I'm sorry."

MaryJo sat up beside him. "Sorry?"

"It was so damn fast. So intense. It can't have been much for you."

Her fingers worked in among his hair, massaging. "You're not going anywhere. Not now. I'll call and leave a message, okay?"

"You want to go with me?"

She couldn't have gone if she'd wanted to, with the evening-class schedule she was working on. A new group, as close as she came to professionals, a real joy to work with. "I can't," she said. She got up and stood over him, naked. "Seriously, I want you to stay home. Your body's trying to tell you something, Wil."

He laughed, reaching a hand for her to heave him to his feet in front of her. "Horseshit," he said pleasantly. "It's probably trying to tell me it needs food."

"Stay?" she asked. "Please?"

"How about if I come home early?" He followed her as she walked bare-ass through the kitchen and stopped to grab an apple from the icebox. "Will you join me? Please?" Her smooth machine functioned flawlessly on the stairs.

"I don't know," she said. "You're not much good to me in your shape."

122

Dousing the studio lights, he locked the front door behind him and walked the half block to the boardwalk, turning south past the pier. The ocean breeze had brought the heat down a few notches and swayed the tops of the tall palms. As always, the skaters were out, zipping through dusk on humming urethane.

Making a left on the northern branch of Venice Boulevard, he strode the half block to the West Beach Café. Opposite the entrance to the restaurant, Charles Strauss was closing up shop at the Venice extension of his gallery.

"Hey, Charlie." Wil paused to chat before he crossed the street. "How's it going? Working late? On a Monday, yet?"

"You know how it is, Wil." Strauss had to be the only man in Venice who wore a white shirt and a business suit to work. "The business doesn't keep hours."

Strauss sometimes had the distant look of a man who sees the world from a different angle than his fellow beings, yet Wil had always found him easy to get along with, a man whose ego didn't conflict with those of his artists.

"I'm headed across the street for a drink with Leon," Wil said. "Want to join me?" The dealer might know more about the stolen pieces than Leon himself.

Strauss checked his watch. "Sure, Wil," he said. "Just a few minutes. I need to see Leon anyway."

The restaurant was relatively quiet on a Monday night. Weekends, it was noisy with the regulars: a handful of artists who, along with Leon and Wil, had colonized Venice in the late fifties and sixties and had survived, more or less, the winnowing process of the marketplace. But the West Beach wasn't cheap, and most of its patrons were young, affluent professionals from the west side of town, who came to the beach attracted not only by the artists, but by the movie people and other creative hotshots from the new Venice studios.

Tonight there was a single noisy corner and it had to be Leon's. Wil led the way and found his friend holding court. He had hoped for quieter circumstances.

"Hey, Wil!" Leon squeezed out from his seat and gave Wil a big hug. "And Charlie! My dealer, man!"

Leon and Strauss had a stormy relationship, which broke out constantly in feuds—both public and private. It was an open secret that

Leon wasn't averse to sneaking a piece out through the studio now and then.

"Hi, Leon," said Strauss. "I need to talk business with you sometime."

"Sure," said Leon. "How's about tomorrow?"

Wil watched Charlie swallow his annoyance. It looked like one of those days for Leon, mercurial and liberal with the expression of his moods. There were six at the table, eight with Wil and Strauss. Wil recognized the Mosers, Luke and Nancy, a young couple from the Fox Hills area who were new collectors. Social collectors, Wil suspected. He nodded at them when Leon introduced him.

"We've met," he reminded them, "a couple of times. Maybe at openings someplace." The guy was a lawyer who liked to trade services for art, and his bouncy wife did the rounds of the studios with university extension groups.

Directly across from Wil, Lee Lawrence smiled and saluted. He could afford to smile. He owned the joint. Wil made an effort to return the greeting pleasantly. Not that he had anything against Lee personally. It was principle. Wil knew he was too old and too smart to have principles, but he couldn't help it. Sometimes they made him prickly and stubborn. Lee was a symbol as well as a prime mover of the changing Venice scene. His pink T-Bird covertible was conspicuously familiar in the flow of Venice traffic, as were its owner's flowing hair and handsome profile. Lee had made good business marketing his image with his products. Tonight, with casual grace, he wore a loose shirt and baggy pants pieced together out of different layers of leather and velvet. Three heavy gold chains clattered at his wrist.

"I hear you're opening up some kind of a shop down there on Windward, now," Wil said. "You bought another studio?" It could have been Bernie Trost's place.

"A boutique, yes, right next to my own place. I think the traffic will bear it now, don't you?"

Judging from the traffic up on Main, a half mile north, Wil guessed it would. People seemed to be making money hand over fist, west siders pouring in to make the scene. He swallowed the first response that came to him and looked across at Leon. "Hey, Leon, you're contributing to this disaster, as I hear," he said. "You're doing interiors, these days?"

Leon grinned. He made no secret of the fact that he had been working with Lee to create the interior of the new boutique, and he was

124

known to turn his talents to whatever brought in the cash. Lamp shades and all. "You haven't heard? Applied art's going to be in again next year," he said. "Besides, there's some of us work for a living, Wil. One thing I never could stand was..."

"...a tight-ass purist," Will finished for him. They both laughed, and Wil ordered a fines herbes omelet from the menu. It was an ancient bone of contention the two of them had gnawed over for years, with cheerfully bared fangs. "Decorator," he muttered.

"Intellectual elitist," Leon retorted.

Sandy giggled. She took care of books and telephones and business for Leon, along with his more intimate needs. She could have been a sister to the woman sitting next to Lee. Jackie. She had to be a model. Skinny and elegant, almost obscenely young, they shared twin smiles— those easy, attractive smiles behind which lurk a tough intelligence and a solid instinct for the jugular.

"This space is going to be a knockout, Wil," Sandy said. "Listen, we've even got Dick Corman working on the lighting. Can you imagine?" He could. Barely. Dick had devoted fifteen years to exploring subtle effects of light in pure environments. And now this? "It's going to be the first space ever put together by an architect with a designer and two artists. You can't believe what these guys are doing."

"I'm sure it's going to be a knockout," agreed Wil. "Did I say anything?" He wanted it to sound light, and was irritated by the trace of annoyance that crept into his voice.

"I guess it could turn out to be good for business," said Strauss. "You think?"

"Your business, maybe. What happens when some great Lee Lawrence stops by my place with a checkbook and wants the studio, huh?"

Lee laughed. "Next week," he said. "For now, I've got cash-flow problems."

"Pitiful sad," said Wil good-humoredly. "May they last forever."

"Drink, Wil," said Leon. He waved at the waiter for another bottle and poured the last of the white Zinfandel into an empty glass. "What the hell difference does it make? It's all overblown, this art stuff, anyway. Bullshit, I say! It's a bunch of crap. Excuse me," he added, nodding across to Nancy Moser. "You're as much of a con man as the rest of us, Wil."

"That's what you guys are selling us? Crap? At those prices?" asked

Moser. He feigned an enjoyment of the joke, but Wil sensed an under-current of anxiety. Like most husbands whose wives drag them feet-first into collecting contemporary art, the guy was scared of being had.

"Sure." Leon laughed. "It's all a big rip-off. You didn't know?"

Charlie Strauss leaned across the table and put a hand on Nancy Moser's. "Didn't I tell you?" he said. "Never believe a word you hear from an artist. Leon, you're smashed."

Leon wasn't. Wil had seen him smashed, and knew that he had a good long way to go. He was somewhere between being a good man who was genuinely scared of losing it, and a terrific artist who had shined it on and thrown a lot of it away. He was usually much too charming to let it show. Even now he pulled himself out of what could have been a nose dive.

"Well, babe." He spoke to Sandy but his smile was for Nancy Moser. "Why don't you tell the folks who dropped by the studio today?"

Sandy shrugged, obviously pleased.

"You mean Steve?" she said. "Steve Martin? Such a sweetheart!"

"Steve Martin," he said. "The guy's going to buy a new painting, folks. I sent him to you," he added, for Charlie Strauss's sake. "Cross my heart."

"I didn't know he collected," Nancy said.

"Steve? Sure. One of the best Hollywood collections. He has a couple of my things already."

It was nicely done. Leon moved in circles now where he didn't need to drop names, but he had done it easily and made up the point he'd come close to losing with Luke Moser. He smiled around the table inno-cently and went on with barely a pause. "Wil," he said, "what was it you said you needed to talk about?"

18

W IL'S OMELET arrived at that moment. Damn Leon, he thought. The guy was impossible. Still, if he wanted to play, why not? He cut through the middle of the omelet and waved a piece on his fork.

"Your paintings," he said. "The ones that got lost. I wondered when you'd plan to collect on the insurance?" He watched for a reaction and was happy to see the smile exchanged for irritation. In his own sweet way, Leon Drake had been doing business—with Lee Lawrence as well as with the Mosers. High on the image he'd been projecting, he was caught off-guard by Wil's question.

"Insurance?" he repeated.

The herbs worked magic on Wil's taste buds. He broke open a dinner roll and spread butter on it, relishing the moment in which silence gathered around him. Stealing Leon's thunder was no mean feat. "Insurance," he pursued comfortably. "Someone must have had the things covered, right? The museum? I was just wondering, you know, how much you make on the deal when your paintings get ripped off. Market value?" He paused again for a mouthful. "I mean, how do they work these things out? I'm interested."

For a moment, Leon seemed at a loss. Then he snapped back into character, superstar artist, smiling. "Hey, pal," he said with a shrug. "I don't mess with those things. Ask my business manager here." He

127

glanced at Sandy. She shrugged, nodding over toward Strauss, and Leon passed the buck. "Charlie, answer the man's question, okay?"

Charlie was momentarily nonplussed. "Listen," he said. "We haven't got around to thinking about that. We want those paintings back."

Wil didn't suppose for a moment that they'd given it no thought, but it wasn't the time to challenge the assertion. "Well," he said lightly. "I sure hope you find them. I was talking to Stu Ray about them just this morning. He blames the County." He smiled blandly around the table.

"Whoever," said Leon. He slapped his hand down on the tablecloth to announce a change of subject. "Did you guys all see my new show at Charlie's, down on Melrose?" He needed to take back the initiative, Wil thought. My good old buddy's insecurities are showing.

"My God, I flipped when I saw them." It was Nancy Moser, fluttering, happy to have settled safely back on firm ground. "Luke, you've got to see this show. Those things are enormous."

They were. Wil had been at the opening the previous week. Catching up on ground that could have been lost to the neo-expressionist crowd, Leon had spread himself large, his forms beginning to take on almost identifiable shapes. The brushwork was looser, more aggressive than it had been in the past. But if the work had taken off, in Wil's opinion it hadn't landed anywhere yet. He missed the assurance of Leon's finish.

"Listen," he said. "Another time." He finished his omelet and laid the knife and fork across the plate. There wasn't anything more to be achieved, not with Leon in this mood. "I've got to get back to the studio."

He was on his feet.

"Already? That was all? You made it sound like some big deal." Leon put on a show of outrage, looking at his watch. "It's not even ten. You can't chicken out on us like this, Wil. What do you say?" He appealed to Sandy and the others. "This man's going to break up the party. Stop him, someone."

"Some of us," Wil said, "have to work."

"Right, Wil." Leon laughed and slapped his hand on the table a second time. The glasses bounced. "Hey, folks, this guy just quit a cushy teaching job and went off to drive a truck. Such a romantic!"

It was the undertone more than the words that made Wil pause as he was leaving—an unaccustomed jeer that no one else had missed: There was another uncomfortable silence around the table.

128

"For Christ's sake, Leon," said Lawrence. "Don't be so goddamn bumptious."

"Listen," said Wil, "this character's an old friend of mine. No sweat. Leon, good night. Good night, people."

Charlie Strauss got up to leave with him and they stopped outside in the street. A car rushed past on its way toward the ocean, and its red brake lights flashed before it reached the stop sign.

"What's eating the guy?" Wil asked. "He's as nervous as a cat."

"Menopause, maybe," joked Strauss. "No, it's just a mood, I guess. The price of greatness," he added, with understated irony. Together, they crossed the street to the parking lot behind the gallery. "Why the interest in those paintings, Wil?"

At least Charlie had been listening, Wil thought. They crossed the street and stopped in the gallery parking lot. "I found them," he said casually.

"Found them?" Charlie scowled, perplexed. "Jesus, where?"

"Can I tell you later in the week?"

"Later? Why not now?" Strauss took him by the elbow, turning his face to the light. "What is this, Wil? Sometimes you're harder than hell to read. Why didn't you say something?"

"That's what I'd planned to do, if Leon hadn't gotten so obnoxious." He hesitated. "Can I ask you not to mention it to him for a couple of days?"

They had reached the car—an elegant old XK120 Jaguar whose license plate read CHAS ART. Second only to the gallery in Charlie's life, it was a sleek red beast, pampered into a perpetual high polish. Strauss stroked the leather roof and studied Wil curiously. "I guess you know what you're doing," he said. "I'd really like to know where those things are, but if there's no harm done..."

"I can't see that it would hurt," said Wil. He chuckled. "Make the bastard wait awhile longer. I take it they really were insured?"

"Of course they were," said Strauss. "Leon would never let anything go out if it wasn't. Nor would I, for that matter. Forty thousand apiece, we estimated." Wil whistled through his teeth. "You're surprised? That's about the going rate....Oh, shit," he said. He was busy with his pockets. "Locked myself out."

Wil leaned over the windshield and peered in. "The key's in the ignition," he said. "You don't have a spare?"

Strauss laughed. "I never needed one," he said. He pulled out the billfold from the pocket of his suit and found a small, flat length of steel with a hook. "A couple of shakes with this..."

He bent down, jiggling the tool in the keyhole, turning gently. "Presto!"

"Nice job, Charlie," said Wil. "Where did you learn that trick?"

"It's a breeze. Got tired of locking myself out of desk drawers and filing cabinets. Can I give you a ride?"

"I'd rather walk." Wil opened the car door and watched Strauss lower himself into the bucket seat and roll the window down. "Has anything else disappeared that you've heard of recently?"

Strauss frowned. "You working with the FBI these days?" He leaned across to retrieve a tweed cap from the glove compartment and turned the rearview mirror to square it on his head.

Wil chuckled as he closed the door and leaned down to look in. "Well?" he asked.

"It's not unusual," said Strauss. "Things go astray from time to time, when you ship them. It's a business loss. I've even had things ripped off from the gallery walls. Sometimes it's hard to know why: they don't seem to have any special value." He flashed a deprecating smile. "I find some of them hard enough to sell myself."

"Maybe you hired a kleptomaniac."

Strauss cackled at that and looked at his watch. "You're sure about this, Wil?" He seemed worried now.

"Leon's pieces?"

"Yes." Charlie scrutinized him carefully.

"If you'll go along with it."

Charlie shrugged. "I guess." He sighed. "I'll have to take your word for it. In any case, I think I've had it for the day. Got to hit the road." Unmarried—uncoupled in any way and content to remain so, as he frequently asserted—he was reputed to own a small house up in the Palisades, but most agreed that his real home was the business. His life was spent in one or another of the galleries or on the road. He knew his job and wasn't much interested in anything beyond it.

Turning the ignition key, he listened for a moment to the sweet growl of the motor as he nursed the accelerator with his foot. "Are you going out to this Barbara Corton thing on Wednesday?" he asked.

"The preview, whatever? Sure. I wouldn't miss it. Are you?"

Strauss stroked the gas pedal one more time for the pleasure of the sound. "It looks like I'll be flying to New York again that morning, so I guess I'll probably wait and see it over the weekend. She'll have the bugs worked out by then, I hope," he said. "It's only three days, right?" Wil nodded. "I don't have that much faith in technology—especially when artists get their hands on it. Something always goes wrong. See you, Wil." Strauss waved distractedly, and the car's roof gleamed under blue fluorescence as he backed out into the street. Churning up an eddy of dust, the Jaguar turned at the traffic light and was gone.

Wil headed back toward the studio through the alley, deserted now that dusk had given way to darkness. Some blocks ahead, the headlights of a car approached from the east, flooding the big Schoonhoven mural with momentary, traveling light, confusing the shadows of the real colonnade with their ironic, trompe-l'oeil repetition in the painting. Then it passed the intersection, leaving the alley in darkness once again.

A half block from home, Wil was surprised to see lights burning in the clerestories and paused in his stride to scan the high windows. He clearly remembered having switched them off. MaryJo? But even supposing she'd decided to come, it was way too early for her to be back.

In the distance, a telephone rang three times, then stopped. His phone? It could have been any one of the studios or apartments on the block. He hurried on, and was fifty yards from the door when the lights went out.

Wil stopped dead. Down the street a ways, a panel truck was parked illegally outside the studio's freight entrance, two wheels up on the sidewalk. He broke into a run, silent on sneakers, following the length of the east wall, stopping again in the truck's shadow, waiting to regroup his senses.

The big double doors of the freight entrance were still secured on the outside with a heavy padlock, leaving only the front door for an exit. Hugging close to the wall, Wil moved farther down the alley and found the front door closed.

He inched closer, putting his ear to the wood. Nothing. There was only the unsteady pounding in his chest and the sound of his own breath.

He'd left the door locked, but the handle now turned easily in his hand. Wil released it slowly and leaned back against the wall. He was sweating, and his shirt stuck to a clammy patch in his lower back. Taking another breath, he turned the handle for a second time. The door performed, opening easily and silently. He stepped across the threshold, backing against the wall and shutting the door against the street light as he moved.

More silence.

His eyes adjusted to the glimmer of reflected light. Short of a person hidden down behind the shadow of a couch, the living room was empty. He moved through the near darkness into the kitchen and through it, to the studio.

For half a moment, before his eyes readjusted to the different light beyond the kitchen door, he was beginning to think he'd gotten away with it. Then he was blinded by a sudden burst of light.

"Stand where you are. Don't try to move."

The voice was quiet, confident, distantly familiar. Wil closed his eyes and swayed, disoriented. It had to be the stand of floods he used by the worktable. He started to bring up a hand to cover his eyes.

"Keep the hand down."

Behind the glare of light there was total darkness. He stood still, crimping his eyes, trying to resolve some definition and was rewarded only with what he took as the outline of a head, a semicircle of reflected light. At least he could make a guess at where the bastard was.

"Take three steps away from the door and then stop," said the voice. Wil worked at it, trying to remember.

Did the man have a weapon? There was no way he could be sure. In any case, his heart and his head were both conveying the same message: Be smart, they said. Do what he says.

The body reaction was something else again. With a bellow that surprised himself, he used the three steps forward to gain impetus and launch his full weight forward toward the light source.

The lights spun out of his path, the powerful bulbs exploding as they crashed to the floor. He was left falling through darkness, head forward, throwing up hands to protect his face. On the way down, he collided heavily with something, a chair, he thought, that crashed into his ribs and spun away from him. He ended up in a pile on the floor, unable to move for the moment and hoping only for time to catch a second breath.

"Shit!"

Left without light in unfamiliar territory, the intruder would have been at a disadvantage if Wil had been standing. As it was, he closed his eyes to focus what strength he had left, then swung his right arm in an arc toward the sounds that reached him, hoping to catch a foot. He

132

caught hold of a handful of material, a pants leg, perhaps, and held on for an instant before it was snatched away.

"Shit," said the voice again. "Lie still, fuckhead." What felt like the point of a boot socked into his ribs where they had caught the chair and Wil let out a yelp of pain. He flung out the arm a second time, rolling over, using his knees to bring himself up again.

"Shit!"

Wil's head filled with noise and lights. Somewhere, a ragged end of brain activity reported a sharp crack at the back of his skull.

He stopped struggling then.

19

I T WAS the phone that penetrated Wil's unconscious state and brought him back to his senses on the studio floor. When he moved his head, the space tilted sickeningly around him and he swallowed down an acrid mouthful of bile.

The studio was dark except for reflected light from the alley. Above him, close by, the massive length of lumber that he'd hoisted earlier still loomed, dangling from its chain, and a touch of chill in the breeze across his face told Wil the door had been left open. His head ached massively, with a concentration on the spot where the phone still shrilled insistently inside it.

He managed to pull himself to his knees and fumble his way through the gloom on all fours toward the sound. Where had he left the damn thing? It had to be there somewhere.

It was. He had dumped it on the floor to leave himself more work space on the table, and it kept on ringing till he pulled the receiver off the hook, sinking down on his back again. He brought what he thought would be the right end to his mouth and tried to speak. The words wouldn't come.

"Wait!" was all he managed. His voice came out in a croak and he laid his head back down, closing his eyes for a moment. Mistake. Space heaved. The bile surged back to his mouth.

"Hello. Hello. Wil Garretson? Who's there?" The voice chattered like a squirrel's, close to his ear.

"Goddammit, wait!" The words echoed painfully inside his skull and he winced.

"Wil? What is it? What's happening there?"

He knew he recognized the voice from somewhere, but he couldn't place it.

"Who's this?" he asked.

"Wil? It's me, Madison. Are you there?"

"Yeah." He decided he was. He pulled himself up to a sitting position and leaned his torso against the leg of his worktable. "More or less. Someone just raided the studio and beat in my skull..."

"They what...?"

"Yeah. Bashed my head. Second time in two days, remember? I'll have oatmeal for brains at this rate."

Madison thought about that for a moment, then asked, "Are you okay, Wil? I'd call you back later, but I don't think I can. This is urgent."

"Wait." Wil pulled a handkerchief from his pocket and rubbed at the sore spot in back, then felt around above his head for a light switch. The light came on with a new flood of pain and he tightened his eyes against it.

"Okay," he said. "You'd better tell me, Madison."

With his vision adjusting, he could see the results of his work with the handkerchief. Fresh blood. Not a whole lot, but more than a scratch. He began to check out the studio from where he sat.

"It's Don," said Madison. "Don Henschler. I had this wacky call from him. He's been trying to get through to you for hours. When he couldn't reach you, he called me. He saw us drive back together and thought I might know where you were."

The chill Wil felt in the small of his back had little to do with the draft. The racks had been raided. Elevated slightly from the floor, they were built in under the loft, and were rarely used since he'd moved from canvas into three-dimensional form. It was his personal store of paintings from the period that he wanted to keep, protected from the dust of the studio by a white sheet stretched in front of them. It was loose now, turned back in one corner, revealing the edges of the paintings.

"What was the message?" he asked Madison, wincing with the sheer effort of trying to concentrate on more than one thing at a time. He checked the handkerchief again. At least the blood was fresh enough to make him think he hadn't been lying there very long. He checked his watch. Nine-forty.

"Crazy stuff. He went on about some Jasper Johns and the Kline we picked up this afternoon. He's scared shitless, man. I told him to get out of there...."

"Where is he?"

"He's in his studio, at Ray's. He said he was too scared to move and I told him I'd go over—"

"Where are you now?" Wil got to his feet unsteadily and dragged the telephone cord across the studio floor as he went to the racks, taking stock.

"Gas station. I'm on my way there now and, wouldn't you know, the fucking tank was empty. I thought I'd try you one last time."

Wil tried to keep thinking straight, but ideas were fading out before he had a chance to focus on them. "Did you call the cops?" he asked.

"For what? To tell them my friend Don Henschler's scared? Be serious."

"How long till you get there?"

"Ten minutes. Maybe fifteen."

If Henschler had been trying to call him at the studio all evening... "Madison?" he said. "Get going. I'll be there in thirty."

He dropped the receiver back in place and hurried to the bathroom. Listerine. He soaked a wad of cotton and dabbed at the wound, the sharp pain instantaneously overwhelming the throb inside his head. He was in no condition to drive.

The silver Buick bounced down out of the parking lot, crashing what was left of his brain against the skull. He crossed the light to Main Street, turned north as far as the freeway and accelerated down the ramp. Hitting seventy-five in the fast lane, he leaned across and pulled a crumpled fishing hat from the glove compartment, fitting it carefully over his head to protect the wound and hold the swab in place.

The freeway danced in front of him, all red glare and glitter leading toward the high, stacked lights of downtown. Wil followed the Santa Monica toward the Santa Ana and dropped south at the Santa Fe exit. The green digits on the dash read out ten-thirteen. "You'll make it," he told himself. "Take it easy."

In time for what?

He was three blocks from the warehouse when he saw the black-and-white angled across the street, its red and blue lights squirting splashes of garish artificial color over the pavement and cinder-block walls. The street was liquid with reflections.

Slowing down a block from the activity, he edged across the intersection into the clamor of alarms from up ahead. He nosed up to the chain-link fence at Stu Ray's place, doused his headlights, and climbed out.

The noise was ear-shattering now, and Wil staggered slightly, disoriented, as he put weight on his feet, and fought with the swinging car door to regain his balance. He paused to take his bearings.

Don Henschler's studio in back was still closed up and dark. But the door by the Raiders' loading dock was open, and the entire alarm system was activated, piercing the night sky with its din. The yard was awash with light, both from inside the building and from the spot- and headlights of a second police car straddling the entrance. They had Madison spread-eagled over its hood, his legs way out behind him. One cop was frisking him while another stood a short distance off with a weapon trained on his back.

"Hey, officer," yelled Wil. He reeled, bringing his hand to his head with the effort of trying to be heard above the din. He slammed the car door. "Wait! Officer!"

"Stand back." The gun swung around toward him as he came in through the gate. He stopped. At the same time, a third cop came out from the warehouse and turned to look back as the sound was suddenly shut off and they were left in a curious, momentarily silent tableau. Light glowed in high spots on the leather of the policemen's belts and holsters. Then the two car radios stuttered into life together and both were ignored.

"Wil? Is that Wil Garretson?" Madison Grant was still stretched over the hood of the cop car. "Tell these guys who I am, for Christ's sake, before they kill me dead."

Wil walked forward slowly. Instinctively, he kept his hands stretched out to his sides at shoulder height, to show that they were empty. He paused a short way from the group.

"Officer," he said. He spoke to the one without the gun, the one with the mustache that obscured the lines of his lip. A neat badge on his shirt read simply SCOTT. "The man works here. I'll vouch for that. He came to help a friend who could be in great trouble. He called me a while back..."

"You own this place?" asked Scott. "They called the owner."

"I don't own it, no. But the owner's a friend of mine, too. If they called him, he'll be here. Has anyone looked in back?"

A fourth cop appeared on the loading dock, holstering his gun. "Looks clean inside," he called.

"Just take a look in back," Wil insisted. "The small building behind."

Scott looked from Wil to Madison and turned to nod quickly to his partner, a Hispanic whose dark, expressive eyes belied the obligatory blank expression. His ID tag said GUTIERREZ. "Take a look, okay?" said Scott. He turned back to Wil. "You have some ID?"

Wil went to his pocket carefully for his wallet and held it up, open at the driver's license. "We have to go through this rigmarole?" he asked.

"Take it out, please."

He slid it from the plastic folder and passed it to the officer, who held the beam of his flashlight on it for a moment. He turned the beam up into Wil's face. "If the guy works here," he said, jerking his head toward Madison, "how come we find him trying to break into the building?"

The question, Wil noticed, was addressed to him, not Madison. But it was Madison who answered.

"It was the studio I was trying to get to, man," he said. "Not the warehouse. The whole place was busted wide open already when I got here."

"What triggered the alarms?"

"How the fuck should I know?" Madison turned away, disgusted. "If someone else was in the warehouse, man, they're long gone now. Maybe they heard me coming."

"Hey, Scott!" the voice came from the studio door. "You better get in here."

At night, the interior of the loading dock looked bleak and dirty as they marched past. The cinder blocks of the small building beyond, in shadow, seemed to absorb the ambient, bluish light. The door hung open now and the cop led the way.

It was the light Wil noticed first. Intensified by the black-out curtains that had been drawn across the windows, the glow of the ultraviolet tubes radiated from a light-stand set up in front of the easel. Then the Kline. It was the picture he and Madison had picked up that afternoon, clamped upright on the easel under the UV light, its single black image jumping away from the white ground which now glowed and pulsated

138

with that eerie intensity that UV gives to whites. And finally the jumbled heap of vibrant, blue fluorescence on the studio floor.

In ultraviolet light, it had the disconcerting look of a headless, limbless torso, until the flashlight beam traveled up the length of it and found Don Henschler's face.

The dizziness hit Wil in a rush again, his head turning dangerously, the nausea rising in his gorge. He grabbed hold of Madison's shoulder for support.

"Get the lights, Gutierrez." It was the cop named Scott who spoke first.

"You okay, man?" asked Madison.

Wil grunted in response, and the three of them waited in silence in the semidarkness, the second flashlight tracking down the switch by the door. The dazzle of light from the overhead tracks looked unreal, colorless when Gutierrez switched them on.

White shirt, blue jeans. The dead man's features were pallid, bruised around the eyes, and hollow of life.

"Jesus," said Madison.

Scott was down at Henschler's side, his fingers searching at the throat for some last sign of life. Madison glanced from the prone figure to Wil's face, taut and white. "You okay?" he asked again, alarmed.

Wil shook his head, speechless.

The quiet exchange of radio communications and the buzz of static occupied the two cops, and Madison took Wil by the shoulders, shaking him gently for a reaction. "It's not your fault, you know that?" he said, repeating, almost fiercely: "It's not your goddamn fault."

Wil looked at him without expression for a moment, then shook his head again, slowly, and somehow his brain kicked in and began to process information. He looked around.

20

"WHAT THE fuck was the guy doing?" Madison asked quietly. He gestured toward the ultraviolet tubes.

The Kline on the easel would have been enough to tell the story, without the photographic gear and the lights. That wasn't all. A second piece stood over by the heater—a Jasper Johns *American Flag* from the fifties. Wil squatted down to take a closer look at the surface, and turned to break off a wedge of waxy blue color from the rim of the encaustic pot. With a gentle survey of the surface with his fingertips, he determined that it was still not set completely hard. The detail was un-believable—from the substructure of collage, built up with newsprint and cardboard, to the texture of the surface itself, heavy with drips of waxy paint and thick, rhythmic brushwork. Aside from its freshness, even the quality of the color was convincing enough to pass muster.

"A fake?" said Madison.

Wil nodded. He'd known Don Henschler as a facile technician, a brilliant mime: He had built these qualities into his work. But this was an unadulterated forgery.

The studio, which had been so neatly laid out hours before, now looked as though a tornado had hit it. There was a plastic garbage bag left open on the floor, its contents spilling out. There were photos, stained with paint and tacky at the edges where they'd been taped to the

140

wall, details from the original Jasper Johns. In a crazy pile on the work-table, there was another jumble of materials—close-ups of the reverse and the edges of the original, a big folder stuffed with color charts and notations, printed materials to simulate the collage Johns had painted over, clippings from magazines and newspapers from the fifties.

"Bad news," said Madison quietly.

Stu Ray was at the door, mad as a hornet, dragging a bevy of patrol-men. He broke through the barrier and stormed into the studio, pausing to gaze around him in dismay. "Christ, Wil, what happened?" he asked. He looked from Wil to the Johns, to the heap on the floor where they'd laid a dropcloth over Henschler's body, and back again.

Wil stood there, shaking his head. "I wish I knew," he said. "Don Henschler's been killed."

Before Stu could react, the cops at the door parted and a wave of new figures swarmed into the studio, making it suddenly small. The man at the head of the phalanx leaned down to lift a corner of the dropcloth, stared awhile, then looked up and paused to take stock. He wore a light summer suit and tired white shirt, with a striped tie in a full knot at the collar.

"Okay, which one of you guys is Scott?" he asked the cops. He moved away to one side, beckoning the man to follow while the team got started. He listened well, head forward, undistracted by the activity around him. His face was deeply lined, symmetrical, and he wore his wavy hair neatly cropped, a little long in the back where it curled up over the collar. Wil thought he could be older than the few streaks of gray suggested. When he was through with Scott, he gave a few instruc-tions, gesturing, and the cop came over to herd them into the yard.

Outside, in the cooling air, Wil found a curb to sit on and Stu stood beside him, kicking disgustedly at a trash barrel. "Why me?' he said.

"It's not you, Stu," Wil pointed out. "It's Henschler."

The point was either missed or ignored. "What the fuck happened in there, Wil? I mean, what in God's name went down?" He spoke fast, under his breath, his face turned away and staring at the rooftops. "How did he die?"

"I don't know, Stu," said Wil.

"Then what's with the Johns, for Christ's sake? And the Kline?"

"How many guesses do you need?" asked Wil.

Stu snorted angrily. He reached into his pocket for a cigarette and lit it, blowing the smoke away from him. "That Johns moved through here a couple of months back," he said. "We shipped the damn thing out to Tokyo. The guy's been using me. Shit!" He stared into the air for a long while, smoking nervously, chewing at his thumbnail. "What will you tell them, Wil?" he asked.

"I'll tell them what I see and what I know," said Wil. He glanced sideways at Madison. Not the Leon Drakes. Not Sally. He'd decided on that. "If you're smart, you'll do the same."

The cop in the light gray suit came to the door. "Mr. Garretson, please?" He beckoned and Wil followed him back into the studio, where they stood together out of the traffic, close to the door. "Mr. Garretson, my name's DiPaolo." He was brisk, polite, but the steady intensity of his eyes suggested that he wasn't to be fooled with. "I'm a lieutenant with the Los Angeles Police Department. I need to ask you some questions. Just the preliminaries. We'll need a full statement later."

"Sure," said Wil.

"Sam, excuse me." One of the cops came by with a small, zip-sealed plastic bag. "I thought you'd want to see this."

DiPaolo turned away from Wil and poked at the contents. Then he turned back and held it up for Wil to see.

"A syringe?" he said. He was a man who asked questions with his eyebrows—but this one was rhetorical. Wil grimaced and pulled at the rim of his fishing hat. DiPaolo turned back to the investigator. "Horse?" he asked.

The man nodded. "Looks like it." He hurried away.

"So. A heroin overdose, maybe," said DiPaolo. "You think your friend was a junkie?"

Wil's stomach turned. "To tell the truth, I barely knew the guy," he said.

"I thought he put in this distress call to you?" said DiPaolo.

"Not directly." Wil wanted to have the record straight. "He called a third party, Madison Grant, who called me. He works here too."

DiPaolo looked at him thoughtfully. "Are you feeling okay?" he asked.

Wil patted the hat down over the crown of his head and nodded. "I'm not used to this," he said.

The lieutenant pointed to a pair of stools where they could sit together. "Okay, start from the top," he said. "You work here yourself?"

"If you can call it that..." said Wil. DiPaolo raised an eyebrow. "I've

142

known the owner here for years," Wil added. "I came to help out when one of his other workers died. Another young guy, an artist."

The eyebrow moved again. "Tell me."

Wil went back over the facts that had come out in the *Times,* and DiPaolo excused himself for a moment to pass on a rapid series of instructions to an aide. "So you were asked in to take this other person's place?" he asked, returning.

"Listen," Wil told him. "The art world is a tiny one. We're talking two hundred fifty folks, a hundred fifty of them friends. And that's without too much exaggeration. We watch out for each other."

"And tonight?"

"I thought I'd be helping Ray out." Wil explained the sequence of events since the call from Madison.

"Then all you did was walk in here with the officer and find the body? No other involvement?"

"None." Wil was surprised the lie came out so glibly.

"Then where's the guy that got the call, for Christ's sake?"

"Your guys had him spread out over a car when I got here," Wil explained. "He's black." He left the lieutenant to make the connection on his own.

DiPaolo scowled and sniffed at the pervasive smell of chemicals and paints, looking uneasily around the studio, his eyes alighting finally on the Franz Kline canvas. "I don't know from modern art," he said. "So who's going to tell me what's going on around here?"

"A couple of things I can tell you," said Wil. "The painting over by the wall's a fake. It looks like this guy made it." He nodded to the body on the floor.

"You're sure?"

"Take a sniff," said Wil.

"Honey?"

"That's encaustic paint you smell. It's pigment mixed with melted wax and painted on the canvas while it's hot. The guy who made those paintings did them in the nineteen fifties. Name's Jasper Johns. They're history now. Except that on this one here, the wax is still not set."

"Valuable?"

"A million dollars at a guess, for an original."

DiPaolo nodded, rubbing the contour of his cheekbone with a forefinger. "Anything else?" he asked.

"The other painting." Wil nodded toward the easel. "That's an original, also very valuable. But it looks to me like the guy had it set up ready to make a fake. Look at the lights." He pointed, explaining how it would have to be done. "If this kid was hooked on drugs," he said, "he'd found a way to earn the money to finance them. So long as he could find a way to market them."

"Tough job?"

"You need contacts. You can't put an ad in the paper for this stuff."

"And what about this place?" DiPaolo's gesture included the warehouse and the garage along with the studio.

Wil hesitated. "Talk to the boss," he said. "He's your man."

DiPaolo grunted. "What's the owner's name?" he asked.

"Stuart Ray," said Wil.

The lieutenant looked at him with interest. "Are you feeling okay?" he asked. "You're looking pretty shaky."

"Terrible," Wil said. "It's getting to me. I don't think I can last much longer. Can the statement wait?"

"We have your address and telephone?" Wil took out a card and watched as the lieutenant read through it. "An artist, huh?" He nodded. "I should have known. Okay, why don't you get on home? We'll let you know when we need you again. I appreciate your help. Oh, Mr. Garretson...?" Wil paused by the door. "Since you're on your way... Would you stop in the yard and have the black fellow..."

"Grant. His name's Madison Grant."

"...have Mr. Grant come in. Thanks, now."

Outside in the air again, Wil took a deep breath. Stu Ray and Madison were sitting together in silence on the loading dock.

"Hey, Madison," he called. "The lieutenant wants to ask some questions, okay?"

Madison slipped down from the dock and Wil walked with him toward the studio. "Sometime," he said, "we'll need to talk about those Leon Drakes, okay?"

Madison paused in his stride and gazed at Wil suspiciously through thick lenses. "You didn't tell them, huh?" Wil shook his head. "Why not?"

Wil realized that he could offer no good rational explanation, even to himself. "I wasn't sure they were relevant to Don," he said. "The cops have more than enough to do their number on. Besides, I guess I'm an old poker player. It's almost second nature to hold something back."

144

The few uniformed cops who remained on duty gazed at Wil incuriously as he crossed the parking lot. It wasn't only his head that was throbbing—it felt as if his entire body ached along with it, and Venice seemed as distant as the moon. He willed himself awake for the half-hour drive, and willed MaryJo to be there, waiting for him.

She was. Waiting and angry. Waiting and sick with worry since she'd come back to Wil's to find the broken lights on the studio floor, the signs of struggle, and Wil gone. But he was already asleep, face-down on the bed, before she'd finished cleaning out the wound.

21

S ALLY WAS out of the shower in the downstairs bathroom and half-way dry when she thought she heard a noise by the back porch. She put her head around the bathroom door and yelled, "Blanca?"

There was no response. She'd left the kitchen radio tuned to *Morning Edition,* and the comforting drone of a soft male voice continued. She rubbed at her hair with the towel and tried again. *"Buenos días, Blanca!"* It was the only Spanish she knew. Otherwise, she communicated in single words and gestures, smiled as she offered lunch, and paid in cash three times a week at the end of the day, with an occasional twinge of guilt.

She thought she heard the same sound again.

"Blanca!" Still no answer. Sally froze, her whole body listening, her heart beating. She was hearing things, she told herself. "Blanca?"

There were none of the usual noises Blanca made as she collected the cleaning things she'd be needing from the broom closet. Sourdough?

"Rick?" she tried. Could he be back for something? He'd left at six for the airport in the BMW—aloof, a stranger with a brown briefcase and important things to be done. She had kissed him, wanting to want to kiss him, and watched him back out of the driveway, feeling vulnerable and alone. Then she'd gone around checking the latches on the doors and windows.

Rick wouldn't be back. Rick never left anything behind.

"Blanca?" She called louder, unable to control the sudden new surge of fear. The anchorman's voice was replaced by a snatch of 1920s band music, then a woman's voice, and she strained her ears for the sound of something beyond it. Nothing. She reached for the robe that hung on the back of the door.

"Don't be a goddamn fool," she told herself aloud, the sound of her own voice ringing strange in the empty corridor. Reaching the kitchen, she paused by the door to the laundry porch where she could catch a glimpse through the panes of the back door. Another sound, unidentifiable. The movement of a figure. There was someone outside the door and Sally knew it wasn't Blanca. Blanca knew where to find the key. She held her breath. The panes framed sections of blue jeans, blue workshirt.

Petrified, she watched in photo-realist detail as a hand wrapped a bandanna around the butt of a pearl-handled gun. Then she moved. She heard the shatter of glass and turned to run, slipping on the tiled floor of the kitchen, cursing. She made it as far as the bathroom and ducked in, leaving the door a fraction open, panting, trying to control her breath so she could listen.

The back door closed, and boots made heavy footsteps on linoleum in the laundry room. Then the radio stopped. A short silence, and there were footsteps in the hall.

"Mrs. Horan? Hello!"

The male voice chilled her. She shut the bathroom door quietly and turned the lock. She wanted clothes but she'd left them all upstairs, so she rewrapped the robe around her, tighter, partly for warmth, she was shivering, partly out of the desperate need for some kind of protection, however slight. She brought the collar high around her neck.

"Mrs. Horan?"

The handle turned and there was a knock at the door. Where was Blanca?

"Mrs. Horan?"

She cast around for a weapon, opening the mirror cabinet. Scissors. The only ones she had in here were a tiny pair she used for trimming nails. She grabbed them and started on the cabinet under the sink. Nothing. Wait. A can of aerosol deodorant. She grabbed that, too.

There was a sudden crash, amplified in the tiny enclosed space, and the whole door shook. A second, and the wood around the handle split and bulged.

"Get out of here, damn you!" Sally screamed. She shook the deodorant can, shook it and shook it, screaming, "Get out! Get out!"

The third kick splintered the wood and the door gave way. A hand with a silver-and-turquoise watch band reached through the gap and she stabbed at it with the scissors, tearing the flesh, screaming.

"Shitbitch!" The man's voice, enraged.

She stabbed again, but the hand was gone, there was blood all over her own, and the robe, and the door was falling in on her, the room suddenly filled with the stink of synthetic pine and the stifling mist from the aerosol can. And then the huge, angry mass of the man was on top of her, overpowering, swearing, forcing the weapons out of her hands and bringing them crashing into the bath behind her.

He had her pinned to the tub and his breath came back to him slowly as he relaxed. The blue eyes looked as pale and milky as the turquoise around his neck.

"Blanca!" she yelled. "Blanca!"

The man lifted his weight from her slowly, smiling, and the first thing she noticed was the Walkman headpiece, draped around his neck. "There's no one there, Mrs. Horan. I met Blanca at the gate. She won't be coming today. Get up."

He grabbed her hand and pulled her upright, then for the first time looked at his own. "This needs to be washed," he told her. "Do it."

Sally hesitated, shrugged, and ran water in the sink.

"Disinfectant," he said.

"I don't have any."

"Look." He nodded to the still-open cabinet and reached in for the bottle, then winced as she splashed it over the wound, and pulled a clean guest towel from the rack, using it to stanch the flow of the blood.

"Bandage," he instructed. She took a wad of gauze from the shelf and taped it over the wound.

"Now, walk."

He followed close, his good arm round her neck, and guided her down the corridor to the den. Sourdough managed to dodge in ahead of them, and the man paused to scoop the cat up from the floor.

Indoors, he seemed larger than he'd appeared out there on the mountain. His boots were still shined immaculately, and his hair brushed perfectly in place. The Walkman headpiece put out strangled sounds of music.

148

"I know you," she said.

"I'm flattered," he said. "We hardly met." Back in control, he carried himself with easy confidence and beamed at her with patronizing self-assurance. Absurdly, it seemed to Sally especially insulting that he should be holding her cat.

"Sure hope I didn't scare you," he said.

"Listen," said Sally, "I want to know what you think you're doing here."

The man didn't answer but he dropped the cat and pushed it aside with his boot. "Sit down," he said.

She didn't. She went to the telephone and started to dial. The man took the receiver from her hand and cradled it again. Then he turned around to look at her and slapped her hard across the face. He ripped the loosely knotted belt away and grabbed her robe at the shoulders. Before she knew it, he had stripped the whole thing from her in a single gesture and flung it to the other side of the room, leaving her naked in front of him. Then he grabbed her hair.

Her first reaction was to scream for help again, but when she tried, her voice had disappeared. More than anything, she was frightened by the casual ease with which he could humiliate her. He loosened his grip slowly.

"Don't hurt me," she said. "Please don't."

The day was already warm, but she felt incredibly cold. She used an arm to cover her breasts and put the other hand down between her legs. Sourdough yowled.

"Sit down, I said."

When she wouldn't, the man raised a knee to her chest and shoved her back into Rick's leather chair. Her skin felt doubly naked against the shock of its cool surface.

"Listen up," he said. He leaned down over her and grabbed at her crotch, pulling hard at the hairs. Shocked beyond speech by the brutal intimacy of the gesture, Sally was nauseated, too, by the smell of his cologne. "You spread your legs for some horny kid, and that's poor taste, is all. You fuck me over, that's bad judgment, lady. You understand you're in trouble?"

She nodded. He released his grip and stood up, smiling down at her. She brought her knees up across her body to protect herself and held a hand to the stinging cheek.

"I need some property returned," he said. "Garretson has it. I need to know where it is—unless you'd like to see those Polaroids reach the cops."

There seemed no point in arguing. "I've no idea where it is," she said.

He stood beside the chair with hand raised, ready to bring it down across her face again. "I don't know," she said again, instinct insisting she remain calm. "He told me he'd found the paintings in the studio," she said. "He didn't say he'd moved them. It's the truth."

Watching her closely, the man lowered his hand to his own crotch, stroking himself with a smile. He played with the zipper for a moment, then pulled his hand away. The smile had gone. "I can give you half a day to call him off and get the property returned. He's your problem now. Don't let him get to be mine."

"Returned where?" she asked.

"I'll be in touch," he said. "Expect a call. Or a visit." He seemed to have caught some glimmer of thought in her eye. "I'll be watching you," he added. "Stay honest."

What if the thing was taken out of her hands? "The police," she said. "They've been here...."

The man stood and looked at her, his casual inspection crude as rape. He didn't move or speak. When his eyes at last came to her own, it seemed to Sally that they passed right through without pausing to make contact.

"I told them as little as I could," she told him. "I tried. But they know I'm lying." Sourdough jumped up on the chair and she pushed him back down.

The man still said nothing, but he turned and picked up a framed photograph of Sally from the desk. It was one Rick had taken, catching her in an unguarded moment by a waterfall in winter. Yosemite. The water was frozen into ice. Beside it, Sally was wearing a yellow parka and her eyes were glowing. Five years ago. Without taking his eyes off her, he broke open the frame and pulled out the picture, then tore it in half, and half again, quarters, and then eighths. He let the pieces fall to the floor. One of them, she noticed, came to rest on the toe of his boot.

"I guess you lied well enough to your husband, Sally," he said, "fucking around." He grinned. "You have the talent. Better learn to lie better to the cops. Meantime, get word to Garretson. I'll be in touch."

Sourdough scuttled out the door ahead of him, and Sally listened to

150

the echo of the man's boots on the tile as he strode back down to the kitchen. The porch door slammed and the cat gave an anguished yowl.

"Sourdough!" Sally grabbed for her robe and ran down the corridor, wrapping its folds back around her. She met the cat limping back into the house. She picked him up and hugged him, running a hand through his fur. "Sourdough, dumb cat!"

A car started in back.

"Oh, Jesus Christ," she said. "Oh, Jesus!"

She was still trembling, back in the kitchen, when she picked up the telephone and dialed for Wil.

22

THE TELEPHONE stopped ringing before Wil's head had done more than register the call. He opened his eyes and winced at the sudden light, a flash of pain. He closed them again and tried to sort things through.

The memory cells were blank, and the only thing he knew for sure was what the nagging ache in his belly told him: Nothing in his life was right. After a brief struggle, Wil surrendered to the idea that his deductive powers refused to function, and turned instead to more immediate facts.

At least the room was his. Once he'd adjusted his eyes to the light, he registered the sunlight streaming in above his head, making a brilliant rectangle on the opposing wall. Okay, that was wrong. It was late. On a normal day, he was awake at six, before sunrise. He scowled and turned away.

The sounds on the stairs materialized into a vision of MaryJo. Already dressed for the day, she came and sat down on the bed beside him.

"Sally called," she said. "I told her you weren't fit enough to talk." Sally. Of course. The internal eye brought her face into focus. Once he had that, firmly, the rest of the story followed, its parts stacking up like a crazy card house, ready to collapse. "She wants you to call back. You don't know how near I came to forgetting to pass on the message."

152

He remembered the white-blue face of Don Henschler, dead on the studio floor. Jesus! The Raiders. He had said he'd be there at eight. He brought his head up too fast and put it down again. It throbbed with pain.

"Let me take a look," she said. He turned over, chin propped on the pillow, and closed his eyes as her fingers made a delicate inspection. "Don't move."

She came back with the kit from the medicine cabinet and got to work. "I want you to promise me that you'll get this seen today. Professionally, okay?"

He nodded into the pillow.

"Aside from that, stay home. If the police need you, they can find you here." The wound was ugly but superficial, so far as she could tell. She cleaned around the edges of the two-inch break in the skin with a gauze pad. At the outpatient department, they'd probably need to cut some of the hair away and stitch it up.

"I'm okay," said Wil. "For God's sake, don't fuss."

"That's fine for you to say. You didn't have to look at yourself last night, and you're not much better this morning. You're staying home, right?"

He nodded again. What else could he say? He wasn't about to spend the morning arguing with MaryJo. "You're lying," she said.

"You want to tie me to the bed?"

"I'm serious, Wil. Listen, I'm sorry you're hurt, okay? You set yourself up for it, but I'm sorry. Now lay off."

"I can't."

MaryJo's fingers tightened in their work, then started up again, quickening, angry. "You have to," she said. "I'm not going to sit around and watch. We've always kept our noses out of each other's sense of integrity, okay. But now I'm actually scared to be in the studio. It's too painful, Wil. Don't lie to me."

He stared down, squinting at the close weave of the bed sheet. "Okay, then, here's the truth. I'm going out. If I stayed home for no better reason than to keep you from worrying about me, I'd never be able to forgive myself."

"What kind of macho talk is that?"

"Macho?" MaryJo had still not finished but he pulled her hand away and sat up. "This is real, babe. It may be a nightmare, but it's happening to me. I'm in it."

The bottle of disinfectant fell to the floor and bounced off the rug, and MaryJo got up abruptly. "You don't have to be," she said. "Nightmares happen inside some person's head."

"So what? It's no less real for that."

"Then tell me when it's over."

He reached for her hand and held it. "So don't expect me to be rational every moment of my life," he told her gently. "I've never expected that of anyone I loved."

"This is different."

"Different? Why?"

"Because of the risk."

"Maybe that's why I need to do it."

"I mean actual, physical risk. You have some kind of a death wish, Wil? Two people killed? This is crazy." He thought of the piece he'd started in the studio. A hanging man. A death wish?

"No," he said. "Goddammit, it's a life wish. You die when you give up."

She bent over him and held his head between her hands and kissed him hard between the eyes. "Listen," she said, "I love you, Wil. Get it out of your system and wake me when it's over. Don't wait for me tonight."

Then she was gone.

He resisted the impulse to call her back and lay for a few minutes, listening to her steps across the living room, the sound of the street door closing, feeling the emptiness of the studio space. Then he checked the bedside clock. Nine-thirteen. What the hell, he thought. Late is late is late. Stopping in the bathroom to rinse cold water over his face and head, he went to put water on for coffee while he punched out Sally's number on the kitchen phone.

In the studio, the heavy lumber sagged from its chain, its angle vaguely alarming, off-vertical, yet not far off enough to be toppling. It could work.

"Hello?" Sally's voice was guarded, distant.

"Is something wrong Sally? It's me. Wil." He brought the coffee down from the cabinet and spooned some into the filter.

"Wil, thank God. I've been trying to reach you. Your friend said you were sleeping late."

"Out cold," said Wil, without exaggeration.

"Listen," she said, "I'm scared out of my mind. That guy was here, the one on the mountain? The one who changed the tire?"

"He was there? At your house?" The wall backing the telephone was as empty of ideas as his head, but at least it helped him concentrate.

"He must have been out there, waiting for Rick to leave. He showed up at the back door while I was in the shower, and broke his way in." She told him how it had happened. "He wanted the Leon Drakes back, Wil. He knows you have them."

Now he knew why he'd kept them. He had chips to bargain with. He watched the water flood the grounds and start to drip. "That's pretty much what I thought," he said. So far as he was concerned, the guy could have them back. They weren't worth another ounce of spilled blood. But not out of Madison's studio. He would have to move them. Maybe after work Madison could help him take them back to Jim's. "So when does he want them?"

"He said he'd call me. You're going to give them back?"

"Sure," said Wil. "Why not? When he calls, just tell him you've talked to me. Tell him I've had enough already—I said he could have them back, no problem, if he gives me half a day to arrange it. Tell him we don't want trouble."

"Will, I'm scared."

Leaning his shoulder against the doorsill, he looked through into the studio again. A death wish? "Enough to tell the whole story to the cops? And Rick?"

The hesitation was more pronounced this morning than it had been before. It was a while before she came up with the answer: "I don't know."

Things were beginning to take some kind of shape, he could feel it. "There's a possibility," said Wil, "that we could continue to beat around in the bushes just enough to flush him out and leave it to the cops to work their side of things and catch him." Without anyone else getting hurt in the process? "I think you're right," he added. "What happened between you and Jim is incidental."

"We could keep it quiet?"

He poured coffee into a mug and drank. "Well, even if the cops found out, it might have nothing to do with their case against our man." He told her about the raid on his studio and the note sheets he'd left on the bulletin board. He told her about Don Henschler, the fakes and the drugs. And Don lying dead on the warehouse floor. The cops...

"Oh, Jesus," she said. "Wil..."

"The guy's showing signs of panic," Wil said. As soon as he'd said it, the whole dam broke loose: Suppose he'd done nothing? Would Don Henschler still be alive? His head began to whirl with imponderables.

"What does that mean?"

It means I'd better be damn sure what I'm doing. "It could be good for us. If we're lucky he'll play it right into the hands of the cops. Here's how I see it: He knows you've come to me for help—maybe he followed you back to town. I don't think he would have had the time to recognize me at Jim's, but say that he figures it was me. He comes to my studio the following night and he finds, not the Leon Drakes he was looking for, but all my notes. With all the stuff I've pinned up on the bulletin board, it isn't hard to guess that Garretson's trying to ferret out some truth about this whole damn business."

"And Don Henschler?"

Nothing had been moved from the night before. The light-stand still lay where it had crashed on the studio floor, glass fragments from the bulbs scattered everywhere. "Don was trying to reach me," said Wil. "All evening, Madison said. Suppose he called when the guy was here, and the guy picked up the phone. He's some cool customer, okay? Why not? There's Don, all ready to spill the beans and the man recognizes his voice—so now he knows he's in trouble unless Henschler goes the same way as Jim Sewell. Don had to be a weak link anyway. Our folks are already worried about him. So he's a terrific forger. But the guy's hooked on drugs, freaking out at Jim Sewell's death. It would have taken just a little shove from anyone to push him over the edge."

The scenario sounded possible. The timing could have worked out. "Who is this man?" she asked.

He tried to reconstruct the picture from the details Sally had given him. "I wish I knew."

"So what do I tell him?"

"Tell him I'll work with him," Wil said. "Tell him we'll do everything he says. Or there's another way. Don't even wait for his call, let him find me. Fly out to Chicago and meet Rick. That way, you'd be a whole lot safer."

A long pause. "I'm going out to the Valley," she said. "To the Bird in the Bush."

156

The coffee ended up tasting bitter and the blank wall was devoid of inspiration. Wil waited, but no argument came. "Then we'll be in touch this evening. I'll give you a call. Take good care, okay, love?" He hung up and stared at the numbers on the teephone before he stabbed at them again.

Stu Ray climbed out of the van he'd brought back from the airport and waited for the security guard who'd come with him to unlock the rear door. The yellow tapes of the police lines still surrounded the studio in back and two uniformed cops had been stationed by the door. Stu's insides were still churning with poorly hidden rage.

Reaching into the van, he grabbed his overnight bag. "Wait here," he told the guard. "I'll have someone out to help you in two minutes."

Vaulting up on the loading dock, he strode in past Clusky's office, barely pausing as he went. "Hey, Clusky!" he yelled. "Get someone out there to unload that thing. I just brought it in from Customs."

He pushed open the door to the office suite and let it slam behind him.

"Hi, Stu." For some reason, even the woman's blond hair and piping voice annoyed him this morning. He couldn't forgive anyone.

"Yeah," he said. "Don't forget that I'm headed out at eleven. The Corton job. I'll be gone until Thursday. Hold calls for half an hour, till I get myself sorted out."

The telephone rang before he reached his office and he paused in his stride to watch her answer. She punched the hold button, frowned and looked up at him. "It's Wil Garretson," she said. She punched again. "Mr. Garretson, hold the line a minute, please; I'll see if he's here for you."

She recognized the signs as the muscles bunched in Stu Ray's cheeks and took a breath. "You want to talk to him?" she asked.

Stu banged the door to his office without answering her, and picked up the phone from his desk. "Wil Garretson?" he said. "You're fired. Stay out of my life."

"Listen, Stu—"

"You listen, Wil." Stu's temper was blown. "You come in here with some bullshit story and within a day you manage to fuck up a business I've taken fifteen years to build—"

"Stu, you can't blame me for—"

"You snoop around asking questions which are none of your god-damn business—"

"Stu—"

"Don't argue, for Christ's sake, you think I'm stupid? You snoop around like some goddamn gumshoe from a dime novel and next thing I know my folks here start getting killed. Jesus Christ, Wil! Heroin? Fake Jasper Johns? Homicide cops crawling all over my goddamn warehouse? Just stay the fuck away from here...."

"Listen, I just happened...."

It wasn't the moment for logic. "You just happened! Christ, you're a one-man marvel, Garretson. Go happen someplace else!"

He slammed down the receiver and left Wil staring at his own. It buzzed back at him. He held the cradle down for a minute and then punched in Stu Ray's number once again.

"Ray's Raiders."

Wil threw his voice up a half an octave, feeling foolish. He didn't want to get cut off before he had started. "I'd like to speak to Madison Grant." It seemed the effort was successful. At least there was no hesitation in the response.

"Hold the line; I'll page him."

Wil waited, making parallel pencil lines on the telephone pad. He filled in some of the blanks between them and made a tiny Mondrian in black and white. He blinked at his doodle, remembering the piece at the County show. He'd known it was wrong. At the time, he'd put it down to a bad day for the artist.

"Yeah?"

He'd been looking at another Don Henschler. "Madison?"

"Yeah."

"Madison, don't react, okay? It's Wil Garretson." He wrote himself a note.

"Okay. What's happening, man?"

"I got fired."

"So I hear. Stu talked to me last night, when you'd left. Knew before you did, man. It's hot out here today." He chuckled.

"Listen, I need to get those Leon Drakes moved back into Jim's studio this evening. I don't want anyone to know they've been at your place. Can we do it?"

"I don't have a key."

"I do."

158

Silence, for a beat. Then: "Okay."

"And, Madison?"

"Yeah?"

"Take a look at the board. Tell me what time Raul leaves for the Valley this afternoon?"

This time the pause was longer, more uncomfortable.

"Madison?"

"Yeah? Listen, Wil, you're talking about a security run. I mean, armed guards, that stuff. No fooling, huh?"

The red ink.

"Trust me," said Wil.

"This is still for Jim?"

"For Jim and the rest of us. There's someone out there fucking all of us over. Trust me?"

"I guess I have to, don't I?"

"I guess so," said Wil.

23

No ONE HOME. Sally hung up after the tenth ring at Paula's and resigned herself to spending the day alone. But out. The house felt violated, raw.

She worked quickly with the broom on the back porch. Not for herself—at that moment, she couldn't have cared less about the scattered shards of glass that covered the floor—but for Sourdough. The cat had hung around while she was on the phone to Wil, licking his wounds and pausing to gaze at her from the countertop, reproachful for her lack of sympathy and critical of the general indignity of her behavior. Finally, in no mood to tolerate the vagaries of the human species, he'd left in a huff before she was off the phone. By now he was in none of his favorite places and not responding to her calls.

"Damn cat!"

She swept the last remains of glass into the dustpan and set out fresh bowls of dry food and water for his return.

The man had left a neat hole where the pane had been, next to the chain and latch. Even though it seemed pointless now, Sally relocked the door and set the chain before she ran upstairs to change, stopping briefly in the guest room to search the street through the slats of the Levelor.

Nothing.

160

First thing was to dump the robe she'd been wearing in the laundry hamper and get back under the shower to wash his touch from her body. She wanted half an hour but allowed herself a bare two minutes, switching off the faucets and passing on the hair dryer, alert for sounds before she tucked a towel around her and tiptoed over the landing to the bedroom.

She ruffled her hair into some semblance of order and searched through the closet, furious to find nothing she could wear. Frustrated, she settled on a summer dress and pulled it off the hanger. It was wrong. She stepped into it anyway, pulled the zipper halfway, and posed in front of the full-length mirror in the dressing room, smoothing down the light material over her belly. She hated it. Shoulderless, armless, it left her feeling exposed in a way she wouldn't have felt a week ago.

Damn Rick, for being in Chicago.

Unzipping the dress, she put it back on its hanger and tried the yellow jumpsuit. Then a shirt and a simple pair of white cotton pants. She felt fat. Everything fitted wrong. She gave up in disgust, sorting impatiently through the racks for anything that had sleeves and shoulders. When she had it on, she barely bothered to check it out in the mirror, ran a hairbrush through her hair, did a rush job on her make-up, and left the house way overdressed for the heat.

She looked both ways up the street before she left the driveway. If anyone was watching, there was no immediate sign. Still, she continued to watch in the mirror as Woodrow Wilson twisted down and met Mulholland by the freeway, half expecting the spectral limousine to materialize in the shimmer of haze and dust. But the street unfolded its usual shifting scene of pastel surfaces, devoid of traffic other than parked cars.

On any other day, she would have taken the freeway out to Tarzana, but today, for reasons she didn't stop to analyze, she found herself following Cahuenga as it led into Ventura Boulevard—a street she normally avoided like the plague. Already steaming with heat and smog, the strip seemed to wallow unashamedly in its garish commercialism as she ran the broad gauntlet of its rows of shops, and restaurants, and billboards.

Out beyond Sherman Oaks, she watched street numbers for the gallery, then overshot it by half a block, made two lefts, and parked in the alley that ran behind it. She left the air conditioner running while she waited another couple of minutes in the car, watching for any sign that she might have been followed. Then climbed out, locked up, and walked around to the main entrance on the boulevard. A bell chimed somewhere in back.

"Good morning."

The greeting was returned with a brief, incurious glance and a nod from the young woman buried in folds of black clothes at the reception desk. Her hair, cropped short and shaggy, was dyed red. Too red. Its aggressive brilliance combined with the effect of a near-black lipstick to exaggerate the natural pallor of her face. The result was a trendy air of doom.

Sally turned her attention to the gallery space—a simple, rectangular storefront, split by a dry-wall divider into two smaller showing rooms. The first was filled with third-rate imitations of Hans Hofmann: inept attempts to juxtapose a fluid, lyrical use of color with severe hard edge, the paintings managed nothing more than listless cliché. Wil's instinct had been right: a schlock operation.

A glance into the second space confirmed the impression of the first. This was wallpaper, tidy abstractions in bland colors that disappeared mercifully into the walls—the kind of stuff the third vice-president's designer might buy to take care of the secretarial pool. So what was with Jimmy Sewell? Sally couldn't imagine how he'd fit into an operation of this kind.

She was alone. Not surprising. No matter what kind of art they showed, in this obscure location out in the Valley, foot traffic could hardly be what kept the place afloat. So maybe she could find out what was behind the front.

Her mind made up, Sally's footsteps echoed on the wood floor as she crossed back to the reception desk. "Is the gallery director available?" she asked.

"The gallery director?" The shock of ultra-red hair shot up and bristled stiffly, like a cock's comb, while the young woman looked her over. "You have a meeting with her?"

"No. But I'd like to speak to her. I might be able to bring some business her way."

The receptionist shrugged as she lifted the phone and dialed a single number, sighing heavily and scratching at the roots of her hair with a pencil while she waited for a response. "Judy?" she said. "There's someone out here asking for you." She listened. "No," she said, "I don't know who it is. Who are you?" she asked Sally.

Sally went to her bag and brought out a business card from her wallet. It gave her name and a telephone number, nothing more.

"Sally..." the girl said. "How do you pronounce this...? Horan? Sally Horan." She smirked.

There was a brief squawk at the other end of the line. "She says she'll be out," the receptionist announced.

The door in the second gallery opened and Sally walked back to meet the director. Young—youngish, Sally revised as she got closer—she was dressed with a contemporary flair and an eye for quality that contrasted markedly with the art she kept on the walls. She was attractive, with the kind of skinniness that Sally had given up envying because she knew she'd never achieve it. This woman wore it like a business decision. Around her eyes, though, there were signs of wear that betrayed a kind of hardness.

"Hello," she said. She smiled and held out a hand that lacked warmth, not strength. "I'm Judy Townsend."

Sally knew the name, but she didn't know from where. She doesn't trust me, she thought. The message came from somewhere behind the cool gray eyes. "I'm Sally Horan." Her own name opened doors in the art world—thanks as much to Rick and their collection as to her reputation as an artist. "I'm looking for something for a client, and someone suggested I come out here to see you. I've never been to the gallery before."

"A client?" The woman sounded doubtful as she led the way back to her office.

"Yes, people ask me to do a little art consulting now and then," said Sally vaguely. "Anyway, I didn't see anything in the gallery, but I thought maybe you would have something else in back."

Judy Townsend waved her to a chair in front of the desk and crossed the room to close a second door that led to the back room. Sally glimpsed rows of packing cases and the corner of an open rack. The design of the office, too, she thought as she looked around, was incongruous with the work in the gallery—it might have been a totally different eye. Behind the simple white parsons table Judy used for a desk, a big Ellsworth Kelly print picked out the basic black-and-white motif of the décor.

"I'm delighted," said Judy, without great delight. She sat down across from Sally and grasped one leg at the knee to ease it over the other.

"You just happen to have hit us at the worst possible moment. We have a big shipment going out and I don't have much to show you. What kind of work are you looking for?"

"Well, you know these people," Sally apologized. "They're looking for quality art but they don't want to pay for it. I've been trying to turn them onto some young locals, rather than buying prints. Strange thing, I took them to see Jim Sewell just last week, before he died...." Feeling stupid and clumsy, she allowed the sentence to tail off and watched the woman across the desk.

"Jim Sewell?"

"Yes, what a terrible thing. You worked with him, didn't you?"

Judy Townsend simply stared at her. This time, it could have been genuine confusion, Sally thought, or outright hostility in the eyes. "You must have it wrong," said Judy. "I never met the man."

Yet Wil had found the number high-lighted in Jim's journal. "Funny," said Sally, "I could have sworn it was Jim who mentioned you. Who else do you handle?"

"Listen," said Judy, her chair easing back another few inches from the desk. "Any other day I'd be more than pleased to show you what we have in back. But today, as I told you, we have a lot of things going out and everything's a mess back there. Consultants," she said—and her voice made clear what she thought of them—"mostly call me for an appointment. That way I can be sure to have the time they need."

Sally ignored the hint. "I like the prints," she said lightly, scanning the walls. "How much do these things go for?" She got up and wandered from a Jasper Johns flashlight to the Ellsworth Kelly and a De Kooning clam digger. In Judy's office, the severe décor transformed each one of them into an elegant statement in black and white.

"Most of them," said Judy, "aren't for sale. They're part of my own collection."

"Beautiful," said Sally. She turned to the single print whose brilliance in color set off all the others. "I see this one's dedicated." It was a Leon Drake—a familiar print from the mid seventies. This one was an artist's proof, and the message in big neat letters printed across the bottom read: "For Judy, with much love." Of course. The wheels began to turn. Some years ago, Judy Townsend had been one of what art folks in the know had jokingly dubbed Drake's sex-retaries.

"An old, old friend," laughed Judy, lightly now.

"He lost a couple of paintings recently, I hear."

164

"Did he, now? That doesn't sound much like the Leon Drake I used to know. Who's he got paying for them?" Judy asked.

"Cynical?" asked Sally.

Judy laughed again. "You could say that. Have you seen Leon's show at Strauss?"

Sally shook her head. She hadn't. Now that Judy mentioned it, the idea filled her with relief, supplying a ready-made answer to a question that had been hovering in the back of her mind: Where to go from here? "Can I ask you something, Judy?"

"Sure. Ask me anything. Delighted." Only the eyes were guarded.

"This friend of mine's been asking for advice. She's probably crazy, really, but she's been playing with the notion of opening up a new space. Nothing ambitious, to start out. Somewhere to show emerging artists, okay? She doesn't want to go downtown—that scene's old hat, and MOCA dosen't seem to be helping the galleries there, like it was supposed to. The ones that opened up a couple of years ago are closing their doors already. Anyway, she's been thinking about the Valley. Something different. There's nothing out here that I know of, aside from you and Orlando..."

She paused, but Judy waited her out, watching her over splayed and pointed fingers. "The thing is this: Could she make it? I mean, financially? What do you think?"

If Judy was as exasperated as she had every right to be, Sally thought, she kept it carefully under wraps. "You're asking me for advice? For this friend? I'd say, forget it." She laughed with easy scorn. "Listen, I've been in this business for ten years and I still wouldn't make it. Not on shows. Especially not on your emerging artists."

"Really?"

"Nobody buys that stuff. Good God, we're still nurturing the buyers for the blue chips in LA. If they're ready to take a risk at all, they go to New York or Europe. But even if you could sell it, your margin of profit on that kind of work is far too small to support your operation."

Sally didn't argue the point. Successful dealers had something going in the back room—primitives, some of them, or designer contracts. There was one who dealt in erotica on the side. "So what do you do to support your habit here?" she asked. "You have to be doing okay."

None of your goddamn business, the gray eyes said. "I get by," she said vaguely. "I've taken a long time developing contacts. Now that I have them, I know what to look for. I travel a lot. And buy."

"Blue-chip?"

"Sometimes," said Judy. "Whatever I know I can sell."

"And the gallery?"

Judy shrugged. "It's a bona fide," she said. "And a space to work. People you deal with like to know you have a professional setup."

"Not very encouraging for my friend, then?" asked Sally.

"Listen, unless she has some secret formula for taking care of the overheads, forget it. It's as simple as that. Welcome to LA."

Sally sat back. "That was pretty much my conclusion. Seems like bleak advice."

Their eyes met and locked for an instant and Sally had the impression of—what? Challenge? The competitiveness that marks the relationships of some professional women?

"Well, listen," said Judy, rolling back her chair. "I hate to do this to you, but we're going to have to follow up another time. There's things I simply have to take care of before lunch."

"Oh, of course," said Sally. "Maybe I'll stop by to see the Strauss show...."

"Good luck," said Judy dryly. "Just don't expect to pick up something cheap." She showed Sally to the door and listened to the footsteps fade, and the street door close behind her. Then she hurried back to her office and picked up the telephone.

24

WIL GARRETSON dabbed at the gathering beads of moisture on his forehead and stared up at the still-growing hulk that occupied the museum's original courtyard. The new Anderson building stretched along three hundred feet of Wilshire, its glitzy façade of glass block, limestone and green terra cotta successfully blotting out the sad low profile of the earlier structure. Wil squinted into the sun and tried to shut out the construction noises from his throbbing head, scanning the flow of museum visitors headed toward the steps.

"Hey, Wil?" Bernie Trost sauntered down from the other direction in shorts and an open-necked white shirt, a bulky envelope under his arm. "What's cooking?"

"Me," said Wil with a grin. "I feel like a fried egg. Jesus, it's hot."

Trost held out a hand. "Let's get inside," he said.

The museum was much more crowded than Wil had expected. The impressionists from the Russian collections were drawing the people in, and perhaps, too, with the new extension, word was getting around: There's art in Los Angeles. Walking the length of the Hammer wing, he and Bernie picked their way through the scaffolding and joined the line at the cafeteria. Wil had passed on breakfast, and now settled for a bottle of mineral water, wincing at the sight of Trost's chef salad.

"Here it is." Trost tossed the envelope between them on the smooth pink fiberglass of the tabletop. Beige and pink. The whole damn museum had been built in beige, thought Wil. Thank God for change.

He picked up the envelope and slid out the fat Manila folder it contained. "So why don't you tell me what you found," he said.

"What's better," said Bernie, "is you should tell me. What's happening, Wil?"

"Later," said Wil. "Give me a minute. Eat." While Bernie ate, he leafed through the stack of newspaper clippings and notes, carefully dated and taped down to eight-by-eleven sheets that had been taken from a three-ring binder. The earliest entries went back to the seventies. Wil scanned the headlines and read through a few of the articles. They were art thefts, mostly, but they also included notes on insurance claims on loss or damage, and the usual dealer shell games with expensive art works—now you see them, now you don't. There was a whole collection destroyed by fire in a highway accident. There was a story, too, on the theft of the Monets Madison had mentioned the previous afternoon.

"How does it look?" Bernie asked. He was through with his salad by the time Wil closed the file, and pushed his plate aside.

"It's good," said Wil, stuffing the package back into the envelope. "What ties them all together?"

"Geography," Bernie said. "They're all local—or originate locally. And every one of them involves either transportation or storage, like you said. But I've done my bit. You mentioned murder?"

Wil's mind was moving ahead and he ducked the question for the moment. "We'll come to that," he said. "It'll make more sense when we've gone over some other things. This all hangs together somehow. I tell you, Bernie, it's like working on a piece: I'm getting a sense of the whole shape of it before I can see it all, and I know that it has to be bigger, much bigger than the sum of everything I've put together to date. That's why I thought your files could help. If I'd known last night what I've learned since, I would have asked you to check into forgeries, too."

"Fakes? How do you put fakes together with the transportation business?"

Wil looked at him for a moment, scratching at his beard. Outside the window, two pigeons strutted fretfully across the colored awning of a sunshade, eyeing him, asking questions with their heads. A bearded black man in a bright red shirt leaned against the railing and the sky was a Los Angeles orange-blue. The world was right, out there—or at least in its usual state of wrongs.

Not so the art world. Wil turned his attention back to Bernie and checked his watch. Twelve-forty. There was still some time. "I think I can show you how," he said. "Let's take the elevator to the show upstairs. I want you to take a look at something for me."

They followed the construction maze back over to the Ahmanson wing and showed their cards at the desk. "Before we see this thing," said Wil, fastening the little yellow admission pin to the pocket of his shirt, "let me give you a scenario." They crossed to the elevators and Wil pushed the button. "You have one of my pieces, right? We traded, a while back. Your catalogue introduction for my tabletop piece?"

Bernie nodded. "Sure."

The elevator doors slid apart and a little knot of tourists from Japan stepped out. A battery of assorted cameras. An incongruous tartan cap. Wil went ahead and punched the button for the third floor. "Okay," he continued. "Now suppose for a minute that you'd done the same with Andy Warhol. The Warty Bliggens Museum of Art in Blanksville, Texas, calls you up and says, 'Mr. Trost, we would like to borrow that Warhol for our theme show on canned foods in April.'" Bernie grinned. "'Sure, you say, no big deal.' So the time rolls around and the Raiders show up at the door to pick it up and ship it off. Okay?"

Bernie spread his hands. "You said it."

The doors slid open and they stepped out onto the third-floor balcony. Hooking an arm through Bernie's, Wil led him to the balustrade, where they leaned together, overlooking the huge cubic footage of the atrium and its dull expanse of beige travertine marble. Looking down, he felt the dizziness come back and turned the other way.

"Okay," he went on. "Now the Raiders come back three months later and drop the piece off at your place. If you're a museum, you stop and examine every detail, every mark on the stretcher bars and imperfection on the surface. You check it out against the condition report to make sure this is the very Warhol you shipped. But what if you're Bernie Trost? Don't you just give it a quick once-over to make sure that it looks pretty much like it did when it left, then stick it back on the wall without bothering too much?"

"A switch?" Bernie asked. "You mean they keep the original and send you back a fake?"

"Would it work?" asked Wil. "On you?"

Bernie frowned, as though trying to visualize the situation. "It could," he acknowledged.

"And you're a critic," said Wil. Bernie winced. He'd never liked the term. "Okay, then, a writer. You know about art. But what about your average collector?"

Bernie didn't respond immediately, thinking through the scenario. "You'd need an incredibly good forger," he said slowly. "And versatile, if you wanted to turn it into a business venture, right? From what I've read, most of them do just one artist, two or three, tops. And there's a limit to the amount of phony Warhols you could sic back on the collectors—let alone the amount of real ones you could feed into the market with a shady provenance."

"How about Johns? Franz Kline?"

"Same thing, I guess."

"Mondrian?" Bernie didn't answer, thinking, and Wil risked a dizzying glance down at the bald white head of a Chinese sculpture, way below. "You know a young artist by the name of Don Henschler?" he asked.

Bernie nodded. "The guy who did those things he called combinations?" he asked. "Before the appropriation people came along. He put two artists together on one canvas? Funny, but the joke got tired. Yeah..."

"He was killed last night," said Wil. "I was in his studio. The guy was a dope addict. He had a Jasper Johns flag almost completed. Brilliant. He was all set to start on a Kline. Supporting his habit, I guess. He's been working at Stu Ray's for nearly eight years. Bernie, at that rate, half the collections in Los Angeles could be shot through with fakes, if the guy was as good as I think he was. Come here."

He led the way into the gallery and they stopped by the Mondrian. "I looked at this thing the other night," said Wil. "Something wasn't right with it and I stood here and said to myself, well, hell, everyone has an off day. But now..."

Together, they stooped and looked at the painting closely. Wil would have liked to have slipped it off the wall, to take a closer look at the back and edges. He could be imagining the lack of vitality, the way the paint just sat there, on the canvas. "Is that Mondrian? Or Henschler? What do you think?"

Bernie had his reading glasses out. "I see what you mean," he said. He shook his head. "It just seems impossible, Wil. It boggles the mind."

"I haven't told you the half of it yet." They took the slow way down to the lobby, the stairs, and Wil told Bernie the rest of the story, taking his time. With Bernie there was no reason he could see to hold anything back. Not even Sally. He laid the whole thing out, piece by piece, in the deserted stair well between the third floor and the plaza.

"So it's not just fakes?" said Trost.

Wil shook his head. "That's why I asked for the files," he said. "There could be thefts, insurance scams, whatever turns a buck."

"And you think it was Jim Sewell threw a wrench in the works?" Bernie suggested.

"I'm still not sure whether Jim was a symptom or a cause, but yeah, suppose he did a couple of jobs for them, for the ten grand, and then got smart and greedy. To show how smart he was, he stole the Leon Drakes from under their noses. They got mad."

"That would make sense," said Trost. "So what are you planning to do?"

"I'm going to keep throwing wrenches in."

They'd reached the plaza level and Bernie stopped, his eyes wandering from the file under Wil's arm to his face, and back again. "You're serious," he said. "For Christ's sake."

"Damn right."

"It's a risky business, Wil. And it seems like the cops have all the leads they need. . . ."

"They don't know the art scene. What made you keep all this stuff?"

"Fascination with the vagaries of our little corner of the world," Trost said. "But it's more than that. I've always thought that it goes to the core of things."

Wil laughed. "Values," he said. "As opposed to value."

"Values? I suppose that's it, when you come down to the bottom line," said Trost.

"Money and profit," Wil said, tapping the envelope again. "Greed. You have another half an hour? I've got a date in the basement with a friend."

They bumped into Fred Aaron stalking out of the elevator with a clipboard under his arm. He gazed at them blankly for a moment, smoothing the tight hair at the side of his head with the flat of a thin hand.

"Hey, Fred!" said Wil. You could never tell for sure whether the guy had recognized you or not. The two lenses of his glasses glinted a double reflection of the skylight grid in the atrium and he offered the approximation of a delighted smile. "Wil Garretson," added Wil.

"Of course!" said the curator. He juggled the clipboard to his other hand and reached out the right one for Wil to shake. "Sure. It's good to see you...."

"This is wonderful," said Wil. "Just the man we need. Can you give us a couple of minutes, Fred? You remember Bernard Trost?"

"Of course, we've met. I don't have much time...."

"I'd have called anyway. I just wanted to ask you about the Mondrian in the Benson collection upstairs," said Wil. "Bernie and I are both worried it's a fake."

Aaron's face tightened and his eyes seemed to darken into a still more opaque blue. A relative newcomer to the LA art scene, he was sensitive to the memory of the famous Pollock and De Kooning. "We don't talk much about fakes around here," he said, smiling faintly. "Besides, I didn't curate this particular show."

Aaron checked the watch on his wrist, already starting to move on, and Wil fell in step with him as he headed past the information desk. "Did you take a look at it?"

"Not closely, no. If you think I should, I will."

"I think you should." Wil made an extra couple of steps to edge around in front of Aaron, forcing him to a reluctant stop. "How the hell could someone get those other fakes past you, Fred? You're the expert."

Aaron stepped around him and increased his own pace. "They didn't," he said. He checked his watch again. "Really, I have a meeting coming up."

"Tell us how."

"If it's any of your business." Aaron shrugged and stopped abruptly, not bothering to conceal his annoyance. "You want the truth?" he asked. "I guess that's good, because most of the people out there aren't interested in the truth. They prefer the rumors. Here it is, one time. Are you ready?" He took a breath. "It got out that those pieces were purchases. Bullshit. The rumors always get things wrong."

"They weren't?"

"They weren't. They were a gift—initiated before I even came on board. It was a collection I didn't know, one of these tax write-off deals, and the donor wanted to remain anonymous. I went to see the work in

172

the man's collection and the pieces were good. Genuine paintings. I still can't believe I was wrong. On my say-so, the museum accepted the gift. They were delivered, and the two of them sat in crates down in the basement for a year before they got hung in the show where they were spotted." He winced. "My mistake was not to reinspect them closely enough while the show was being hung. The egg on my face was enough to last me for a lifetime. Now, if you'll excuse me..."

He'd reached the top of the steps down to the atrium and clearly didn't want company any further. "I'll take a look at the Mondrian," he said. "Thanks for the tip."

Aaron's glasses glinted one more time before he clattered down the steps and disappeared. "Damn," said Wil. "Now we're late, too."

They left the Ahmanson and retraced their steps around behind the Hammer wing. "Who is it we're going to see?" asked Bernie.

"Barnett Newman."

"I thought he was dead."

Wil laughed. "This one's Barnett Newman, the well-known museum guard," Wil explained. "He's head of security now. Climbed up through the ranks. An old friend from the days when I used to work down in the basement here."

"I never knew that."

"Yeah. Well, that was fifteen, twenty years ago, just after the museum first opened."

The elevator in the Bing Center brought them one flight down to the art-rental gallery. Newman was rocking on his heels, already nervous, waiting at the corner of the long corridor that leads from the board room past the administrative offices, down to the loading area at the far end.

"Hey, Barn," said Wil. "How's things with you?"

"They've been better," the security man said grimly. "This is more than my job is worth." He passed Wil a visitor's badge and looked at Bernie Trost. "Who's this?" he asked. "He wasn't in on this deal."

Wil put an arm around his shoulder. "Listen," he said. "Who's going to know? He's a pal. Give the man a badge."

Newman reached into his pocket grudgingly. "Only for you, Wil," he said. "Five minutes, okay? That's all you get."

The corridor was a canyon of giant packing crates, ready for shipping or recently arrived, each one stenciled with a maze of cautions and instructions. Newman led them briskly down toward the staff entrance but made a left before they got halfway. Here, the short passage ended in huge double doors, with a security booth guarding the entrance.

Newman paused and looked in on the darkened room. "Hey, Thelma," he said. The woman in uniform sat in front of a bank of black-and-white television monitors whose cameras panned along the ranks of deserted stacks. Rows of sharp red lights blinked in sequence on the computer boards in front of her and a service revolver rested on her hip. "These guys are with me," said Newman. "Two minutes, okay? I'll be with them."

"I can't let them through that door without they sign in," the woman said. "Not even with you, Mr. Newman."

She passed a clipboard out and Newman turned away while Wil signed, Jackson Pollock. Bernie glanced at what he'd written and added his own signature. Willem de Kooning. The security woman took the clipboard back and punched the code in for the electronic lock, and one of the great steel doors cracked open.

The clutter inside the storage vault was the flip side of its high-tech, open-sesame entrance. The racks were crowded, confusing, their logic determined not by chronology or school or national origin, but by size —and the registrar's numbering system. "This is madness," said Wil. "Where else would you find a Degas drawing in bed with a Sol Lewitt?"

"You said it, friend. I don't know how they ever put their hands on anything in here," said Newman. "You're lucky I just happen to know where they put these mothers. I had to bring the cops in to see them, last year. Can you believe, they wanted to dust the frames for fingerprints?" He laughed, and stopped to sort through a rack at the far end. "I guess these are the things," he said. "Is this what you were looking for?"

He pulled the Pollock out and together they stripped the clear plastic sheeting from it. They did the same with the de Kooning and set them up, side by side, against the edge of the racks and stood back to get a better look.

What they lacked, Wil thought, was the energy of the original, the spark that had made the work new and vital. Technically, the impersonation of the artist's voice was superb.

"Damn, but they're good!" said Trost.

Side by side, they studied the two pictures in silence for a while. What would have been close to a million dollars' worth of art, if they'd been real.

174

"Hey, Barnett," said Wil, "could you do me one more favor? Could you track down the records and find who delivered them here? What shipping company, I mean."

"I don't know, Wil." Newman was hesitant. "Maybe. I have the feeling that I've done a lot more than I should have already. I have your word: Anything illegal shows up, so far as the museum's concerned, I'll be the first to know?"

Wil nodded. His gut feeling told him that it had to be the Raiders. More inclined than not to trust Fred Aaron's eye, he would have bet the gift had been the originals. But they could be anywhere by now; what they were looking at here was two Don Henschlers.

"Listen," he said. "Thanks, Barnett. I don't know how to say it..."

"Don't let it touch the museum," said Newman. "Whatever it is. That's the best thanks."

He dropped them off at the desk in the rental gallery, and Trost was thoughtful as they headed for the elevator. "Isn't there one serious problem with your scenario?" he asked.

"What's that?"

"Suppose the whole thing's been going down like you say, they have this terrific operation with this genius forger. Even supposing he's not the only source of business, why screw the whole thing up? Okay, so they bump Jim Sewell off when they find out that he's been double-crossing them, I'll buy that. He's just a carrier, and there's others where he came from. Maybe they need to make a point, for the sake of the other drones. But Henschler? A man that talented? And they own him. There must have been some other way."

Wil stopped and turned. "I've thought about that," he said. "But suppose they've decided the water's getting too hot? I mean, it's taken me one day to get this far. How about the cops? Suppose these guys have decided one last sweep and that's it? It feels to me like they're burning bridges, friend. Which leaves a person seriously uncomfortable in the region of the belly."

Outside, at the corner of Wilshire, the shade of the magnolia offered little protection against the heat. Its tough leaves had baked brown in the sun, curling at the edges. The two stood together briefly, shaking hands.

"Are you sure there's nothing more I can do?" asked Trost.

"For now," said Wil. "Are you headed out to Barbara's show tomorrow?"

"Tonight," said Trost. "I'll be spending a couple of days. And you?"

"God knows," said Wil. "I'd hoped to."

They were headed in different directions, toward their parking spots, when Trost called back. "Hey, Wil!" he shouted. "I forgot Tristate! You interested?" Wil came back. "I went to the address they gave for their offices before lunch," said Trost. "There's nothing there. Bare walls, a ragged carpet, and a desk lamp sitting in the middle of the floor."

"Did you try the building manager?" asked Wil.

"Claims he never heard of them," said Trost. "The office hasn't been occupied in more than a year."

25

THE COLOR was overwhelming. It was like driving naked into the warmth of tropical waters, alive with a flickering diversity of form and light. Sally looked into the painting and felt Jim's touch all over, and her knuckles whitened as she told herself for the hundredth time that he was gone. She hadn't even allowed herself to mourn him.

Shaking her head hard, she forced herself to look around. There were no more than half a dozen paintings in the Leon Drake show at the Charles Strauss Gallery on Melrose, but what they lacked in number they more than made up for in size and power. Drake was working on a scale that was new to him, she remembered now, from Friday's review in the *Times*. "Heroic" was the word the reviewer had used.

Accustomed to her always visceral response to paintings, she was startled by the sensual assault these huge canvases made on her body. The surface of her skin sent back reverberations wherever it touched her clothing.

"Sexy paintings, huh?"

Sally jumped. She hadn't been aware of anyone else in the gallery and started at the sound of the voice at her elbow. It was a student. Had to be, she thought. He was standing close, with a notebook and a pencil. Smiling, his face and eyes had the same intense clarity of Jim's.

"Oh God!" Sally said. It could have been Jim, the way he moved his body, too. Sally shifted uncomfortably on her feet and stepped back a pace or two.

"Did I scare you? I'm sorry. They are sexy, though, aren't they?"

"No," she said, denying her own response. "Sexy? They are beautiful." Yet, feeling them out, she also found something missing. Heart? Soul? It was like being made love to with more skill than passion.

The student laughed. "This guy makes a fortune," he said. His eyes wandered down to the outline of Sally's breasts and scurried away again. "They're not his, of course," he added.

"Not his?"

"Not Drake's," he said confidently. "The man never paints anymore. He brings guys in to do the work for him."

"I didn't know."

"He hired a friend of mine."

Sally moved down the gallery to the next painting on the wall and he followed her. The reds and yellows swam below the surface of the painting, leaving her dizzy and bewildered, and he was standing too close again, like a puppy dog, as though he expected something. Harmless enough, yet she found the simple fact of his being there overwhelming. For a moment, the big, empty space heaved. "Listen," she said. "I have to go...."

She turned and left him there with his notebook dangling, and walked quickly away to check out the gallery office in back. It was past one o'clock and, hoping Charlie wouldn't be gone for lunch, she ignored the woman at the reception desk and poked her head around the corner into Charlie's private office.

"Charlie?" she said.

He was there, a half-eaten sandwich left on its open wrapping on the desk in front of him, a can of soda perched by the conference phone. He looked up from the paper he was working on and gazed at her for a moment through his glasses.

"Sally?" he said. "That you?" He put down his pen and scrambled from his chair. "Sally Horan! It's wonderful to see you! My God, it seems like years." With a kiss on both cheeks, he brought her into the office and sat her down. "Excuse me, I was just in the middle of..."

"Go ahead," she said. "You're sure I'm not in the way?"

He moved the sandwich to a desk drawer and shuffled the papers together, tidying. "Are you kidding? How's Rick? I don't see enough of him, either."

"Rick's fine, Charlie. Thanks. He's in Chicago for a conference. Too busy, as always."

Strauss smiled sympathetically. Immaculately as he always liked to dress, he worked in an inelegant sprawl, surrounded by heaps of files and magazines and papers, with open racks of work behind his desk. He looked more like a librarian than a dealer.

"I stopped by to see the new Leon Drakes," she said.

"Oh, yes, they're fabulous, aren't they?"

Sally jerked her thumb toward the gallery. "There's a kid out front says he doesn't paint them himself anymore."

Strauss laughed at that. "A budding artist, I'll bet. It's funny," he said, "I must have heard that one a hundred times. Leon paints. I just wish he would spend more time on it, and less on his other hobbies...."

As if on cue, the door burst open to the secretarial area from the parking lot in rear, and Leon Drake's voice breezed through the intervening space.

"Hey, gorgeous," he said. "Is the chief in session?"

"Speak of the devil," said Sally.

"Don't bother to show me in...."

It was too easy. The timing was too perfect. There was something about it that pricked the surface of her skin—something her instinct took to be a warning and her mind repressed immediately as paranoia.

Leon walked right in, a package wrapped in plain brown paper under his arm. The iris pattern on his Hawaiian shirt was powder-blue and orange against a midnight background, and his white cotton pants bagged fashionably at the hips and thighs. He stopped short at the door when he saw Sally. "Am I interrupting something?" he asked. Then he smiled. "Sally Horan, am I right? I'm not usually wrong about a face—and never wrong about a face as beautiful as this one." He kissed her easily, surprising her on the lips before she could turn her mouth, and squeezed her hand a little longer than he needed, his smile addressed directly to her eyes.

"Come on, Leon," she said. Releasing her hand, she tried to match his ease. "You don't need to flirt with me."

Strauss chuckled uneasily at the desk.

"Flirting? Who's flirting?" Leon appealed to Charlie: "Was I ever more serious in my life? Here," he told him. "I brought you something. It's the drawing I've been promising to let you have." He propped it up against the wall. "Now, Sally. About lunch..."

So what did he want with her?

"Isn't that strange?" She ignored the suggestion. "I just ran into an old friend of yours." The Townsend woman could have called, of course. He would have had time to drive in from Malibu. But why?

"You did?"

She nodded, watching his eyes carefully. They held hers, smiling still, and she found herself wanting to believe him.

"That's not hard," he added with a laugh. "That's how most of my friends are, these days, Sally. Old." He brushed at the gray that salted his hair at the temples.

"Judy Townsend," she persisted, though he hadn't asked.

"Judy!" he said. "Amazing! How long has it been?" He turned to Strauss as though he might supply the answer, but Strauss simply shrugged. "Not at the Bird in the Bush? God knows how she ever came up with a name like that. How's she doing?" She would have told him, but he didn't wait for the answer. "Charlie," he said. "I stopped by to go over a couple of things with you. Now I'm not so sure. You may be out of luck."

The desk chair squeaked as Strauss inched around to face him. "What can I say?" he protested. His smile was a fraction less convincing, though, than Leon's, and Sally sensed a dynamic between the two that she didn't fully understand. A kind of resentment? But the moment passed before she'd had a chance to catch it. "Sally's all yours," Strauss added with mock generosity. "That is, if she'll have you. Get out of here, will you? Let me do some work. Go sell her one of the new pieces."

The student was still busy taking notes. Either he'd been given an assignment, Sally thought, or he was more impressed than he'd made himself out to be. He caught one glimpse of Leon and made tracks across the gallery. "Mr. Drake," he said. "I'd like to introduce myself. My name is Ron Friedrich. I'm an artist. I just wanted to tell you how much I liked the work." A sidewise glance at Sally dared her to challenge his sincerity. She smiled and turned away.

"Well, thank you, Ron," said Leon. "That's nice to hear. You're a student?"

The kid was finishing up at UCLA next year. "Listen," he said. "I've heard you sometimes hire students for studio work—building stretchers, that kind of stuff. Any chance you'll be needing someone?"

Drake gazed at him thoughtfully and reached an arm across his shoulder. "You want to make my paintings for me?" he asked confidentially. "Find out how easy it is? You want to do Leon Drakes?" He chuckled, and Sally was happy to see that the kid had the good grace to blush. "Well, sure. Leave your name and a telephone number with Charlie Strauss's girl in back and write down what you can do. And a reference, okay? A teacher, maybe. If I need any extra help, I'll have my people call."

He patted Ron's shoulder and pointed him in the right direction for the office. "The price of fame and fortune," he told Sally. "No one believes you can get it up anymore. Now, what can I sell you, honey?" He swept an arm expansively around the gallery.

Watching the slender back disappear, she thought again of Jim. She turned to the canvas on the wall in front of her and thought of the two he'd hidden in his studio. "Wil told me I shouldn't miss the show," she said.

"Ah," he said. "Good old Wil." His eyes searched hers, speculatively she thought. "So now you're here, you like it?"

"I'm overwhelmed. I find it disturbing." And Leon. She found him disturbing too. He seemed serious for a moment, his eyes wandering moodily through the detail of the painting.

"Disturbing?"

She looked for the words to say what it was she meant. "They're terrific paintings, but I miss the more delicate touch," she said, "the nice control of your earlier work. When men let the feelings out, it always seems to end up looking like there's a lot of anger underneath." She paused to glance at him. "Some cruelty, maybe."

Self-hatred. The notion popped into her head unasked, and she weighed it, surprised, while Leon continued to stare in silence at the surface of his painting for a moment. He turned to watch as a woman came in at the far end of the space, hesitated on the threshold, looking around, then turned and left. That broke the spell. "You win some, you lose some," he joked, and laughed. "Anger, huh? You're a perceptive lady, Sally. You're sure you're not up to a late lunch?"

She looked at her watch, doubtful. "Well..."

"I'll buy," he said. "Better, on second thought, I'll make you lunch at the studio. You can see what I'm working on and we'll crack a bottle in front of the Pacific. All you can see is trees and ocean. I promise, you'll love it."

Last week, she'd have jumped at the chance to see the Leon Drake studio. Today...She had to keep asking herself why. What did the man want with her?

But Leon took her hesitation for assent. "I'll drive you there and bring you back to your car," he said. "We'll hop on the freeway, twenty minutes is all. No strings."

Bruised. Bursting. That's how she felt, inside and out. She wanted everything to stop happening, not to be forced into decisions she wasn't ready to make. She wanted the hours to consume themselves and leave her alone, but she forced herself to smile. "Are you sure you have time?" she asked.

"For you, honey, anything. Come on." He slipped an arm around her waist and stopped by Strauss's office on the way to the parking lot. "Charlie," he said, "we'll talk business later. Maybe around four, when I bring Sally back to her car."

"The studio tour?" asked Strauss.

"I couldn't resist," she said.

"Watch out," he said. "Don't trust him farther than you can throw one of those paintings in there."

"I won't." She laughed. "I can handle him, don't worry. See you later, Charlie." But he came out to the alley with them, and opened the car door for Sally.

Leon drove a white Corvette. With the car's hardtop removed and the wind lifting his hair, he cheerfully ignored the speed limit on the westbound freeway, one hand straying restlessly along the back of her bucket seat—a man who seemed compelled to act out the image he'd created for himself. She found herself understanding him a little more, feeling almost sorry for him.

She pictured the paintings again. Until now, Leon had been the quintessential East Coast image of the Californian: all ease and style and surface, nothing underneath. What she sensed in the new work was perhaps no more than the struggle finally to get something said, a kind of frustration, a self-directed irony and anger. The disappointment of a man at mid-life so successful in his own facility, he couldn't get a solid grip on anything anymore. Who felt it slipping away from him.

They burst back into sunlight from the curving tunnel that squeezes the Santa Monica Freeway into the Pacific Coast Highway. The wind and the traffic made talk impossible, and Sally reached in her bag for sunglasses and gazed out over the brilliant blue ocean with an irresistible sense of the unreal. Since Sunday, her life had slipped uncontrollably from one dream into the next, each one less familiar than the last. Even her own house had become the stage set for a melodrama. The white Corvette, the ocean, Leon Drake with his movie-star face—it all had a flickering polish that left her rootless, gasping for something solid herself.

Failing anything else, she held on to herself, hands tucked around her body. Jim was gone. Two days. She went back over them, astonished. Two days out of forever. Rick was gone, but would be back. So where was she?

The car shot past the Topanga turnoff and soon veered off the highway into an obscure canyon whose dusty lane looked barely used. A half mile up, they came to the studio, a castle of stage-prop materials poking up into the sky—aluminum siding, chain link, plywood boards, juxtaposed in a house of cards whose structure seemed to defy the laws of gravity. Sally was surprised to hear herself laugh out loud.

"You like it?"

She nodded. "Frank Gehry, right? It's crazy," she said. Acting, that's what she was doing, she decided. Playing parts that were unrehearsed, undreamed of.

A gate led into a cactus garden, Japanese in its sparse precision, with a path that followed steppingstones across the sand to a great bronze door. You stepped inside, not into interior darkness, but into light that was almost more intense than the light you left. White surfaces, windows, polished metals, skylights all worked together to collect the brilliance from outside and intensify it through their interaction. Set off by occasional plants, small thrusts of green among the overall white, the effect was breathtaking.

"Come on in," said Leon. "I'm famished."

It was almost too perfect. Coming into the open kitchen and dining area was like finding yourself bodily transported into a David Hockney painting, all fresh, clear color and simple line. There were two large white plates already prepared with food in the refrigerator.

"You must have been expecting someone else," said Sally. "What happened to her?"

Ignoring the question with a grin, he brought the plates out and set them down on a glass-topped table, where the window looked out over the Pacific. The plates were perfect, artworks in themselves, with avocado slices, fresh, skinned grapefruit, shrimp, lemon chunks and greens. Then he brought two glasses from a rack, and a bottle of chilled Chardonnay.

"Come," he invited. "Sit."

The view was as spectacular as he had promised. A line of brush obscured the beach houses that lined the Coast Highway down below, and the elegant, spare frames of a grove of eucalyptus seemed to uplift the whole vast expanse of the sky above the ocean.

"I could sit here for hours," said Sally. "How do you get your work done?"

Drake laughed. "When we've eaten," he said, "we'll go see the studio. You'll understand. The wine's good?"

"The wine's perfect."

She listened to the easy flow of his talk, conscious of the sound of cutlery on the plates and the classical music that filtered from some distant part of the house, the delicate pastel colors of the napkins, pink and mauve, the sharp, clean pattern of Leon's shirt.

Seductive. That was the word she was looking for. The whole place was seductive, like his paintings. Irresistible. It had something to do with the magic of light, the attraction of surfaces. Like Leon himself.

"So what's this with Garretson?" he asked. He dipped a small slice of avocado into the dressing and held it for a moment on his fork. "You guys an item, like they say?" He grinned at her.

Sally never drank at lunchtime. She drank very little anytime. Now when she looked up from her plate, she found the shimmer on the horizon brighter than she would have liked. "Hey," she said. "Look, don't get the wrong idea. I'm a very much married lady."

Yet, listening to herself, she realized that her tone was a little off, defensive, not as light as she had intended. Leon's expression, though, was adamantly cheerful. "That's what they all say, sweetheart. But I never knew a married woman yet that wasn't ready for some instant light relief. A husband may be nice people, but he gets to be a fucking bore—or at least a boring fuck—"

He broke off, dabbing the paper napkin at his lips, and the silence was palpable. "Look..." Sally started.

But he'd gotten the message. "...forgive the expression," he ended lamely. "I'm sorry." He reached across the table for her hand, but she pulled it away.

184

"Come on, Leon," she said. "For Christ's sake. That kind of stuff might work well on your floozies in their twenties, but give me a little credit, okay? It sounds like you tried it on a hundred of them."

The façade collapsed for a moment and gave way to an almost laughable dismay. Somewhere under the immaculate bronzed exterior, she thought, was a small boy scared of being found out. Whatever it was, he covered it up with charm and a rueful grin. "You're right," he said, "forgive me."

And she might have left it there, but some perverse impulse swept her on, telling her that she had the momentum, now, that she had to use it. "What's with those paintings, Leon?" she asked. Was this why she'd come? Or was it the wine? "I heard you'd lost a couple of them."

The reaction was hard to read. A pause, a flicker behind the eyes. A small knot at the forehead, quickly unfolding into the familiar smile. "Jesus, Sally, not you too? I'm beginning to wish I'd never heard of the damn things. Where did you find out about them?"

Keep Wil out of it. Be easy, gracious. She brought the glass to her lips again and smiled across the table, listening to the words flow out. "I guess maybe Rick mentioned something about them. I thought it was Rick who said something at dinner last night, but I wasn't paying that much attention."

Somewhere at the far end of the house, out of sight, a telephone rang and Leon's eyes responded to it briefly. "Well, no, they haven't found them yet," he said. "No great loss."

She looked down into her glass and couldn't believe when she saw that most of the wine was gone. She could feel it setting off soft, disconcerting fireworks in her head. "Am I crazy?" From some great distance she heard herself pursue it, recklessly, without being able to stop. "Somewhere in the back of my mind I seem to have heard Rick saying they'd been found. Is that possible? Some totally off-the-wall place? Jim Sewell's studio?"

That was it. She heard herself say it and sat there, listening to the silence, wondering what she'd done.

"But that's crazy," Leon said. He was serious now, intent. "I would have heard. Jim Sewell? The kid that got killed?"

"He worked for Ray's Raiders," she said. This time she set the wineglass down and slid it a little way from her over the glass-top table.

"You're kidding, Sally?"

Now that she tried to think about it, she could no longer focus exactly on what she'd hoped to gain from this. "I don't think so," she said. "I shouldn't have said anything. I wish I could remember exactly what I heard. Maybe I'm just getting different things confused."

Whatever, she'd pushed it too far, and Leon wasn't about to let it drop. "You said they found them at this kid's place?" he said. "Who? Who found them, Sally? And where did they take the damn things? Did they say?"

Change tone. Change tactic. Sally took refuge in a little gush and giggle. "I don't know," she said. "This is silly, Leon. It's all just scuttle-butt anyway. Let's drop it. It's just something I heard."

"The kid ripped them off from Stu Ray's place?" he persisted. "Is that what it was?"

"Listen, I don't know, I promise you. Leon, I had no idea you would take this seriously, it's just a scrap of gossip. Drop it. Show me your studio, okay?" Drake's eyes were focused somewhere on the horizon. "Okay?" she said.

He eased himself back from the table and looked at her. "Okay," he said briskly. "I'll check it out with Rick this afternoon. Let's go take a look."

Sally's heart took a leap against the inside of her chest and settled down to a fast drumbeat. How could she have been so stupid?

"Rick's out of town," she said hurriedly. "But don't. Please don't. I'm sorry I said anything, but don't talk to Rick." She leaned across the table to touch his arm. "Listen, Rick would be mad as hell if he knew I'd been quoting him to anyone. Even you."

"Come on, Sally..."

"I know, it seems ridiculous." Damn the wine. She was flirting a little now, and watching herself look foolish. "Spare me a scene, okay? I'll ask him about it when he gets home and get back to you. I'll call him in Chicago. Leon? Please?"

He looked at her, doubtful.

So goddamn smart. She thought she'd turn the tables on him and had turned them on herself. The man was playing with her; she was playing along. And the wine made itself felt when she stood, jogging her hip against the corner of the table, clumsily, setting off a rattle of utensils.

"Please?" This time it was she who reached out to him. "You'll show me the studio?" She took his hand and brought him away from the table, and he stood there for a moment, smiling, pausing for long enough to kiss her lightly on the lips.

"Out of town, huh?" he said. "Not a word."

A small door off the living area opened to a corridor that led to the north end of the building. To the left, as they reached the end of it, Leon paused by the door to an airy business office, spacious, well equipped, with two desks, each with its own computer terminal, and a printer pumping copies into a neat stack over by the wall.

"Hey, Sandy," he said. "How's it going?" The woman sat at one of the desks, the telephone receiver cradled between head and shoulder, patching up the polish on her nails.

"I'm on hold," she said. "Art Services."

"Right," he said. "Sandy, this is Sally, Sally Horan. Sally, meet Sandy. Right-hand person." He laughed.

Sandy grimaced and flashed a fistful of brilliant rings. "Texas called," she said. "They're ready to go. Finally. We're scheduled for a year from this October. And the Dallas piece sold."

"That's it?"

The woman hesitated, with a glance at Sally, then shrugged. "Your shipment came in," she added tersely. "They say it'll be delivered by late afternoon."

"Okay," he said. "Thanks."

The studio was an enormous space, double-story, whose light was filtered in from above through north-facing skylights. It had the quiet, concentrated atmosphere of a light industry, a crew of maybe half a dozen people so busy at their various work stations that they scarcely bothered to look up.

"Hey, Leon? You want to check this out?" A young woman in white coveralls, her hair pinned up under a baseball cap, called him over where she was working with an oversize brush, preparing the surface of a huge stretched canvas with gesso.

Sally watched as he went over, squatting down and testing some parts of the surface with his fingers, pointing out areas that still needed work, nodding slowly, joking.

"So it's true," Sally said, when he got back. "You don't make them all yourself?"

"Are you kidding?" Leon was surprised. "Putting together the stretcher bars, stretching the canvas, painting in the ground—that stuff takes hours. I do the easy stuff, when these guys are finished." He pointed to a pair of canvases laid out flat, in another part of the studio. "Here, I'll show you."

The composition of the diptych was already beginning to emerge, although with none of the detail that would later bring it to life.

"How do you see these things, to paint?" Sally asked. "How can you get any perspective on them?" Lying flat, the canvases were so large you couldn't see them head-on, except at the edges.

"I lie down and look up," he said. He pointed to the roof. Two large mirrors were installed, some twenty feet high, reflecting the pictures on the floor. "It's an idea I had Frank build in for me. Want to try?"

He pulled a mat to the edge of one of the paintings, sat down, and offered his hand to help Sally down beside him. Then they both lay back, side by side, and gazed up at the mirror until silence threatened to develop into intimacy.

"They're incredible." She had to say something, if only to break the silence. "If only I could paint like that..."

"You like them, huh?"

"They're beautiful...."

She felt better now, in the studio. Safer. Not that hers measured up to this in scale, but the smells and the shapes of things were familiar, known quantities. And perhaps she expected no more than to have to offer a few polite platitudes and hear some in exchange. It took a while for Leon's response to surface, and when it did, it shocked her.

"Bullshit!" he roared. One of the assistants laughed at the far end of the studio. Leon rolled over on his side to look down at Sally, and propped himself up on one elbow. "You were right before. It's anger. I look at what I do and I see a bunch of crap."

"Crap?" She closed her eyes, reeling, and Leon's face swayed dangerously close above her.

"Wallpaper. Look at it, woman. Look at the rest of it." He swept his free arm around the studio, in the direction of the stacks. "You ever see so much crap?"

"It's fantastic work," she said. Let me up.

He didn't. "You think so? What can I tell you, Sally. I'm a fraud. I've got the world bullshitted into thinking I'm a painter and I'm nothing but a fraud. Jesus!" He leaned down close to whisper in her ear. "What do you say we get it on, huh, Sally?"

She winced. "For Christ's sake, Leon..." She wriggled underneath

188

him, looking around the studio where the assistants went on working, unperturbed. "Let me up."

Then suddenly Drake was laughing, getting to his feet, changing as abruptly as he'd done before. The charm was back. "Come," he said. "I want to show you something. Come."

When she hesitated, he reached down and offered a hand. "Don't take me seriously," he said. "That's a mistake. I joke around a lot, is all. Come on."

The room he wanted to show her was a tiny one, a study. Its walls were covered with clippings, reproductions—some of them pages simply ripped from coffee-table books. Most of them were impressionists, and the flood of color suddenly made it clear what he was after in his own work. It was like her own small bulletin board, filled with fragments that had caught her eye.

"Don't get me wrong," he said. "I love what I do, but I guess, like everyone else, there's times I feel like a fraud. Even these guys must have felt it, once in a while." He waved his hand around the walls. "I tell you what," he added. "You want to see some art? You want to see art, you come out to the ranch with me tomorrow. I'll show you art."

"The ranch?" she asked.

"My ranch. Out in the Coachella Valley."

"Isn't that where the Barbara Corton thing is happening?"

"Same place," he said. "I offered her my spread. You'll get to see her show, too. Come with me. Please."

"You have to be kidding. After today..."

"No propositions, I promise. There'll be others there." Sally couldn't believe it. She stood there shaking her head. "Okay," he said. "I understand, but think about it. Don't say no, okay? Not yet. I'll drive you back to town."

26

"DANCE FOREVER." It was MaryJo's voice, cheerful and self-assured. "We'd love to hear from you. If you wish to leave a message on the tape, please wait for the beep."

Wil didn't. He hooked the receiver back in place and looked up and down the street. The mix of heat and smog was suffocating where he stood at the intersection, and he fought for air as he watched for the Raiders truck to turn north toward the freeway. His eyes were wet and raw, and he dabbed at the stinging corners with a handkerchief, managing only to make them worse. His head was swimming, too, and the wound from last night still throbbed steadily.

Bum day by any standards, Garretson, he thought. The digits on his Casio read out at five minutes past two.

The commercial traffic thundered past in an endless stream, its color and contour blurred by the rusty haze that melted steel and concrete into a single chimera of unstable light. What the hell was he doing out here, anyway? All he had to show for two days out of his life was a sick void in the belly and an aching confusion in the head. He should be teaching. He should be back in the studio.

A truck horn blared not ten yards from him, and he jumped back farther on the sidewalk. Making little boxes? Tight-ass, invulnerable, ironic little scenes that everyone in the art world had come to recognize and love instantly? He thought of Sally, remembering the rust-red scratch and the smudge of blood across her forehead. He thought of Jim Sewell, twisting out from the cliff. He thought of the piece that was waiting for him in the middle of the studio floor and he felt that familiar itch of excitement, knowing that the work was headed somewhere and yet now knowing where. He felt it like a power gathering in his hands.

It was ten past two before the truck with Ray's logo pulled out on the main thoroughfare a block south of where he stood, adding a trail of visible exhaust particles to the already laden atmosphere. Raul. Wil gave the driver a good half block to spot him, stepping out with one foot from the curb and waving both hands. He heard the hiss of brakes as the truck swerved toward the sidewalk and bumped to a stop a few yards up the road.

He ran to catch up with it and pulled the door open on the passenger side.

"Garretson?"

It wasn't Raul. It was Madison, peering down at him through round lenses. "Jeez, I thought I'd managed to shake you for one day. You bumming rides these days?" There was a rivulet of sweat running down the side of his cheek and the top of his skull gleamed with moisture.

"I'm going with you." Wil had to yell to make himself heard. He grabbed the metal frame of the door and swung himself up into the passenger seat. "I thought this was Raul's run?"

Madison laughed. "Got stuck with it," he said. He slammed the truck back into first and climbed up through the gears, lumbering out into the traffic lanes and up toward the freeway ramp. "You needn't have worried," he added. "You could have come down to the Raiders. Stu Ray left town before lunch. He won't be back until Thursday, they told me in the office."

For half a second, Wil had a question on the tip of his tongue, but it slipped his mind before he got it out. He sat there, worrying at it in the din of traffic, perplexed, while Madison navigated the series of freeway transitions east and north of downtown until the traffic settled into a steady northward flow on the Golden State. Wil watched the ribbon of concrete ditch where LA keeps the thin layer of caked mud that passes for its river.

He turned to find Madison looking at him. "You're crazy, Wil," he yelled. "You know that? You look terrible. I never saw anyone look so bad." Wil reached out through the window and twisted the wing mirror to look at himself. Besides the red lining that rimmed his eyes, his skin was clammy and pale at the temples. He leaned back in the seat again and closed his eyes against the light. "You know where you should be?" asked Madison. "You should be home in bed."

The two of them should get together, Madison and MaryJo, he thought wryly. Take care of his health. "Thanks, Madison," Wil said. "Kind thought." They drove in silence awhile longer, then he glanced across the cab. "Where did he go?" he asked.

"Who go?"

On the far side of the river, one by one, the faces of crudely painted cats stared out from the storm-drain covers. Territorial graffiti covered the concrete wall of the embankment. Wil thought about Raul and his spray can. "Stu Ray. You said he left town."

"Went up to the desert on the Barbara Corton job, I hear. He took a couple of the guys along with him."

"Are you going up there, Madison?"

"You kidding, man? Where would I get the time?"

Wil clearly remembered writing the date in his book two months ago. He remembered the announcement that arrived in the mail last week. A deep blue with a fluorescent glow. Another life. It was something he had been looking forward to—one of those events that shake the art world out of its socks for a day or so, and bring everyone together. But now ...He surrendered to the traffic and sat silent, watching the pictures in the windshield unfold like a movie screen. They passed the zoo turnoff and followed the long curve that leads into the Ventura Freeway west, a long drag through the Valley—Studio City, Sherman Oaks, Encino— whose four lanes clog at all hours of the day.

"You've been out to the Bird in the Bush before?" asked Wil. Madison nodded. "What the hell kind of operation is it, anyway?"

Madison glanced across his shoulder, sideways. "Some kind of gallery, I guess. Who knows? You don't hear much about it. We pick up or deliver there two, three times a month."

"You know who runs it?"

"Some trendy dame." Madison grinned. "You know the type. Snotty. Tight-assed. Dressed in a half million bucks of designer stuff with jewelry up the kazoo. I forgot her name."

Wil closed his eyes and tried to refocus his thoughts. They came up with red ink. Of course.

"Where's the guard?" he asked.

Madison treated him to a jaundiced stare. "What guard?"

"No, listen," Wil said, the memory coming back. Despite the cab's heat, he felt a sudden chill down near the base of his spine. "On the phone, you told me this was supposed to be a security run. There was supposed to be a guard."

"What's often supposed to be at Ray's place and what is, there's a difference," said Madison.

He started to laugh but Wil cut him short abruptly: "Don't bullshit me, Madison," he said. He fought down the sense of dread that had begun to surge up from his gut. "These things aren't just happening, for Christ's sake. What happened to Raul?"

The idea sank home. The truck lost speed and dropped a lane to the right. "Are you serious, man?"

"Tell me."

"It's like this," said Madison. "Clusky calls me to the office after lunch. He's hopping mad, right. 'Hey, Madison,' he says. 'Fucking Raul never showed up for this run. I want you to take it.' So I take the sheets he throws at me and I look them over. 'You want I should check the load?' I ask. 'No need,' he says. 'Raul took care of that before lunch. It's all locked up and ready to go.' Then I remember. 'This here's supposed to be a security run,' I tell him, 'so where's the guard?' 'Fucking guard took off early,' he says. 'Get moving.' 'I'm not leaving without a guard,' I say. By this time, the guy's hair's bristling around his collar, you know Clusky. 'Listen,' he says, 'Stu Ray's not here. He's taken half the fucking staff with him. I'm short-handed, what do you want, the U.S. Army? Get out of here.'"

"So you left?"

"So I left. He's the boss, man."

"Was that typical?"

"Typical? No. The guy was mad."

"Just mad?"

Madison stared out the windshield, leaning forward, spreading his weight out over the wheel. "Funny," he said. "I had the feeling he was..." He paused, searching for the word along the vanishing lines of the freeway up ahead.

"He was what?"

"Embarrassed. Like it was something he knew he should never have approved. And knew that I knew."

So what could have gone wrong? "This gallery," Wil asked, "they ship mostly locally?" If the place wasn't known in the art world, it was a good guess they handled down-scale stuff.

"I'd say the opposite," said Madison. "Their shipments are mostly national or international."

Wil frowned. That didn't figure at all. "So what is it you have in back today?" he asked.

"God knows what's in there," said Madison. "I didn't stop to ask. It's a crate that Stu brought in earlier from Customs."

Wil looked back over his shoulder, but the blank wall of the cab told him nothing. He picked up the clipboard and worked back through the shipping papers. "Whatever it is," he said quietly, "it's insured for a million two."

The truck jerked and lunged as Madison lost the gas pedal and picked it up again.

"Smells wrong, huh?" asked Wil. The driver doesn't show up after lunch. The guard leaves early. A shipment of a million dollars-plus, to some hokey gallery in the valley. "Let's make a pit stop," he suggested. "What would it take? Five minutes? Ten? I think we've got to take a look in back."

"You're nuts, Garretson. It could cost me my job to screw around with this kind of load...."

"It may have cost two other people's lives. There was Jim, remember? And Don Henschler?"

"Oh, Jesus." Madison set the indicator and swung off the freeway at Forest Lawn, bumping down the cloverleaf and pulling up under the bridge. "Let's check it out," he said. He reached under the dash to punch a code on the dusty electronic pad and jumped down from the cab. The two of them walked on opposite sides to the back and met by the big double doors, where Madison tested the lock and pulled the right door open. It swung slowly back, allowing the sheltered light from under the bridge to mix with the interior gloom.

"Jesus," said Wil. "Wait."

The scene was hard to make out in semidarkness. At first sight, the heap at the far end looked like no more than a confusion of rags, but the stench of human excrement was unmistakable. Wil pulled the handkerchief from his pocket and held it over his face as he climbed aboard.

Even so, he gagged.

"Wil?"

He had to force himself to adjust his eyes to the scene.

A confusion of limbs, where the bodies lay in a tangled heap, one atop the other. The one below was wearing the blue uniform of a security guard. On top, it had to be Raul.

Raul with the spray can. Raul who'd worked across from him yesterday, setting screws in a packing crate. He lay face-down, a pudgy figure whose definition seemed to have been lost in death. The face—if face there was—was mercifully hidden.

Their blood was everywhere. It spattered the walls and floor. It soaked the packing crate and the wrapping materials that spilled out from the splintered wood. Whatever had been in the crate was gone.

"Hey, Wil?" It was Madison, anxious. Wanting to know, or not to know.

"Stay out. I'm coming."

"You want I should...?"

"No. Stay where you are." Wil stepped away slowly, examining where he'd placed his feet and backing to the open door.

"Now," he said. "Help. Get me down from here." He leaned his weight on Madison's shoulders and lowered himself carefully to the pavement. "Close the doors."

"Listen, man..."

"Don't argue, Madison. Close up."

The rough concrete wall of the freeway bridge had the refreshing feel of reality where he leaned against it. El Loco. Top name on the roster. Charlie Brown. Frogtown. Gato. Wil read through the list like a requiem. He heard the clang of the doors and the clatter of bolts.

Then Madison was beside him, awkward, pained. "Raul?" he asked.

Wil nodded. "They're both in there. Raul and the security guard. Both dead. The crate's empty."

"You're sure they're dead?"

"There's half of their heads missing."

Wil rested his head against the wall and waited for the nausea to pass.

"I don't believe this, man," said Madison. "Raul?"

For Wil, it cost a massive effort of self-discipline to move. He was rooted, heavy. His legs told him they were going to stop right there, by the concrete wall. "We've got to move," he said.

"You're a fucking maniac." Shaking his head, jaw clenched, Madison turned to the big rectangle of light where the bridge opened out to a view of the mortuary on the hill. A car accelerated out from the stop sign behind them, the sound of its motor reverberating against four sides of concrete.

"I'm all right," said Wil. "We're going to drive this truck on to the gallery as though we'd never stopped. We're going to find them when we get there."

Launching a foot in a sudden gesture of frustration and despair, Madison kicked the wall, cursed, kicked it again and turned on his heel in the dust. "Fuck it," he said. "Jesus Christ, Wil. Fuck it." He marched around to the driver's door and climbed back in the cab.

With the engine hot, the ignition wouldn't catch and he turned the key till it screamed. He floored the gas pedal and worked at the ignition again until the motor roared. "Raul," he said, and repeated the name like an incantation: "Raul, Raul, Raul." He turned to Wil, weeping, wiping at his eyes. "I knew the guy. This guy was my friend."

"I know."

There wasn't anything else he could trust himself to say. He sat there, watching as Madison swung the truck around, back up the westbound ramp to the freeway.

27

THEY DROVE past the Hollywood Freeway interchange, past Laurel Canyon, Coldwater, Woodman, each staring ahead in his own particular silence. Van Nuys. Sepulveda.

Wil looked down at his hands and found the knuckles frozen, white, the fists clenched hard like rocks. He made himself release them, slowly, along with the bunched muscles in his neck.

There are times, he thought, when it pays to numb yourself. If he couldn't shake the vile image from his head, at least he could tough it out. With conscious deliberation, he rejected a creeping sense of guilt and settled for cold anger. He set his jaw, set his mind, and stared ahead unseeing...until the image of Raul returned, unasked, crushing the Coke can as he left for lunch. "You reckon they'll need a lowrider?" he asked. And the smile had said more than the words about the man—vital, full of feeling, with an edge of bitterness.

Watch out, Wil thought. I'm coming.

"Tell me," he said—they'd passed the San Diego Freeway before he could trust himself to speak, and when he did, the sound of his voice was strained—"tell me in tiny detail what happened this morning at the Raiders."

Madison's face had frozen, too, into a hard, ebony mask, and the creases in his forehead darkened as it softened into a frown. "Listen," he said. "I don't know how much I remember. I was working...."

"Use your eye. It helps."

There were fragments. Madison put together those he'd registered as the morning's events went on around him. He'd seen Stu Ray stalk in, irate, yelling something at Clusky as he passed the office. That was maybe around ten, ten-thirty. He was dressed less formally than usual, and carried a flight bag, blue, slung across his shoulder. He slammed the door from the warehouse to the office suite. Five minutes after Stu arrived, Madison was paged to the warehouse phone. That was Wil. And it must have been while he was on the phone that Raul passed by with the dolly, whistling, wheeling it out to the loading dock and, within two minutes, back inside to the lock-up—the special vault behind Clusky's office where they kept small valuables in transit. As he remembered it in his mind's eye, the crate was no more than thirty-six by thirty, plastered with labels and various international shipping symbols. The wineglass. The umbrella. A stenciled address. Nothing out of the way.

"You were working in the warehouse all morning, then?"

"Pretty much, yeah. I did a short stint out on the dock, loading up for the Chicago run."

"Nothing else? No one else that you remember?"

Madison thought back. There was the little red foreign job squirreling into a parking space. The words exchanged with the security man who was idling by the door to the lock-up. "Brad showed up, before noon," he said.

"Brad?"

"Yeah, Brad. You saw him there yesterday. Or you saw his car—the Alfa."

Wil remembered the encounter, too, in the corridor. The man Clusky had been yelling at. It hadn't been light enough for him to get more than a fleeting glimpse. Yet now the secondhand images and phrases collapsed together into sudden insight and Wil's heart took a jump against the side of his ribs.

"Tall, right?" he guessed, on impulse. "Blond hair and pale blue eyes? Neat look?"

"That's Brad. You saw him?"

Jesus. Wil sat forward. "Did you ever see him with a Walkman? Earphones with orange pads? A little tape deck?"

"Sure. The guy's a certified freak for country music. Cowboy boots

198

and jeans, silver belt buckles with turquoise, the whole...Hey, Wil?" The sickness was back, the throbbing head, with a vengeance. "Are you okay?"

Wil didn't answer. He realized suddenly that he'd stopped breathing and exhaled slowly, drawing in another breath. Impossible. "This guy hangs around with Stu Ray?" he asked.

"Wait, here's our ramp...." Madison slowed and followed the curve of the inside lane at Hayvenhurst, pumping the truck's brakes as it coasted down the ramp to the light.

Stu Ray?

A mural on the concrete wall of the underpass showed a sardine can with its top stripped back to reveal a crush of freeway traffic. For Wil, the image floated in and out of focus. "Brad," he said. His fists were rocks again, and he breathed the tightness out, muscle by muscle. "Tell me."

"You think Brad...?" The question hung in the air, unanswered, as Madison pulled away from the traffic lights. "Listen, man, I already gave you all I know. That's it. He hangs around Ray's like he owns the place. Cool cat. Clusky doesn't like him. You don't get the feeling that Ray likes him that much, either, but he never did anything to get him out of there. Word is, they have some kind of business deal. Aside from that, there's nothing I can tell you."

"A business deal?" Stu Ray?

"That's the talk, okay? I sure as hell don't know if it's true or not."

Impossible. Wil settled back, his heart a steady, pulsing throb in chest and ears, and waited for clarity to come. It didn't. What came was a tangle of images, half-certainties, ill-formed guesses and wild insights.

The truck came to a stop at the red light on Ventura Boulevard.

And where was Sally? The walls of the buildings at the four corners of the intersection seemed swollen, soft with heat. She was out there somewhere, swimming in this soup that passed for a summer day. How could he get word to her?

The light turned green and Madison made a right onto the boulevard. Three minutes later, they made a left and pulled in to the alley. Madison backed the truck up to the gallery's freight door. "This is it," he said. He set the brake and wiped the sweat away from his eyes under the glasses.

"Okay," said Wil. "Let's get to it."

A small bell push and a voice box were set in the brick to one side of the freight door, and Wil rang the bell while Madison unlocked the truck from the cab and came around the back to set the door ajar. It seemed like a twenty-minute wait.

An electric crackle, then the voice came through the plastic grille: "Yes?"

"It's the Raiders." Madison leaned forward, speaking into the box. "Delivery."

Another crackle. "Hold on."

Wil waited, hand on the brass knob, and listened to the turn of the lock and the sliding back of bolts. Then he pulled the door toward him as it began to open and found himself face to face with Judy Townsend.

They stood there and stared at each other, wordless, for a minute. Wil said, "Judy?"

It was a while since he'd seen her. Her eyes were half closed against the flood of light from outside, yet he hadn't remembered a face so filled with tension.

"Wil Garretson!" she said. She brought a hand up to her forehead, blocking the sun. "Wil? Are you kidding? Is that you? For God's sake..."

Wil Garretson with the Raiders, Judy Townsend at Bird in the Bush? Ironies he'd have enjoyed at any other moment, but he turned to see Madison waiting at the rear doors of the truck and swallowed down any pleasure he might have felt. "Is this your space?" he asked.

She nodded. "But Jesus, Wil, what brings you here? It has to be ten years." Sensing something wrong, she held out a tentative cheek for him to kiss. He returned the old affection briefly with a hug, and stood back, serious, steadying her with firm hands on her shoulders.

"Listen, kid," he said. "It's great to see you, but we have a problem here." He nodded his head back toward the truck.

Gray eyes, he remembered. She started a small, nervous laugh but stopped when she saw his face. "Serious?" she asked. He wasn't smiling anymore. She looked quickly to Madison and found no reassurance there. "You guys..." she began, but her voice trailed off into silence.

"I need the phone," said Wil. "We're going to have to call the cops."

"What's the problem?" Judy asked. "I don't understand."

He put an arm firmly around her shoulders and led her back into the gallery. "It's trouble," he said. "Is this the office, in here?" He brought her to the desk and wheeled the swivel chair back for her, sitting her down. "There's no way I can make this easy," he said. "We have two men dead in the truck.... No, wait. Hold on...." She wanted to get up,

200

but he held her gently in place. "It looks like they got bushwhacked. The painting's gone. I'm sorry."

Judy went limp under his hands. She sat there without expression for a moment, white as the wall behind her. "Dead?" she said. "Who's dead?"

"Wait," said Wil. He was already on the office phone, dialing 911. "We need help," he told the officer on the line. "What? We have a delivery truck with two dead men...killed, yes...and a stolen painting. What? Yes, a painting. Work of art. Name? My name's Wil Garretson." He spelled it out and waited. "I'm at...What's the street address here, Judy?" He read the number off the sheet of letterhead that she pushed toward him. "It's in back, in the parking lot. Telephone?" She wrote it large on the stationery, and he read it off again. "And, officer...I want to be sure that a Lieutenant DiPaolo of the LAPD is informed." He spelled that out, too. "Division? He said he was with Homicide....He answered a call out Vernon way, does that do it? Tell him it's a Ray's Raiders truck. He'll know....Yes. DiPaolo."

He put the receiver down and stared at the number he'd found circled in Jim Sewell's book. Bird in the Bush. Judy Townsend. The picture he'd been assembling in his mind expanded dizzyingly, losing the focus he thought he'd finally begun to find. Judy Townsend was a professional. She knew what the hell she was doing. He couldn't see her happy running some schlock gallery. That wasn't her style.

"For Christ's sake," she said. "Will you tell me what's happening, Wil?"

"You're okay?"

She nodded. "I just don't believe a word I've been listening to. Or the world's gone crazy."

"Listen," he said. "I can't leave Madison alone out there. Are you up to it? Let's talk outside, while we wait."

But the sound of the first siren was already greeting them as they crossed the threshold, wailing into life out on the boulevard. Another broke in on the first, and the two of them arrived within seconds of each other, squealing into the parking area and bouncing to a halt, their sirens dying simultaneously into a sudden, odd silence as the cops piled out and converged on the panel truck in pairs.

Before they reached it, two of the officers had to split from the phalanx to head off the three or four onlookers—five, maybe six, now starting toward the truck. The two men from the second black-and-white stopped to check Madison out before they had him open the doors wide and stand away while they took a look at the scene inside. One of them was out again in a moment, pale, Wil thought, and running for the patrol car. He reached inside and radio voices crackled.

"Mr. Garretson?"

There were ten, twelve people now, one of them arguing loudly with the cops, and others coming out from the rear doors of the Ventura Boulevard storefronts. A third cop car arrived and sped through the parking lot to cut them off. The officers piled out and held the people back.

"Mr. Garretson?"

"I'm Garretson." The sunglasses reflected a tiny double portrait of himself.

"I'll need a report from you." The cop had a printed form on a clipboard, and a ballpoint ready. He jammed a black shoe down on the fender of a parked car and steadied his knee to rest on. "Full name?"

Solve a problem, fill in a form, Wil thought.

"You'd best talk to the driver first," he said. "I just put the call in for him. Would it be all right with you if I took care of the lady?"

The cop glanced at Judy, huddled against the wall, white cotton against white-painted brick. "We'll need you, too," he warned.

"Of course, I understand that. I'm sure Ms. Townsend will appreciate the kindness."

He pointed the cop toward Madison. By this time, the crowd was thirty people strong and growing. Urging, pushing, arguing them back to the edge of the parking area, the uniformed cops unrolled a yellow plastic tape that read: POLICE LINE—DO NOT CROSS, and sealed off the area from the alley. Meantime, a line of other vehicles had begun to form, lights flashing, edging down the narrow alley through the crowd. Out there, among them, a paunchy man in a business suit was yelling, red in the face, about how he needed his car.

"Let's get inside." Wil took Judy by the arm and steered her back to the office.

The door closed off the confusion from outside. Here, everything was cool and orderly and silent, the white walls gleamed and the pictures exercised their quiet control over the space. The limits of reality were once again as clear-cut and defined as the hard, clean edges of the desk-top. The domain of art, Wil thought. Untouched by human hand.

"Wil...?"

One more call, he signaled with a forefinger, picking up the telephone to dial as she reached into a drawer to find a pack of cigarettes. She lit one nervously with a silver lighter and raised her chin, inhaling the smoke in one quick, breathy swallow. "For emergencies," she explained. "I quit."

Wil listened to the phone ring twice before the tape kicked in. "This is Rick Horan," the voice said. "Please leave a message..."

Wil shook his head slowly, replacing the receiver. "What was it?" he asked.

"What was what?"

"The shipment."

"Wil..."

"What was it?"

She looked at him and shrugged. "It was a Monet. A tiny piece, very late."

"Yours?"

"Are you kidding?"

"Whose, then?"

The cigarette sent up a thin column of smoke toward the ceiling. She was very still now, deep in the swivel chair. "A client."

"Someone I know?"

A small squeak from the chair as she shifted. "Some clients," she said, "like their privacy." She was still very pale, shaking slightly where she held the cigarette between her narrow fingers.

"Jesus," said Wil impatiently. "Privacy? The shipment's gone, Judy. You want to know what's in the truck instead of it? A bloody mess. Two people who were walking around, living and breathing just this morning. You talk about privacy? I'm talking massacre. Don't give me privacy."

She pulled at the white filter tip again and blew the smoke away. "Let me get something straight," she said. "You're working for Stu Ray? Wil Garretson, working for the Raiders?"

"Okay," he said. "I could sit here all day explaining. I started out trying to help a friend, and I got in deeper than I'd planned to. That's not important. What's important now is to help find out who's gone berserk—and stop him."

Judy stared at him a moment longer and then shrugged. "Listen, Wil, I feel as sick as you about the guys in there, but I don't see that my client's name can help. Maybe if the cops want it...He can't have anything to do with this. I was expecting a piece of art to show up here and it didn't show."

"That's all?"

She didn't answer.

"Judy . . . ?" She returned his gaze steadily, jaw set, with something mixed in the gray of her eyes that blocked off all communication once he got beyond the surface. "There's more," he said. "These are the third and fourth of Stu Ray's people to get killed in the past three days. You heard about Jim Sewell?" A flicker of light in there, in back of the eyes. "Sally was here, am I right? Sally Horan?"

She was scared, Wil thought. That was it. "I don't know what the woman thought she was doing here," she said. "She came in here and lied herself blue in the face."

"She told you about Don Henschler? Another of Ray's people?" Her eyes told him she knew what he was talking about. "These guys are foot soldiers in someone's war, Judy, and here you are, sitting in the middle of it. You've got to know more about this than you're letting on."

She stared at him, unblinking, shaking her head. "I don't. Believe me, Wil, I don't."

"Stu Ray?" he insisted. "I mean, is Stu involved in this?" It didn't make sense. They guy had a first-class business going, why would he risk it? And even if he had been ripping off art from himself, it wouldn't make sense to start killing his own best people.

"Ms. Townsend? Ms. Townsend, please . . ." A voice from the storage room was followed by a knock at the office door.

"Brad?" Wil went on, ignoring the sound. "You know this character, Brad?"

"Ms. Townsend . . ." The door opened and the cop was standing there with his clipboard.

"You'd better go, Wil," she said. "Come in," she told the officer. "Can we talk in here?" She stubbed the cigarette into a shower of sparks in the plastic wastebasket as Wil got up to go.

It was early to be looking for DiPaolo. Would he even come? Wil wondered, looking at his watch. This time of day, it had to be close to an hour's drive out from the city.

Outside, they'd zipped the bodies up in bright blue bags and were lowering them from the truck's tailboard on stretchers, locking down the aluminum legs to bring them to the waiting coroner's wagon. The

204

wheels rattled on the uneven surface of the parking lot as Wil asked his question.

"DiPaolo?" The plain-clothes officer who seemed to be in charge of directing operations was sweating freely in the full glare of the sun. His white shirt was stained dark with moisture, and he used a handkerchief to dab it from the back of his neck. He already had a line of others vying for attention. "You're asking the wrong guy," he said. "First off, I don't know the guy. Second off, I don't know whether he was called, or if he's coming. You got something to say, friend, you say it to me. Wait there." He turned to answer another question, though, and Wil backed off.

Where was Madison? He searched around the other side of the truck and found him squatting in the shade by the front wheel. "You told them about Brad?" he asked.

Madison looked up and squinted against the sun. "Sure," he said. "I told them."

"Well?"

"They wrote it down."

"The woman in the office, what's her name?"

"You mean Doria?"

"Doria. Call her. Find out where he lives."

"You're crazy. You're going looking for him?"

"This could take until midnight. I'm not waiting around, are you?" Wil hunkered down beside Madison, out of the sun. "Listen," he said. "There must have been several people around Ray's who would tell the cops that Brad was there this morning. You, for one. What does that suggest?"

"The man's crazy," said Madison. "Or he doesn't care."

"If he doesn't care, the way I see it, it's because he's already planned his exit. He's on the move."

Frowning, Madison took a few moments to work out the scenario. "Pick up every fucking piece he can round up?" he said. "Then split?"

Wil nodded. "That's one way to make sense of it," he said. "Come on. Let's find a telephone."

They walked past Judy's office and down through the gallery to the front, where the woman at the reception desk returned Wil's stare. "You know what we have to do?" he asked her. She shook her scarlet comb at him and grinned a surprising mouthful of braces. Somehow they made her look more human. "We have to find Brad," he said. "Can we use the telephone?"

"Brad who?" she said.

"Yeah, right. Brad who?"

28

THE YELLOW cab left the Valley under a shroud of orange-brown haze and followed the ascending curves of Laurel Canyon to Mulholland, waiting in a small knot of traffic at the light. Ahead and below, the city of Los Angeles suffocated under a thick blanket of the selfsame haze, and here at the summit the eucalyptus and the scrub brush seemed to breathe with extra effort. The dirt that had been swept down to the surface of the road by the previous winter's rains swirled up in eddies of fine dust with the passage of each car.

At least there was a specific target now.

Wil stared grimly at the sheet he'd torn off from the memo pad at the gallery and drummed his fingers on the hot vinyl of the seat while the aging Datsun ahead of them dawdled over the intersection and started to putter down the canyon at eighteen miles an hour.

"You can't get past this putz?" he asked.

The driver had long, stringy hair that fell from a wide bald circle in the middle of his head. "You got it," he said. He grinned back in the rearview mirror and sank his foot on the gas pedal, roaring past on an inside curve and steadying down to an honest forty-five through a gauntlet of angry horns.

Brad Michaels. The name meant nothing to Wil, but he was sure now that he was right.

The cab sped down between the steep sides of the canyon and passed the junction where Hollywood Boulevard dead-ends into the hill. The Crescent Heights address was half a block below the Sunset strip and the street was quiet outside the big old Spanish apartment house. The building was grand-Hollywood style, from the prosperous days, and the subtropical foliage that landscaped its façade grew roof-high between the street and the peach paint job with its elegantly scripted lettering, leaving the whole exterior in heavy shade.

The yellow cab's ancient air conditioner wheezed as it idled, double-parked.

"I may need to head downtown in a couple of minutes," Wil told the driver. "Can you wait for me here? Drive around the block a couple of times, if you need to."

The driver looked over his shoulder with a sigh. "I'll need a deposit."

"A deposit?"

"Listen, man, you get screwed once too often in this business. You give me a twenty, I'll wait. Ten minutes."

Wil sorted a twenty from his billfold, passed it over, and climbed out, slamming the door behind him.

Michaels. The name was stenciled on a length of blue metal tape that was stuck to one of the rusting mailboxes. Reading it, Wil felt a sudden tug at his gut, as though this simple label changed the man from chimera to reality. It looked relatively new, but the apartment number had long since disappeared from the box, leaving only a small rectangle of rust to show where it had been. Wil reached two fingers down inside, fishing for one of the mailers that were visible through the grille. No luck.

The wrought-iron gate below the arch was open and Wil walked through into a spacious central courtyard. Inside, another bed of the standard big-leafed greenery was topped by a murmuring fountain—the stylized figure of a seated nymph. Deco. Wil's footsteps echoed loudly on the floor, whose tiles were each handcrafted with the care and passion for design of another era. Following the court to the right, he found a small plaque embedded in the stucco. "Manager," it said.

His knock at the door intruded suddenly on the peaceful afternoon, and left the slow drip of the water more insistent, more precise as he waited. It was a while before a tiny window opened in the middle of the door and a pair of eyes gazed out at him. From behind came the sounds of afternoon TV.

"Yes?"

"Forgive me," said Wil. He realized now that he'd counted so confidently on Brad's being gone, he had no idea what he planned to do if the man was there. A confrontation? "I'm looking for a friend...a Mr. Michaels? He forgot to give me an apartment number...." The door opened halfway and the TV sounds flooded out into the courtyard. The woman who stood there in front of him was short, Hispanic, guarded in her stance.

"A Mr. who you look for?"

"Michaels."

A little plump, she had dimples in her cheeks even when she didn't smile. She wore a satiny pink shirt tucked into her jeans and her hair was gathered in a pink scarf around her head. She was barefoot.

"You a friend of his?" she asked.

Wil nodded, aware of the tightness growing in the muscles around his neck and shoulders. The sound increased by decibels in volume as the commercial started, and the woman turned to yell a few words over her shoulder. A child's voice came back, whining a complaint, but the sound went down.

"Michaels, huh? Then I guess he forget to tell you he was planning to move out of here," she said. The relief was instant, tangible. "He forget to tell me, too."

Of course. Things falling into place.

"He moved?"

"Moved out today," she said, with a gesture that described how fast he'd defected from the fold. "Never said nothing," she added. "Just sent a van here for his things."

The Raiders?

"Everything?" asked Wil. "The furniture?"

"No furniture," said the woman. "Is rented furnished. Just his things." A howl went up from somewhere in the depths of the apartment, but if it worried her she didn't show it. She was leaning against the doorsill now, arms folded, apparently at ease. A gold cross dangled at the end of the chain around her neck, bouncing off against a smooth, moon-pale expanse of breast.

"How about the van?" Wil asked. "Did you see the van the man came in?"

She frowned. "Is not my business," she said shortly. She clearly thought it wasn't his business either. "You a friend, or you from the cops?"

209

"A friend," he told her, smiling. "Did he owe money?"

"I had his first and last," the woman said, shrugging. "And his key money. You ask me, your friend's crazy. I'm not sorry to lose him. This place, we get all the tenants we need." She tossed her head scornfully. "We got a waiting list."

"Can I see his place?" Wil asked.

"What for?" she said. "Is nothing in there anyway. I was in there myself. Nothing. Is all gone."

Wil looked around the courtyard. What would he hope to find, anyway? "Did he live alone?"

The woman nodded. "Alone," she agreed.

"No friends? No visitors?"

Another shrug. "I never see no one," she said. "Is not my business, okay? So long as the neighbors not complain. Nice quiet place, you see."

Wil did. "Even so," he said. He felt in his pocket for his billfold and pulled out a ten. "If I could just take a look..."

The woman took the bill and folded it into the pocket of her jeans, shaking her head. "I get you the key," she said.

Climbing the terra-cotta tiled steps to the balcony, Wil paused by the apartment door. He looked at the key in his hand, the Yale lock in the door, the dark-green-painted wood. Suppose the man hadn't left? He closed his eyes, shook his head, and opened them again, overwhelmed by the power of his sense of Brad's presence on the spot where he must have stood a hundred times, going through the same series of motions Wil was repeating now. A killer.

Get it over with. He put the key in the lock and pushed the door inward into darkness.

Stepping into the relative cool of the apartment, he took some moments to let his eyes and ears adjust before he went to the windows and pulled back the draperies. It was a dark apartment anyway, shaded from sunshine by the massive greenery that grew at each of the windows: "Studio apartment"—a euphemism, Wil suspected, for a single room with kitchenette and bath.

The sad, sparse furniture looked as though it could have been there since the fifties—bare sticks of chairs with vinyl upholstery tearing at the corners, a kitchen table with a beige Formica top, a green sofa with its stuffing falling out below, and a coffee table creased with the dark brown burns of cigarettes. Wil was puzzled by the absence of a bed, until he discovered a rusting mechanism that creaked down into place when he opened the door of what he'd thought to be a closet. The sheets and blanket were roughly tucked in under a thin mattress. In the corner of the room stood an old TV with a rental sticker peeling at the top.

The manager was right. There was nothing left. If anything had been there in the first place, Wil thought. He glanced in the drawers and closets and checked the icebox in the kitchen: half a can of orange juice and an open quart of milk. Wil had the impression it had never been used for more. By the stove, a jar of instant coffee stood next to an unwashed yellow coffee mug.

It was as if no one had lived there, Wil thought. A zero. But a zero whose absence left behind a frightening sense of power.

Pulling a stool out from the kitchen counter, he sat down and looked around him. He'd already begun to reach for the wall phone when it shrilled into sudden action, startling him from his seat as it broke into the silence of the apartment like a summons from the dead. It rang three times. Wil stared at it. It rang a fourth time, and he picked up the receiver.

"Yes?" he said.

There was a cough, a hesitation. "Brad?"

He could almost swear he knew the voice, from the single word. But he needed more. More words.

"Yes."

He waited, but this time there was a longer pause, then the line went dead. Wil rested his finger on the cradle, waiting again, as though half expecting the caller to ring back, but the instrument persisted in its silence.

Sally. He dialed her number and the tape kicked in again, after the second ring. He looked at his watch and checked his options as he listened to Rick's voice. Then the beep. "Sally," he said. "I'm pretty sure I've found out who your caller is. After what's happened today, I'm laying odds you won't hear from him. He has bigger stakes at this point, and he's burned too many bridges. It's a hundred to one that he'll sacrifice the Leon Drakes, but in any case, just to be sure, they'll be returned to Jim Sewell's studio within an hour from now . . . six-thirty, say. Listen, I don't dare wait for you outside your place in case you decided to stay out. I'm going back to the studio. If you hear this, call me there. If you don't get home, I guess you'll be calling anyway. I need to know where you are."

Five twenty-eight.

The cab would be long gone by this time—it was twenty minutes, half an hour since he'd left it. He searched the yellow pages for a number, called a new cab and hurried out to the street to wait, returning the key to the manager on the way.

So Brad was gone, he told himself. If that was true, the immediacy of the threat seemed gone with him. But the larger question loomed like the thunderstorm that spawns the lethal tornado. Brad was a nothing. A mechanic. It was enough to look at the space he lived in: The man hadn't the imagination or the knowledge to blue-print and engineer the plans behind this operation—let alone to market the product.

The problem now was the guy who'd wound this killer toy up and let him run.

The alley behind Jim Sewell's studio shimmered like an assemblage of loose particles, hanging together as if only by precarious luck in the haze of the late afternoon. Jim's stall in the garage was still unoccupied, and Wil swung the wheel of the big Buick to ease it into the shade.

Madison was waiting. "Come on in," he said. "Take the weight off. I have a cold beer in the icebox."

"I can't stay," said Wil. But he caught the can that Madison lobbed in his direction. By force of habit, he wandered into the studio to get a sense of what Madison was all about. "You talked to Clusky?"

The police had impounded the truck, and Madison had called in to the office for help. "Pump him," Wil had said, when he heard that Clusky himself was driving to pick him up: "Get what you can."

"I talked to him," said Madison. He followed Wil into the studio. "Didn't get much. Clusky's a tight-lipped mother. He said if he'd talk to anyone, he'd talk to the cops."

Some blow-ups from videotapes, framed, a chiaroscuro of dark colors, luminous lights, the chaos of an inner city teeming with life and dreams.

"You asked him about Brad?"

"I asked. From what he said, he knows pretty much what I knew before. Brad has some kind of deal going with the boss, which gives him a say in the way things get done. He hasn't been much in Clusky's hair until recently. He got uppity. Clusky got mad because he couldn't get Stu's support, is what he says."

Wil realized he'd been moving at a near-run through the studio. He slowed himself down, pausing at the bulletin board and flipping through

212

layers of newspaper clippings, images from the weekly magazines. "You think he was telling the truth?" he asked.

"Hey, Wil. Clusky's a crusty bastard, but I'd trust him with my life."

The Inferno. Descending circles sketched in a storyboard that took up a whole wall. "Is this what you're working on now?" Wil asked.

"Yeah. Was working. Past tense. I haven't looked in the studio for two days straight." Madison took a swallow from his beer.

"That's it?" He looked around restlessly, wondering where Madison had stashed the paintings.

"There's one more thing," said Madison. "I lied. Turns out I'll be going out to the desert thing tomorrow afternoon. There was a message waiting when we got back to the warehouse. The Corton lady ran out of high-tension wire. Clusky's madder than hell to lose another hand for half a day."

"And no one got through to Stu? About Raul?"

Madison shook his head. "They're still trying to get him. No one's been able to find him yet."

Wil stared moodily at his beer can before he swallowed the rest of the tingling liquid down. "Okay," he said. "Let's get it done." He dropped the empty can in the trash and followed Madison to where he'd slid the two paintings behind a storage rack. Together, they grabbed them by the stretcher bars, face to face, and walked them out into the alley.

"Let's hope the fucker's not out here, watching us," Madison said. "Jesus, I'm spooked."

"He won't be." Wil sorted through his keys and opened the door. "Okay," he said. "Let's go."

They left the paintings propped against the wall, side by side, face out, brilliant with color even through the plastic wrappers. They were there if they were needed.

"So could I catch you, then, tomorrow?" asked Wil. "In case." He slammed the Le Sabre's door and Madison leaned down at the window, laughing.

"I leave the warehouse at two," he said. "Then out to City Lights— it's a neon yard in the east Valley. Sunland. I won't be leaving there before three. You'll find it in the book. See you there."

"Who knows?" said Wil.

"Me. I know. I can't get rid of you. Wherever I go, Wil Garretson shows up."

Wil grinned and backed out into the alley, watching as Madison closed his studio door behind him. Then he turned onto Washington and headed west.

Back at his own place, Wil stopped by the laundry porch and stripped to the skin, dumping his clammy clothes in the washing machine. Naked, he went through the day's messages on the tape. Bernie Trost, from after lunch. Fred Aaron: Major panic, he was right about the Mondrian. Charlie, no message. Nothing from MaryJo. No word from Sally. He dialed her number and listened to the first words on her tape. Then he stopped on the way upstairs to see if MaryJo had left a message on the kitchen counter. Nothing.

Up in the bathroom, he stepped into the shower and let the water run cold.

Still toweling dry, he wandered back down to the studio and gazed at the piece he'd started there. He measured himself against it, in tension with it, breaking away from it, surprised at the wallop of its emotional impact. The scale felt right. He wanted himself right in there with it.

Seven-fifteen.

He lay down on the studio couch, planning to do no more than rest his bones for ten quick minutes before sorting out some dinner from the icebox. When he laid his head back, though, he was surprised by the huge heaviness way up under the skull, the swirl of images that came and went, just beyond his reach.

Somewhere he lost it. He barely had time to wonder if he was going to fall asleep when the telephone rang.

Then he was wide awake. How long had it been? Ten minutes? An hour? He was surprised to see the light already fading in the clerestories.

"Wil?" It was Sally. He looked at his watch.

Eight-thirty. Jesus.

"Sally," he said. "Did you get my message?"

"Wil..." There was a note of urgency in her voice that brought him right back to the surface. "Wil, I need to see you. Right away."

It came to him with absolute clarity now. "Listen, Sally," he said. "Before you say anything...Since we talked this morning, too many other things have happened. There's no way we can hold out any longer. We've got to hand it all over to the cops. Everything..."

"Wil," she said. "I'm there."

"There?"

There was a pause. "The police. They brought me downtown."

Wil's head whirled. "They what?"

"They picked me up," she said. "They were waiting for me when I got back home."

"Are you okay?"

"I'm not sure. I'm surprised how calm I feel. Spacey. They want to question me."

"You have a lawyer there?"

"You think I need one?"

"Yes," he said. "You do. Do you have someone I can call for you?"

"There's one person..." she said. "My friend Paula's husband." Kenneth. He'd always acted as Rick's attorney when he needed one.

"Give me a number, love," said Wil. "I'll call him."

"I have a home number." He took the number she gave him, and an address for the downtown police headquarters. Robbery-Homicide, she said. "I'll be there," he said. "I'll make it in...maybe half an hour. Hang on."

A woman's voice answered at the number Sally gave him.

"Ken's at dinner at the moment," she said. "Can I have him call you back?"

"It's urgent," he said.

Then the guy was on the line. "Listen," said Wil, "I'm calling for Sally Horan. Yes. No, I'm afraid not. I'm a friend. There's a whole lot of story here that I don't have time to fill in for you. She needs a friend fast, a lawyer. Here's the address."

"Isn't that...?"

"Police headquarters, yes."

"Can I ask...?"

"Not if you're a friend. Ask her. She's in trouble."

Wil had clothes on in three minutes and was out to the Le Sabre in five. He scraped the wing against the brick wall as he turned out onto Speedway.

"Oh, shit!" he said aloud. He'd forgotten to tell her about Raul and the security guard. Terrific. He'd forgotten to tell her about Brad Michaels.

29

THE WOMAN lifted Sally's right forefinger off the pad, pressed it down, and rolled it around firmly on the printed card. It had her name already typed at the top. Sarah Beatrice Horan.

She wondered if it was Sarah Beatrice Horan who'd been up on the mountain there, with Jimmy Sewell.

Shutting out the noise and the confusion, she stared at the marks on the white card until they lost all definition. She struggled in vain to remember instead the contour of Jim's face, and wondered where they would have put him. It seemed strange that his body would have simply gone away. When she closed her eyes, she visualized a wall of drawers such as those she'd seen in television scenes of city morgues, and shuddered. Of everything Jim Sewell had been, she thought, all that was left was scads of printed forms like this one. Reports and statements copied out in triplicate.

"The left hand, please."

The uniformed woman dropped the right one in her lap and said it a second time, louder, before the sound penetrated. Sally lifted the left hand automatically and let the woman take it, too, as if it weren't her own. It belonged to this strange other, this waxen figure sitting there in the space she normally would have occupied—a stranger with the placid inanimateness of one of those Duane Hanson visitors you brush against in the corners of museums, lifelike in every tiniest detail but life itself.

The second hand dropped back in her lap and she looked at the ink that remained on its fingers, rubbing at the stuff with some solvent and a Kleenex they gave her to clean up with. On the card, flattened out like that, the fingerprints filled each one of the little boxes, edge to edge. Somehow, she wouldn't have expected them to look so square, nor so large. She had imagined them oval and small, like the tips of her fingers.

She got up, standing there at the counter, gazing into the pale, fluorescent green light of this peculiar purgatory of uniforms and typewriters, paperwork and Styrofoam cups. In a moment's strange euphoria, a giddiness, she decided that it was after all a relief to be a cipher, a nothing, a smudge on a printed form. She felt that she deserved it. That this was the punishment she'd earned for too much wrongful happiness. Or for betrayal. For betraying Rick, then Jim.

The least she could have done would be to have the guts to face it right away.

"Sit over there."

The woman was finished with her now and pointed toward a row of seats where she found a place between a snoring Japanese man in a business suit, head tilted to the flickering white neon strips on the ceiling, drunk out of consciousness, and a belligerent Latino kid in white shirt and black pants who shifted away from her uneasily when she sat.

It wasn't a relief. She was scared. Her eyes stung in the flat, raw light, her belly ached and her fingers were stained with ink she'd never be able to get off. Her hair was stringy. She stood out ridiculously in a summer dress she wished she'd never paid four hundred dollars for and she clung to her bag as if someone were about to steal it.

"You understand your rights?"

The question was addressed to someone in the row of chairs behind her and, overhearing it, she realized that she didn't. She'd never needed them before. Could she have refused to have fingerprints taken? They went right ahead, even after she told them she was waiting for her attorney. "Things will just go faster, Mrs. Horan," the woman explained tonelessly. It was late, she wanted to get the job done, you couldn't blame her, she wanted to get home. "You don't need to answer any questions yet."

Sarah Beatrice Horan...

...sat on her fiberglass chair in a line of others, repeating the name to herself, and waiting, angry, watching a slack-waisted, sweating detective amble past in front of her with a cigarette in the corner of his mouth. She thought she'd gotten past her own humiliation, but she couldn't get over the inefficiency, the rudeness, the lack of simple human feelings. She didn't belong here. This wasn't a part of her life. She wasn't a part of theirs. She got up, sick to her stomach, and sat down again.

When Kenneth Stone arrived, escorted by a plain-clothes officer with an ID badge, she barely recognized him. A stranger in a pinstripe suit. A bewildered friend who didn't know what she was doing here. Paula was a good lunch pal, but it was rare that the four of them got together otherwise and several months at least since she'd seen Ken. And now he stood there hiding his embarrassment with a puzzled smile and business-like expression, tall, distressingly like Rick, pink flush in his cheeks, vaguely angelic.

"Sally...?" he said.

"Hi, Ken."

Thanks to Paula's gossip, Sally knew more about his erection and its sometimes erratic performance than she knew about him or his work.

"Sally!" When she got to her feet, he gave her a little formal hug, then kissed her cheek and stood back, brief case dangling. "For God's sake!"

Somewhere behind the clatter of typewriters, a woman wailed as though the world would end. Another officer in street clothes, a clip-board under his arm, came searching for Sally along the row of chairs. "Mrs. Horan? Mrs. Sarah Horan?" He had a sheaf of pink telephone messages in his hand. The top one, Sally read upside down, said "Gar-retson."

"I'm Sally Horan."

"Yes, Mrs. Horan." His plastic ID was clipped to the pocket of his brown-striped shirt, below an array of ballpoints. "My name's Lieutenant DiPaolo. I understand you have an attorney present? Have you had time to talk?"

She shook her head.

"Okay, I can give you a couple of minutes." He checked his watch. "You're going to meet me in there." He pointed with the clipboard to an open door. "Why don't you two get started? I have some calls to make."

He hurried away, and Ken took Sally by the elbow to bring her into the office. It was a tiny space, windowless, equipped with a single gray metal desk and four gray chairs. The calendar on the wall had a picture of Mount Fuji, and the ashtray had spilled half its contents on the desktop.

Sally sat down, crossed her legs, and took a breath. "We don't have time to be coy," she said. "Are you ready for this?"

She laid a hand on his arm and he nodded, planting himself on the chair beside hers as she started a bare-bones sketch of what had happened to her in the past three days. Once the first few words were out, she was surprised to find that she could tell it quickly, accurately, unemotionally, as though it were something that had happened to someone else.

He was good, she thought. Unlike Paula, he was most often withdrawn with others—talking quietly and fast, and only when silence was impossible. But he could listen well, as he did now, with a small, professional frown of concentration playing around his forehead. When she had finished, he simply opened his brief case and pulled out a legal pad.

"Listen," he said. "I need to ask you this first: Have you told me everything? I mean, the truth? There's nothing you're holding back?"

Sally shook her head slowly, thankful that he gave no sign of judging her. "Does it sound like it?" she asked. "Isn't it bad enough as it is?"

He grinned and reached for her hand and she was grateful, again, for its warmth. "I've heard worse," he said. "So you're a human being, Sally, like the rest of us."

That was all. It wasn't the worst thing in the world. He'd said it—and it hurt much less than she'd expected. The difference, though, was that his ego wasn't at stake, as Rick's would be.

"Thanks, Ken."

"Okay, we don't have much time, so we'll stick to business. For the moment, here's how I see it: With a lot of rigmarole, I could probably get this session postponed for a while. It's not worth it. I know that all the feelings get in the way and tell you otherwise, but you've done nothing serious enough to want to hide and, believe me, your cooperation will earn you a whole lot of good will. If you stall them, it only irritates without helping. What I'd suggest is that you get it over with. Given all the circumstances, I think even the cops will understand."

She allowed the trust to come slowly. "What about Rick...?"

"Let's leave Rick out of it for the moment. In a way, it's lucky he's out of town. We'll sort that one out when he gets back—I'll help, if you want me to. For now, just tell the story. If I know Rick, his first concern will be for your protection." Funny, she hadn't thought about that since arriving home, late afternoon. With the police, at least she'd felt safe. "You've been threatened, Sally. The best thing you can do is help the police lay their hands on the guy behind it. You're vulnerable. Remember that."

DiPaolo poked his head around the door with a question mark. "You're ready?" Kenneth nodded and the lieutenant came in, sitting down across the desk with his clipboard and a long brown envelope. He reached inside and pulled out two snapshots, laying them out like playing cards in front of Sally. Beside them, he placed a black-and-white glossy photograph, eight-by-ten. Sally steeled herself.

He sat and looked at them for a moment in silence, weighing his words. "I'm not going to bullshit you, Mrs. Horan," he said. "You don't look to me like that kind of woman, and I mean that as a compliment. Fair enough? This"—pointing to the black-and-white—"is a police department picture of a drawing found in James Sewell's studio. These"—he pointed to the color shots—"were hand-delivered to the front desk at this station just three hours ago."

Sally barely glanced at them. She knew what they were: the Polaroids. Ken picked up one of the color shots. She glanced at him sideways, but whatever thoughts he had were lost behind an expression that carefully concealed them.

"So someone has it in for you." DiPaolo shrugged. "No big deal. But from a news-file picture," he continued, pulling out another one and laying it beside the others, "the sheriff's folks out in San Bernardino county had a Mrs. Norah Coats, at the general store in Nine Palms, identify you as a woman who came in to ask for change for a telephone call last Sunday, at the time James Sewell's death was reported."

He brought out her fingerprint chart and laid it side by side with another photograph, and a flight of butterflies took off in Sally's stomach, leaving it hollow with anticipation. "I don't know how much you know about police work, Mrs. Horan, but we have miraculous ways of enchancing latent fingerprints these days. This"—he said, pointing to the thumbprint on the right hand—"is identical to this photographed print we recovered from the stock of the rifle found in Sewell's camper."

DiPaolo ran a hand back through his hair and looked at Sally for a moment.

"I'm a practical man, Mrs. Horan," he said. "I'm leveling with you now because I'm asking for the same from you. There's an obvious inference here and I don't want to make it yet. I'm giving you credit, right? I need your help, not your problems. I assume you know that Jim Sewell worked for an outfit called Ray's Raiders?" Sally nodded. "Did you know, Mrs. Horan, that since your friend died, three other people working for that company have been killed?"

"Three others...?" Sally's heart jumped and her mind began to race. Wil had told her about Donald Henschler. Now three? Jesus. "Three?" she repeated.

"Three others. From the same outfit," DiPaolo went on, nodding. "There was a Donald Henschler, last night. And today, a man named Raul Ortega, and a security guard."

Sally looked back at Ken. "This is crazy," she said, shaking her head.

"From what she's told me," Ken started, "my client certainly knew nothing about this...."

He was waved down by DiPaolo. "We can screw around with the legal technicalities all night, Mr. Stone. That's not the point. The point is, what we've got here is a problem of frightening dimensions. What we need is information to resolve it. Ortega was supposed to deliver a painting to a gallery this afternoon." He consulted his notes. "A Monet. It never got there," the lieutenant continued. "Neither did he. He was shot at close range in the head, in the back of his own truck, along with the security guard who'd been assigned to protect it."

Sally winced. "Oh, dear God," she whispered. "What did I do?"

"You didn't do anything." Ken leaned over, taking her hand. "Sally..."

But DiPaolo kept looking across the desk at her intently. "God knows, you're right in the middle of it, Mrs. Horan."

Silence followed as Sally met his gaze. His face offered no judgment, but allowed her no excuse. He was right, she knew. Ken cleared his throat. "My client's in a delicate situation here," he suggested. "I should perhaps explain..."

DiPaolo waved him down again. "Listen," he said. "I'm not stupid. I understand that your client wants to keep an indiscretion from her husband. But, to put it simply, the time has come for her to tell the truth." He turned to Sally. "The rest of it's up to you, your husband..." He shrugged. "Some things matter less than others, Mrs. Horan."

Sally crushed her eyes closed and opened them again. It made it easier, having told Ken, but the void still looked pretty dark and bleak now she had to step out into it. Ken laid a hand on her arm. "My client is prepared to make a statement," he said. "Is this for the record?"

The lieutenant signed and nodded. "I'll make notes," he said, "and write it up later. What's important now is the information. Mrs. Horan...?"

She found herself focusing on the picture of Mount Fuji as she talked, an overly pretty shot whose colors verged close on the gaudy. The snow-cap rose to its perfect peak against a clear blue sky, and in the foreground, real or not, a sprig of cherry blossom cut across one corner of the view. She tried to tell the story with the same sharp, dreamlike outline of detail, right down to the burst of lining from the sleeping bag and the shards of the broken thermos glinting in the sun.

It may have been twenty minutes she talked, or half an hour, and at the end she was surprised to hear her own voice stop. She emerged from silence to the sound of DiPaolo rattling small change in his pocket. "Can I get you a Coke?" he was asking. "Coffee?"

She stared at him, realizing that the telling had left her empty, totally depleted, wrung out of emotions. There wasn't anything left for her to feel. She simply shook her head.

"This man," he asked, "the one who came to your house... We think we've got a line on him from another source. You're sure he's the same one that helped you change the tire? The chauffeur?"

When would it stop? She glanced across at Ken. "I wouldn't mistake him."

"And you never saw him anywhere before?"

"Never. I'm sure."

DiPaolo clicked the end of his ballpoint in and out. "The one thing we still lack is a picture. Can you help our police artist put a composite together?"

Her shoulders slumped a protest. "Tonight?" she said. "Really? I don't think I can see straight."

DiPaolo allowed himself a small smile. "I understand," he said. "To-morrow?"

"Tomorrow I can do better than that," she said. "I can make you a picture myself." She could feel the lines of the tight jaw, the bunch of muscles under the skin. "I'm an artist."

"So I hear," said DiPaolo. He made a note to himself on the side of

222

his notepad, then looked at her closely again. He was tired, too, she saw—a tiredness that reached deep under the skin, below the surface of his eyes. A tiredness you could hear in his voice, when you listened close. "Mrs. Horan, understand, please: We need to consider every alternative. Your husband—he's also engaged in a business that has to do with artists?"

Ken began to interrupt, but this time it was Sally who waved his objection aside. "Let's get it over with, Ken, okay? I won't last much longer. My husband's a business manager," she told the lieutenant. "Yes."

"On the weekend, now, you saw him last ... ?"

"Saturday morning, when I left. Around ten."

"And again ... ?"

She tried to get the thoughts straight. "When I got back. Around seven, on Sunday evening. But you're not suggesting ..."

"It's just the information that I need, Mrs. Horan. Did you contact him, call him at all in between?"

So did she? The dates and times were getting confused. "Not on the weekend, no. Oh, yes." She'd left that out. "I called from San Bernardino, yes. Otherwise he would have expected me to be in Phoenix, with my friend. That was around noon on Saturday."

"He was home then?"

"He was at the office. It's not unusual for him to spend most of Saturday there. I'm lucky if I see him on a Sunday."

"You spoke to him personally? Not a secretary? Not a tape?"

She remembered, yes, she'd spoken to the secretary in Rick's office. He had gone to lunch. DiPaolo made a note.

"Aside from Jim Sewell," he asked, "did you or your husband have any other contact with Ray's Raiders?"

Sally looked at Ken again, and pointed to her watch. He simply shrugged and nodded.

"I believe Rick handled the books for Stuart Ray. And we both run into him, of course, at various events."

"Events?"

"Art openings, benefits ... That kind of thing."

"Did you know any of his other employees? Let's see ..." He checked through the papers. "Madison Grant?" She shook her head. "The two that were killed? Donald Henschler? Raul Ortega? No?" Sally shook her head again. She kept shaking it.

"I know you're tired, Mrs. Horan. Just a couple more things. Did the company ever do any work for you? They package and transport art-works, I believe. You have a collection?"

Sally nodded. "We have a small collection. On a very rare occasion, yes, we used the Raiders. Not often. It's not that kind of a collection."

"What kind of a collection?"

"Not an important-enough collection to be lending work out to exhi-bitions," she said.

There was a silence. The lieutenant started to shuffle through the file again and Sally leaned forward over the desk to rest her head in her hand.

"Ken," she said. "Help!"

Ken looked at his watch. "Listen, Lieutenant," he said. "Time's get-ting on. My client has been thoroughly co-operative but she's obviously exhausted. If you need to follow up, she'll be available. Why don't we call it a night?"

DiPaolo brought the papers back together into a pile. He sat back in his chair and thought for a moment, pinching his nose and staring up to where the red second hand made a long, slow circle around the face of the wall clock.

"Mrs. Horan," he said. "You've done the right thing, and I want to thank you for your help. Now, you said that your husband's out of town?" She nodded. "At some point," he went on, "—I have to be frank—we're likely to have to talk to him. In my experience, it's best you should do that first. You understand what I'm saying?" She nodded again, and he tidied the edges of the papers together, tapping the sheaf down on the desktop. "Okay," he said. "We'll sleep on it. You'll bring that sketch by for me in the morning?"

30

"THIS ISN'T a joke, this isn't high school, this isn't a game...."
The cop at the Impounded Vehicles desk was hectoring a new
batch of kids. "We're talking state business here. I ask for a license, you
bring me a license. You don't bring me no note from your teacher, hear?
You bring me a license." The door behind him opened, allowing a brief
glimpse of banks of black-and-white television monitors, flickering.

Where was Sally? When Wil had asked for her, all they would tell
him was to wait.

"Get on out of here," the cop yelled. "You kids, get on out." They
trooped out, muttering, half a dozen of them, bent on trouble.

The lobby was smaller than Wil would have thought for a metropoli-
tain police center, but still a babel of language and angry humanity,
sweating and edgy with the heat of a night that refused to cool. The few
yellow seats at the edges of the room were taken, and the lines at the
counter grew longer by the minute. Wil leaned back into the corner he'd
carved out for himself and stared at a black-framed picture on the wall,
into the unsmiling blue eyes of a cop who'd been killed in the line of
duty.

He'd been waiting a full hour, a reluctant eavesdropper in two dozen
melodramas whose meanings he could only begin to guess at. In the far
corner, a Mexican family was huddled around a weeping grandmother

who kept dabbing a handkerchief to her eyes. Across from Wil, a thin southeast Asian man and a pregnant woman argued in high-pitched voices, with poison as sharp as chips of flint in their eyes. At one moment, a kid, thirteen perhaps, burst in with a bloody face and nose, and ran the length of the lobby before disappearing out on the street again, apparently unnoticed. Others were silent, stolid: a bag lady sat unmoving with her shopping cart, staring ahead with a smile that belonged to a reality other than the here and now.

It was well past nine when Sally finally emerged from one of the anonymous doors marked "No Admittance." She was pale under the neon light, the dark make-up around her eyes streaked and smeared, and in this improbable tableau of inner-city drama she looked as misplaced as the man who walked two steps behind her in his immaculate pin-striped suit.

"Sally!"

Wil's voice was drowned out by the noise.

"Sally!"

She seemed to have heard and searched him out in the crowd, too tired to respond as he stumbled through a couple of lines to meet her. "Sally," he said, "are you okay?"

She said, "Fine," but almost at once the tears began to gather in her eyes. She made one last attempt to hold it all down with a smile, but then she lost it. Fell forward, literally into his arms. Grabbed on to him and let the whole flood out. Wil stood there, rocking her.

"Wil Garretson?" It was a while before the attorney spoke. He stood a little to one side and raised his voice when he saw that Wil could barely hear what he was saying. "I want to thank you for calling me," he said. He made to offer a hand, then found that both of Wil's were occupied and offered a small smile instead. "I'm Kenneth Stone. Let's get Sally out of here."

Wil released her slowly and she shook out the hair behind her. "Okay?" he asked.

She nodded, accepting the handkerchief he offered, and he led the way around the corner to the outer lobby where a concrete retaining wall shut off a good part of the sound. The three of them stood together in a wedge of light.

"How did it go in there?" asked Wil. Sally shivered and he pulled her in tighter under his arm.

"Okay, I think," said Ken. "We told them everything—including

226

whatever Sally knew about your part, I'm afraid. I'm sure they're going to want to talk to you."

"Of course."

"Meantime, I've got her off the hook for tonight. Tomorrow, she's promised to stop by with a sketch. They'll also want to have her sign a statement."

"A sketch?" asked Wil.

"The fellow up on the mountain. The one that broke into the house."

Brad Michaels. With luck, Wil thought, his own report could wait for the morning. "They know who it is?" he asked. "Are they looking for him now?"

Ken nodded. "They know the name," he said. "And the lieutenant thinks they have a good line on him." He pushed the big glass door to the street and urged them both ahead of him.

"No, wait," said Wil. There was one last thing, to be sure. "They put the Raul Ortega murder together with Jim Sewell and Don Henschler?"

Stone paused and looked at him, his shadow echoing the action on the mosaic mural at his back. A tricycle, a little schoolhouse, kids. A kindly cop in a black-and-white. A few yards away, in the real world, a drunk perched precariously on the wall, a brown-bagged bottle in one hand, baying insults at the passing cars. "They did," said Stone. "Yes. You knew about that?"

An RTD bus rolled by, drowning out the last of his words.

"I was there," shouted Wil. It seemed to him that there was nothing he could add. "Let's go."

He took Sally's arm and the three of them crossed the street to the park-and-lock, where a small posse of black kids sauntered past in black jeans and white T-shirts, confident of their turf. Somewhere out there, Brad Michaels strutted with the same freedom and power.

"I'll drive Sally home," said Kenneth.

They shifted out of the path of a backing car. "I can't go home," said Sally, with surprising calm. It was the first time she'd spoken. "Not without Rick there, not after this morning. I was going to call Paula..." She was surprised, herself, to find how the night air revived her.

"Of course," said Ken. "She'd be delighted. We'd both be delighted."

"Sally..."

"But listen..." Her words came out at the same time as Wil's, and Sally broke off, realizing that she hadn't talked to him since morning and had lost all track of what he knew and what he didn't know.

227

Glimpses of the day began to rush back. There were Leon, Judy . . . She remembered now that she hadn't mentioned the visit to Leon's studio to DiPaolo. There was the invitation out to the ranch. She'd almost forgotten about that. "Listen," she told Ken, "there's so much I need to talk about with Wil. . . ."

Stone kicked at the tire of his Continental. "That's fine with me," he said. "If it's okay with you. But you'll call me first thing in the morning, Sally, right?" His glasses glinted in the streetlight as he looked from one to the other of them, then smiled, and offered Sally a small kiss goodnight.

The business district of downtown was cavernous, empty by this time of night, and the freeway was a straight shot to the beach. Silent, Wil nudged the Le Sabre up to sixty in the second lane and maintained the speed.

"Why?" Sally asked. Her head was clear again, working. "That's what I don't understand. Why?"

The dashboard lights glowed green with a couple of points of red and the freeway opened out in front like a great wide concrete ribbon splashed with a thousand traveling lights. "Why what?" asked Wil.

"The man . . ."

"Michaels?"

"Whatever . . . He said he'd give the Polaroids to the police if I didn't help him recover the Leon Drakes. Then he never gave me the chance."

It had been on Wil's mind, too, and there was an answer that fit in neatly with his scenario. "The guy's setting brush fires," he said. "These people had a cozy operation going, maybe for years—until something happened. My guess is that you're the smoke screen for some last big effort . . . a grand slam. Maybe that was the Monet. . . ." He tightened his grip on the wheel, remembering Raul.

Sally's memory served up another picture. "Leon Drake likes Monet," she said.

"What's that supposed to mean?"

"I had lunch with him today," said Sally. She told him how Leon had shown up at Charlie Strauss's place, on Melrose. "The man's off his head."

"Leon? How so?"

"He's off at tangents. You don't know where he's going, from one

228

moment to the next. Among other things, he wanted to make love to me on the studio floor, in front of a bunch of other people."

Asshole. Wil had long ceased to share the world's amused tolerance of Leon's sexual insecurities. "I hope you threw it back in his face," he said. "Leon's one of those men who have to try it on with every woman they take a shine to." He took his eyes off the road to try to gauge her reaction at a glance, but found her only thoughtful. "What else?"

"I went slightly crazy myself," she said. "I told him I'd heard on the grapevine where his paintings were."

She fell silent, hands in her lap, and Wil waited while he scratched at his beard and focused carefully on the taillights up ahead. Fatigue was taking its toll on the corners of his vision, leaving it frayed and imprecise. Single points of light stretched out into long, blurred lines. It was only when silence threatened to edge over into oblivion that he said, "And?"

Her thoughts tumbled back in order and she picked up the thread where she'd left it. "He wanted to call Rick, to check it out," she said. "I didn't want to bring you into it, so I told him I thought it was Rick who'd mentioned them. He wanted to call."

"Just what you needed," said Wil. "How did you dissuade him?"

"I guess I strung him along."

From this raised perspective, the streetlights picked out the city's grid in a million tiny points that shimmered against the darkness, and Wil eased his foot down on the gas pedal, watching the needle climb to sixty-five on the dial. The studio called him like a refuge from the craziness beyond its wall.

"He claims to hate his art," Sally said.

He'd heard that story before. "So how did you get around to Monet?" Leon's infatuation with impressionist painting was an old one. Why now, thought Wil?

"He has a whole roomful of reproductions at the studio. God knows what he has out at the ranch. He wants me to go out there with him tomorrow, to see what he calls some 'real art.' He's going out to the Barbara Corton thing."

Asshole. For Christ's sake, what did he have out there? "What did you say?"

"I didn't say no."

Wil thought about Judy Townsend and the Bird in the Bush. That was an old connection. He tried putting Leon together with the work Jim Sewell had stolen. With four dead people. It made no sense. He tried putting him together with Don Henschler and the Jasper Johns. With heroin. With Brad Michaels. Leon and Stu Ray? It made less sense. He tried telling Sally about it and it still didn't work.

"You went to see him last night," she said. "Before your studio got broken into."

"He knew I was out," said Wil. "He was the only person who could have. Does that mean something?" And Leon had been furious when he wanted to leave early.

"You think so?"

Wil beat on the steering wheel with his fist. "This thing's got me crazy," he said. "I've known the guy for twenty years and sit here wondering whether he's involved in murder!"

"Four murders."

"Four murders, then. And God knows what else: forgery, grand larceny, insurance fraud...I mean, Leon may be an occasional asshole, but a killer?"

No, that was it, that was the difference. Brad was the killer, he reminded himself. The cops would be taking care of Brad. Brad was on the run. It was the bigger thing....

"Let's find out," she said.

"Find out what?"

"What he's got up there. He can show me his real art."

Real art, fake art. The bigger answer. There was the Barbara Corton thing. Stu Ray was headed out there, with half the Raiders. And now Leon Drake. It seemed, with a logic he didn't stop to analyze, the next step along the road. "Let me do it," he said. "I'll go up to the Barbara Corton show with the Raiders truck and call in on Leon at the ranch."

They had left the freeway now, making a right on Pico, coming up over the crest to glimpse the glitter of reflected lights on the ocean and the outline of tall palms against the orange street lights.

"I'm not staying in Los Angeles by myself," she said. "No way."

"You don't imagine I'd let you go with Leon, for Christ's sake?"

"Who's to let?" she asked. "What is this, Wil? Besides, I know the guy's a pussycat once you get below the surface. He fantasizes himself as the great seducer, but he's not a rapist. He's going to have a houseful anyway. I'll have lots of company. If it's being safe you're thinking of, I'd much rather be up there."

230

His instinct told him she was right about that. Besides, if he hitched a ride with Madison, he could still walk the mile across the mesa to check things out at the ranch. "What about the police?" he asked.

"They didn't tell me not to leave town, if that's what you mean," she said. He laughed. "They just asked me to drop off the sketch and sign the statement. I'll work on the sketch tonight, or tomorrow morning, drop it off, and then take off with Leon."

"Let's think about it, okay? When does Rick come home?"

"He should be back Thursday."

Wil's eyes went to his rearview mirror as they headed back along Ocean. Behind them, the headlights were anonymous, sparse. There was no other vehicle in sight on Speedway when they pulled into his parking spot off the alley, nor was MaryJo's Honda parked in its usual place, when she spent the night.

Nor a message where she'd have left it, on the floor inside the door. Wil double-bolted it behind them, and checked around the studio carefully. By the time he got back to the kitchen, Sally was already on the phone. "I'm calling Leon," she told him. "It's a tape."

"You're sure you want to do this, now?"

"I'm sure. Wil? What's that?"

She was looking through to the studio, where the giant length of timber was still hanging from the chain.

"An idea," he said. He searched the refrigerator for food and pulled out a loaf of French bread from the freezer. There was cheese.

"Leon, this is Sally Horan. If the offer's still open, I'd like to go with you. You could pick me up early afternoon at my place. Call me around noon..." She checked out the time with Wil and he nodded. "...or a little later, if you need directions to my house or you've changed your mind. Otherwise, I'll expect you. Okay? See you then."

There was soup, too. Wil set Sally up with a drawing board in the studio and emptied the soup in a pan with the flame on low. He checked the messages on the tape. A call from Charlie Strauss, on his way to New York. It could wait, he said. A call from Bernie, leaving for the desert. No word from Michaels. Nothing from MaryJo. She meant it. Wake me up when it's over, she'd said.

"Some idea," Sally said. She had switched the studio lights on and looked up at the piece. "What happened to the boxes?" she asked.

"Sometime," Wil said, "I'll tell you. Get to work." By the time he'd heated supper and brought it through on a tray, Sally was already well ahead with the picture. Tight forehead. Tight muscles in the cheeks. A chin and jaw that were tense with angry, undirected power. She was back at work on it when he turned on the news at eleven.

"I wonder if we made the headlines?"

They had. "Four dead in bizarre art-world killing spree," ran the teaser. Then they cut to commercials.

Wil sat beside Sally on the couch and laid an arm across her shoulder. She put the pencil down and it rolled off the drawing board to the floor.

"The normally quiet world of Los Angeles art has exploded in violence in the past two days," the announcer started, after the break. "Sunday, The Late Report first broadcast news about what appeared to be the accidental death of a young artist in the San Bernardino mountains. Last night and today, the bloody sequel to this death took the form of three more killings. . . ."

The shots that followed had the same eerie feel of a déjà vu. These were people he knew, their faces at once familiar and strange on the little screen. The Le Sabre, parked in front of the warehouse, appeared in the first clips. Then he and Madison, in the Valley, shadowy extras, walking on at different moments in the drama.

"Meanwhile," the announcer went on, "the company that seems to be at the center of this storm, an art transportation business known as Ray's Raiders, continues to operate. . . ." One of Stu's trucks rolled out from the chain-link gate toward the camera. With the light reflected off the windshield, Wil couldn't tell who the driver was. ". . . and police are still unable to report any significant leads in the case."

Wil stood to turn off the set and stopped short, shocked by the sudden image of his face. It filled the screen for an instant, then gave way to a long shot.

"In a possibly unrelated incident," the anchorwoman continued, "there was a violent episode of a different kind in the art world today." Wil stepped back from the set. It was the Kent Twitchell mural, shot from across the freeway, with a news reporter standing in the foreground. As the camera panned again, it focused on the center of the forehead, where it found a shock of red. It followed the tracks of dripping color down across the face.

"This many-times life-sized portrait by a Los Angeles muralist was vandalized, perhaps during the night or in the early hours of the morning." The camera reversed and left the whole screen filled with the single image of the face.

232

"Oh, Jesus, Wil!" Sally was horrified.

The impression was unmistakable: a gunshot wound between the eyes, a stream of blood. Wil put his hand to his forehead.

"From the Harbor Freeway, this is Chuck Simon reporting."

Wil switched off the set and forced a grin at Sally. "Sticks and stones," he said. "Symbols can never hurt me. Let's see how it's going."

The picture was a simple head-on portrait, lightly worked in pencil. Unconsciously, perhaps, Sally had given it the flavor of a police sketch, a dehumanizing quality that left the image threatening and cold. Hit first, was Madison's phrase. Before thou gettest hit.

"Are you ready?" he asked. She looked up from the drawing. "For bed," he said.

"Wil..."

"I take the couch. You take the bed up in the loft."

The work lamp caught the highlights in her hair as she looked at him. "Couldn't we...I mean, can you...Can you just hold me?"

He shook his head slowly, smiling. "Well," he said, "you caught me on the right night. I don't know that I could do anything else if I tried." And he helped her from the couch and held her on the way upstairs.

31

S HE LAID her head on the flat of his chest and despite the fact that she said she'd never be able to sleep, she was off within what seemed like moments.

For Wil, sleep came harder and much later. The minimal light that filtered through the slats of the blinds gave the familiar space he'd built and changed over the years a barely tangible definition. Tonight, it felt new—a space that needed to be rediscovered, redefined.

Once before they'd slept like this, with the sword between them, on a stolen night in a graduate studio at Otis. He remembered the night-long protest of the broken spring in the mattress, the specific darkness, the filtered sound of mariachis from the Mexican restaurant down below, and the outline of the student's work against the wall. He remembered the sudden flood of the cold ceiling lights when the janitor came in to clean and found them there, stared drunkenly, switched off the light and left—remembered her worrying for hours that the breach in studio rules was going to be reported, that the Dean himself would show up any moment at the door.

But mostly he remembered the need, the particular weight and perfume of her body, the rhythm of her breathing, the fit where she lay against his body—that peculiar rightness of it that had haunted him and

234

that was right again now. And was timed as wrong—more wrong—than it had been back then.

When sleep did come, it came fitfully. He must have half-wakened ten times through the early morning, unable to judge the time because he'd closed the blinds on the clerestory. His mind kept recalling the list of things that needed to be done. But there was Sally. He didn't want to wake her.

Now, when he finally woke to full consciousness and the blinds could no longer contain the growing daylight, he found her dark hair making wide, abstract brush strokes across the white sheet, and mingling with the short curls of his own hair where it tufted over his T-shirt. Down there, under his shorts, where her thigh was hooked unconsciously across his own, that arrogant, independent-minded piece of the male body was hot and hard between their separate flesh, pulsing taut at the urgent intervals of its own wanting—in part with sheer lust for Sally, and in part, Wil realized practically, with the simple burden of a bladder filled to bursting.

He slid from the bed and went through to the bathroom, pausing to twist the rods on the Levelors, one by one, until the light poured in. By the time he came back to the bedside, Sally's eyes were wide open, and for the first moments of the day, their green had a depth and clarity—a kind of innocence of the world—that made you think you saw right through into the soul. By God, Wil thought, in a rush that overwhelmed him: I love the woman. It was there, that simple. Something he had lived with and knew he always would.

The eyes had a sudden doubt, a question, a sleepy sadness. She opened the bedclothes for him to come back in.

He sat down beside her and kissed her on the lips. "Sally," he said, "you have to know that if I come back in, it's not going to ever be the same. We won't be able to go on pretending to be good friends forever."

The sadness blossomed into a smile that caught him somewhere in the gut and left him breathless.

"I have MaryJo," he heard himself say. "You have Rick."

She shook her head. The telephone rang. He climbed into bed beside her. It rang a second time. They were twins, in the T-shirts he'd found for them last night, white against white sheets, and the sun made the room brilliant with clear light. It rang a third time, and a fourth, then stopped.

Leaning over her, he held the contour of her cheek in his hand and brought the weight of his body forward, kissing her again. Then watching the light change in her eyes as he offered her a hand and raised her upright, sitting, while he pulled the T-shirt over her head and dropped it on the bed. She laughed a little, starting to cover her breasts with her hands but he held them, laid her back down again, stripped off his own shirt and ran a firm hand the length of her torso, from the shoulder down, watching the surface of her skin respond to his touch.

The words that came to his head seemed pitifully inadequate and he left them all unsaid. They made love silently, with concentrated passion —yet with the depth of familiarity of old lovers, with that sense of coming home at last. They made long love, ungreedily, not wanting it to end, as though preparing for the eventuality that they'd never make love again. And when it was over, they lay together, silent still, unable to realize the event in words for fear the reality would be too fragile to outlive the moment.

"Wil..." she said finally.

"I know. Don't let's say it, okay?"

Then the telephone rang again and he broke away from her, twisting to lift the receiver and decided not to. He turned back to Sally and kissed her. The phone still ringing, she pulled the sheet back up to her chin and stared at him.

"Wil...?" she said. It stopped.

He laid the tips of three fingers on her lips to quiet her. "Forgive me," he said. "Okay? Forgive yourself. We're human beings....No, let me finish—it's something I want to say. I've loved you for as many years as I've known you without ever having laid a hand on you, and I'll be goddamned if I let you feel guilty now—or if I feel guilty myself—for this small miracle happening, even if it happened in the middle of whatever else is screwing up our lives at this particular moment. Let's just be happy that it happened and let it go. We'll keep it somewhere in the back of our heads and one day, who knows, it'll light up some other dark moment down the road. It was meant."

She rubbed the moisture from her eyes with the back of her hand and smiled again. "You're right," she said.

"Damn right, I'm right." He gathered her up and held her close to him. "So we'll let it go, okay? We'll let it go and get on with all those other things."

236

It was Wednesday. The day of the Barbara Corton spectacular.

Sally had found the coffeepot and the drip grind by the time Wil was out of the shower, and he could smell it brewing. Winding the towel around his waist, he left the bathroom and found her wrapped in the white robe he had given her to wear that first day when she came to him. She was standing in the studio, staring up at the pictures on the bulletin board.

"So what's this piece?" she said.

"You don't remember it?" he said. "It was the transition between the paintings and the boxes."

"But all these images...? You didn't tell me."

"I had to check it out. I was spooked by it myself when you first came in—it was like some voice from the past. This piece was called *Murder at Flat Rock Springs.*"

They stood together and looked down the row of glossies. "And the boxes?" she asked, when they reached the end. "You wouldn't tell me last night...."

"I was through with them anyway. They'd gotten too closed, too self-contained. I'm looking for something...dirtier, I guess."

Sally turned to look at the tilting chunk of wood. "That's it?" she asked doubtfully.

He laughed. "Not exactly," he said. "Just wait. I'm not ready to talk about it yet."

"Not even to me?"

Wil smiled, and ran a hand through her hair, sitting her at the drafting table. "Not even you, love," he said. "Get the drawing done, okay?"

"Paranoid?" she asked. Some artists hate to talk about new ideas before they're ready because they think someone's going to rip them off.

He shook his head. "You kidding? Chalk it up to simple superstition," he said. "Are you ready for coffee?"

Back in the kitchen, he was pouring out two cups when he heard the key fit into the lock at the street door, and Wil closed his eyes and rested his forehead against the cold refrigerator front. MaryJo. She'd been calling. Down in his gut, he'd known it. He was still naked but for the towel he'd wrapped around his waist. In the studio, Sally was naked too, underneath the terry-cloth robe. It would have been absurd to try to have her hide.

237

"Hey, Wil!" He was going to have to explain. The door began to rattle against the bolts he'd shot last night when they got back and had still not opened this morning. "Wil, let me in, okay?"

He tightened the towel around his waist and went to the door. "I'm coming," he yelled. "Hold it."

The bolts slid out and he turned the thumb lock to let her in. MaryJo stopped short at the threshold, key in hand. Dismayed, Wil looked at her and saw a stranger. Beautiful, but as if he didn't know her anymore. Hair pulled back. Black leotard, fitting tight across the hips and thighs, breasts rounded out into two small mounds by the material's pull. The thin lines on her forehead were tensed into horizontal creases and her eyes were anxious, puzzled.

"My God, Wil! You had me scared out of my mind. I've never known you to bolt the door before."

"Hi, babe."

When she came into his arms, he held her a little too tight. "Wil, are you okay?" she asked. When she tilted her head toward him, he knew he was somehow overdoing the fervor of his kiss. Kicking the door closed behind her, she loosened the towel and dropped it to the floor. He was limp. "Hey, babe?" she said.

"Wil?"

The voice came from the kitchen.

"Wil, are you there?"

MaryJo stiffened, stepped away, and stared at him in disbelief that changed rapidly to anger.

"Listen," he said. "This isn't what you think, okay?" Naked, he stooped to pick up the towel and sensed Sally's presence behind him. MaryJo was staring over his shoulder. "Just wait," he said. "Okay?"

She didn't. She slapped him hard across the face. "You prick," she said. "You first-class shit." She slapped him again. Then she turned and left and slammed the door behind her.

32

THERE HAD to be some tie-up on the freeway. East of La Brea, they were headed into four solid lanes of red brake lights flashing on and off. Mostly on. There was nothing to do but sit and curse the traffic and jerk along in fits and starts. By the time they made the transition to the Harbor Freeway, it was past eleven-thirty and the ramp was jammed solid. When they passed the bend, they could see that the accident had blocked all but a couple of carefully policed lanes of the Harbor Freeway up ahead, a hundred yards north of the intersection, where a chicken truck had rolled and spilled its load. The birds were everywhere, squawking and shedding feathers, and the cops seemed bent on chasing them one by one.

"Goddammit..." said Wil. Any other time, the scene would have been a farce.

"Easy, Wil."

"Easy, hell. It's all going to get away from us, Sally. I can feel it go."

"So? That could be better all around."

They would have cut up through the Sepulveda Pass to the Valley but the drawing had to be dropped off and Wil was curious, too, about the Twitchell mural. They made it past the chickens, and Wil slowed past the mural as the rest of the traffic sped away ahead of them and left them staring at the wide red stain that ran from the forehead fifteen feet to the chin. The hairs on the face stood out with the thickness of fingers, and the pores were pitfalls in the surface. Now, vandalized, this giant other self stared out at Wil balefully—a warning that hit with the force of mocking contempt, shocking, somehow more real than reality itself.

"It hurts?" asked Sally.

Wil nodded, shuddering and accelerating toward the next exit ramp. "It's truly strange," he said. "It does. It gets me right in the middle of the forehead."

She watched him drive. "I always had this image of you as being somehow invulnerable," she said. "Larger than life—like the picture. In control of everything. Then I walk right in and screw it all up for you."

They'd both avoided the subject, but he knew it was on her mind. "You mean MaryJo?" Years of work at the barre had given her a vicious arm. "Maybe we'll patch things up. What about Rick?" he asked. "When we've sorted this mess out, you'll have to sort things out with him."

"We'll see. When he gets back."

Instinctively, out of a kind of self-preservation, he reached for the easier level of the mundane: "Does he stay in touch when he's away?"

"If he called last night or this morning, he'll be wondering where the hell I am."

"Would he worry?"

She frowned. "I'm not sure. He might. I suppose I've always been there, in the past, when he wanted to reach me. In any case, he's sure to have left a message on the tape if he called."

"You can't call him?"

She wasn't sure that she wanted to, and Wil could read the ambivalence in her hesitation. "If I could remember the hotel," she said. "I have it somewhere at home."

They left the freeway at Third and cut through downtown, turning south again to come back up Fourth one-way. Sally ran into the police headquarters with the drawing while Wil idled the old Le Sabre around the block. As if in siege, an army of the dispossessed and the alienated swarmed through the four streets that surrounded the building, dreadlocked, unwashed and uncared for, incoherent, shuffling, dull-eyed, without hope. Instead of making the second pass he'd planned on, Wil stopped in the red zone after the first time around, and waited for her at the curb.

She ran down the few brick steps and tumbled into the front seat.

240

"My God," she said. "It's a war zone here."

Watching for the break in traffic in the mirror, Wil eased the Buick out from the curb. "Did you see DiPaolo?"

"No. They said he was out to lunch," she said. "But, listen, they took the drawing out and I took a kind of objective look at it. You're right, you know. This man's not the one to call the shots."

"It's in the picture?"

There was a small knot of lines that gathered between her eyes as she looked at the drawing in her memory. "What's in the picture is a man with the wrong kind of intelligence—more a cunning. I wouldn't say he had the patience or the foresight to plan over a period of years. The guy's impetuous. He's the kind that acts on impulse. I should have seen that when he was there."

"You did," Wil pointed out.

They passed through the northern end of Pershing Square and headed up the hill past the public library, whose pyramid roof glimmered golden in the sunlight. "Okay," he said. "Then who?"

"Stu Ray? At least he has to know more than he's told you. Why's he holding out?"

Wil stared ahead moodily through the windshield as he drove. One thing was certain: He couldn't go on simply trusting the old pegs he'd always used to pin down what the real world was about. The ground had shifted, revealing gaping cracks he'd never known were there.

Stu Ray. Good old irascible Stu. Stu, who had more information at his fingertips about the movement of artworks in Los Angeles than anyone else. Who seemed to feel so threatened that he flew off the handle at a moment's notice. Stu, who was giving Raul and Madison their orders. And Don Henschler.

They pulled off the freeway at Mulholland and drove in silence up the hill to Sally's house, nosing into the driveway behind the Celica. Wil killed the motor and they sat in silence, looking up at the white façade.

"It looks quiet enough," said Wil. "Let me check around in back." He opened the car door.

"Wait," she said. "I'm staying with you."

Sourdough mooched around the corner and greeted her with an indignant yowl. "Oh, God," she said. She bent to scratch the animal's head. "Can you believe, I forgot this creature's food last night." This morning, too. It was past twelve-thirty.

They followed the side path and came to the rear door with its broken pane of glass. Wil reached in, unhooked the chain, and opened the door from inside. "You know someone to call, to come and fix this glass?" he asked. "It's an open invitation."

The house was silent, stuffy with trapped heat from the Santa Ana. Sally took care of the cat, and they checked through each of the rooms together, opening windows as they went. The place was empty.

Back in the kitchen, Sally looked at the blinking light on the tape machine. "Oh, Jesus," she said. "Can you do it, Wil? I don't think I've got the nerve."

He let the tape squawk back through the messages and punched the start button. There were several hang-ups. Then Paula: "Sally, honey. It's late Tuesday night. Ken drives me crazy. He refused to breathe a word, but he told me you might need a friend. What's up, for Christ's sake? Give me a call when you get home?"

There was Leon Drake: "Hey, great! A woman of poise and class. Since you called, I'm guessing I've been forgiven for yesterday. See you at your place, around three. I know the way."

Then there were two more hang-ups before Rick: "Sally, it's Rick. I'm concerned about you. It's nine A.M., your time. Either you're not home, or you left the damn machine on. I called several times last night and again this morning—you'll find the hang-ups on the tape. Last time was around eleven. What's happening? I'll keep trying, okay?"

Sally listened to a couple more hang-ups and switched off the answering machine.

"You think he's given up?" she asked.

"Brad? Yes. I thought so yesterday."

"Thank God." But she stood there, her hand resting on the telephone, and Wil put an arm around her waist. "Call," he said. "You'll feel better."

Sally dug out the number of Rick's hotel from the basket by the telephone and stared at it.

"What should I tell him?" she said. "About this afternoon?"

"Tell him the truth. You're going out to Barbara's event with a bunch of friends."

She dialed the number and waited.

"Regency."

"Yes. I'm calling for Mr. Rick Horan. Will you put me through to his room?"

242

"Yes, ma'am."

The phone went through a series of clicks before it began to ring in the room. Five rings. Six. The operator came back on the line again. "I'm sorry. Room 510 doesn't seem to be answering."

"Can I leave a message?"

"Sure thing."

"Tell Mr. Horan that his wife called to say not to worry, everything's fine. I'll call him back this evening, around ten. Chicago time. Thanks."

"You bet. I'll see that he gets the message."

Sally hung up the phone.

"Sally...," said Wil.

"Don't tell me," she said. "I can handle it. Let's get some lunch."

Sometimes you forget about the mountains in Los Angeles. They shimmer in the background like a Hollywood set, put there to hold the desert back from the Pacific Ocean. Too often, as in the past few days, even the closer foothills fade into the haze. But today the mountains were back, looming, imperious, clear.

Wil kept his eye on them sideways as he stooped to fill the Le Sabre's tank. Over beyond, the desert flattened out and reached toward Las Vegas.

He wanted answers. At ten bucks, he lost patience and slung the nozzle back in place on the pump.

"Some sight, huh?" said the man in the cashier's booth, his eyes planted firmly in the distance. He refocused them on the credit card and passed it through the machine.

"Some sight," said Wil.

He looked at his watch as he pulled out from the gas station. Two thirty-five. Half an hour, and Sally would be hitting the freeway in Leon's car. Stu Ray was already there. Merging back into the traffic, Wil put his foot down on the gas pedal and watched the speedometer move past sixty. Madison had said he wouldn't leave before three, but Wil wanted to be sure.

It was nearly five minutes to when Wil turned into the customer parking area at City Lights. The lot was empty.

"Anyone home?" yelled Wil. He walked down between rows of towering hulks, the glittering signs of half a decade back. Stacked up like this, they had the appearance of beached whales, awkward and lifeless and out of their element. At the end of the yard, the half-door to the office was left open, but there was no one at the desk. Wil tried the neighboring warehouse and was rewarded with a stubbled face that peered at him with watery eyes.

"Where's the manager?" asked Wil.

He found the manager of City Lights dreaming out by the chain-link fence where he, too, seemed enraptured by the distant silhouette of the San Gabriels. He was a short man, stout, with abundant waves of hair left over from the hippie days. A soft camouflage hat was crushed down over it, leaving long curls cascading over his shoulders.

"Did the Raiders arrive?" Wil asked.

The man turned to look at him unhurriedly. "They called," he said. "They're running late. Be here in a while."

"You're the manager?" asked Wil.

"That's me. Gus Larson. Who the hell are you?" He stuck out a flabby hand. Wil knew the name.

"Have we met?" he asked. "I'm Wil Garretson."

The manager grinned. "We met," he said. "Years ago. I used to be in your racket."

Of course. Neon work, way back in the sixties. "Sure, Gus, I remember. You still working?"

"Working?" Gus grinned again and fanned an arm to indicate the yard. "Working? Man, I'm the resident genius around here." He burst out laughing. "If you mean art, no. I gave up on that stuff years ago. For myself, anyway. I still get the occasional artist in here. Most don't know their ass from their elbow, so I help them out."

"Like Barbara?"

"Corton?" He roared with laughter again. "Yeah, I got her set up. I was up there with her last week. Should be a good show."

He looked up at the mountains again, nodding wistfully to himself.

"You're not going to be there?"

"Hey, are you kidding?" The blue eyes, almost hidden under the tough sprouts of his brows, turned to Wil again. "I got too much to keep me busy right here."

A pickup with the Raiders logo turned in from the highway and pulled up at the office. Madison climbed out.

"Hey, pal," Gus yelled across the yard. "You'll find it all inside." He waved a direction and turned back to Wil. "You with this character, then?"

244

"I'm hitching a ride out there with him," Wil said. "I hear there's a heap of neon out there?"

"Yeah. It's the owner's wife." Gus returned Madison's wave and stretched an arm to point him toward the office. "She took a shine to our Barbara's work and gave her the run of the yard. Barbara unearthed some crates that had gotten waylaid on the way to the New Orleans World Fair. Some clown went broke and they never got there. Someone cashed in on the insurance, someone else took the write-off, and Barbara got the tubes. That's how it happens, man."

"What's she doing for power out there? She must need a good deal of juice."

Gus grinned again. "Donated," he said. "She liked the idea of a natural source, so she got the owner of one of those wind farms twisted around her finger. She smiles nicely and says please and he jumps. We're talking megavolts, project that size. I got her hooked up to the main line Friday."

Madison emerged from the office and waved a sheet of paper. This time, Gus pointed him toward the warehouse. The resident genius left the footwork to others.

"High-tension wire, she needs," he explained. "You always think you have enough of that stuff, then you run out."

"How does it work?" asked Wil. "Does the wind farm sell its own electricity?"

"Sort of, in a way. It's like a bank, see? It pays in the power to the electric company, feeding it in through a meter. Then it can draw on its account, feeding out. Like when you pay your money into the bank, you don't get your same money back. Just money. Same principle. The guy's just letting her draw on his account."

"Nice guy."

"Nice lady." Gus Larson's belly shook where it drooped over a thick leather belt.

The man with wet eyes stuck his head around the warehouse door. "Says here she needs another transformer," he yelled.

"Load it up!" Gus shouted back.

"She's all set up, I guess?" Wil asked.

"She still has a gang working out there, stringing up tubes. A couple technicians for the kliegs."

"Kliegs?"

"Oh yeah. She's flooding the whole valley behind the piece with light.

245

Then there's this pyramid at the top. There's people say those things are supposed to give off some kind of a discharge. Energy, they say. That's the effect she's looking for."

"Live and learn," said Wil.

"You bet."

Looking back at him as they pulled away, Wil had the impression that Gus would rather be going with them. He thought again about Stu Ray. It was like that, with any artist who'd dropped out. Most had regrets when they saw someone else's work going up. Like giving up smoking. Once you've had that high of getting something made, you're hooked for life. You don't give up.

33

THREE O'CLOCK came and went with no sign of Leon. Ten past. Sally was already packed and waiting, refusing herself the comfort of checking through the guest-room blinds every second minute. The house felt too large. She sat on an upright chair in the dining room and waited, wishing that Wil hadn't had to leave so soon. His absence already gnawed at her, like an emptiness. She mustn't let that happen....

Three-twenty.

The telephone rang. She'd set the answering machine.

Leon? He could have been delayed. She dashed back to the kitchen and turned up the sound in time to hear the end of Rick's taped announcement, annoyed to feel her heartbeat racing out of control again.

It's okay, she told herself.

The caller paused for what seemed like an interminable second after the beep, and Sally stood there, willing him to speak. Him?

"Sally?"

It was Paula.

Sally let her breath out slowly and waited with a finger on the switch. Did she want to talk to Paula?

"Sally, I don't know what's happening to you, honey, but I sure wish you'd let me help. Are you there?" Sally shook her head. "If you're there, please pick up, okay?"

247

There was something inside her that wanted to and something that rebelled. She couldn't. Then she thought she heard the sound of a car outside the door and turned the sound back down. By the time she got to the front to answer Leon's ring she could feel the moisture gathering in the small of her back and she was breathless, angry with herself, since she'd worked so hard to be ready in good time: She needed to be cool and poised.

Then she was in so much of a hurry she forgot to check through the fisheye lens that it really was Leon and realized as she began to open the door that she hadn't and half-closed it, felt too foolish, opened it again and stood there, confused and unsure what to say.

It was Leon. The white Corvette was parked in the driveway behind him, roof down, glowing in the sunlight.

"Oh," she said. "It's you."

"You were expecting someone else?" he asked.

"No. I was just wondering if you were planning to come at all."

He looked at his watch. "I'm late," he agreed. "I'm sorry, Sally. Some things came up at the studio. Are you ready?"

"Sure." She hoped it sounded easy. "Just a couple of things. Maybe you could take my bag to the car?"

She went back to the kitchen to find the message light blinking. Paula had evidently given up. Tearing Rick's hotel number from the notepad, she dropped it into her bag and stopped by the bathroom to check her face in the mirror. All morning, she'd tried without success to see herself as Wil saw her. What she saw staring back at her was a face that was tired around the mouth and eyes, accentuating the tiny lines which had already started to appear.

"Sally?"

"Ready. I'm coming."

In the hall, she found him running his finger across the surface of a piece he'd done maybe fifteen years before. "Resin," he said. The color glowed through several layers of subsurface. "Can you believe, I've forgotten how I did it."

"I saw another earlier piece of yours yesterday," said Sally. "In Judy Townsend's office. A print."

She watched him, but there was barely any reaction beyond the smile. "Judy," he said, hoisting Sally's bag. "Judy, Judy. Great gal. Let's go."

Outside, it was the irony that fed her a jolt of pain as she watched Leon Drake load into the trunk of his dapper Corvette convertible the

248

same bag Jimmy Sewell had thrown in the back of a battered Datsun pickup with its cheap little camper shell. And that was, what, four, five days before?

"It's great," Leon told her, pausing with his hand on the ignition, "that you're coming. Bless you, Sally."

Who was this man? she wondered. What did he have to prove to her?

A stranger. She watched his face as he concentrated on the curves, headed down toward the freeway. The profile was so familiar, you almost felt you knew him. But under the surface, nothing. He reached forward for a pair of sunglasses and put them on, turning to smile at her—and, with the shades, the smile seemed a part of the armor, polished, impenetrable.

"This car," he yelled. "It's a wonderful drive, but you can't hear very much. A real conversation killer." He shrugged an apology with his smile and picked a cassette from the caddy by his door, feeding it into the tape deck. Sally recognized the sophisticated paranoia of the Talking Heads.

The idea had seemed simple yesterday. Let's find out, she said. Today —strange car, strange man, strange destination. Things falling apart. People. Rick in Chicago. Ken Stone in his office in Century City and Paula in Encino. DiPaolo downtown LA. Wil on this same freeway, headed in the same direction. Wil. Who made love to her, this morning. She felt him, down where she'd welcomed him inside her—another stranger? No, she thought. Not Wil. She looked around, as though the Raiders truck might be on their tail. Where was it? Ahead of them? Behind? As though it mattered, she told herself. It was traveling at some other intersection of time and space. A mile? Ten miles? Another world away. It was someplace else.

And Jimmy, too. Someplace else.

They hit traffic east of downtown but had broken loose from it by four o'clock and headed east on 10. Leon drove fast, with easy concentration, alert for the Highway Patrol. The sound of the wind and the freeway traffic made talk impossible, and Sally surrendered unwillingly to the necessity of isolation, resting her head back on the headrest, closing her eyes against the sun.

Where was the man whose picture she'd made?

With a growing, aching void where her stomach used to be, Sally tried to sort them all out from each other but the faces seemed to take a life of their own, collapsing, all these men, into a single picture—a kind

249

of composite man, strange, distant, unknowable. "Psycho killer, *qu'est-ce que c'est...*" Why French? she wondered. "Better run-run, run-run-run away."

"A penny!" She realized suddenly that Leon had been yelling at her through the wind.

"A penny?" she asked.

"For your thoughts."

Funny, there was a kind of innocence, a boyishness about him, too. "You wouldn't want to hear," she shouted back.

She looked up ahead, at the mountains that had taken Jimmy Sewell. They carried the horizon on broad shoulders, waiting, patient, she thought, biding their own time.

Past San Bernardino the car continued east through the San Gorgonio Pass to the point where wind farms fill the hills and valleys with their forests of towers and swinging blades. Ignoring the Palm Springs exit, Leon finally slowed and left the freeway, turning north through the desert into the Coachella Valley.

Ten minutes north, they left the highway, turning up into the hills. The white car trailed a plume of yellow dust where it had drifted across the tarmac of the narrow road, and sped up through foothills—giant piles of boulders, spewed out from the maw of some ancient volcano and left here to weather over millions of years. Between the boulders, cactus and parched scrub brush found meager lots of dirt to put their roots down, and the occasional century plant sent up the stalk of a long-dried blossom.

"You know this country?" Leon asked.

She shook her head. "Barely," she said.

"A little further up, it plateaus off. It's not so barren up by the ranch."

They turned off the hardtop past a warren of mailboxes, passing under a rough wooden ranch sign that spanned the access road.

"Abandon hope," grinned Leon, nodding up at the sign, "all ye who enter here." The weathered skull of a steer returned his grin, with vacant holes for teeth. "It's the old Bar T that's subdivided now into maybe twenty properties—mostly weekend homes and mountain retreats. And my place. It's wonderful. We're barely in sight of each other, let alone hearing."

Small comfort, Sally thought. From here, the desert stretched for countless miles below and the sky seemed infinite above. "How long have you had the ranch?" she asked.

"Maybe seven years." He came to a near stop. "Over there's where Barbara Corton's doing her number," he said.

It was about a half mile off the road, a hill rising out of the wilderness floor, almost a perfect cone. Shading her eyes, Sally could make out a small knot of vehicles at its base, where the sun angled dazzlingly off chrome parts.

Was Wil there yet?

Leon slipped back into gear. The gravel road soon gave way to a dusty trail, narrow and filled with potholes. The Corvette yawed and rolled for another half mile before they reached a screened electronic gate.

"The clicker's in the glove compartment," he said. Sally reached in and touched the pressure pad, and the gate swung open to admit them into a compound, a manicured oasis, rich with trees and plants. A swimming pool glittered turquoise in the sunlight and, beyond it, the wood retainers of a small corral.

"This is incredible," Sally said.

Leon grinned. "It may not be much," he said. "But it's mine. Sam Beckman built it, the movie mogul? Then his kids grew up and he got bored, I guess. Or divorced. Who knows? I bought it from him."

Down by the wood frame house, a couple of cars were already parked. "Lee Lawrence, the designer," Leon told her, pointing to the pink T-bird. "He's up here for the show. He probably brought his friend. You'll meet her."

"Who else?" she asked. Parked beside the T-bird, the high-slung jeep with its battered cab looked like a relic from a scrap yard.

"Jon and Janice," he said. He opened the door for her and took her arm. "Kid artists. They'll bring the bags in for us, don't worry. They stay here all year and keep the place up for me. It's a great deal for them. Food and lodging. A little cash. They look after the horses and the animals. Hey, Jack. Down!" An oversized, scraggly shepherd mutt had jumped him as he opened the car door, offering generous licks from a lolling pink tongue. "This one here's Jackson Pollock. He's a stray."

"Jackson Pollock?"

He laughed. "Fits, huh?" He gestured over toward the paddock. "The horses are Leo and Angel. A Renaissance pair." He checked his watch. "Let's get inside," he said. "I've got a couple of things that need to be taken care of."

If Leon was a crook, she thought, he'd chosen an improbable setting for it. Peaceful, removed. A tiny paradise. Inside, the house was done in southwestern-ranch style—white, terra-cotta-tiled, and sparsely furnished with simple wood chairs and tables and low, ample couches covered in soft pastels. There was art everywhere, on the walls and tables. Sally paused by the door to gaze into the large white spaces of an old Sam Francis. Vestigial passages of blue and yellow at the edges served only to allow you to define the dizzying expanse of white.

"Real art?" she asked.

"Not that stuff," Leon said, an edge of irritation in his voice. "That's not what I meant. I'll show you later. Jon! Janice!"

"You have a studio up here?"

"I'll show you that, too. Janice!"

"I'm here." She was very pregnant, straw-haired, calm. She had a comfortable, freckled country face with a beatific smile, and she wore one of those voluminous Indian print dresses from the sixties. "Hi, Leon," she said. "Welcome home."

The man who followed her in was slightly shorter than his wife, bearded, trim at the waist. His blue jeans were well worn and his boots scuffed and dusty from the stables.

"Hey, Leon!" he said.

Leon returned both greetings with a nod, preoccupied. "I see that Lee's arrived already."

"He arrived an hour ago with Jackie. They're long gone. I saddled up for them and they went out riding."

Leon laid an arm around Jon's shoulder. "This," he said, "is Sally Horan. A friend. She'll be sleeping upstairs, okay? Front room. There's a couple of things I need to do in the studio, so I'd like you guys to get her settled in." He turned to Sally with a smile. "Give me half an hour?" he said. He hurried down a short flight of steps and disappeared.

"That's the main suite down there," said Jon. "Leon has his studio there, right next to his room." He stuck out a hand. "Sally, hi! This is my wife, Janice. Leon likes to think he owns this place, but it's really ours. We tolerate him, when he gets up here. If you need anything, Sally, you check in with us. I'll get your stuff from the car."

He came back with Sally's bag and led the way upstairs to a darkened bedroom, where the shutters were still closed. "We weren't expecting you," he explained. "But the bed's made anyway." He laid Sally's bag on it and crossed the room to throw the shutters open to a flood of light. "The view's incredible," he said. "Enjoy it! And don't forget—anything you need..."

The door closed behind him and she sat for a moment on the crisp new counterpane that covered the bed. The room was beautiful, anonymous. She felt suddenly more alone than she could remember feeling since that very first night she'd spent away from home, as a child, on an exchange in France. Excited, strangely awed by the unfamiliar environment—not its opulence, it wasn't that... but its curious perfection.

She unzipped the bag and retrieved her bath things from the top, then went to the bathroom and switched on the light. One whole wall was mirror; the rest—walls, floor and ceiling, were tiled in matte black slate. The tub, in the same material, was sunk into the floor, and the ceiling-mounted shower, uncurtained, had a huge irregular black slab of slate as its base, surrounded by a bed of black pebbles where the water drained. A single plant, its leaves a glossy green, stood in a black clay pot in the center of the room.

"My God!" she said aloud.

The bedside clock showed ten past six. She stripped off the clothes she'd traveled in and turned on the shower. Soaping away the grime of the highway, she watched the suds being swept down by the water, settle among the pebbles, and rinse away. Then she tilted her head to the ceiling and allowed the water to stream down through her hair.

She rubbed herself dry and wrapped the towel around her. Padding barefoot across the tiles and the pale brown carpet in the bedroom, she stepped out into the brilliant sunlight on the balcony and gazed down over the mountainside where it fell to the desert floor.

Jon was right. The view was incredible.

Her elbows resting on the balcony, Sally watched a hawk spread its wings as it drifted into a thermal, and rise in lazy circles way above the canyon.

Closer to home, to the south side of the house atop an outcropping of rocks, she was surprised to see an orange wind sock.

The plastic tube was half-filled with still air, faintly obscene, rising and drooping lazily in an indifferent breeze. Below it, spaced at intervals, was a row of electrical fixtures that she took to be landing lights.

253

A runway? Leaning farther out across the wooden railing, she managed to see back along the path of lights to the yellow belly of a helicopter.

Jesus! Sally closed her eyes and stepped back from the railing. Her head seemed to take a swing out over the precipice, dizzy. Then the fear gripped her, hard and cold, a knot like a boulder in the abdomen. Jesus!

They came into view, from the unseen rear end of the helicopter. Two men. One of them was Leon Drake. The other was Brad Michaels.

She stumbled over the threshold back into the room and froze, her back against the wall. Leave the bag, get some clothes on. Move.

But she stood there.

It couldn't be more than a mile to the Corton site. If she could just get out of the compound before Leon came looking for her again. He'd said thirty minutes, and it had to be more like forty-five already.

Now.

She ran to the bed and ripped the clothes from the bag, tossing things aside until she came to a sweat suit. Bra. Undies. She dropped the towel and tripped on the elastic waistband of her panties, then fumbled with the bra and pinched her nipples as she shoved her breasts down into the cups. Sweat suit.

The laces of her tennis shoes were in a knot. Jesus! She tried to force her feet into them anyway, but it didn't work. Another minute, two minutes, sorting out the tangle.

Her purse?

Forget it. She raked both hands through her hair instead of the brush.

The door handle worked silently, and Sally stepped out on the landing, stooping to where she got a view of the front door. It was closed. Holding on to the rail, she took the stairs one at a time, on tiptoe, cursing the creak of the wood beneath the carpet.

She had reached the bottom step when the door burst open, three feet from her.

"Sally?" Her face must have registered its shock. "Did I scare you? Gee, I'm sorry. I'd no idea..." Leon closed the door behind him. "Are you ready for the tour? Are you okay?"

He reached for her arm. "I'm fine. It was just...I wasn't expecting the door to open suddenly, like that."

"You want to sit down awhile? A drink?" He was solicitous, kind.

"No, really. I'm fine."

Outside had to be safer than in. She let Leon take her arm as he

254

opened the door again. A motor started close by and, as they stepped out into the sunshine, she saw the jeep pull away from its parking place, with Jon at the wheel and Janice in back. Next to Jon, the man was gazing out at her with the same blank smile with which he'd stripped her yesterday.

"They're leaving?" Sally asked.

"They're just headed down for some supplies. Don't worry, they'll be back."

"Who's the guy?" she asked.

"The guy?" he said. "That's Brad. A friend. You'll get to meet him later."

"Leon..." she said.

He stopped to look at her, turning her toward him with a smile.

"Could we..."

"Could we what, Sally?"

She took a breath and it all came out in a rush. "Could we drive over to the Corton site? I mean, why don't we go on over while it's still light?"

Leon looked doubtful. "I don't see too much point in that," he said slowly. "There's nothing happening there till dark."

Her eyes were searching everywhere now, desperate for inspiration. "I'd like to meet some of the people," she said.

"Come on, that's bullshit, Sally. We didn't come out here for that. You see too much of all those folks in town. Out here..." His eyes followed the horizon line, out over the valley. "Out here it's different," he said. "Come on, I'll show you around."

34

W IL CHECKED his watch as the pickup rolled across the rough track to the foot of the hill. It was six-fifteen, getting ready for evening—though the sun still had a good hour to run. The coffee stop had taken longer than he'd bargained for, and he was impatient to check out Sally's situation. He craned his neck to find the spot where he remembered Leon's ranch to be.

It was over there, somewhere, at the ridge of the hill, looking down across the Coachella Valley.

Madison found a spot to park alongside the dozen other vehicles that were clustered around Barbara Corton's base of operations. A flurry of dust flew up around the cab when he braked, and started to settle back on the windshield.

"Watch out," said Madison. "It's Stu."

He was right. Stu was right there, with Barbara, waiting for the delivery. Madison, he'd expected. He was sweating it out in the heat, and the anger showed on his face when he saw Wil in the cab.

"Jesus Christ, Garretson!" he yelled. He ripped open the passenger door and started to pull him out. "How many more times do I need to warn you off? What the fuck are you doing, riding in my truck?"

"Take it easy, Stu..."

"Don't easy me, Garretson." He turned to Madison. "You know the law," he said. "The equipment isn't even insured for people who aren't employees...."

"Lay off of him, Stu—"

"Lay off! Jesus Christ!" Ray lunged his weight at Wil and shoved him off-balance.

"Hey, Stu!" It was Barbara this time who tried to calm him but he elbowed her out of his way and lunged again. Caught in the chest while he was still off-balance, Wil went down and landed in the sun-warmed, gritty dust in front of the pickup and Stu was after him again. He held his hands up to protect his face and got kicked in the belly instead. He rolled with it, and the boot glanced off, its heel catching him in the lower ribs.

"Stu...Hold it, man!" He managed to grab the boot and brought it around in an arc, swinging Ray off-balance, too, and bringing him down "Listen..."

Then Madison and Barbara were there, between them, standing, holding them off from each other on the ground. They lay still for a moment, panting, hot.

"Get Garretson out of here!"

"Stu, no one's going anywhere, for God's sake!" Barbara squatted down beside him, catching his arm. "I thought you guys were friends for a hundred years."

Wil pulled himself up to lean against the pickup. "Leave him be," he said. "The guy's got a lousy temper, is all. Stu..." He got up, offering a hand to pull Ray up from the ground. Ray took it, heaved himself up, glared at Wil, then walked away without another word.

"Let's get this thing unloaded," Madison said. He went around the back and jerked the tailgate open.

"Wil...?" Barbara Corton was unhappy, leaving it like this. "What the hell is happening around here?"

Wil dusted himself off. "When I know myself," he said, "I'll tell you. Meantime, the next best thing is to move ahead with the show. Do you have everything you need?"

She looked over the load in the bed of the truck. "I think so, yes."

The hill she'd chosen rose two hundred feet above them from the wilderness of scrub. Behind it, the mass of the mountains climbed to an extended ridge and made a clear outline against the intense blue sky. On the next slope to the south, in almost surreal elegance, stood the power source—a field of wind generators, maybe thirty of them, ranked like a great, silent army of hi-tech giants. Their blades swung idly now, uncoordinated in the lackluster breeze.

The two-way radio crackled and Barbara unhitched the unit from her belt.

"Barbara?"

"Yeah?"

"Barbara, Bernie here."

Wil recognized Trost's voice. "Say hello from Wil Garretson," he said.

"We're going to need that last stretch of cable awful soon now," Bernie's voice crackled on. "Has it come in yet? Over."

"Bernie? Yes, it's here. We'll unload the transformer that we need down here, then we'll ship the HT wire around the other side in the pickup. Is there access up the hill? Over."

"Yeah, Barbara. Some of the way. I think we can run it out from the end of the road okay. Over."

"Great. I'll check in when the pickup's on its way. By the way, Wil Garretson just arrived. He says hello. Over."

"Garretson? Is he there?"

"Sure is."

The radio crackled again in her hand.

"Will you give him a message?"

"He's listening," said Barbara.

"Wil? That information you were looking for? I got it. You're in for a shocker. Check the glove compartment of my car. The door's open. We'll talk later. Over."

Wil nodded. "Tell him thanks," he said.

"Wil says thanks," said Barbara. "Get back to work, Bernie. Over."

"And out," he said. Barbara hitched the radio back on her belt and went to the rear of the pickup to help get the transformer unloaded.

Bernie's car was a yellow Volvo that he'd driven for twenty years. It was soaking up what remained of the heat and light of the day in the parking area and the door was unlocked, as he'd promised. Wil sat down in the passenger seat, his feet stretched out into the dust, and turned the latch on the glove compartment.

Inside, there was a small, neat pile of papers, service manuals, warranties. At the top, in an unmarked envelope, Wil found the photocopy of a legal document, folded in four. He unfolded it and ran his eye quickly down the page. Tristate. Articles of Incorporation.

Wil read on, and the cold knot in his belly turned to solid ice.

"Madison!" he yelled.
Wil stuffed the Xerox into the pocket of his pants.
"Madison!"
"He left already," someone shouted back. And Wil could see from here where the pickup had left a trail of dust around the curve of the hill. He checked to see if Bernie had left the keys in the ignition, then slammed the Volvo's door and scrambled up on the fender of the pickup truck next door, gazing out across the mesa.

God help me, he thought. He checked his watch again. They could have arrived as much as two hours ago.

He had to reach Sally.

He'd been here only once before—Leon generally kept it private from the rest of the art world—but he remembered that Barbara's hill was located to the south and west of Leon's place, one of the last in the range of foothills before the final drop to the desert floor. From here, even with the gain in height, the ranch was hidden from sight, but Wil gauged pretty much where it had to be and picked out the shortest way along the trails. A mile. Maybe a little more.

He looked back at the horizon. Evening had already begun to encroach on the daylight, and it looked to be another half hour or so before the sun went down.

He'd run it. Ten minutes. To track down a vehicle he could use was going to take more time than it was worth. He set off at a steady lope down the rutted dirt track that cut a path through the sagebrush down toward the ranch.

The light continued to fade. Fast—faster than he'd expected. Within minutes, the potholes and bumps that were clearly visible when he started out became dangerously difficult to distinguish from the rest of the uneven trail. He zigzagged north a ways, conserving energy with a steady pace, then east, and north again before he came to the electronic gate within fifty yards of where he'd calculated it to be.

The gate was shut. The eye of a closed-circuit camera reflected the setting sun from behind it, and Wil remembered the bank of monitors stacked over the refrigerator. The bell from the gate rang in back, he remembered, behind the kitchen, and one of the kids who looked after the place would check on the closed circuit before they buzzed you in. Farther down, though, there was a gap in the fence he'd climbed through on his morning run and he followed the trail on down to where it used to be. It was still there.

Once in the compound, he scrambled back up to the driveway and slowed to a fast walk as he continued on toward the ranch house past the two cars, side by side—Lee Lawrence's Thunderbird and Leon's white Corvette.

The front door was unlocked, but despite the growing dusk there were no lights.

"Leon?" he called. "Anyone home?"

He pushed the door open farther and reached for a light switch, peering into the house. The run had left his heart rate high, and the sweat was cold where it gathered at the base of his spine. Close to the mountaintops behind him, the sun had lost its warmth and cast long shadows from the west.

"Leon? Sally?"

Wil walked on into the sitting room and waited for some responding sound. But the house was silent, dark, its white walls and corridors returning only the sound of his own voice, unanswered.

"Leon?"

He put his head around the corner of the door to Leon's suite and found it similarly in darkness. The kitchen was deserted, too, as was the guest suite in the back part of the house downstairs—though a tangled pile of designer clothes on the bed was added testimony to Lee Lawrence's arrival.

"Leon? Sally?" Wil called once more upstairs before he left the house and jogged around the side past the tennis court to the crest of the little hill beyond it. Leon had put a bench up here, from which he liked to survey his empire. Above it, the wind sock flapped uneasily at the top of its flagpole.

Inherited from the previous owner, the fabled heliport that Leon never used was a standing joke among friends. But the helicopter resting on the landing pad below was real enough. Wil stared down at the plexi bubble that enclosed its cockpit and the long, slow torque of the rotor blades at rest. Jesus, he thought. No. The pain sliced through his chest like a knife.

"Sally!"

As he searched around, fighting down the desperation, a new scenario began to lock in place with a sudden and dreadfully sequential logic. Jim Sewell, shot from the cliff, and Sally, arriving at Wil's place on Sunday afternoon. The Leon Drakes in Jimmy's studio. The call from the pay phone: It was Leon who'd known when Wil would be out of his studio the night Henschler was killed, and Leon who'd lost his cool when Wil left early from the West Beach. The Bird in the Bush was a perfect front for international sales, and Leon had the contacts needed to pull it off. He had Judy Townsend running the place. So it was no coincidence, surely, that he'd run into Sally at Charlie Strauss's place on Melrose. All it took was one quick call from Judy.

"Real art," Leon had said? Wil felt the chill in the breeze, now, coming down from the mountain, and he shivered. He'd been so goddamn smug, so cocksure about Sally coming out here. He'd encouraged it.

"Sally!" he shouted, listening to the name reverberate through the dusk.

He scanned the compound one more time from the top of the little hill. A timer must have tripped the underwater pool lights at that moment, for they went on suddenly and silently, conjuring a hard-edge rectangle of translucent blue in the area between the tennis court and the paddock. Behind, up by the stables, a single bulb was lit above the door.

Wil ran down the hill and skirted the tennis court. The surface of the pool was unrippled and the pool house was deserted.

"Sally?"

The stable, on the far side of the small corral, was a long, two-story structure built into the hillside. Half of its first floor was open to the weather, and bales of hay were stacked in an open section in the middle, with tack strung up along the walls in back. Wil pulled a pitchfork from the rack and hefted it self-consciously, examining its three steel tines. This was crazy.

Armed with the implement, he moved quietly ahead into the stable. to the right, a passage opened the way to a pair of stalls, their doors left open now that the occupants were gone. To the left, a second corridor led through a door that had been propped ajar with a worn salt lick. Beside the door, the tiny red and green lights of a security system blinked in rapid sequence.

His heart pounding wildly, Wil ran a hand over the cold surface of the aluminum panel and stared at the lights. More craziness. The secur-

261

ity itself would have been surprising in a stable, but the heavy fireproof door and the construction of the walls suggested more than a stable. The place was a vault.

Inside the fireproof door, a second, lighter door was held closed by a hydraulic hinge. Wil pushed it gently.

The dim glow of bare bulbs in the stable left him unprepared for the brilliance of the interior space. Initially blinded, he took some moments to adjust and was still unsure he wasn't imagining what he saw.

A gallery?

And Leon was there, with Sally. For a moment the three of them stood and looked at each other in stunned silence.

Sally moved first. "Wil!" She stepped firmly away from Leon and held her arms open for a hug. "This is incredible! What a great surprise!" But if her voice expressed delight, her eyes were telegraphing other messages. Wil switched his gaze to Leon, wary, and he firmed his grip on the pitchfork with his right hand as he hugged Sally to him with the left.

"Wil?" Leon was bewildered, half-smiling. He looked from one to the other of them. "Jesus, man, what the fuck are you doing here?" He halfway laughed, then stopped. "My God," he said. "What's with you both? What's with the weapon, Wil? You Tarzan, me Jane? I surrender." He raised his hands and started to laugh again.

Wil kept his arm around Sally but took his eyes off Leon long enough to glance around the walls. If he'd thought there was nothing left to surprise him, he'd been wrong. He was stunned. There were no more than half a dozen paintings hung, but each one was a miracle in itself. A Matisse, an early one, Wil guessed, hung alongside what had to be a Delaunay and a Kandinsky. Opposite, two Monets from the Water-lily period, both small, managed to occupy the whole length of a wall with an incredibly powerful presence.

"Leon..." Wil stepped forward, half in front of Sally, leaving her protected.

The movement wasn't lost on Leon. "Wil," he said. He held his hands out in front of him. "Wil, hold everything, man. Just tell me what you're doing here."

"You want me to believe that you don't know?"

"Listen, Wil, you come muscling in without a single word of explanation or apology, and you expect me to tell you why? Is this some

jealous-lover act? If it is, it makes you look like the country yokel, pal."

Wil gestured around the room. "How do you come by this stuff?" he asked.

"If it's any of your goddamn business," Leon said stiffly, "I buy it."

"You buy it?" Wil stood there staring at the Matisse. "That thing alone must be worth a half a million."

Leon looked behind him. "Six hundred grand," he said calmly. "So now it's your business how I choose to spend my money?"

Money? Is that what it all came down to? "You mean this junk is worth four human lives?" He felt Sally shift behind him.

Leon stared at him in silence. Then: "Four lives? Are you out of your skull? What in God's name are you talking about?"

Wil checked them off on his fingers, holding his hand out toward Leon. "I'm talking about Jim Sewell," he said. "The kid that tried to rip you off. I'm talking about Don Henschler. He was used until he was no more use, and then disposed of. I'm talking about Raul Ortega and a security guard..."

Leon shook his head slowly. "Come on, Wil," he said. "I can't believe my ears. You're hallucinating, pal. First off, I don't even understand half of what you're saying. Listen, this Jim Sewell I heard of. Sally was on my case about him yesterday. I never met the guy in my life, but you tell me he stole my paintings. Okay, so where are the fuckers? The other three, I never heard of before yesterday—and then only what I heard from Judy Townsend."

The silence was underscored by the distant roar of an air conditioner and the quiet suck of air. "Then for Christ's sake, Leon, where do you get these things?"

Leon looked around the walls and shrugged. "A little all over," he said. "Judy travels for me. You remember Judy? That woman's a treasure, I tell you."

"She has a new one coming in for you? A Monet?"

Leon nodded. "The one that was stolen from the Raiders, right. Looks like you know my business pretty damn well," he said.

"Tristate?" asked Wil. He took the photocopy from the hip pocket of his pants and waved it in Leon's face. "That's your business?"

"If it's any of yours." Leon was cold. "Look," he said. "Let's not make a big deal out of this. Okay, Wil, so you unearthed my disgusting secret. I made money. I turned my art into capital, is all. Then back into

art. So I used real estate to do it. Shameful, huh? I've been doing it for years. I went in with Lee; we've been buying up everything in Venice we could lay our hands on."

"You've been selling out your friends, for Christ's sake, Leon."

"Don't get moral on me, Wil. It stinks like envy."

It made sense. Goddammit, it made sense. Wil shifted, uncomfortable with his pitchfork, searching for the only card he had left to play. "What about the helicopter, Leon? The one that's sitting on your pad out there? The one that was used to shoot Jim Sewell off the cliff?"

"Shoot Jim Sewell, Wil? What in God's name are you talking about?" There was no doubting Leon's bewilderment. "Jesus, that thing's not mine. I just let them use the bloody pad for once in its life. Stu Ray flew it with Brad. They wanted to come up that way today, I said yes. For the fun of seeing the bloody thing used. That's a crime?"

Wil looked slowly around the gallery walls and shook his head before he turned to look at Sally. At least she was safe. "Stu's over at the Corton site," he told Leon. He felt wasted, tired and sick and sad beyond expression. "I have to go."

35

"YOU'RE NOT going anywhere, for Christ's sakes, until you let me know what's happening. Put that damn thing down."

Leon took the pitchfork from Wil's hand and led the way back into the stable. He closed the fire door behind them and scrambled the code on the electronic lock before striding out into the early evening light. The vault of the sky was a sheet of acetate blue, punctured with early stars and backlit by the sun from behind the mountains. Outside the fence on the far side of the corral, a pair of horses stomped and whinnied, hitched loosely to a horizontal bar. Their saddles and bridles were still in place.

"Damn," Leon said. "It's Lee and Jackie. I wish they'd unsaddle those animals and not leave the tack for Jon." Over by the cars, the ranch wagon was still not returned to its place. "Damn," he said again. "He's not even home. Let's get inside."

Wil held him back with a hand on his arm. "Wait," he said. "I still don't know where this Brad is. He left with Stu? I didn't see him over at the site."

"He left with Jon," said Sally. "I saw him."

Leon made a circle in the dust with the toe of his boot. "Some of the guys are staying at the San Marcos, down in the valley. Brad said he wanted to grab a ride down there."

"Was he planning to come back?"

"Not to the ranch." He scratched the circle out and kicked the dust away. "Not until they come by to pick up the chopper in the morning. What's all this about?"

Wil didn't answer, but gazed over toward the spot where Barbara's mountain raised its impassive crest above the mesa, waiting for the night. Sally hooked an arm through his. "You don't have to go," she said.

God knows there were things he'd rather do. But he looked at Sally and balled his fist into the flat of his stomach. "Right here," he said, "is where I know they're not going to wait until morning. For Christ's sake, what's the man doing up here?"

"Call DiPaolo," she suggested. "Call the local cops."

"What is this, for Christ's sake?" said Leon. "There's no phone, not up here. First thing I did when I bought the place, I had them all ripped out. The closest place is down there in the valley. You need to call the police, you'll have to get down there."

The lights of the towns had begun to glitter, way down on the valley floor. "We'll do that," said Wil. "Meantime, will you come with me, Leon? I may need help with Stu. He's not listening to me much these days."

"Leave the ranch?" Leon's eyes were on the stable. "For what?"

"Trust me. I'll tell you while we drive." Wil looked at his watch, impatient to be moving. "Or stay if you want. I just need the car. We don't have time to stand around here telling stories. Keys?"

He held his hand out.

"Wait," said Leon. "I'm coming."

They piled into the small car, with Sally crowding into the bucket seat on Wil's lap. The sound of the Corvette's motor cut through the evening air and Leon hit the headlight switch as he backed across the driveway. "Now," he said. "Shoot."

He listened intently as he drove. The headlights brought out details of the low growth on each side of the narrow track, but the glow of twilight was still powerful enough to cancel the beams as they dipped through the troughs in the surface and bounced up out of the ruts. Once in a while, he shouted a short question, nodding as Wil came back with the answer. Ahead, the outline of Barbara's base took the shape of a circle of parked pickup trucks and a commotion of small lights.

A hundred yards short, Leon brought the car to a halt in the middle

266

of the trail and sat for a moment staring through the windshield. "You really believe all this?" he asked. He turned to look at Wil and Sally, eyes sliding between the two of them.

"There's a lot of it you can't argue with," said Wil. "I just told you what happened."

"But Stu? You have to be kidding, Wil. I mean, Brad I don't know too well, he seems like your average shithead redneck. But Stu? So he picks weird friends..." He laughed. "He picked us."

"We can only ask him, right?"

Leon steered the car to the center of the circle up ahead and pulled up in an eddy of dust.

"You can't park here, man." It was Madison, with a flashlight. It was that close to darkness now. "We'll be using this space. Why don't you guys park further up, beyond the truck up there?"

"Madison," said Wil. "Give us a break. It's me, Wil."

The flashlight jumped to his eyes. "Wil?" The beam ran the length of the car and back to Sally's face. "No shit."

"We're looking for Stu. Have you seen him?"

"What's the matter, Wil? You don't know when to quit?"

"I'm asking, right?"

"It's hard to keep track of anyone round here, man. I seem to remember seeing him a while back."

"Brad?"

"Haven't seen him, no."

Wil strained his eyes to where most of the activity was concentrated behind the parked vehicles, on the mountainside. "Wait here," he told Leon. Sally climbed out ahead of him and he took her arm, dodging the clumps of scrub brush.

Bernie Trost had returned from the other side of the mountain and sat in a director's chair in front of a small panel of switches and pinpoint lights. Above him, someone had strung a tiny bulb from a cable that led to a generator in back of a nearby truck.

"Bernie?"

"Hey, Wil!" Trost turned around and waved a hand. "You found the Tristate thing?"

"Thanks, Bernie."

Bernie looked around. "Is that Leon back there? You're still talking? What happened?"

"Forget it, Bernie. I'll tell you later. For now, we need to find Stu Ray. Have you seen him?"

"Stu?" Barbara Corton was there with a clipboard in one hand and a stop watch strung from a ribbon around her neck. "Stu left. He went down to the motel to catch a nap and pick up a sweater. He said he wanted to be back before the show starts."

"When's that, Barbara?"

She checked the watch. "Should be an hour, maybe ninety minutes, if everything goes right. It has to be absolutely dark, aside from the moonlight." The sliver of a new moon and the evening star were already sharp against the deepening blue of the sky.

Wil pushed the light button on his own watch. "How long ago did he leave?"

"Maybe forty minutes, an hour. He drove down in the Raiders pickup."

"The San Marcos?"

"Is that what it's called? It's where a whole bunch of art folks from LA are staying. They picked it because they can get a straight shot up the hill to the piece.... I'm supposed to be down there for a party later in the evening."

"How far?" asked Wil.

"Twenty minutes, I'd guess. I've got to go."

She called out a couple of instructions to Bernie and disappeared in the equipment truck. Wil took Sally by the waist and walked her back toward the parked Corvette. "Listen, love," he said. "I want you to stay up here with the gang, okay?"

"I'm coming."

They crossed through the headlight beams and Leon tooted his horn. "Okay," Wil shouted. "Sally, you're going to have to do what I ask, this one time. You don't have a choice. The car's not big enough for three of us—not for that distance over these roads. Besides, you know most of these guys and you're in better company here. It's safer." He gave her a squeeze that was supposed to say more than he knew it could. "Don't give me a hard time on this," he said. "We don't have any to waste."

Sally looked away, to where the sun had set behind the mountain. "You'll take care, Wil?" she asked. "I'm going to be in agony up here."

"When we get to the valley," he said, "the first thing I do is call the cops. Don't worry." He brought her hand quickly to his lips and held it there for a moment.

268

"It's not only that." She risked a quick look where his eyes shone in the darkness, then looked away again. "I don't want you to leave."

"I know." He joined Leon in the car. "Drive," he said. "You know where the San Marcos is?"

Twilight had given way to darkness, and the Corvette picked a slow path over the wilderness trail to the paved surface of the road down to the valley. When they reached the valley floor, Leon headed north for a half mile and then sped east toward the lights of Desert Hot Springs. The road was straight, with roller-coaster hills and dips where the flash floods wash between them after rain.

"Wasn't that my jeep?" Leon glanced back at the retreating red lights of the high-sprung four-wheel drive that roared passed them, speeding in the opposite direction. "Jon and Janice. They're late. And driving too damn fast. They told me they'd be back by seven." He looked at the digital clock set in the dash. "It's way past eight."

"Worried?" asked Wil.

"Listen," said Leon. "I don't know what to think anymore. It's not like the two of them, is all. They devote their lives to doing the right things for that baby."

The San Marcos was the only motel this far north toward the foothills. A rough U-shape, its open end faced the downslope of the huge valley, offering a panorama of the desert-community lights and the black hulks of the mountains opposite. The pickup Madison had driven out from Los Angeles stood parked among the row of cars angled in from the street in front of the motel.

"Stu's here," said Wil.

"And Brad?" Leon asked.

A short flight of steps led up to the motel courtyard, where a mismatched assortment of patio chairs and lounges stood in small clusters on the cracked concrete around a diminutive kidney-shaped pool. In and around the cactus and parched border plants, red and green garden lights reflected their colors in splashes on the stucco exterior.

Beyond the pool, a semicircular red neon sign on the wall read "Office," and Wil knocked at the sliding glass door beside it. Judging from the darkness inside, they were expecting no more business for the night, and it was a while before the door slid back.

"You need a room?" The narrow oriental face absorbed the lights, half-green, half-red, from the garden.

"Maybe later," Wil said. "Right now, there's a friend of ours staying here, a Mr. Ray? Stuart Ray? Could you tell us what room he's in?"

The manager looked doubtful. "Listen," said Leon, "we're all together, in a party. Up the hill." He jerked a thumb toward his property. "You've heard of the artists working up there?"

He evidently had, nodding agreement as he checked the reservations book. "Number eleven," he said. "Mr. Ray."

"And Mr. Michaels?" asked Wil. "Mr. Brad Michaels?"

He checked the book again. "No Michaels," he said. "No Mr. Michaels here."

"You're sure?"

"Here, check for yourself." He held the page of the book open while Wil checked through the names. No Michaels.

"Thanks, anyway," said Wil.

"No trouble, huh?" The man had picked up the tension they'd brought with them. "Nice place."

"No trouble," said Wil.

Outside, the underwater fixtures flooded the pale blue depths of the pool with light and bounced the water's shifting highlights off the surrounding buildings. Room number 11 was over the far side of the court and the draperies were drawn. "Are we ready for this?" asked Wil. He paused by the edge of the pool. "Do we call the cops now, or after we've talked?"

"After," said Leon. "This is Stu Ray, right? Our old friend Stu? He gets a chance to talk first."

There was no sign of lights switched on in the room, but a faint edge around the curtain suggested the glow from a window to the street on the other side, a bathroom light, or possibly a TV running in the dark.

"Ready?" asked Wil. He tested some pressure on the sliding door, but it wasn't going anywhere. It was locked. So he thundered at it with his fist. "Hey, Stu!" he yelled. "Open up! Stu Ray!"

They waited a few beats and repeated, both of them yelling. Then a lamp went on somewhere.

"What the fuck's going on? Wait!" Then the door slid back a foot and Stu stood there, barely awake, with the light behind him. "You guys crazy?"

Wil pushed the door wide and he and Leon walked in together, edging Ray back toward the bed in the tiny room. Leon pushed open the closet door. "Nothing," he said. He moved on to the bathroom.

270

"What is this?" Stu was still blinking the light from his eyes. There were heavy circles under the neat blond brows.

"You tell us, Stu," said Wil. "No more games." He pushed Ray down on the bed and stood above him. "There's just this one last chance to let us know what's happening. Now. We've reached a point of no return."

"For Christ's sake..."

Leon had finished his quick tour. "No one?" asked Wil.

"No one," said Leon.

"Then there's just the three of us. Old friends. No more excuses."

"Listen, Wil, if I knew what this was all about myself, I'd help you. Okay?"

Stu Ray tried to swing himself into a sitting position, but Wil shoved him back again. "Then I'll tell you, Stu," he said. "There's something stinking rotten in your business. It stinks like death. Do we talk about Don Henschler? Forgery? Do we talk about art getting ripped off from the Raiders trucks? Leon's stuff? Do we talk about three of your kids getting killed in the past three days? A security guard? You tell me you know nothing. Is that what you're going to tell the cops, Stu? Because that's where we go next. The three of us."

He fell silent, watching Stu's face. It was gray. "If you're looking for options, Stu," said Leon quietly, "forget it. There are none. There's just the truth left now."

When the fight finally left him, it was as if he fell inward on himself. The tough outer structure that he cultivated for the world seemed to collapse. "I'm scared," he said simply. "I'm scared shitless, Wil."

"Me, too," said Wil without sympathy. "So tell me."

"What's your stake in this?" Stu asked.

"A friend. That's the short answer, I guess. A person who got hurt." This time he let Stu sit up. "What scares you, Stu?"

"You're on to Brad?" Stu asked.

Wil nodded. "And?"

"The man's gone wild. I couldn't stop him, Wil. I tried." He shook his head in disbelief.

"Brad was your man?"

"I guess, if you look at it that way. Not really. More like the other way around." His eyes couldn't quite meet Wil's. Something in them shifted slightly every time they came close to contact. "Okay," he said. "I can only ask you to believe me this time."

"Try me."

"I've only just begun to understand the thing myself. Here it is—just the facts, no apologies, okay? A couple of years back, I made the all-time mistake. I got in over my head when I bought the warehouse. The business was about to fold. Ask Rick Horan. He followed the thing all the way. He was all set to file a chapter eleven for me when this Brad came along out of the blue with two hundred thousand cash and bails me out. He bought into the business. I never liked the guy and I wanted to buy him back out, but I've been forced to work with him. A sleeping partner," he added bitterly.

"And for two years, you haven't suspected anything?"

"No, it wasn't like that, Wil. I'm not stupid. For two years I've suspected there were things going down I didn't know about. Suspected. I haven't had a scrap of hard evidence."

"You let Don Henschler use your studio. You had no idea what the guy was doing in there?"

"Why should I? You rent a space, you rent the goddamn space. When he saw I wasn't using it, Brad suggested the deal with Don. Said he was interested in the work, he'd pay half the guy's rent."

"And when people started getting killed?"

"You're talking Monday, man. Two days ago...I come to the office Monday morning and I hear about Jim Sewell. For all I knew, the kid just fell off of a cliff. Then Henschler, Don—it just blew my mind. The first time I put it all together was yesterday, when I got word about Raul Ortega and the security guard."

"You were out of town then, already?"

"I was at the helicopter rental place out in Ontario. When they told me I put the phone down, went outside, and threw up in the parking lot."

"Brad was with you then?"

Stu nodded.

"So what did he say?"

"The man came out laughing. He didn't even bother to deny that he'd been fucking me over for two years." Stu managed a straight glance in Wil's direction. "He told me all I needed was to keep my mouth shut for another day. He told me he'd kill me if I didn't."

"You believed him?"

"Wouldn't you?"

"And even then you flew up with him?"

"I had no choice. I'd have gone right back to LA, if he hadn't forced me."

"So what's with the helicopter, Stu? You been doing that long?"

"Once in a while, these past two years. Brad used to be a pilot in the navy."

"A limo? You know anything about a limo?"

Stu Ray shrugged. "The guy has these fantasies about himself," he said. "He sometimes showed up at the Raiders in a limo. Why?"

Wil was still telling him how Jim Sewell died when the telephone rang.

36

THE RING was a sudden, shrill summons that brought ice into the room.

"You're expecting a call?" Wil asked.

Stu Ray shook his head and reached out for the telephone. "Hello." Then he covered the receiver with the palm of his hand and looked at Wil. "It's Brad," he said shortly. "Yes, this is Stu Ray. Where are you? Yes, he's here...."

He listened for a moment longer, then handed the receiver wordlessly to Wil.

"Yes," said Wil.

"Garretson?"

"Yes."

"We never met." The voice was hard, edgy.

"Not yet."

"You know who I am?"

"Yes, I do."

"I've got a friend of yours here." Sally. Fighting back the wave of panic, Wil forced himself to stare at the light switch set in the pale green wall of the motel room and said nothing. "She needs to talk to you."

There was a moment's silence, what sounded like a scuffle, then Sally

274

was on the line. "Wil?" she said. She sounded calm enough, but strangely distant. "Wil, I'm in a mess up here...."

"Where?"

"Up the hill. I'm back at Leon's place. On Lee Lawrence's car phone. I'm sorry, Wil, there was nothing I could do...."

He kept his voice carefully even. "Are you hurt?"

"No, I'm fine."

"Do the others know? Back at Barbara's?"

"No."

"They saw nothing?"

"They just didn't know."

"We'll get you out of there...." Before he'd finished, it was Brad's voice back on the line.

"Garretson? I want keys."

"Keys to what?" Wil already knew. He wanted the keys to the stable. He glanced at Leon, who was alert now, tense. "You'll never be able to get out. Not with the paintings."

Brad ignored him. "All I need is one person to bring me the key and the combination. I want you, Garretson. You bring them here to me. No one else. I'll trade them in on your lady here."

"Listen, Brad. Do me a favor, just listen to me for a moment...." But the line was already dead as he spoke. "Shit," he said. "For Christ's sake, let's go." He was halfway out the door when Stu called him back. "What about the cops?" he asked. "This guy's a killer. Where's your head, Wil?"

There was an irony in there somewhere, Stu Ray keeping his cool while Wil lost his, but Wil hadn't time for it. The guy was right. "Listen," he said. "Follow us. Call the cops from here—the local guys. And Di Paolo, down in Los Angeles, he'll know what to do. You remember him? Okay. Make sure that word gets to him fast, whatever it takes. Then follow us up to Leon's place." He paused at the door. "And, Stu..."

"Yeah?" His friend looked up from the telephone.

"Don't take no. From anyone."

"I won't."

Leon spun the Corvette back across the gravel, crashed into first and squirted rocks from under the tires as he headed for the stop sign at the end of the road. Drifting through it, he took his foot from the brake, changed up, brought his foot down on the gas pedal again and raced back over the hardtop toward the base of the hills.

"It must have been Brad," Wil shouted.

"What?"

"In your jeep, going back there. That must have been Brad."

Leon nodded. Behind them, the colored lights of the motel dropped farther from sight, as time and again the needle of the speedometer edged past eighty, the little car bouncing clear off the tarmac at the top of the ridges. Up ahead, the soft light of the new moon set a glow on the heaps of great boulders, distinguishing their outline from the massive background of the mountains beyond.

"Don't kill us both," yelled Wil. The two wheels on his side of the car slid off the tarmac onto the gritty surface of a turnout, churning up a shower of dust and jolting the car off course.

"I know the road," Leon shouted, grinning.

The Corvette whirled up more white dust in the moonlight as it left the paved section of the road and dodged the jutting rocks and the potholes. Up ahead, the lights of Leon's compound made a beacon in the growing darkness, and three bone-shattering minutes later the car roared through the open gates.

The silence was so intense, it almost hurt the ears when Leon cut the engine. Then Leon nodded his head at the T-Bird. "Lee," he said. "What did he do with Lee and Jackie, for Christ's sake? And with Jon and Janice?"

"You worry about them," said Wil. "Give me the key. I'll take care of Sally. What's the sequence on your security?"

"You mean you're going to let him get away with it?"

"What's your idea? Hand him Sally on a plate?"

"What about the cops?"

"You want to bet Sally's life on the cops' getting here within the next ten minutes? He's got the chopper there, and there's nothing inside you couldn't carry under one arm. No way, Leon. Give me the key."

The key turned out to be a pair of keys, each a small cylinder with a single tooth. Drake had them on a chain around his neck. "You've got the sequencing system first," he said. "You saw it, on the panel by the door. The number's eight-five-nine-one. That cancels the alarm. Then insert the two keys simultaneously in the other panel and turn. That releases the locks. Then push the steel door."

276

Wil took the keys without a word and opened the car door.

"I'll come with you as far as the pool house, Wil."

They stood together by the car and gazed up toward the stable.

"You there?" yelled Wil.

"We're up here." The voice came from the doorway, and Wil could just make out two figures under the raw bulb that hung outside. "Just you, Garretson." The figures backed into the stable as Wil and Leon made their way past the backside of the small pool house and stopped. Wil noticed that the horses still stood stamping in the shadows on the far side of the corral where they'd been before, restless, unhappy to have been left sweating under the saddle.

"Goddammit," said Leon under his breath. "How come those guys left them there like that, for Christ's sake?"

His answer came from the pool house itself. The lights were doused inside, but there was a sudden angry knocking at the wall.

"So who did you shut in the pool house?" Wil called.

"Guests." Brad laughed. "My guests," he said. "They stay there until after I've left."

Lee Lawrence. Jackie. Perhaps Jon and Janice, if he hadn't left them down in the valley.

"Are you okay, Sally?" shouted Wil.

"She's okay." Brad moved her forward into the light again. Her hands were strapped behind her, and a gag had been jammed into her mouth, held in place by a length of cloth. Brad held an arm around her throat, with a handgun pointed to the side of her head. "She can't talk, but she's okay. I need the keys. Come close enough to throw them. Garretson, you come alone from there if you want the Horan lady safe, okay?"

Wil started slowly up past the corral fence and stood a dozen paces from the two of them.

"Throw the keys carefully."

They made a jangling silver arc and landed within a yard of Sally's feet.

"Now the numbers, Garretson."

Wil shielded his eyes from the light and repeated the instructions Leon had given him.

"Back down," said Brad. "Way back to the pool house."

Wil kept his eyes on the man as he backed down the slope, using the corral fence as a handrail, guiding him. There had to be something he could do. He could think of nothing, and he was too far away by the time Brad slowly released his grip from Sally's throat.

"Bring me the key," he told her. He put his knee in the small of her back when she didn't move and shoved her forward. "Bring it," he said.

There was a sudden, intense flash of light from the shadows up on the little hill beyond the pool, and it was a moment before Wil recognized the crack that followed it as gunfire. Then Brad's gun jerked and fired as he was moving, bringing it around in line with Sally's back. A bullet smashed into the rocks behind the tennis court, whining off in a ricochet into the night. The two sharp sounds were followed at once by the high-pitched panic of a horse and the stomp of nervous hoofs.

Sally screamed. Behind her, Brad's head blossomed red, like a sudden flower in the half-light. Then his body tumbled forward, crashing down across her and knocking her to the ground.

By the time Wil reached her, she was soaked in blood.

It was seconds more before he was aware of anything but the blinding relief of realizing that Sally was unhurt.

Then suddenly action erupted all around them. A pickup truck thundered through the main gate in a cloud of dust, and Stu Ray climbed out with a yell. Leon Drake let the prisoners out from the pool house, shouting at Lee to get back in the house. And, across on the far side of the corral where the horses stood, a figure materialized from the dark behind the tennis court, released the halter, and vaulted up into the saddle.

Wil glanced up at the wind sock over the hill where the shot had come from.

"Take care of her," he told Stu. "I'll be back."

"Wil..." It was Sally. Hurting, even though she wasn't wounded. He had to take his hand away from her by force.

"I'll be back," he said.

"Wil!"

He ran down through the corral and climbed the fence. He had learned to ride as a youngster, but it was thirty years since he'd been thrown by a horse and decided forever after to treat the whole species with a healthy distrust.

He jerked the reins loose from the post, pulled them back over the

278

horse's head, then grabbed the knob of the saddle and hauled himself up.

The animal needed no encouragement. Spurred by the gunshots and the release of its mate, it set off like a maniac in its wake. For a hundred yards, all Wil could do was cling to it, and pray, and watch the stirrups flailing out to the sides.

Knees, he remembered. Use the knees.

He squeezed the great body between his legs and pulled in on the reins until mercifully the creature seemed to calm to the rhythm of its own movement, settling down to a pace that might have seemed easy to a rider. To Wil, though, tossing on the smooth, hard flanks of the enormous animal, and fighting to get his feet into the stirrups, it was a jarring nightmare that refused to end.

Who was it? The anonymous brown figure offered no clue, nor the small white blur of the face turning back to look at him.

Wil turned his head for a glimpse behind. At a glance, the ranch was a blur of lights, but the head lamps of what Wil guessed had to be the jeep began to dance away from it.

Stu and Leon.

They'd never catch up with the horses, not over this terrain.

Up ahead, the rider continued south at a steady gallop, but swung around to the west someway before he reached the lights of Barbara's command post, heading around behind her hill toward the highway. He rode more easily than Wil, maintaining an effortless lead.

A glimpse. It was all he wanted.

Once he found the stirrups, Wil concentrated less on staying in the saddle than on conveying to the horse the need to increase his pace.

Then the man turned again. Wil saw the glint of the rifle as he raised it with one hand and fired two lazy shots, more to discourage the pursuit, Wil thought, than to hit the target.

Nonetheless, he brought the reins a little closer in, checking the horse's stride. The narrow sliver of moon and the myriad stars cast a pale light on the tufts of sagebrush, the rolling balls of the tumbleweed, and the occasional darker stump of a barrel cactus. Miraculously, the creature underneath him never seemed to falter in placing its pounding hoofs.

Had he gained some ground?

If so, he was losing it slowly now. He lost sight of the horse and rider up ahead for a moment as they followed the curve of the low western slope around into the canyon that separated Barbara's hill from the higher one behind it. First one, then a second of the tall wind generators loomed out from the horizon, silver with moonlight, their blades turning slowly in the evening breeze. Then there were more, as the natural curve of the hill brought the riders around to the south.

There were perhaps two hundred yards between them when Barbara Corton threw the switches on the kliegs.

The piece was designed to be seen indirectly, as an ethereal glow, from the other side of the hill or down in the valley. On this side, the megavolts of brilliant light washed through the canyon in a single, blinding instant.

Wil's eyes fixed for that one second on the image of the teeth of the horse ahead as it reared up, screamed and toppled, spilling its rider. Then his own mount faltered, rose into the air and fell back down, crashing his body into a spiny bed of sagebrush and bolting off with a thunder of terrified hoofs.

The lights stayed on.

Wil lay still, panting, waiting for his eyes to adjust and testing out sore limbs. Everything hurt—but there was nothing broken. He struggled to his knees, then to his feet, staggering, using his hands to block the light from his eyes.

He scoured the landscape. The other rider was on foot now also, and had gained a precious fifty yards on the climb toward the wind farm. No gun, that Wil could tell. Had it been lost in the fall?

"Hey!" he yelled. "Wait!"

The echo filled the canyon, but the man climbed on without pausing to look back. There was no sign of either horse.

Wil started to run. "Wait!"

He picked a way between dark patches of those weeds and shrubs that somehow contrive to subsist in this hard, parched ground, and the going proved easy enough until he reached the foot of the hill. On the steepening slope, his feet began to slide out from under him as he climbed and his hands stung, bleeding, where he steadied himself on whatever looked strong enough to hold him.

Halfway up, he paused for breath, gasping, searching the skyline. The man had disappeared beyond the crest, and for the first time now Wil heard the prolonged and eerie music of the blades in the wind above him, churning the turbines with their huge, inexorable grace. It sounded like a thousand aeolian harps, or the sigh of the distant dead, come back to mourn.

He scrambled to the crest of the hill and stopped again.

The stout aluminum towers stood ranged in rows. Their stems were thicker than he could have imagined, seeing them from the valley. A door at the base of each allowed access for a man to climb half the height inside, to the point where it narrowed and an exterior ladder led onto a tiny platform at the top.

They were taller, too—dizzyingly tall, when seen from the base. Directly above him, the blades cut the wind with their peculiar sound, a slicing of metal through air that riffled and throbbed with the singing of the turbines.

Aside from this movement in the space above, the field stood in utter stillness. Behind him, the valley was still flooded with light, and for the first time Wil could make out, at the summit of Barbara's hill, the pyramid of blue neon that outlined its natural form.

He turned back to the wind field. The man could be anywhere in this forest of metal, hidden behind any one of the fifty columns in their stolid rows.

"Is anyone there?"

He repeated the question, more for the comfort of the sound of his voice than because he expected a response. Then he started into the field, walking slowly ahead between the rows. The little service doors were closed and padlocked, identical, each with its rectangular peephole, like repeated images.

Except one. Without a padlock.

The door was closed.

And suddenly Wil was overwhelmed by the dreadful surge of knowledge.

37

"CHARLIE?"

Wil came up on the door silently and whispered through the peephole. Even the whisper seemed to amplify immensely in the hollow cylinder of the tower.

"Charlie."

He called a little louder. There was no response but the sound of sudden movement and the clang of boots on the metal ladder.

Wil ripped open the door. "Charlie!" he yelled, and the sound of his voice came back at him, ringing with the echo of the enclosed space.

There was total blackness above him. Fumbling in the darkness, he found the base of the ladder and began to climb. He counted twenty rungs, and rested. Above, he heard the sound of a metal door swinging open and glimpsed the quick shaft of light, blurred by the movement of a figure against a patch of sky. Enclosed in the narrow tube, Wil took a deep breath and went another fifteen steps, then fifteen more, slower this time, and found himself at mid-point.

The door opened out onto the night sky, cold, split by the blades that turned with slow regularity, their sound at this distance like the sudden, rhythmic rush of a whip through air. A glance at the ground below made Wil's head swirl—and the transition platform from interior to exterior ladders seemed large enough for a single foot at most.

He clutched a rung of the second ladder and swung his weight out onto the platform.

Now.

He moved steadily on up, afraid to look down. Afraid of what he knew he would find when he reached the top. Step by step, with the overpowering whine of the turbine seeming to grow fuller with desperate sadness at each rung.

"Hello, Wil."

He reached the top. Charlie Strauss was sitting on the service platform that ran alongside the turbine, his back propped almost casually against its casing. Almost casually, too, he held a handgun in his lap.

"Hi, Charlie." Sick to his stomach, Wil hauled himself over the top and sat there, dizzy with the effort of the climb and the incredible drop beneath them. He perched opposite Strauss. "It's unbelievable," he said.

Above the glow of the valley which Barbara had used as the backdrop for her piece, the blue neon pyramid seemed to hover mystically above the earth like some spaceship come to carry them away.

They watched it in silence for a while.

"I couldn't let the bastard kill her. Could I, Wil?"

"You couldn't. No."

There was a new sound now, the stutter and feathering of helicopters coming up toward them from the desert floor. Two of them, Wil saw.

"He was a terrible mistake." Charlie Strauss seemed not to have noticed the aircraft.

"Brad?" asked Wil.

"Yes, of course Brad. You know I didn't kill anyone? Not until now."

"I guess I knew that. I could have figured it out."

"The man went mad. He wanted everything."

The sound and the lights began to make a mockery of Barbara's piece, shattering its effect. The choppers searched this way and that, their lights crisscrossing the ground they'd covered on the horses, around behind the mountain.

"And you, Charlie. What did you want?"

"To start with? I wanted a terrific gallery. I wanted the best gallery on the West Coast. That's what I got."

"At a price."

"It seemed like a small one, in the beginning, Wil." Strauss smiled absently out across the desert. "A lost piece—genuinely lost. I found it before the insurance check came in. It was just a matter of not telling anyone. Not hard. I sold the piece years later. The insurance check meant a lot, in those early days."

"Ten years ago? When you started?"

Strauss nodded. "It wasn't easy, starting up the gallery. Just a little bit of fiddling helped. It didn't seem any worse than that. It got to be a kind of a game, doing not much more and not much different from what others were doing. Bending the rules a little here and there. Not hurting anyone. It was like always figuring out new ways to play the real against the phony. It was like an art form, really."

He fell silent, and they looked out over the valley.

"An art form?" said Wil.

"Yes. Remember, the early seventies? It all had to do with values, when you get down to it. The funny thing is, it was all an act. None of it was worth much in my book, but you had people lining up to join the game. Falling all over themselves to buy whatever anyone said was art. And don't say the artists didn't join in, too. They loved it. There's so much trash around and so much that looks alike. So much that's phony—and so few who care about the difference."

"Don Henschler?"

He grinned. "The kid was good," he said. "I had others before him, but none so good. A genius, really, in his own way. Until Brad got him hooked on drugs. You knew about that?"

Wil nodded. "And Jim? Jim Sewell? The Leon Drakes?"

"Jim Sewell was a live wire. Dangerous. Too smart for his own good, really. I'd always managed to hide behind a variety of smoke screens before. But Jim Sewell wasn't content with a nice cash bonus from time to time. He wanted more. He managed to track us down through Judy Townsend."

"Judy?"

"Not her fault, you could say. We used her as a shipping conduit. Mostly there was no need for her to know what was passing through her hands, but she wasn't too fussy, anyway. There's few people that are, when you think of it. No, Judy was happy to have the work—and the commissions. Still happier to have the international contacts that I gave her."

"So Jim tracked you down?"

Strauss nodded. "I think that gave Brad what he was really looking

284

for. A reason to kill. It was like it was something he'd been waiting for all along, and I never knew it."

"And you went along?"

The light from Barbara's pyramid reflected blue on his face as he turned to look at Wil. "If you mean did I actually help him kill Jim Sewell—no. He hired his own help for that job. God knows where....But short of going to the police myself, there was no way I could stop him. He staged the whole thing like some elaborate performance piece." He shuddered. Even in summer, the desert air gets cold at night.

"You made him, Charlie. You made Brad."

"I did, I guess. He looked good and tough at first. Just out of the navy. He looked like what I needed. Quiet. Discreet. Someone to keep the distance between me and the folks I had to deal with. Like Stu. The poor guy never knew. And all his kid artists. Eager as hell to make a buck, most of them. It was too easy, Wil."

"I know." He was right, Wil thought. Charlie couldn't have done it without help. Everybody's help.

"I fucked up with Brad." The choppers were close now, sweeping low to the ground. "Looks like I ruined Barbara's piece, too."

"You did, Charlie. You screwed it up for all of us."

The lights came closer, sweeping the undergrowth, following who knows what traces they had left, coming up the hillside. A four-wheel drive, emergency lights flashing, made it to the bottom of the road that led to the towers. Wil heard its wheels skid on the gravel road.

"I'm sorry, Wil," said Charlie. The light from one of the choppers swept cross his face, and its sound swallowed up his words.

"You're what?" yelled Wil. He couldn't believe his ears.

"Sorry," Charlie shouted back. "I'm sorry."

The helicopter settled, hovering between their tower and Barbara's pyramid, blocking out the view. The noise was deafening.

"It's not enough," said Wil.

He got up, his figure outlined in the spotlight from the chopper.

"Police." The amplified voice was disembodied, alien under the huge canopy of the desert sky. "Stay where you are."

"I suppose that's it." Strauss rose, reaching pleasantly toward Wil, smiling, as though to shake his hand. But the gun was in his own.

"Charlie! No!"

The force of the first shot set Wil tottering on the platform edge.

"No!" The second exploded in his ears as he threw the weight of his shoulder into Strauss's chest and watched him tumble backward into emptiness. Falling himself, he clutched the metal guard rail and crashed face-down against the wailing turbine.

THERE WERE six of the new pieces, lit from above and standing at intervals the length of the gallery. Close to life size, rearing with agonized energy, toppling, the figures were shown in life-and-death struggle with the material world that seemed to engulf them.

"Is it a part of them, all of this stuff? Or are they part of it?" Sally asked. Limbs were devoured by struts and I-bars, beams, door frames— the detritus of the world man builds around him.

"Both, I guess." What he saw, sometimes, when he looked at the new work, was the image of Jim Sewell, falling back from the mountain face; the rearing horse; Charlie Strauss, tumbling out into the darkness that he'd chosen for himself.

"They're fantastic, Wil," said Sally. "Painful."

"Too close to the bone?"

"Tough to take. You've kept it all in perfect little boxes until now."

He'd spent the day and half the evening installing. Six months of work, a new gallery, and work whose connection with everything he'd done to date was so deep, so raw, so personal, he wondered who would see it other than himself. "I'm scared out of my mind," he said.

287

"But they're great."

Wil smiled. "No one likes change as much as they pretend to. Especially with an artist. People will come here thinking about the boxes and freak out. They'll say I'm jumping on the neo-Ex bandwagon."

"Watch," she said. "They'll love them."

The last of the installers was finishing the clean-up job with a broom and Wil stopped by to collect his jacket from the reception desk. "So how come you showed up on the wrong night for the opening?" he asked.

"Sheer blind luck," said Sally. "And you, Wil? How are things going?"

It was eight months since the Barbara Corton evening. Eight months since they'd agreed to cut the cords.

"As you see," he said. He slipped the jacket on and somewhere back in the office someone coughed, the sound echoing down toward them through the gallery spaces. "I've been working, not much else. MaryJo up and left for Philadelphia."

"She did?"

"I told her so often she should get back into a professional company, she finally believed me." He grinned ruefully. "It just happened to be in Philadelphia."

He took her arm and they walked together to the door. "You heard that Rick and I finally split up?"

"I heard about that," he said. "I was sad, but not surprised."

"You were sad?"

"Of course. You'd put a lot into it. Both of you." He took a last look around the gallery. "So what's next?"

"Dinner?"

"I wouldn't turn you down," he said.

288

About the Author

Art critic, poet, dean, and the author of *Chiaroscuro* (1985), Peter Clothier was born in England and graduated in languages at Cambridge University. He taught his way through Germany and Canada, arriving in the United States in 1964. He studied as a poet at the University of Iowa's prestigious writing program, where he also taught the translation workshop while completing a doctoral degree in comparative literature. Moving to Los Angeles in 1968 to teach at the University of Southern California, he published two books of poetry before discovering a special love for the work of a new generation of visual artists. Ten years a dean of the arts at Otis Art Institute and Loyola Marymount University (both in Los Angeles), he has recently turned to a lifelong interest in the thriller to further explore the endlessly fascinating labyrinths of the world of contemporary art. Clothier is a regular contributor to *Art in America*. *Dirty-Down* is his second thriller.